Antoine Archange Raphael

A

Stranger's

Wonderful

Chronicles

(15 short stories)
Book II

Property of the author

From the same author

Essay:

The Haitian Drama, history taking the wrong turns (the English version)
Le Drame Haïtien, une tournure inquiétante de l'histoire (the French version)
The Sources of Values, their claims and their failure, an essay (the English version)
Les Sources de Valeurs, leurs prétentions et leur faillite, un essai (the French Version)

Stories:

Derrick, the Young Wise Man, story(English story)
Derrick, le sage jeune home (The French version)
Big Ninny's Home, the confrontation, story (the English version)
La Maison de Nini, la confrontation (the French version)
Mutual Discovery, at the end of the tunnel (English novel)
Marcel, le jeune esprit positif, short stories, books I, II and III (the French version)
Marcel, the young positive mind, short stories, books I, II and III (the English version_
La découverte mutuelle, au bout du tunnel (the French version)
Harmony and Contrast, the female impact, books I and II (English story)
L'harmonie et le contraste, l'apport féminin, books I and II (the French version)
Le Rêve, sous l'empire de l'amour (French Story)
Dream, under the influence of love (the English version)
Voodoo, within the limits of the law (English story)
Le vaudou, dans les limites de la loi (the French version)
Concern, the sources of values under fire in Cows Island (English story)
L'altruisme, les sources de valeurs vivement critiquées in L'Ile-aux-Vaches
The wonderful stranger's chronicles, short stories (the English version).
Les merveilleuses chronique d'un étranger, short stories (The French version).
Chasse à la vie, (French story)
La main Invisible, (French story)
Le petit Coin de l'Office (French Story)
Livre de poèmes (French version)
Book of poetry (English version)

This book is dedicated
To all lovers of mankind,
To the known
And
Unknown benefactors

TABLE OF CONTENTS

Introduction

Since adolescence, the reporter, Brian Clifford has always betrayed some bent for mystery. This tendency, undoubtedly, has motivated his professional choice to become a journalist. He strongly believes in the possibility of the *bizarre*, the *unique*. For, according to him, the world abounds in mysteries to decipher; otherwise, absolute truth and total knowledge would have belonged to the past.

Indeed, occasionally, new data, in almost all the fields of cognitive activities, baffle the mind of our most sagacious researchers.

Mr. Clifford has distinguished himself by his enquiries on the *UFO*, the *Sash Quash*, the *Killing Tree*, and the *Voodoo Hibernation* —to say the least.

He has also realized the fact that many *extraordinary affirmations* are bogus until proof to the contrary.

However, he has revealed strange occurrences *about a Mysterious Stranger* to the public (for the first time), which seem to stand up to criticism.

Men and women, of different backgrounds, have mentioned the *stranger's appearance*, who has shown up in time to get some people in distressful situations out of a tight corner. Where does that stranger come from? What is his real name? Does he assume various identities?

Nobody knows. For some unexplained reason, he has always disappeared, soon after his good deeds, without leaving any sign of himself, besides his beneficiaries' testimonies.

Mr. Brian Clifford has reported these men and women's accounts, who have benefitted from that *stranger's munificence*.

He leaves it to the readers to assess the values of his reporting.

He made his first visit to Sabina Musa, formerly Mrs. Sabina Kalia, a graduate from the State University, with a doctorate degree in sociology. She happens to practice objective-mindedness and wouldn't deliberately lie. However, she puts her credibility on the line by reporting exactly the facts from her own personal experiences.

She often said to herself, "If I make a mistake, they shouldn't ascribe it to me".

She heads an organization aiming at defending women's right throughout the world and at promoting them to the social hierarchy.

That day the reporter, Brian Clifford, had visited Doctor Sabina Musa, an extremely beautiful woman, she beckoned him in her sumptuous office.

She seized that opportunity to let the visitor know that cleanliness in one's appearance and place of environment betrays not only the person's nature, but also a sign of respect for others.

A stranger's wonderful chronicles, Book II

The journalist said abruptly, "Doctor, I thank you for receiving me on this short notice.

"However, I hasten to get your account for which the big shots of the magazine I represent seems so anxious.

"Therefore, my advancement depends on you."

Doctor Sabina Musa cut in mellifluously, "Listen, Mr. Clifford, the subject fascinates both of us.

"I feel happy to tell you about it. I have no shame to express the truth."

After a short pause, she summed up her attitude in these terms, "It's my nature."

"Dr. Sabina Musa, allow me to record our conversation. I may even do better; why don't we put it on video? It would look as if I take your testimony on the spot."

"You have carte blanche, Mr. Clifford. My story looks bizarre, unheard-of but true.

"Some people from the public will have doubt about my accounts; others will believe me.

"However, I can't deny the occurrence of the events and my story.

"If I fall into madness, my account of it happens to express of the true, the way I remember it."

"Then, Doctor Sabina Musa, let's start this story from the beginning."

The reader may enjoy reading this first episode by obtaining Book I of the saga.

Introduction

Book II started with a case in which Brigitte Donation had experienced a narrow escape.

(16)

A

Narrow

Escape

By Antoine Archange Raphael

*S*tudents from Preston High School, according to the investigative reporter Brian Clifford's account, were wait-ing for the school bus assigned by the Department of Education. It was three PM. The students headed for their family homes. As usual, the adolescents bubbled over with energy, spoke loud, touched and teased each other. Finally, the bus arrived. They rushed getting on it to occupy their favorite places.

Only Brigitte Donation remained seated on the public bench. Her schoolfellows paged her at the top of their voices, but she ignored them. At last, the bus left towards downtown.

Soon, it would stop every two blocks to drop students who would leave it, as noisily as they had entered it, while they had lost awareness of Brigitte's image expressing deep sadness.

She had hiccups, looked up and only seemed to become conscious of reality.

She understood that she had missed the school bus, the last one for that Friday evening, until the following Monday.

"How stupid am I!" she thought. "How will I go back to my parents' home located at two hours walk (at least)? Well, I will reach home late at night.

"Good! Daddy and mammy have turned grumpy, since their unemployment."

Then, she remembered the lousy family situation and burst out crying.

A stranger's wonderful chronicles, Book II

A soft hand rested on her shoulder.

She briskly turned around and saw a young man, in his early twenties. He looked at her with such intensity that she thought she could deal with a mentally disturbed person.

"Sir," she said, "what do you want?

"Who has given you the permission to touch me?

"I am only seventeen, therefore, a minor. I don't intend to look for a man.

"If you don't stop, I will scream to draw people and the police's attention. They will arrest you for attempted rape."

The man's face broke into a smile.

"Ms. Brigitte Donation," he announced, "my name is Renault Pinzon. I do not intend to hurt you.

"I know that you are seventeen, and that, soon, you will complete your secondary studies."

"But, sir, I don't know you."

"Ms., please, don't act so formally.

"I feel very close to you. I come to you as a fellowman, therefore as your brother."

"I don't quite follow you, my dear sir. You use a very strange language."

"I may understand your behavior, my beautiful Brigitte, since you are so young.

"However, I feel very close to you, to such a par that I believe that I belong to your household.

"Would you believe it?"

For one reason or another, Brigitte had no longer fear of Renault Pinzon. Anyway, his presence took her mind from her sadness.

The man advanced, "Brigitte, contrary to your first reaction, I don't suffer from any mental disturbance. I simply look strange. For example, you may not believe me if I told you that I have the ability to grasp someone's life just by looking at him.

"I know the alpha and the omega of reality."

"You have expressed an impossible occurrence," cut in the young woman.

"Do you want some proof?"

"Yes, I do."

"Brigitte, you are dazzlingly beautiful. However, for a split second, your face has betrayed the mask of death."

"What!"

"Well, let me tell you the cause of my deadly impression of your face.

"Your parents no longer work, as a consequence of widespread inflation.

"Such despairing eventuality has taken them by surprise. They have no savings, no equity shares, no real estate investment, beside the family house.

A stranger's wonderful chronicles, Book II

"Your parents won't have money to pay the next month mortgage and they will claim bankruptcy. If nothing positive happens in the nearest future, your family will become homeless."

"But, it's incredible, Renault," astonished the female student. "You represent a danger. You spy on people to humble them."

"That's not all."

"What else?"

"Remember what I have said about my impression of your face which has given me the picture of a death mask."

"Yes, I do. However, you have evidently made a mistake. I am alive"

"Not for long."

"What do you mean? Do you intend to kill me?"

"No, I don't.

"You can trust me. I will save your life as well your siblings and parents'"

"You confuse me."

"Remember, your father bought a handgun last Monday. He lets the family know that he intends to protect the house against burglars, above all since thieves have recently rubbed people at gunpoint.

"However, he rather intends to kill his entire family, including himself."

"His mass killing will prevent him from facing the disgrace he could undergo soon."

Brigitte couldn't believe her eyes and ears.

Deep in her heart, she felt that Renault had told the truth.

She wondered, "God, Creator of even and earth, what can we do to save ourselves from such nightmare?"

Then, she said, "Renault, do you have a cellular phone? Mine isn't working, since I didn't have money to reconnect it."

"Yes, I have one, but you can't call your house. Your father has disconnected all the telephonic units to make any assistance impossible. He behaves as if he has taken his own family hostage."

"Then, what should we do?"

"I will take you home. You will make more than two hours to reach your parents house on foot. By then, your father would believe that you have found out about his deadly plan and that you would stay away from that home.

"He would ignore you and would kill your mother, your siblings and himself.

"Once we reach home, don't use your key. Ring the doorbell. We will enter together.

"What will happen...?

"We will see."

The car proceeded at a moderate speed. Some point in time, it overtook the school bus.

Many of Brigitte's schoolmates recognized her and started to lend her bad intentions.

A stranger's wonderful chronicles, Book II

"Oh! Look guys! Isn't it Brigitte Donation?" inquired Elizabeth Adour.

"Ah! I see," observed Maurice Colon, an admirer turned down by Brigitte.

Then, after a short pause, he added, "She goes to bed with wealthy men. Why shouldn't she? Nowadays' women…"

"Watch your language," cut in Antoinette Pepin, another Brigitte's schoolmate. "Women don't behave all the same way. I will never sell my body."

Brigitte, ignorant of their gossips, waived them good-bye. Then, she lost sight of them.

Suddenly she panicked and, against her better judgment, she pointed out. "Renault, I feel uncomfortable sitting in your car. You may be a serial killer or a mental patient escaped from the asylum!"

"I don't sink into madness, Brigitte. As I know your address, I wouldn't waste my time to wait for you in the neighborhood of your school, if I intended to harm you."

"But, Renault, you must understand me. You may invent this story about our father who has lost his mind and has wished to kill all of us today.

"Additionally, why do you want to help us?"

"Brigitte, let me repeat it: I come to you as a fellowman, as your brother, as another human being who believes that his presence on earth would serve no purpose, if he had to spend it just to eat, drink and enjoy money.

"Brigitte, you must believe me. I have never forgotten that my mission has to go beyond the routine I have just mentioned."

After a pause, he added,

"However, many people that I have met have cast doubt about my intentions. Actually, I have never ceased to amaze myself; for, I fulfill my beneficial activity in a natural fashion."

"Yes, Renault, I will acknowledge that you possess great human qualities provided that you have told the truth.

"Yet, you must understand me. Men and women don't make sacrifice for their fellow creatures' beautiful eyes only.

"Furthermore, how would you help us?

"We live in a house estimated at three hundred thousand dollars or more.

"In addition, we must pay our monthly obligations, not including school tuition, health care…

"Frankly, Renault, you want to embark on an impossible mission."

The car parked in front of the house. Renault got off, went around the vehicle and helped Brigitte to join him.

As agreed upon, she pressed on the doorbell.

The father appeared.

"Who is this man?" he inquired.

The student didn't answer at once.

A stranger's wonderful chronicles, Book II

She looked around and saw her mother and her siblings sitting together on the sofa. Then, and only then, she understood that Renault had told the truth.

She lingered a look at this one who made a positive gesture with the head.

Finally, she opened the door wide, put her arm under Renault's, before entering completely the living room.

"Dad, Mom, my brothers and sisters, let me introduce my unexpected friend Renault to you."

"What do you mean?" asked the father.

"Well, we have met by accident. As the school bus had left without me, he volunteered to drive me here. On the way, he made some disturbing revelations."

"What are you talking about, Brigitte? Have you given yourself to prostitution?"

"Renault wouldn't allow that. He practices wisdom like Confucius and some kind of ancient morality."

"Ah! This is your lover."

"I don't know yet. However, he comes to see us to make the same revelations to the whole family."

Renault went straight to a cabinet, opened it and took the gun out.

"Sir, what are you doing?" yelled the father. "You have no right to search our home. Do you come from the government?"

"No, I don't come from the government," replied the visitor. "However, as a man, it's my duty to remind you that you have no right to end your family's life and yours. On behalf of mankind and society, I will not allow you to kill these potentially great professionals.

"Remember, each member of your family is unique and irreplaceable.

"If you kill them, you will do harm to mankind.

"Brigitte, alive, will become a philosopher and a sociologist who will conduct very salutary researches.

"Milton will become a renowned physician.

"Marilyn will emerge as a great literature professor.

"Gabrielle will turn a chemist and will embark on researches that will help healing many diseases.

"Benjamin will become a great lawyer, a congressman and will have a positive impact on the national jurisprudence.

"Finally, your wife, Andrea, expects another baby. She is two month pregnant."

"But who are you?" astonished the father. "Have you spied on our family?

"Has Brigitte given you so much information on us?"

"No, dad, I have given no information to this man on my family," protested the daughter. "I have just met him.

"However, for some unexplained reason, he may grasp reality in its totality.

A stranger's wonderful chronicles, Book II

"Actually, he told me that he knows the alpha and the omega of reality.

"He has made revelations about me I thought to be impossible for someone, beside me, to know.

"Additionally, how would I fathom my siblings' ideals and my mother's pregnancy?

"Actually, the way my mother looks at me, she has just learned about her own pregnancy. Undoubtedly, she hasn't seen her period…"

The father, Mr. Jules Donation and even the other family members burst out crying,

Renault close his eyes: he couldn't believe that distress would reach such level. Then, he remembered that the human administration, throughout ages, has never helped the masses to improve themselves. These have always experienced, from time to time, bitter days.

In the meantime, the rulers have wonderful moments and never stop holding summit conferences on crises they don't intend to solve.

Why do they behave like that?

Jules Donation's voice pulled Brigitte's accidental friend from his thoughts.

"Mister…"

"Call me Renault."

"Renault, I have no other alternative. I have exhausted all my resources. We have nothing in the house. We start undergoing the pangs of hunger…"

Renault went to Jules and put his hands on his shoulders, before saying, "Jules, believe me, I understand everything.

"My friends, like you, I feel sad; for, I know that many, like you, vegetate. But I can't help them all.

"Listen, earth will always represent a valley of tears, unless men and women of goodwill get together to impose their good intentions, regardless of wealth, colors, beliefs and backgrounds. Nobody in this world should go without food, shelter, access to education and health.

"I try to do my best.

"What I require from my beneficiaries and that I will ask you for, is to spread this manifestation of brotherhood you will receive from me.

"Tomorrow is Saturday. Mr. and Mrs. Donation, you will go with me at the XPN Bank. I will help you paying off your mortgage."

"What!" screamed Jules. "You have alluded to a loan amounted to two hundred and fifty thousand dollars or more."

"Renault, you have thrown us into confusion," pointed out the wife. "You may embody Lucifer. We would rather die than sell our souls to Satan and his assistants."

"Mom!" exclaimed Brigitte

"We don't want to die, mom!" screamed the other siblings together.

"Listen, Renault, let's go back to normalcy," pointed out Jules. "Why would you like to help us? Like my wife has said, you may embody Lucifer or sink into folly.

A stranger's wonderful chronicles, Book II

"We don't even believe that you have a great fortune to help us."

Renault raised his hand. Everybody kept silent. He argued once more,

"I only want to help. An invisible but benevolent force put me in Brigitte's path. This meeting, I know, would have many rami-fications.

"However, I don't embody Lucifer and I don't sink into madness. I am Renault.

"Well, enough innuendoes. Let's cling to reality. You have nothing to eat. Let's go to the supermarket. After having your fill, Mrs. Donation, would you still take me for Lucifer in persons?

"I don't know," answered shyly the woman.

"My dear friends, stop imagining; stop worrying. Let's go to the super-market."

That evening, Renault sat down at the Donations' dining room to have supper.

The spouses happened to be cordon bleus.

Some point in time, the visitor said to the couple full with perplexity, "You have recently worked for an investment firm?"

"Yes," replied the wife, after she had got over her surprise.

"But, Renault, how do you know something like that?" inquired the husband.

"Brigitte hasn't made any mistake about me. She has a good head for grasping the truth. However, let me repeat it once more, I grasp reality in its wholeness, as well as its past, present and future elements.

"It's another way to tell you that I know the alpha and omega of reality.

"Frankly speaking, in some extent, you should rejoice at your dismissal, although, you, Jules, has thought of taking your leave of this valley of tears.

"In a way, this dismissal has taken a great weight off your shoulders, for ten years or so you spent at the office of exchange, you didn't have one peaceful moment.

"You lived in a constant state of uncertainty.

"Tell me if I have told the truth or I don't, the stock exchange intense activity badly affected your judgments."

"You have told the truth," acquiesced Andréa. "How many times I would like to relax, to spend some peaceful moments with my children; nevertheless, to keep appearances, Jules and I didn't have a choice but to work hard."

"You did have a choice, but Jules and you didn't want to take it into consideration."

"Listen, Renault," cut in Jules, "You try to guess. We did have a dream, but we have never expressed it clearly to anyone else. I challenge you to name such dream.

"This time, you will lose."

"My Renault won't lose!" insinuated Brigitte.

"Ah! It's your Renault," observed Milton

"Oh, la, la!" exclaimed Gabrielle.

A stranger's wonderful chronicles, Book II

"Thus, Brigitte, contrary to the common belief, you have a lover."

"Listen to me, my friends, it is a figure of speech. Dad has challenged Renault, which my mother has undoubtedly condoned. I know that Renault will win."

The mother intervened and remarked, "Children, you must trust Brigitte.

"She has reached the age to have a lover.

"If she presents Renault as a casual friend, you must believe her. She has no reason for deceiving you.

"However, Renault (she turned towards this one), we all would like to see you struggling like a mad man to get yourself out of this challenge.

"For, Jules and I have never said one word about the choice you have just mentioned."

"Andrea and Jules, my friends, if I guess right will you trust me entirely?"

"Yes, we will," replied spouses together.

"You, Jules in particular, you must give me your word that you won't frighten to kill your family and you again."

Jules straight his arm and gave a handshake to Renault.

"My dear friend, I give you my word, as a gentleman," pronounced the former."

Shortly after, he added, "By the way, Renault, I don't want to die any more. You have given me a new heart; thus, I regain interest in life."

"Well, both," went the beneficial visitor, "you have whispered on day, once in bed, that if you had resources, you will open a restaurant in this neighborhood.

"Not only you didn't have enough resources, but also your father, Jules and Andrea's father-in-law did dissuade you from the idea.

"But, at that time, Jules, your father couldn't have anticipated the stock exchange crash. Now, he has regretted his position taken against your idea, above all, he no longer can help you financially."

Jules had tears in his eyes.

His wife potted him of the shoulder to calm him down.

"Listen, my friends, did I guess right, my friends," asked Renault.

The spouses nodded.

"My friends, this is what I anticipated when I advanced, 'Not my Renault'," rushed point out Brigitte. "That man knows everything."

That night, Renault slept like a baby, after having received Jules' *words of honor*.

The morning after, he went and picked up the Donation couple to go to the bank.

However, before he did, he called Brigitte and her siblings, and stated, "My friends, you don't lack wisdom. Stay in the house. Brigitte is in charge. Do you hear me?"

"Yes, replied the siblings together."

"On my return, I want to feel proud of you."

A stranger's wonderful chronicles, Book II

"Don't worry," ensured Milton. "We will behave wisely."

"Well, my children, your parents and I are on our way to the bank without the slightest concern."

Renault asked for an immediate interview with the bank chair-man.

"It's about an extremely important matter," he pointed out to the receptionist.

Once introduced to the chairman, Renault expressed his intentions without beating about the bush, "Monsieur Philip Lamarck, Mr. and Mrs. Donation intend to sell their property to me."

The spouses had their eyes wide-open.

Renault beckoned to them to remain calm.

"Mr. Renault Poison," observed the chairman, "It's impossible for the spouses to sell you their home. They did take out a mortgage from our bank. You must not forget; if the Donations don't pay off the mortgage, they won't have the right to sell their house to someone else."

"Mr. Frank Lamarck, we don't intend to consent to such transaction without satisfying the bank claim on the property," pointed out Renault. "We only want, by coming here, to make the house available.

"By the way, Mr. Frank Lamarck, what is the mortgage balance?"

"Wait just a minute, Mr. Pinzon! I will give you the answer, as soon as possible."

The banker pressed on an electric bell. A female employee showed up. The former passed the Donations'' file to the latter and recommended,

"Judith, do me a big favor to verify the financial situation for this property."

"I will be back in twenty minutes."

Indeed, the female employee returned with the file and a print-ed account. Then, she disappeared without a murmur.

"Mr. Renault Pinzon, I don't have any piece of encouraging news for you.

The Donations' are late in their monthly payments. Actually, the bank will soon send them a letter reminding them of their obligation; otherwise, they could lose the property.

"I am so sorry."

"Mr. Philip Lamarck, the Donations have already told me about that. Yet, I want to pay off the mortgage they owe you.

So, they will have the right to dispose of their property in any way they want to."

"I don't see any inconvenience."

"Tell me the payoff amount?"

"Let's see.

"The payoff exactly amounts to two hundred and fifty thousand dollars and eighty cent."

"Let me give you a check. Fill it out to the exact amount and add the name of the endorser."

The chairman acted as suggested.

A stranger's wonderful chronicles, Book II

When he finished, he remarked, "Mr. Renault Pinzon, you understand that we must verify the check cover, before the release of the property."

"Of course," agreed Renault.

Once more the chairman had recourse to his employee's expertise, by the way Judith.

Few minutes after, she returned and whispered her findings to her superior's ear.

The chairman beckoned to her to wait. Then, he said, "Judith, fill out the release paper for this property; then, bring it to me for signature."

Finally, the chairperson gave the original to Renault and shook everybody's hand.

Outside, Jules Donation observed, "At least, Renault, you have saved us from shame.

"In one month or two, the bank would have put a warning on the property main door indicating its ownership of it.

Thus, when you become the new owner, you save us from displaying our despair."

"What would become of us?" inquired Andréa.

"We will go directly to the notary public in the neighborhood," answered Renault.

"Why?"

"Jules, Andréa, don't deny it. For a split second, you took me for a heartless usurper.

"However, I didn't have the choice but to secure my claim on the property and to return it to you immediately."

The deal went on smoothly at the notary public's office. The Donations regained the ownership of their house.

The same day, Renault and his workers started constructing a spacious pavilion for the restaurant.

Located at the corner of two busy streets, not too far from governmental offices, as well as from the stock exchange building in which had worked the Donations for almost ten years, the place had great charm.

The following Monday, the restaurant had a spectacular opening. Parents, friends, old colleagues, employees and passers-by came in great number.

Jules' father asked abruptly, "Jou, where have you found so much cash to open up this luxurious restaurant?"

"Dad," answered the son, "to appease you, I must tell you that I haven't found any cash.

"Indeed, dad, I still don't live in opulence. However, last Friday, Brigitte came back home with a friend who has helped us a lot."

"A friend!" said the father astonishingly.

"Yes, a friend," cut in Andrea. "Dad, I know the vividness of your imagination capable of inventing a number of scenarios.

"But, this time, Brigitte insists that Renault is a friend."

A stranger's wonderful chronicles, Book II

"Dad, we believe her, since we haven't prevented her from having a lover.

"Don't ascribe her shying away from romance to us.

"Now if she takes Renault as a good friend, we must believe her."

"Where is this Renault?" Inquired Beatrice Pamphlets, Andrea's mother.

"I don't know," rushed saying Jules. "However, he has promised to come here today."

"This Renault may derive from the family's imagination," insisted Beatrice Pamphlets. "To the best of my recollection, no friend on earth will pull a whole family from a mess. I won't believe you."

"Mom, not our Renault," acknowledge Andréa.

"What do you mean, Rea," asked her mother.

"Mom, don't worry. He will come, I am sure of that. You will have your chance to ask him the same question, and you will have the right answer."

Suddenly, some noise came from the street.

The people sitting at restaurant briskly took a look through the window panes. They saw a young man surrounded by the Donations children (including Brigitte)

"Ah!" exclaimed Jules happily. "My friends, finally, you will meet with Renault."

The Donation spouses joined their children to give a warm welcome to the visitor.

A narrow escape

Jules presented him to his parents, to his in-laws and friends closed to the family in these words, "My friends, here is Renault.

"Renault, I have here my father, Joseph Donation, my mother Julienne, ma mother-in-law Beatrice and my father-in-law, Webb Pamphlets...

"Pleased to meet you," said Renault.

"We also feel very happy to meet you," echoed Beatrice Pamphlets.

Shortly after, she insinuated, "They have told us about your friendship with Brigitte."

"Indeed, I met Brigitte by chance.

"She had missed the last school bus for that day. Then, I drove her back home."

"I see."

"Listen Renault, you become a good friend of the family," observed Joseph Donation. "According to Jules and his wife, you have given them financial support to help them get back on their feet.

"How do you explain your great generosity?"

"I may give you a simple explanation. In the name of humanity, I have acted as Brigitte's brother, as well as her siblings and parents'."

"A brother!" astonished Julienne.

"Oh, excuse me, Julienne.

"My friend, the Donation family is composed of human beings.

"They have found themselves in the same bag as I.

"They have, one day, an awareness of living on this planet, by accident.

A stranger's wonderful chronicles, Book II

"It depends on someone like me to help them out.

"In return, they have promised me to spread generosity in their surroundings.

"You see, Julienne and my friends, the explanation is really simple."

Few minutes after, Renault took leave of the Donations and their customers.

Brigitte insisted on seeing him to his car.

They walked arm in arm.

Without noticing it, parents, grandparents, the siblings, the customers looked at them through the windows. A client bent too low and fell down on his behind.

There was a burst of laughter.

Fortunately, Renault's had parked his car at the street corner, far away from the "interested" people's field of vision, which put an end to those curious-minded customers and relatives' imagination.

Brigitte sat down at the passenger's seat; Renault took the wheel and kept silent.

Finally, the young lady observed, "Renault, what will become of our friendship?

"Don't tell me that you will disappear to thin air, with no trace of your visit..."

"Brigitte, our friendship will turn stronger, I think," replied the man.

"You know?

"For one reason or another, I wonder if I can keep living without you."

"Don't worry, my beautiful Brigitte. You will always remain in my mind."

"Stop it! Renault, you are talking with a young lady who will go to college within two months.

"I don't want to refer to your image, the memory of our accidental meeting or else. I mean your physical presence that brings me so much happiness and inner security.

"You shouldn't forget, Renault, I had no fear of you, since our first encounter. You are the only man by which I have felt so great.

"Additionally, you have pulled my family from predicaments and shame, thanks to me. If I didn't deliberately miss the school bus, I would belong to history, by now; for, my father intended to obliterate the whole family, in hope of avoiding the embarrassment of sinking into dire poverty.

"If you belong to reality, and I have all the reasons for believing that you do, how can you have so much kindness to make me happy, and so much heartlessness to leave me forever?"

"Brigitte, I can do nothing.

"You must go on with your life. Soon you will become a professional, after obtaining a PhD in philosophy and sociology.

"You will succeed…"

"I know that you have uncovered my future to the minute details.

A stranger's wonderful chronicles, Book II

"But I won't feel any happiness without your presence.

"Renault, promise me to come back to me after my college studies; promise me to come and visit me once in a while; promise me that you will make me happy…"

"Brigitte, listen…"

"No, I don't want to listen to you. I won't let you go until you make these promises."

The young lady burst out crying and mumbled, "That's not right! How can you turn so heartless?"

Renault patted her on the back trying to calm her down. Finally, he ended up saying, "Brigitte, I promised to make you happy."

The young lady turned close to the man and kissed him tenderly on the lips.

"Now, Renault, you may go. I know that you always embark on benevolent missions. I won't stand in the way of such noble function.

"However, I feel so happy to learn that you will never forget me.

"As a gentleman, you wouldn't intend to delude me with empty hope."

"No, Brigitte, I wouldn't lie to you.

"A lie from me would discourage you for life.

"I would rather make you happy than destroy the existence of such beautiful person.

"See you soon, Brigitte."

"See you soon, Renault.

"By the way, here is my cellular number. Thanks to you, I have reconnected my phone."

"Brigitte, let me give you mine."

She got off the car; Renault drove on.

On her way back to the restaurant, the young woman noticed that she had an envelope in her skirt pocket. She thought that by mistake she had taken papers gathering on the car seat.

She turned quickly to beckon to Renault, but the car had mysteriously disappeared.

She resigned herself to pulling the sealed envelope out of her skirt pocket. She couldn't prevent herself from reading her name on it.

She stopped and opened it.

She had a big surprise at seeing a credit card with her name on it.

She wondered when this wonderful man had the time to do all this.

Additionally, she spotted bank notes and a letter which said the following:

Hi! My beautiful Brigitte,

The credit card will allow you to pursue studies without any problem whatsoever.

Don't also forget to help you brothers and sisters.

Would you believe it, if I told you that I feel happy to make you happy?

A stranger's wonderful chronicles, Book II

It's your Renault, who will never cease to keep a little warm spot in his heart for you!

Signed: Renault.

Then, and only then, Brigitte had no doubt about meeting again Renault and to look at reality with confidence.

Her *accidental friend,* met in the neighborhood of her school, wouldn't let her down.

◘   ◘

◘

The reporter, Brian Clifford, took great delight in the happy adventure of Brigitte's adventure, which he would publish the day after.

More than ever, his belief in the marvelous stranger grew stronger, since other beneficiaries felt encouraged to report their encounter with him.

He already anticipated the exquisite pleasure he would experience during his next visit to "those who are at the mercy of the unknown"

(17)

At
The mercy
Of
The unknown

By Antoine Archange Raphael

*T*he reporter, Brian Clifford, soon after filling out the proper documents at Port-au-Prince international airport, called a taxi and went to BelAir section where stood Felicia's store-restaurant. The woman recognized him not only because of his picture she had seen on TV, but also because of the presence of a cameraman with his powerful movie camera hung at his shoulder.

She gave them a warm welcome and offered them a bottle of cold acassan and bread with peanut butter.

"Felicia!" exclaimed Brian. "I have never tasted something so delicious! After the interview, I would like to have some more."

"That is a promise," advanced the store owner.

Then, after a pause, she went, "Brian, to save time, knowing that you will take the next plane after the interview, let's start from the beginning."

The wonderful stranger, called this time Johnny Burton, landed in the capital of Haiti. Because of his tiredness, he decided to spend some time in absolute tranquility.

A friend had told him about the marvelous places of interest that, despise the country dire poverty, could satisfy his *bents for daydreaming*.

For one reason or another, Johnny Burton felt comfortable in Port-au-Prince. He spent the first day of his arrival resting in his room, taking delight in local foods and having a chat with tourists and Haitians.

At the mercy of the unknown

To his amazement, he could communicate with the latter in patois. "What's going on?" he wondered perplexedly. "Where did I learn this idiom?

"Did I live in this country with my parents during my childhood?

"But who are they?"

The day after, he rented a big car and ventured through the street meanders.

Some point in time, he drove through *Sans Fil* area. He spotted a store-restaurant and parked his car alongside the sidewalk.

He entered the business place and ordered a bottle of acassan and bread with peanut butter.

A nineteen-year-old woman attended him. They looked at each other; then, the waitress' reality appeared clearly to Johnny Burton.

In another room a man, his wife and their children enjoyed themselves.

Children all over the country were in school recess.

From time to time, the man looked at the store-restaurant to see if everything went well.

Some point in time, he yelled, "Felicia, my dear, do you have any problem?"

The waitress didn't respond. She rather went into raptures over the visitor.

"Felicia," said the latter, "it's so tasty what you have served me. Who has the recipe?"

A stranger's wonderful chronicles, Book II

The woman breathed deeply before answering, "Sir, I have no secret to divulge. I take care personally of the acassan cooking, the dour making and other aspects of the operation."

"As a young lady, you do have skills."

"This means nothing."

"I know.

"You came from the Northeastern part of Haiti.

"You have also two sisters who get caught in the hellish spiral of Port-au-Prince."

"My God! You may embody a spirit, a Voodoo god such as Papa Ogou, Baron Samedi—to say the least.

"Nobody knows so much about others.

"Have we ever met before?

"If you spy on me, you will waste your time; for, I live in dire poverty, at the mercy of the unknown.

"I often wonder if I have a purpose in life.

"Why was I born?

"Certainly, not to lead a doggy existence, like this one."

"Felicia, I embody neither God, the Creator, they said, of heaven and earth, nor a Voodoo god," replied the customer. "I only have the gifts for understanding others' reality, just by looking at them.

"I can't offer any other explanation. You must take me as I appear to you."

At the mercy of the unknown

Jerome Lecentre, the store-restaurant owner, played domino with his wife and their three children.

He found the familiarity between the client and the waitress intriguing. "Has she ever met him before?" he thought. "Does he come from the *Department of Labor*, asking questions about wage?

"I remember not having paid Felicia for her services. I must find out what they are up to."

He stood up and went to Felicia. "What's going on?" he stated peremptorily.

The client answered instead, "Mr. Lecentre, Cici doesn't bother me."

Then, shortly after, he added, "It's quite the contrary. We live in harmony."

"You call her Cici. Have you maintained intimate relationship with her?"

"It's my impression."

"Then, that hypocrite had given herself over to prostitution before coming to my house. I had an intuition that she was rotten…"

"Attention, Mr. Lecentre, I said that I knew her. However, I haven't made any other insinuation."

"Listen, if you have already paid for your foods, you have to leave."

"Yes, I will leave. However, I would like to finish talking with Cici."

"No, you must go now."

"In that case, Cici, follow me."

A stranger's wonderful chronicles, Book II

"No," yelled the owner. "I won't allow this. Who will attend the clients?"

"I have no idea, but Cici must speak to me."

Johnny made a motion of the hand and stated, "Cici, we must leave now. Let's go."

The young woman betrayed a short moment of hesitation. Then, she decided to act one way or the other. She locked the cash drawer, handed over the key to her cousin and followed the man for the better or for the worse.

The stranger had packed his car in front of the store-restaurant. He opened the passenger's door and invited Felicia to get on. Then, taking the wheel, he drove away.

Suddenly, he inquired, "Cici, tell me about your sisters and you."

The woman burst out crying.

The man rubbed her back to calm her down. Then, she started, "Sir…"

"Call me Johnny," said the man.

"Johnny, my sisters and I have committed a big mistake. Actually, many, from the country, believe, like us, that Port-au-Prince, that big city, offers plenty of opportunities to everybody.

"In our case, friends and relatives let our parents believe that we could leave with them to the Capital; we would assist them in their business and we would get paid. But, once arrived here, those people have reduced us to some kind modern slavery.

"I must tell you that my cousin has gone as far as to physically assaulted me once.

"Additionally, he has tried to rape me; fortunately, his wife has returned from her business. Yet, she has accused me of trying to seduce her husband.

"My two sisters have experienced the same hardships.

"Johnny, we find ourselves in a hellish situation, completely stripped of our human dignity.

"Phew!"

She had a pause to repress her emotions.

Then, she added, "I don't know why I have to tell you about our tribulations.

"For some unexplained reason, when I saw you coming, my heart palpitated. Then, I saw in your eyes a kind of hopeful expression.

"What does it mean? I have no idea."

"Cici, I will help you out," cut in the so-called Johnny.

"How, Johnny, will you help us?" inquired the young woman.

She took a short pause again before acknowledging, "I don't know about my sisters, since they have reached adulthood; however, I don't give myself over to prostitution. I rather sink into poverty. I have nothing to offer. Then, why would you help me."

"Cici, I want to help you because you embody my sister in humanity."

"I embody your sister in humanity?"

"Of course, you do.

"Cici, a huge brotherhood and sisterhood should unite men and women; for, we belong to the same planet. And all the human beings should satisfy their primary needs such as foods, good shelters, and entertainments."

"In that case, Johnny, you don't belong to this world. Men and women tear each other to pieces.

"Then, until proof to the contrary, I know that you mean to hurt me.

"Frankly speaking, the way I feel it, I don't care if you hurt me."

"You have the right to profess such pessimistic opinion, after having suffered so much in your cousin's home.

"But trust me. I will take upon myself to make you happy."

The car slowed down and stopped by a house with a sign indicating "for sale".

Johnny got off the car and asked Felicia to do the same.

He spotted a man sitting in front of the house and said to him, "Hi! Gaston! Are you the salesman for this property?"

"Yes boss!" replied the so-called Gaston astonishingly. "But you call me by my name.

"Do you know me?"

"Gaston, I know everything."

"You know everything? In this case, I will rank you with God."

"No, Gaston, you should rank me with Johnny.

At the mercy of the unknown

"But let me give you an idea of my divinatory powers.

"My dear Gaston, you haven't received any commission this month; for, you haven't sold any home.

"You have sadness in your heart, since Christmas is around the corner. You have no money; therefore, you won't buy your children any gifts. Your family won't have any Christmas dinner to which you would invite your penniless neighbors.

"Then, you have sadness in your heart."

"It's incredible," acknowledged Gaston.

He turned towards Felicia and stated, "Ms., your lover has extraordinary skills."

"Gaston, you are not the first one to say it," cut in the young woman.

"Well, boss…," started Gaston.

"My name is Johnny."

"Johnny, do you intend to buy this house?"

"Evidently, Gaston, I will, but under certain conditions I will state soon."

"I knew it. Things look too good to be true. You would impose unacceptable conditions..."

"Gaston, don't betray so much pessimism.

"Additionally, you haven't even heard these conditions. They may bring you some extra cash."

"Oh, Johnny, I rank you with God (whether you want it or not).

A stranger's wonderful chronicles, Book II

"For some unexplained reason, your voice has reached my ears like a melody.

"From now on, I will pay more attention to your sayings.

"I mean it."

"Well, Gaston, I mean the following: I do intend to buy this house for Felicia. She thinks of opening a beautiful store-restaurant.

"Employees of the company nearby and others institutions I have seen, on the way, would take delight in her succulent dish, of which she keeps secretly the recipes."

Johnny, then, gave instruction to Gaston and made him in charge of the renovation process.

"As you are familiar with the area, you will gather a team of unemployed cabinet makers, masons, electricians, plumbers who will show eagerness to work at this project."

After a pause, he inquired, "Now, Gaston, as a salesman, you have to tell me the process I must follow, under these circumstances.

"To start with, my dear friend Gaston, how should I buy this house?"

"Well, we will go to attorney Morton Lanester. He has responsibility for selling this property."

"Then, let's go Felicia. Believe me, you will become this house owner soon.

"After the transactions, we will go and pick up your sisters who will live with you and help you with the store-restaurant."

At the mercy of the unknown

"Johnny, whatever you want, I won't have any quarrel with it," pronounced Felicia. "However, I won't exclude the possibility of dreaming such wonderful scenario.

"When I wake up, I won't see any handsome man called Johnny, any Gaston, the salesman of a beautiful house in which I will live with my sisters and in which I will have a nice little restaurant with all modern equipment..."

"Ms. Felicia, I have a similar impression," acknowledged Donald. "We have the same dream."

"Yet, both Felicia and Donald, you make a mistake. How can you have a real dialogue in a dream?

"To the best of my recollection, one person always dreams, and two or more converse."

"Johnny, you come from above," pointed out the salesman. "Your wisdom has no bounds."

At a street corner, he informed, "Johnny, we have reached attorney Morton Lanester's office. I must warn you about his haughtiness and meanness.

"Would you believe it?

"He has never given me a bonus, besides the small commissions I receive if I have the chance of finding buyers for his array of properties."

"Don't worry, Donald. He may be haughty and cruel, but he doesn't lack greed. He won't refuse money. Believe me."

A stranger's wonderful chronicles, Book II

"You do have a good point."

The secretary invited the visitors to sit down and stated, "I will ask Maître Lanester if he would receive you without appointment."

"Ms, don't forget to tell him that I want to buy his property located in BelAir.

"Ms., this is Donald Gaston, the salesman.

"You must recognize him."

"Yes, vaguely

"Well, wait a minute."

Five minutes after, attorney Lanester came to welcome the visitors in person.

Gaston Donald was about to remain in the waiting room, but Johnny beckoned to him to follow him.

"Come, Gaston," he added. "Without you, I wouldn't know the steps to buy Felicia this property.

"And, Gaston, my friend, don't forget that you will also act as my agent."

Attorney Lanester sold the house to Felicia for four hundred thousand dollars.

To close the deal faster, Johnny made money transfer directly to Lanester Firm.

"Well, Gaston, your assignment may start now," stated Johnny. "Here is some money. Take a taxi.

At the mercy of the unknown

"Oh, wait just a minute. This is the new blueprint for the house renovation. It's simple. Go and fetch the workers. When we return, everything must be ready."

"Yes, Johnny. Everything will be ready."

"You will have a big reward."

"I know. I have an intuition."

Then, returning towards Felicia, Johnny recommended, "Let's go and get Mogette and Violeta."

"You know my sisters' names!"

"Felicia, I have to see your innocent eyes to know the story of your life."

Mogette had a gash to her face.

"Mo, darling, what happened to your face?" asked Felicia anxiously.

The sister kept silent.

"Mo, don't have any fear," assured the oldest sister. "You won't return to this house."

"Really!" exclaimed Mogette joyfully.

"I come to pick you up."

"Well, Cici, the man hit me yesterday for a trifle. I dropped a pack of cigarettes, by accident."

"I can't believe it. The man hit you for something like that?" inquired Johnny.

"Yes, sir, he did."

A stranger's wonderful chronicles, Book II

"Call me Johnny."

"Tata, how are you?" asked Felicia (speaking to the other sister).

After a pause, she added, "Oh, my God! You are so skinny. What is happening to you?"

"Cici, I haven't eaten since this morning?"

Johnny whispered to Felicia's ear.

She made an acquiescing gesture. Next, Johnny drove to a McDonald restaurant and ordered foods at the window.

"We are late," stated Johnny. "We will eat in the car, as we drive towards your new home."

Then, turning toward the sisters, he added, "Mogette and Violeta, Felicia has just bought a house in which she will set a store-restaurant. You will help her out in her business and she will pay you.

"From that point on, you will remain independent."

"But, it's incredible," stated Mogette. "Where did you get the money from, Cici?"

"Mo, my dear sister, this is a true mystery. Until ten in the morning, I was a slave. Johnny came and put his fortune at my disposal."

"Oh, Felicia, you have lifted my soul!"

Then, after a short pause, Violeta whispered, "Cici, is he your lover?"

"Tata, I wish he could, from the bottom of my heart. However, I met him this morning. I haven't even got the opportunity to thank him for all he has done for me, so far."

At the mercy of the unknown

The car stopped in front of the house. A neon sign, perched on the upper door fixed frame, announced, *The Store Corner.* A poster on the wall invited the public to attend the grand opening the day after.

Inside, the workers kept a *sharp eye* on Gaston and started being fidgety; for, they wondered if they would receive any pay for a work well done.

A broad smile opened up the salesperson's face on seeing Johnny.

He went to him without any ceremony. "I get so scared, Johnny," he finally said. "They have done their part.

"As you can see, they have accomplished a superior job."

"You are right, Donald," acknowledged Johnny. "I will take care of your buddies."

Then, raising his voice, he pronounced, "Listen, my friends, I did get caught in a traffic jam.

"You must forgive me.

"You have done a good job. I will pay you right away.

"How much do you charge me?"

The workers looked at each other. Then, they whispered few words to Miller Joseph's ears, one of their coworkers who happened to practice wisdom.

Finally, he advanced, "Boss, we did work for four hours straight. Listen, Boss, what would you say if we charge each fifty gourds?"

A stranger's wonderful chronicles, Book II

"Listen, my friends, I know that you have been unemployed for months. I will give you each two hundred gourds, which will allow you to spend a nice holiday with your families."

The workers shouted together, "My God! Johnny, you embody manna from heaven."

Gradually, the workers left over abundantly satisfied, not without shaking Gaston's hand.

In the meantime, Felicia and her sisters, under Johnny and Gaston's amused eyes, got organized and ready for the store big opening, in few hours. They would manage to have supper some point in time and would, certainly, have a chat before going to bed for one of the best night sleep they had ever taken delight in.

Johnny drew Gaston's attention and gave him an envelope filled with banknotes.

The salesman almost lost his faculty of speech. Finally, he said, "Johnny, do you belong to this world?"

"Yes, I do," replied the benefactor.

"But I have a small problem."

"You have a mall problem?"

"How to make my wife and my children believe in the events I have participated in. They will, certainly, think that I have committed a crime."

"Don't worry, Gaston. I will go with you to your home."

52

At the mercy of the unknown

"But, Johnny, we don't live in a pleasant-looking house…"

"Remember, Gaston, as a man, I count among the most adaptable beings on earth."

Shortly after, he added, "Don't worry, my friend, we will go in a few minutes."

Johnny promised Felicia and her sisters to come back to see them the day after, for the big opening. In the meantime, he would visit Gaston Donald and his family, before resuming his hotel room.

The Donalds lived in some kind of huge box located deep in a huge yard overpopulated by many families sinking into dire poverty. To reach their home, they had to walk through a long and narrow passage and often to *flatten* themselves against the wall to let others through, coming from the opposite direction.

Mrs. Donald pulled her husband by his shirtsleeve for a private conversation.

The spouses had a big surprise, when Johnny observed, "Pa enkyete ou man Donald. Se mwen ki vle vini [Don't worry, Mrs. Donald. I have come on my own accord."

Gaston, first, had the eyes wide-open. Then, he acknowledged, "Johnny, are you from this country? You haven't told me that you are my fellow-citizen. But you speak Creole fluently. Where do you come from?"

"My friend, listen to me. I can't tell you about my origin. I don't know it. I have been here in Haiti for three days.

A stranger's wonderful chronicles, Book II

"I speak to the locals in Creole. When did I learn this idiom? I can't tell you.

"But, Isabelle…"

"You call me by my first name?

"Donald…"

"No, darling, I have said nothing to this man," rushed saying the husband. "But, don't worry. He belongs to this planet and knows everything."

Johnny made a large motion of the hand before saying, "Isabelle, Gaston and you, my children, sit down."

The Donalds had four children: two boy and two girls.

"Well, Gaston, tell your wife and your children why I come to your home."

"Isabelle," started Gaston, "the man has bought the house in BelAir for his fiancée. Then, he puts me in charge of the house renovation. In a short time, my friends have thoroughly transformed that house. Then, Johnny has given me this envelope of money by way of income.

"You may open it yourself."

The whole family had a shock when they saw the wad of dollars.

The Donalds kept silent.

They thought they had a family dream.

Yet, they had to face reality; for, a family dream has never existed. His members must have each his or her own dream.

Someone knocked at the door.

At the mercy of the unknown

Isabelle hurriedly returned the money to the envelope and put the whole thing in a cabinet drawer.

One of the children opened the door. Charlton Beaujolais, a merciless extortionist, showed up.

Johnny and the others could see the grip of his revolver, through his unbuttoned shirt.

Gaston had borrowed ten dollars from him, close to a year before. Despite the payment of the debt, this extortionist kept coming back, once a week, to claim "interests" on the debt.

Isabelle, Gaston and the children trembled all over.

"Gaston, who is this man?" inquired Johnny.

"It's Mr. Beaujolais," replied Gaston.

Then, shortly after, he stated, "I have borrowed some money from him; then, he comes to collect interests on the debt."

"Mr. Beaujolais…"

"Who are you?" yelled the extortionist.

"I am Johnny."

"I don't know you."

"You can't know me. It is my first visit in Haiti.

"Well, how much money the Donalds owe you? I would like to pay the principal and the interests today. Then, you will leave these good people alone."

"Let me see…

A stranger's wonderful chronicles, Book II

Well, according to my calculation, Gaston owes me two hundred dollars. "

"Oh!" exclaimed the whole family together.

"Well, Mr. Beaujolais, here are two hundred dollars. Don't ever come back to this house."

"Nobody can tell me what to do," replied the extortionist masterfully. "I will come back, as I please. And don't make me take extreme measures."

"What kind of measures can you take?"

The criminal made a gesture to cork his pistol, but his hand met with empty space.

He turned out quickly and saw his weapon in Johnny's possession.

The latter stood up and let the Donalds know, "My friends, wait for me. I must have a chat with this criminal."

Charlton, frightened, walked crabwise, while Johnny stayed close behind him.

Suddenly, the extortionist had a feeling of floating in the air. Indeed, his feet had no longer contact with the soil. Then, he started to spin around like a windmill.

Next, he saw Johnny metamorphosing into a frightening being. He looked like a man with a cow head and a long pair of horns.

That Lucifer-like creature said in a cavernous voice, "Charlton, the next time you harass these people, you will go straight to hell.

At the mercy of the unknown

"That's a guarantee of daily torments.

"Let me give you an idea of what you will endure,"

Having said that, he pointed to an immeasurable machine, with huge gears, that would crush everything such as trees, rocks, metals, animals, human beings…

"I will drop you there, Charlton," went the demonic creature, "and, day and night, this machine will liquefy your body, from the past, the present and to eternity. And you will keep an awareness of you unspeakable pain.

"Well, go away, punk! Don't ever return to my friends' home. Otherwise, you will undergo the eternal torments, day in, day out, at every minute, at ever second…

"Did you hear me?"

"Yes, Mr. Beelzebub," groaned the criminal.

"Do you want to go to hell now?"

"No, dear Mr. Beelzebub, I don't want to. I won't do any more harm to your friends."

"Charlton, you must use caution. I know the alpha and the omega of reality."

"Mr. Beelzebub, I have no doubt about it."

Next, Charlton took to his heels. While dashing, he received bullet wounds to his calves, fell down to the ground, stood up and kept running towards his car parked, in which were waiting three of his henchmen.

Johnny rejoined the Donalds who inquired about Charlton's lot.

A stranger's wonderful chronicles, Book II

The visitor beckoned to them and asked them to look through their windows.

They had a big surprise at seeing Charlton running away as fast as he could; the more as their windows didn't open up to the street.

Gaston inquired, "Johnny, what did you do to the poor man that makes him run away like a dog with its tail on fire."

"Nothing," replied Johnny peacefully. "Except that I have shown him the hell gate opened up on to the place of suffering from now to eternity, if he doesn't repent."

"The hell gate?" asked the family together.

"Well, my good friends, let me tell you today that I do have magic powers.

"Thus, I can invent all kinds of images, depending on the circumstances."

They burst out laughing.

In the meantime, one of Charlton's henchmen asked him, "Boss, what's going on?"

"Let's go," answered Charlton. "We will talk about that on the way. You should know that I have received bullet wounds to my calves."

A few blocks further, Charlton stopped the car to assess his legs wounds. He didn't have any.

Johnny stood up and announced, "I must go to my hotel room, my friends.

At the mercy of the unknown

"By the way, Gaston, *Bonaventure Firm* has a house for sale. It is located not far from the national library. You are the salesman, aren't you?"

"Yes, Johnny, I am.

"Well, forgive my indiscretion. I waste my time on asking questions. You know everything.

"But, Johnny, what's in your mind? Don't tell me that you have another fiancée?"

"No, Gaston. However, I have new acquaintances.

"What would say, my friends, if tomorrow we go and visit that house?

"Frankly, I don't have the heart to see you live in this kind of box, forever and ever."

"You want to deceive us?" inquired Isabelle."

"No, I don't. Tomorrow I will come to pick you up. You must only secure you identification papers. Tomorrow, you will say, once and for all, good-bye to this hellish life."

"When will you come to pick up us?"

"I will come early in the morning."

"We will place ourselves at your disposal and at your mercy."

"You have shown the right attitude!

"Bye, my friends. I will see you tomorrow."

Johnny left the Donalds' and disappeared.

On the way, he spotted Charlton Beaujolais' car.

A stranger's wonderful chronicles, Book II

He turned on his "listening device" and realized that the henchmen believed that their supervisor in crime reacted under the influence of an illusion created by this *famous Johnny*; witness the bullet wounds to his legs, which had never occurred.

They urged their boss to go back one of these days to the Donalds and to kill them.

Then, they had a shock, and their car had almost collided with other vehicles when they heard Johnny voice make threats,

Listen, my friends, you must let the Donalds alone. Well, let me make you a suggestion: I will hold you accountable for the slightest hitch the Donalds will fall victim of.

Then, from now on, you will act as their protectors, their guardians; otherwise, I will turn very angry. I can make Charlton bullet wounds to his legs reappear. You should know that they were real.

But, this time, they will turn permanent and gangrenous.

A surgeon will amputate both of his legs, and your boss will die shortly after.

By the way, I have the intuition that we will meet again soon, somewhere, and you will try to harm others. At that moment, I will pronounce my last verdict about you.

At the mercy of the unknown

It will have the complexion of a piece of advice, a suggestion. If you accept it, we will be good friends. Otherwise, I will take you for human beings incapable of living in society and I will eliminate you without the slightest remorse.

I must have some rest.

I will invite you, my friends, to use caution. You should also get some rest.

Bye.

Charlton stopped the car alongside the sidewalk. He and his henchmen looked around and saw nobody.

The extortionist insisted, "I have told you. That man has extraordinary powers."

"Now, I believe you," acknowledged one of the henchmen.

"Let's get out of here," suggested the others.

Johnny got up early, in the morning. He would fulfill two important tasks: the Donalds new accommodation and his presence at Felicia's store-restaurant great opening.

By ten in the morning, he was happy to complete the first stage of his projects.

The Donalds took possession of their very first home in the history of the family. Parents and children covered Johnny with kisses, to express their gratitude.

A stranger's wonderful chronicles, Book II

Gaston decided to use one room as his office to organize better his brokerage activity.

From that point on, real estate companies and the prospective buyers would come to his office.

Then, he would enjoy more *prestige*.

As far as his wife, Isabelle, was concerned, she would use the front porch and the solarium to open up a little restaurant and put her culinary talent at the service of middle-income families and other members of society.

Both husband and wife had received some cash from Johnny to start their respective line of work.

It was eleven o'clock when Johnny reached the Corner store-restaurant. Felicia, Mogette and Violeta were busy satisfying a crowd of customers.

Felicia spotted Johnny and stopped all activity to throw her arms around the man neck.

"Johnny, my beloved, tell me that I am dreaming?" she whispered.

"No, Felicia, you are not dreaming," replied the man. "The presence of so many customers is irrefutable proof of your being awake."

"But, at least, when it comes to you, Johnny, I have the impression of living in a state of dream," insisted the woman. "I may not find anyone like you throughout this world."

At the mercy of the unknown

"Yet, Cici, my beloved, I may be unique and irreplaceable; however, my neck around which you throw your arms belongs to my body. My voice you hear comes from a physical source belonging to me."

Felicia gently pulled her benefactor by the hand and suggested, "Listen, Johnny, you will taste the foods and will tell me what you think.

"Come and sit down behind the counter."

As Felicia got the acassan and bread with peanut butter ready, Mogette and Violeta rushed kissing Johnny on the cheek.

The man smiled: his prediction just materialized. Charlton and his henchmen showed up at the doorway.

Johnny beckoned to the sisters to wait for him and went to "welcome" the extortionists.

He invited them to follow him outside.

"Listen, my friends," he said, "remember, I told you that you would meet me again; for, you put in your head that the new store-restaurant needs your unwanted protection for a large fee to collect on weekend.

"However, you should know today that this store-restaurant belongs to my fiancée.

"I mean that she owes you nothing.

"Did you hear me?"

The criminals nodded consent.

Johnny pointed an index finger towards the sky before adding, "Listen to me, I want to strike friendship with you. What do you think?"

A stranger's wonderful chronicles, Book II

"Why not?" replied Charlton.

"We wish it with all our heart," added another henchman. "Apparently, you have extraordinary powers; we may use someone like you."

"Sir, no one uses me.

"However, a considerate man gives good pieces of advice to his friends and relatives.

"There is a big empty building located on *American Street*, between *Avenues A* and *B*.

"You can't miss it. They have put it on sale.

"You have enough money to buy it. Our friend, Gaston Donald, is the salesperson.

"If you buy it and open up an auto parts store, you will render a big service to the mechanics on *American Street* and to public in general."

Johnny pulled a booklet out of his inner jacket pocket and added, "To facilitate your tasks, my friends, let me give you this brochure.

"It contains the addresses and phone numbers of major auto part distributors and manufacturers.

"As your friend, I would advise you not to overcharge your customers.

"Additionally, you may sell parts on credit to car owners who may not have the full amount you will require, on the spur of the moment. Eventually, you will set up installment accounts for those people.

"Of course, you will have the right to make a profit. That's the nature of business.

At the mercy of the unknown

"However, you must not frighten your customers or summit them to torture. You have to exclude violence in your daily dealing with the public.

"You will become a great asset to mankind in general and to your country in particular.

"If you accept my suggestion, I will take you myself to Gaston, then to attorney Roland Jordan for closing the deal. Then, we will remain good friends.

"If you reject my suggestion and that you choose to harm others, as you used to do before (until you met me), then, at our next meeting, I will reach the conclusion that something is wrong with you. I will also conclude that you don't deserve to live in the society of men, women and children, even on this planet, created with the best intention of love, generosity and brotherhood one could think of, then,

"I will eliminate you without further ado.

"Do we agree?"

Charlton stretched out his hand. Johnny shook it.

Then, the latter shook hand with the others.

"Well, let's go back inside," he suggested.

Along the way, he added, "To start with my friend, you will savor good foods prepared by Felicia and her sisters. Let me stop; your palates will be the judge.

"You may eat as much as you can.

A stranger's wonderful chronicles, Book II

"As a gesture of our new friendship, I will pick up the tab.

◘   ◘

◘

"Mr. Brian Clifford, I have just told the whole story," concluded Felicia.

Shortly after, she went on, "I will drive you personally to Gaston Donald and to *Charlton auto part store* to back up my account.

"However, before I proceed, I would like to serve you, as I have promised, another bottle of acassan and bread with peanut butter.

"It's on the house.

"Thank you, Felicia. However, I must pay for what I will buy for my wife.

"She would certainly savor it, the more so as she has an increase appetite since her pregnancy."

After a short pause, he added, "By the way, Felicia, have you ever seen Johnny again?"

"Mr. Clifford," replied that woman, "the day following the store-restaurant opening, I saw Johnny again. He informed me that he would leave Haiti the day after, taking the early flight at the International Airport.

"I felt so sad, asking myself if I would ever see such a marvelous man again. Then, I had an idea. I invited him to have supper with my sisters and me.

"I spent such wonderful time with him.

At the mercy of the unknown

"He left me around four o'clock in the morning after. He promised to visit me more often; for, he confessed that I have appeared to him more and more special and charming.

"Mr. Clifford, that man seems to take us to an extraordinary dimension.

"For one thing, he has the talent to foresee everything, in minute details.

"During our supper, he said to my sisters, and I quote, 'I know what you are thinking. You wonder if you will ever find the man of your dream.

"The answer is yes, my beautiful sisters, the prince charming will come.'

"As he has predicted, my sisters live respectively now, like two doves, with the men of their dream.

"The three of us, we take care of my store-restaurant, from early in the morning, until six in the evening.

"My place becomes the ideal meeting place for good, professional people."

Few hours after, Brian Clifford took the next airplane to the mother studio, in the USA.

He felt so happy; for, many groups of people had benefited from the marvelous stranger.

His next visit would take him to "The philosophers falling into disgrace".

(18)

Philosophers Falling Into disgrace

By Antoine Archange Raphael

*A*s they had the days off, the couple Adrian Beau-séjour and Julienne Maximilien capitalized on their free time to welcome the reporter, Brian Clifford in their shared office. After light meals, they told him their story in a natural fashion.

The year before, they had undergone hardship and had professed doubt about their future; for, they hadn't seen any way out of poverty.

Then, one of these doggy days, they met *with the marvelous stranger.*

They stood up at a street corner, with their two children, Philip and Mina, sinking into despair.

The father burst out crying at seeing his wife covered with blood.

Earlier, as they had taken a walk in a seedy neighborhood, two thugs assaulted the woman with a knife and an iron bar, and took her bag.

However, these criminals would have an unfortunate surprise; for, the bag had no money in it. The family had reached the bottom of poverty, since they had gone into exile from their native country.

By a stroke of the luck, Julienne had always kept her identity papers in her skirt pocket. She felt it to make sure of these important papers presence and heaved a sigh of relief.

A police car arrived; an officer asked the crowd to disperse. Then, he advised the victim to go to the emergency service located miles away from the place of assault.

A stranger's wonderful chronicles, Book II

"I am sorry," added the officer, "but they forbid me to give ride to civilians."

"Don't worry, Officer," said the husband. "We will take care of ourselves."

The police car shot off at high speed, with the sirens on. Apparently, the precinct had announced on their telephonic system the occurrence of an urgent situation requesting police assistance.

The family, not having any money to take a taxi, the husband sank into despair.

His children and even the victim tried to calm him down, but in vain.

He mumbled, "My friends, I take full responsibility for your hardships. I could have used more caution during my professorial career.

"I did try to instill objectivity in the mind of the new generation of students; thus, when it comes the time for them to take over, they will feel ready for starting a revolution of the mind.

"Unfortunately, one my students had ascribed bad intentions to me and had reported my alleged subversive *plans of action.*

"Now, we find ourselves in a foreign country, with no resources, no money, at the mercy of the unknown. Because of my foolishness, my family I love must suffer."

The wife, despite her head wound, say sweet things to her husband.

She patted him on the back and advanced,

"Adrian, you can't accept all the blames…

Philosophers falling into disgrace

"Don't forget that I have taught philosophy at high school for girls.

"We haven't committed any crime; we have expressed ideas in harmony with the curriculum proposed by the *board of notional education.*

"However, we must admit that politicians usually don't give philosophy a warm welcome, above all in a country like ours, in which standstill pervades the mind and smothers it.

"Julienne, you have told the truth," added the husband. "Yet, we could have chosen a different major at the university, such as math, physics, and chemistry.

"Why did we choose philosophy, taken for a *bête noire* by so many?

"Now, let me repeat it, we remain at the mercy of the unknown.

"Undoubtedly, we can't have a new beginning."

"Adrian, my beloved, don't talk about a new beginning," cut in the wife. "Philosophy must respond to the deepest layers of our tendencies. Then, if we could take the clock back and become students again, we would not lose our fascination with philosophy."

A luxurious car stopped.

A handsome man in his thirties got off it.

Graciously, he made his way through the crowd and said, "We live in a small world! My God, I thought that I have suffered from hallucination!

"Don't tell that I have stumbled on Professor Adrian Beau-séjour and his wife, Professor Julienne Maximilien?"

The spouses and their children had such a big shock.

A stranger's wonderful chronicles, Book II

They knew that they were obscure and that nobody would pay them any attention, in a foreign country.

"Yes, I am Adrian Beauséjour.

"It's my wife whom you have designated by her true names, Julienne Maximilien.

"These are our children, Philip and Mina.

"You have gained the upper hand. We don't recognize you. You must refresh our memory, as they say."

The stranger kept silent for a while. He didn't know what to do. Finally, he smiled and suggested, "Listen, get on my car. We will talk further.

"However, we will show wisdom by taking care of Professor Julienne Maximilien's head wound."

The professors and their children looked at each other. They couldn't stop wondering if they should trust this perfect stranger.

Finally, Professor Julienne Maximilien admitted, "We have nothing to lose. Actually, what else can we do? We have no money.

"Let's get on his car.

"As he has said, I should take care of my wound.

"Additionally, we have reached the end of our tether. We may allow ourselves to delude ourselves with illusions; yet, we will wake up from them soon."

The whole family followed the stranger to his car that pulled away, leaving the onlookers perplexed.

Philosophers falling into disgrace

"My name is Arsene Romain," announced the driver and Good Samaritan.

"But, Mr. Arsene Romain…, who are you, really?" started the husband.

"Please, Professor Adrian Beauséjour, call me Arsene.

"This goes for all of you. I wouldn't recommend formalism under these circumstances.

"At certain moments of our existence, we need a true universal brotherhood to climb up the steep slope of adversity.

"Don't you think so, my friends?"

"Well, Arsene, you have said something deep," went on Professor Beauséjour. "I don't know if you behave sincerely or if you intend to add to our misery."

"I don't think I should play game under these circumstances," argued the stranger named Arsene.

"Arsene, you look so strange to us," intervened the wife, "that you frighten us."

"Actually, Arsene," cut in the husband, "I didn't remember meeting you before. You must give us a hint."

He kept silent for a short while, and then, he added, "I must recognize the weakness of my memory in these days."

"As far as we, human beings are concerned," pointed out the driver, "we shouldn't blame our memory whenever we can't remember past events.

A stranger's wonderful chronicles, Book II

"A long time has elapsed since I assisted to one of your classes offered on Saturdays to the public, in the huge conference room of the national lyceum, in the Island.

"The day I attended your lecture, you described well the philosophical activity, based on its multiple manifestations in life.

However, my dear professor, you should know that the idea that has retained my attention has stemmed from the *notion of stepping back*, of which I quote,

Ladies and gentlemen,

In summary, despite the imperative of existence, despite the precariousness of primary *needs, philosophy invites us to consent to a stepping back in order to think over human beings and things.*

This stepping back (or even a pause) intending to reevaluate the real, has been, all the time, the greatest lesson drawn from philosophy.

It posits, as a principle, the inexhaustible character of the human person, the right to profess hope even in a context of ferocious adversity. For, at the end of the day, the man, who transcends reality, who goes beyond his conditions to think and raise questions about these conditions, will be the one who will

74

emerge as one of the architects of a more viable existence in the world, because it will derive from reflection.

Doesn't the world need such stepping back? In this new century, people should consent to a halt to reevaluate the road they have covered and the remaining of the trip to undergo.

We should have reason for worry, since, apparently, we seem to pull behind us the drawbacks of the last century: rampant poverty, hatred, violence, religious fanaticism, economic parallelism, discrimination, administrative waste, couldn't-careless attitude.

We should have the right to ask ourselves if these drawbacks come from instincts imposed by nature or if they are the consequences of our minimizing the role of reason in the handling of our affairs.

We must raise questions about wisdom and ask ourselves if it is dialectical and will predominantly influence our endeavors, as the time goes by, or if it is a "thing" in the past about which we talk as if it is a dying tradition.

Professor Adrian Beauséjour and his family couldn't believe their ears. He observed, "Arsene, you don't come from this world.

A stranger's wonderful chronicles, Book II

"Apparently, you represent an American scientific project; you are a robot. Nobody in this world can memorize such a long quotation from a conference held years ago.

"Undoubtedly, I had expressed myself the day I had held the conference the way you have just mentioned, but I can't memorize such a long quotation. Tell us the truth."

"My friends," replied Arsene, "I have no truth to reveal. I only know that I have a profound intuition of reality; I apprehend the alpha and the omega of existence.

"How can I explain these skills? I have no idea."

"No, Arsene," interjected Julienne, "what you have just said falls in the realm of impossibility."

"Julienne, you have said impossibility!

"Well, this word means nothing to me. I have just revealed my existential truth. I left nothing out.

"For example, I also attended, Julienne, a conference you had held in the *School for Girls* auditorium.

"Here is a quotation from your conference,

The questions that have always drawn the philosopher's attention still exist today: love and hatred, compassion, human dignity, the existential conditions, death, politics, religious attitude, research for wisdom—what have you.

Philosophers falling into disgrace

For example, from one generation to another, they have noticed a total lack of love among our fellow creatures, which has led to bloody wars and other calamities.

None of these questions and topics will go away (despite science gigantic progress). They will also be the objects of our inquiries. We will always raise new questions about them, and thinkers will always strive to shed light on them.

"Of course, my friends," went on Arsene, "you have reason for looking at me with certain apprehension; for, my faculties seem to hypertrophy. However, I give you a glimpse of my reality. You should rejoice, along with me, that I don't represent a danger to my brothers and sisters.

"Anyway, Adrian and Julienne, both, you have left a strong impression on me. From that point on, I have never stopped taking interest in philosophy."

The Adrians didn't have any kind of explanation to offer. They kept asking if they had a family dream, but, they rejected at once such thought; for, dream belongs to the most intimate and personal part of our personality. People can't dream of the same scenario at the same time, and have the same objects of perception.

As the car turned on a sloping street and drove at high speed, Adrian inquired, "Where are we going to?"

A stranger's wonderful chronicles, Book II

"To my home," answered Arsene.

"But we don't want to inconvenience you."

"Why wouldn't you?

"You find yourselves in deep trouble. You need my assistance. As far as I am concerned, my explanation responds to a rigid logic: we should offer our assistance to those who need it, not to millionaires and billionaires."

"But, again, my friend, do you really belong to this world?" insisted Adrian. "I repeat, you may represent a figment of our imagination."

"Adrian, they have mentioned collective hallucination. I think that, theoretically speaking, it's possible if all the members of a group profess the same belief.

"However, we don't have such case now.

"Mina is fascinated by my person (she opened wide her eyes full of surprise).

"Julienne takes me for a sympathetic person (the woman betrayed a dubious face).

"Philip no longer follows our conversation (the boy jumped). His mind wanders in Haiti with his buddies."

"It's incredible!" acknowledged Philip.

"It's unthinkable!" exclaimed Mina.

"I am completely astounded," observed Julienne.

"As for me," argued Adrian, "I run out of explanations."

Philosophers falling into disgrace

"Well, my friends," promised Arsene, "I will calm your worries."

"My dear friend, I would like to see that," cut in Julienne in a dubitative tone.

"You don't incur any danger," insisted Arsene. "I can't hurt anyone. I behave like a machine programmed to help. I have never had entertained evil thoughts.

"Who may remote-control me? This kind of question, I have never ceased to raise it.

"However, I may tell you at once that, for unexplained reason, I can grasp people's reality in its entirety.

"Impossible!" exclaimed Adrian. "Nobody on earth has the gift for knowing the alpha and omega of reality.

"You must act as a government spy from our native country or the secrete administration…"

"Ah! Adrian! I don't blame you for professing some doubt. The Cartesian's theory has thought us that doubt leads to the open door of objective reality. Then, as an enthusiast for Cartesian's philosophy, you take nothing for granted.

"May I tell that, in this chapter, we are brothers? I don't take anything for granted.

"However, how can you deny to have taught, on the 25th of last April, at three o'clock, something about the *Bergsonian Sympathy?*

"What!"

A stranger's wonderful chronicles, Book II

"You said that the *Bergsonian Sympathy* allows us to grasp the inexpressible in others.

"Then, it explains how a mother may realize that her baby suffers from headache; how a woman may discover that her lover dies of hunger, but, being too pride, he has said nothing; how someone may decipher rotten intentions from a stranger…

"Adrian, I may recall all the steps of this presentation you had delivered that day."

"I don't know, my friend, how you manage to do it," admitted professor Beauséjour, "but you have told the truth to the minute details."

"Then, shortly after, they have fired you, telling you that you represent a national danger."

"I don't know what to say.

"Apparently, the government of our native country thought that our teaching corrupts young minds."

"You don't know the specific reasons. Nobody has told you anything about it."

"Did you say the specific reasons?"

"Yes, I did.

"Let me refresh your memory.

"In the warmth of the presentation, you talked about the mediocrity of many world leaders and took as examples those of your own country which, to all appearances, don't conceive of viable institutions.

Philosophers falling into disgrace

"A student named Marcelin Legrand, the eldest son of Tancredo Legrand, the Coordination State Secretary, had reported your statement to the authority that, in his turn, let the Interior Secretary know about it.

"Finally, they decided that you should leave the country or die."

A dead silence pervaded the confined car space. The spouses and their children didn't know what else to do. They still believed that they experienced a family nightmare, of which they would wake up soon after.

They had a shock when Arsene told them they didn't sink into a "family nightmare".

"Not at all," added Arsene. "You are not dreaming. I belong to reality as well as the floor you walk on.

"You live at Julienne's cousin, Laurel Maximilien. Contrary to your expectations, he and his wife, without mentioning their children, have never stopped mistreating you.

"By day, while they are at work or at school, they lock all the room doors and leave you in the patio.

"Then, this morning, tired of sitting and waiting for their return, you thought that a walk would do you some good, to kill time.

"Unfortunately, criminals, under the influence of drugs, thinking that you, Julienne, had money in your bag, had assaulted you. To prevent you from any resistance, one of them hit you hard to your head with a blunt instrument.

"Fortunately, you haven't kept anything valuable in your handbag.

A stranger's wonderful chronicles, Book II

"The criminals remain empty-handed, with a forced laugh; while you, Julienne, you repress hardly a big laugh, despite your wound, after feeling your skirt pocket and perceiving the swishing sound of your identification papers."

"You are incredible," stated the others together. "You have power beyond comprehension."

Then, after a pause, Arsene went on, "But, you too Julienne isn't more innocent than your husband, in the eyes of those myopic politicians."

"Oh!" exclaimed the woman. "Did I commit a crime?"

"No, you didn't.

"However, you caressed the government of your country the wrong way."

"How do you reach such conclusions?"

"Julienne, do you remember a conference you held, on February 5 of this year, by one o'clock in the afternoon? You touched on the viability of human civilization that we may recognize by the more or less important role played by women.

"You went on and conclude in the following terms,

Ladies and gentlemen,

To conclude, let me say that women have the right to require respect and freedom in the bosom of society: they will never receive them as gifts; they have to ask for them.

Philosophers falling into disgrace

The woman put her palm to her mouth betraying her surprise. Then, she added, "Arsene, I take my hat to you."

"Such gesture, as far as you are concerned, falls in the realm of the impossible."

"Why do you say that?"

"Julienne, you have never carried a hat."

Everybody burst out laughing.

The car reached the front of large gate. The driver opened it by remote control; soon after, the car entered a huge yard.

Finally, it stopped.

The whole family followed Arsene to the spacious living room of the house.

"My friends, this is my place," informed Arsene. "Make yourselves at home."

"As for you, Julienne," he went on, "follow me. I will clean your wound to prevent any infection."

After a few minutes, a maid whispered something to Arsene's ear.

"Good, my friend, Margaret has just informed me that she has cooked some foods for us. As far as I am concerned, it's music to my stomach."

Everybody laughed at the top of his lungs.

"Let us go and sit at the dining room table," added the homeowner. "We may continue our conversation there."

A stranger's wonderful chronicles, Book II

Philip had never stopped looking sulky, which drew Arsene's attention. "Philip, what's wrong?" he asked.

"Nothing," answered tersely the boy.

"Well, Arsene, explained Julienne, Philip is certainly angry with us because he believes that if we have chosen another line of activity, he would still live in his country with his chosen friends."

"I don't think so," intervened Arsene.

"What!" exclaimed Philip. "This time, Arsene, you have made a huge mistake. Because of my parents' militancy, we find ourselves in a foreign country. I feel isolated. I have just told you the truth."

"Philip, your surprise betrays your true unexpressed intentions. You know that I am right.

"No, this time, you have made a mistake," insisted the boy.

"Do you want me to divulge the truth? I don't intend deliberately to invade your privacy."

"Listen, Arsene," cut in Julienne, "I know that truth hurts. However, why will Adrian and I have to suffer unnecessarily if Philip has a specific reason for being sulky?

"We would like to know that motive, so we would stop having a feeling of guilt."

"Arsene, I must recognize that Julienne has spoken judiciously," added Adrian. "You must reveal the true reason for Philip's bad humor; for, he would make us guilty with no motive.

Philosophers falling into disgrace

"I don't like people (including our children) to use Julienne and me."

"Go ahead," acquiesced the boy. "You won't find anything new to reveal."

"Philip, once more," said Arsene, "can I reveal the true reason for you sulkiness?"

"Go ahead."

"For the first time in life, you have fallen in love. The girl is Justine Presort."

The boy turned quickly towards his sister and said,

"Mina, how could you have betrayed me? I would never harm you this way."

"I have betrayed you!" shouted the girl. "What are you talking about? When have I done so?

"Frankly, my dear brother, you make no sense.

"Like everybody, I met Arsene, one hour ago. We haven't, so far, gotten the opportunity to have a chat. Then, did I tell him something about your love life?

"Additionally, you have never let me know that you have fallen in love with Justine, one of my school girls. However, she is not my friend.

"Frankly speaking, she has never been. She believes that she stands above everybody in terms of superior essence and she only strikes friendship with wealthy girls."

"Ah! She isn't snobbish," argued Philip, "Maybe…"

A stranger's wonderful chronicles, Book II

"Philip," cut in Arsene, "did I see right?"

"Yes, you did," replied Philip.

"Therefore Adrian and Julienne," added Arsene, "Don't worry. Philosophy isn't at fault.

"But, Philip, let me tell you the whole truth. It will hurt you, but, after listening to me, you will regain your freedom from this love.

"Justine Presort wouldn't serve you as a good wife. She takes herself for a princess admired by all the handsome and wealthy boys in the school.

"Actually, she recognizes that you do have qualities, but she always said to herself that you come from a poor family.

"Believe me, you will suffer a lot if you marry that girl full of herself.

"I would advise you to trust Mina's intuition.

"She has her head rested on her shoulders.

"A month, before leaving her country, a school playboy…"

"One minute!" yelled the girl. "Let me tell you his names: Gustave Delius?"

"Yes," admitted Arsene. "He tried to make a pass at your. And your answer (you may have forgotten), was, 'Gustave, you must look for another girl.

"I take no interest in love game. When the time arrives, I will choose my own prince charming. In the meantime, I must stay in school and study hard to become an independent woman and follow my parents' good examples. Thus, I advise you to leave me alone."

Everybody's eyes were wide open.

Arsene's gifts, whether natural or not, had defied all logical explanation."

After having eaten, Adrian, on his way to the living room, pull Arsene apart and whispered, "We must go back to the Maxi-miliens, Julienne's cousins."

"I wouldn't go back there."

"What!"

"As far as I am concerned, I take your family and you for members of my household.

"However, all depends on you.

"I don't intend to impose my will on you. I have no right to do so."

"Arsene, give me few minutes. I will discuss this matter with my family. I will let you know about our decision."

Ten minutes after, Adrian rejoined the homeowner to tell him that the others didn't see any inconvenience.

However, they hardly found the words of excuse to appease the Maxi-miliens.

"Julienne, according to me," cut in Arsene, "will tell them that you have met an ancient student. He would like you to spend some time with him.

"Those people would feel so happy to get rid of you!"

Few minutes after the phone conversation with the Maxi-miliens, Arsene pointed to a door opened on a huge bedroom to the couple.

A stranger's wonderful chronicles, Book II

Then, he took the children to two separate bedrooms of smaller dimensions.

"My friends, try to have a good night sleep. We will have a busy day, tomorrow.

"To start with, we will concentrate on the schools Philip and Mina will attend."

"Thank you so much, Arsene," cut in the girl. "I have had some apprehension about my future. I have already lost months out of school."

"Thank you, Arsene," Philip said on his turn. "You won't be disappointed.

"I will stay far away from girls (for now) and will concentrate on my studies."

"I don't know how to thank you," pronounced Julienne.

"As for me, I don't know what to say," insinuated Adrian. "I can't understand the reason for so much generosity from you, Arsene."

The latter didn't answer at once. He was dealing with a brilliant philosophy professor who placed great importance on ideas. Finally, he replied, "Adrian, you have expressed wonderful ideas in the course of your teaching.

"You too, Julienne has put forth fascinating and powerful ideas, in the course of your teaching. However, you have always believed that these ideas are purely Platonic; in other words, they suggest transcendent conducts with no possibility for concretion.

Philosophers falling into disgrace

"Well, they find concretion with me.

"I grant terms such as love of neighbor, brotherhood, the similarity between the "*I's*" aiming at well-being, at positive goals, at a better future, at values and their real meanings, at all beneficial ideas.

"My desire to put them in concrete form reminds me that I am a special being, that transcends the existential situation consisting in eating, drinking and sleeping to reach the true dimension for which, as a person, I find myself on this planet.

"I may be wrong…"

"No, Arsene, you are not wrong," cut in Julienne. "You are simply marvelous."

"Arsene, I couldn't say it better," cut in the husband. "Thank you to remind me that our philosophical instructions are not meaningless, vain, like fake jewels."

"Listen, my friends, not only they are not meaningless and vain," insisted Arsene, "but also I will strive to make sure they will keep on spreading.

"Tomorrow, after having assisted my little friends with registering at the high school nearby, I will take you to *Social School Studies* where, both, Adrian and Julienne, you will respectively teach the *philosophy of action* and the *philosophy of thought.*

"Yesterday, I had a lengthy conversation with the dean of faculty, Doctor Marcus Baton. He told me that they need philosophy professors.

A stranger's wonderful chronicles, Book II

"The philosophy department chairman, Doctor Emile Ross, expects to see you in his office in the neighborhood of ten in the morning.

"He will present you, at the auditorium, to your colleagues and students.

"Then, I would advise you to think about making a toast under these circumstances.

"I will be there.

"Next, I will take you to your new home, a unit of my real estate business.

"I specialized in prefabricated houses.

"From that point on, you will keep spreading the good you have received from me."

"You are simply incredible but grand," acknowledged Mina. "I will never forget such manifestation of human transcendence and I will draw inspiration from it until my last day."

"Oh! Nana, how profound are you!" exclaimed the host.

"Arsene, my brother, my daughter has said it all," stated Julienne.

"Then, my friends, have a good night sleep. Remember, I don't intend to harm you."

The day after, Arsene fulfilled all his promises.

The children registered at the neighborhood high school with no hurdle whatsoever.

Then, they accompanied their parents to *Social College,* Adrian and Julienne's place of employment.

Philosophers falling into disgrace

The dean and the philosophy department chairman presented the new professors who received a warm welcome from colleagues, students, parents and visitors.

Julienne concluded her toast in these terms,

Mr. Chairman,

My dear colleagues,

My dear students,

Until yesterday, my family and I were hopeless. Then, suddenly, we find ourselves on the path of success.

I don't know how to thank the person who has made our today's meeting possible.

This man is unknown to us.

This is what we have thought.

However, according to him, he has been our brother in humanity.

He has never stopped having a common destiny with us: to find ourselves on a planet without a clear reason.

These are simple words which I used to take for granted. However, according to our brother Arsene, these words follow closely the dimensions of the real.

A stranger's wonderful chronicles, Book II

A thunder of applause followed Julienne's speech.

On his turn, Adrian said among others,

Mr. Chairman

My dear colleagues

My dear students,

Ladies and gentlemen,

I sense that Arsene's culture is immense.

This man has reintroduced me to the intimacy of my own profession and made me grasp better the nature of ideas I have profusely made a use of, throughout my professorial career. Additionally, he has drawn my attention on the notion of stepping back, which takes incalculable dimension in philosophy, to see better the real and use it with wisdom.

This man has reminded me of my own thought and feeling I used to express everyday in my classroom.

He draws my attention of the fact that overall, philosophy does not develop without any contact with the outside world.

Actually, the elements of reality must set philosophy in motion.

All around the philosopher exist real people whom he can't confused with figments of his imagination.

Philosophers falling into disgrace

A great majority of them suffer want.

Others manage and hold on to their dreams in the bosom of society.

Others accumulate colossal wealth and ensure inordinate power.

Positive knowledge widens intellectual and technological horizons, next to irrational types of conduct such civil and international wars, crimes, injustice, and reduction to dire poverty.

On the one hand, they show, on televised media, picture of the space shuttle, a billion dollar project, engaged in the space exploration; on the other hand, picture of long lines of people with empty boxes, awaiting free food.

On the one hand, governments with an array of experts lead their people to hell.

By the same token, one individual tries to serve as a solace to millions of people throughout the planet.

On the one hand, people mistreat their fellowmen and fellow women; on the other hand, men and women show compassion for lower animals.

Indeed, a very pressing and disturbing imbroglio draws the philosopher's attention.

A stranger's wonderful chronicles, Book II

Thus, he does nothing but awakens his readers and listeners' awareness of what was vague in their mind or not limpid enough to express them in a dynamic way or to make them know to public.

Therefore, philosophy, as Karl Jasper so rightly states, is accessible to everybody.

Yes, my friend, Arsene, disarmingly frank, has shown us the road to transcendence.

Evidently, I can't find more words to express all my thoughts under these circumstances. However, this man has changed me completely.

My friends, here is Arsene. Let him tell you himself about his philosophy of life.,

There was a thunder of applause, which lasted for a long time. Then, students, professors and other staff members and the rest of the audience screamed, "Arsene! Arsene! Arsene…"

The latter had no choice but to respond to the audience enthusiasm and expectation.

Therefore, he walked slowly to the podium and took the microphone.

He had no other alternatives but to make a toast for the occasion.

He declared,

Philosophers falling into disgrace

My brothers and sisters,

As has said a contemporary author, our existence on this planet, is a gift the origin of which gets lost in the mists of time (a round of applause).

Then, since we are here, the planet's future depends on our actions.

From the appearance of homo sapiens to the future, progress, more or less, has always been assured by men and women of action.

From our hurried actions derives this disoriented world, hardly beneficial to the masses, the foundation and the test of our decision.

More than ever, the eighteen-century thinkers' wish to see more philosophers becoming enlightened leaders of the world justifies itself.

Then, Adrian, Julienne and all the philosophers will work hard and will allow the new generation of men and women to approach the real with a more organized, human and rational vision.

Without such lucid approach, the future of this planet will remain somber.

A stranger's wonderful chronicles, Book II

Thank you, ladies and gentlemen, as well as the college authorities, for allowing me this opportunity to express my thought at this great center of learning.

I will never forget this day.

Take care of yourselves.

The speech had received a round of applause.

Of course, the audience started again to scream, "Arsene, Arsene, Arsene…"

◘　　◘

◘

The reporter, Brian Clifford, breathed deeply. He had the impression of immersing himself in an ocean of purity and transcendence.

He took leave of Adrian, Julienne and their children, not without saying, "This is one of the most edifying episodes of the marvelous stranger.

"For the first time, philosophy has played such important part in the 'Stranger's wonderful chronicles'.

"I feel so happy to report this episode…"

The day after, he would visit a certain Josiah Melon who had experienced a bitter deception before meeting with the wonderful man.

(19)

Bitter Disappointment

By Antoine Archange Raphael

*J*osiah Melon, an executive at the Marvel Real Estate Company beckoned to Brian Clifford to enter his spacious office parsimoniously furnished. He had postponed all his engagements for that day to contribute to the *stranger's wonderful chronicles.*

As usual, he started from the beginning, at the precise moment at which the marvelous stranger intervened to limit the damages in the unfolding of some people's lives.

Josiah Melon had undergone a bad experience, when he entered his apartment shared with his lover, Paula Dancourt, since his graduation from *State Architectural School* in the Capital City.

He had met that woman, one day, in the faculty vicinity and had known love at first sight.

Without a murmur, he had implemented the *Bible advice* according to which one has to leave his parents in poverty, to follow the elect of his heart.

The night before, when he reached home, he didn't see sign of his girlfriend. He looked for her everywhere, but in vain. He had no other alternative but to wait for her return. Evidently, for one reason or another, she had to work late in her office.

However, on the dining room tabletop, he saw a folded sheet of paper. His heart started to pound. He unfolded the sheet of paper and read the following,

Josiah,

Bitter disappointment

By the time you read these lines, I will live far away from you.

Don't waste your time looking for me, you won't see me again.

I think that I have wasted a valuable time with you.

Apparently, my dear, you will never guarantee me a positive future.

I regret if my decision hurts you.

However, before anything, I must take interest in number one (I mean my own future).

The sweet words we have exchanged derive from disgusting childishness.

Thus, I say farewell.

You are young; you will find a woman coming from your poor social rank to follow you.

Signed, Paula.

Josiah had a sleepless night. He didn't expect such inhuman reaction from Paula.

They had embarked on a life of intense emotions.

Actually, the night before, she had given herself up, mind and body, to him, and if his memory served him well, she had sworn eternal loyalty to him.

He felt like hanging in the air.

A stranger's wonderful chronicles, Book II

He couldn't find anyone else to appease him. He had turned his back on his parents, had broken up with his schoolfellows, had even given up his dream to become a renowned architect and had happily looked for a clerical position.

That day, Josiah had no way out. He had dug his own grave. As a man, he has no alternative but to commit suicide to free himself from all these pitfalls of existence.

In the morning, he left without his briefcase. Despite the cold, he didn't wear a coat. "What for?" he whispered. "Death goes without temperature. My body will turn hard and cold like marble."

It was five in the morning. He believed that he would have jumped, from that skyscraper under construction two blocks from his apartment, into nothingness, before the engineers and other workers' arrival.

On the way, in front of the building under construction, he spotted a white minibus. He had an instant of hesitation, thinking that an enthusiastic employee had reached the place ahead of him. However, as the driver was sleeping deeply, he concluded that he was the security guard who had nothing to worry about, since the neighborhood, inhabited by people with high incomes, had never experienced acts of vandalism and banditry.

He stood on the roof edge. He didn't feel dizzy.

He thought he wouldn't even have time to suffer. With the tremendous pull of gravity and under the strong impact of the macadam, his heart would stop along the way and his body would burst and spread all over.

Bitter disappointment

He had a shock: he didn't know when, but people realized his deadly plan. In a flash, onlookers invaded the streets. The man surveyed the crowd making gestures.

In the middle of it, he saw his parents, his siblings, old neighborhood friends and schoolfellows.

He also saw Paula!

She remained tense with mixed feelings.

Undoubtedly, she had just recognized her fault, but her repentance would come too late. She would spend the remaining of her life with this bitter taste of disgust she had caused to an ingenuous soul.

Joshua, then, had the ultimate joy to know that *viper* would burn in hell until the last day of her life. Then, in spite of himself, he would come out victorious over that unfortunate love affair.

Apparently, Paula didn't know it, but, with her, that man had his first sexual experience, his first taste of love, his first joy of togetherness.

Indeed, the woman had introduced him and guided him into the burning world of passion.

Unknowingly, she had fulfilled a primordial role in his life. Yet, she deluded him with a deceptive *Eden*.

Among the onlookers appeared police officers who volunteered pieces of advice to the jumper through their powerful loud speakers.

However, Joshua had made his ultimate decision for the last time. He didn't intend to cancel it out.

A stranger's wonderful chronicles, Book II

If he didn't implement it, others would accuse him of cowardice and would take him for a *wet chicken*, a man with no guts. Without jumping to the emptiness and to his death, he wouldn't have the courage to face anyone; but, splashed on the pavement, he would probably receive others' praise and consideration.

And before he could think of any other alternative, such as remaking his life, looking for parents' assistance, trusting society which would guide him to a more rational existence, to get back on his feet and recapture his human dignity, his professional prestige of an engineer, he leaped to the emptiness.

Contrary to his expectation, the pull of gravity left him with all his lucidity and the horrifying sensation to get near the ground fast.

He anticipated his ultimate suffering before turning to a mush made of blood, skin and bones.

"What have I done, my God?" he thought. "Why did I choose the road to despair?

"It's too late now. I should have ignored that wicked woman; with time, I would have found again my serenity and would have set out to conquer another woman worthy of respect and love.

"Undoubtedly, a real woman may madly fall in love with me without knowing it..."

He had seen his mother losing consciousness. He had heard cries of distress and emotion coming from hundreds of mouths.

Bitter disappointment

For a short while, the onlookers could have closed their eyes to prevent themselves from following the deadly trajectory. Then, everything turned black and white.

He thought to have reached his final destination. It wasn't that bad. He felt no pain. On the contrary, he had the impression of entering a neutral surrounding in which he had no disquietude, no ambition, and no will-power.

Definitively, he believed to reach paradise. He rested on a couch.

He looked around the room and admitted that he found himself in a living room luxuriously furnished.

A huge sofa, a loveseat and an armchair, all made of brown leather, displaying their splendor in the middle of a brown-floored room.

In the background spread out a huge disconnected television set.

Joshua said to himself, "If I could go back to the planet of men, women and children, I would advise them to follow the *Holy Scriptures*. They typify the ideals ensuring a life of felicity in Heaven.

Thus, a righteous, just man will always have a reward in the life beyond.

"I understand now the deep sense of the Bible that goes as follows, 'he who laughs last laughs longest'.

It represents the ultimate saving on which one will live in great joy, daily, during an existential eternity."

An absolute silence reigned over the room; Joshua had no idea about the outside that may not exist at all.

A stranger's wonderful chronicles, Book II

Paradise simply appeared like a location without history, without a street used by vehicles, men, women and children coming and going. God wanted it this way; otherwise, a troublemaker, an offender, a guttersnipe would show up and disturb the paradisiacal harmony.

Suddenly, Joshua saw a thirty-year old man; he sat down comfortably, reading a book apparently captivating.

His eyes remained fixed on the pages.

That man's presence, for some unknown reason, seemed to shake a little bit Joshua's belief in reaching paradise and a felicitous type of life.

However, he explained to himself the meaning of this new discovery.

He had seen countless movies concerning life beyond, which made everybody believe that, in heaven, they keep a welcome committee and a guide to lead the new arrived and accommodate them.

"Excuse me, sir," he said.

The man closed his book at once and rushed putting himself at Joshua's service.

"My name is Roland Badour," he said

"My name..."

"Joshua Melon," rushed saying the man.

Shortly after, he expatiated, "You are the oldest child of the Melon family. Despite the family deplorable economic conditions, they have managed to send you to the best schools in the country. You emerged as an extremely intelligent student.

Bitter disappointment

"You have just finished your college studies, with the highest score obtained by a student in your promotion. You have presented a project approved by the teaching staff.

"It consists of a building capable of withstanding severe earthquakes, hurricanes and other natural disasters.

"If they can finance such project, you will revolutionize the real estate industry and, in the end, you will save many lives.

"Unfortunately, you have met with an exceptionally beautiful woman, named Paula Dancourt. You had experienced love at first sight and had given up everything: your dream to become an architect, the Promethean role you could have played in this field of activity, your family…

"You have lost contact with your schoolfellows and your professors, to follow that Venus.

"Actually, as you have never taken delight in intimate relationship, that woman has introduced you to all the exclusive gametes of pleasure.

"You will have a shock to learn that she extremely wealthy. You understand how she manages to take care of the household spending. You content yourself with a simple office clerk position to kill time, until you meet, in the evening, your beautiful mistress.

"Then, last night, you have received a big blow: Venus has escaped.

"Then, you want to kill yourself. Life turns a bitter pill to swallow. The world no longer looks like paradise…"

Joshua made a gesture of the hand and sat half way on the couch.

A stranger's wonderful chronicles, Book II

Next, he argued, "Mister Roland Badu, I have no surprise that you know everything about me. You are God appearing under the shape of a man. You know the alpha and the omega of reality. You have created me; I have awareness of your omniscience."

"Call me Roland," cut in the man. "Stop deluding yourself. You haven't reached paradise.

"You find yourself in my home."

"Sir, what are you talking about? I have jumped to my death from the building top.

"No one could have rescued me."

"You should have paid greater attention. Haven't you spotted a minibus in front of the building in construction?"

"Yes, but the driver slept like a log."

"He feigned to sleep. However, he had never stopped keeping an open eye on your steps towards your death."

"You had watched all my moves!"

"Yes, I had."

"But, how did you manage to save me? How did you guess that I wanted to commit suicide?"

"If you have patience, I will tell you a long story.

"For one reason or another, something drives me to go to places in which desperate men and women like you really deserve a second chance in life.

"Thus, this morning, I got on my minibus and wore a security guard uniform.

"I drove at random. I saw you, and immediately, I had the intuition of your next course of action.

"Then, with an elastic cord I made a slipknot. In the course of your fall, I caught you by the feet."

A dead silence reigned over the living room. Joshua didn't know what to think. Suddenly, his body shook all over.

"But, sir, what do you want from me," he anxiously inquired. "You may suffer from mental trouble. You may intend to torture me before killing me. Apparently, you have tremendous powers against which I have no defense. However, if you want to kill me, why have you rescued me? I beg you not to make me suffer too much. Put a bullet into my head."

"Joshua," cut in Roland, "you do have a vivid imagination. Nevertheless, I have no desire for torturing you.

"Undoubtedly, you have confused me with one of the serial killers they have talked about on TV. Perhaps you have watched too many sadistic movies."

"Then, you may be bizarre; for, a man wouldn't go as far as to save another one."

"You mean that I may practice homosexuality!"

"Do you?"

"No, my dear friend, I don't. I feel in heaven in women's company.

A stranger's wonderful chronicles, Book II

"However, I believe that men and women can help each other without embarking on intimate relationships.

"Don't you think?

"As for me, I take you for my brother in humanity. I make it my duty to help you out."

"You can't help me, Roland. Like the *Egyptian*, I have committed all the sins in the world.

"I have abandoned my parents, my siblings, my childhood playmates, my schoolfellows, my professors...

"I have given up my dreams and have experienced the bitter deception of a person I have loved madly."

"You have committed many sins (as you call them), too many sins.

"However, don't ever forget that man makes mistakes. We often launch into action without an iota of reflection. Reason always arrives too late to enlighten us.

"However, we shouldn't blame reason. It depends on us. It makes itself available to us day and night. Nevertheless, we scorn it; we lock it up in the boudoir of our mind to give ourselves over to the thrill of pleasure.

"Despite the enormity of your mistakes, society and you should not give you a life sentence."

He took a long pause, before going on, "I may help you to get back on your feet.

"Before I do so, I would like to open your eyes on your love for Paula.

Bitter disappointment

"You have made the wrong choice; for, that woman has never had any love to offer you in return."

"Roland, this time I don't quite understand you. You didn't witness that woman's unreserved display of love for me."

"She had put on an act."

"Roland! I forbid you to speak like that about Paula.

"She may have a very important reason to act in such apparent off-handed manner. If I could see her again, she would, certainly, reveal these reasons."

"No, she wouldn't tell you anything."

A deep silence reigned in the room. Discretely, Joshua wept. He didn't know why. An array of contradicting thoughts assailed his mind. Nevertheless, he had the certainty that his *omniscient* benefactor told the truth.

Finally, he calmed down.

"Why do you think that she would tell me nothing about her lack of love for me?" inquired Joshua.

"Joshua, truth hurts. You have an experience of what I have said.

"However, truth has also the virtue of opening people's eyes and to put things in their proper places. Accepting the truth, Joshua, will make you reach happiness in the end, as it will allow you to recognize the very nature of reality and to act in full acknowledge of facts.

"Once you understand Paula's impossible love for you, you will feel a deep sense of relief.

A stranger's wonderful chronicles, Book II

"By the same token, you will get rid of your obsession with that woman."

"Roland, thank you so much for insisting on the positive value of the truth. I fully understand you, now. Please, help me accede to the truth.

"As my friend, don't speak in a parabolic manner. I have almost committed suicide. You have only just saved my life. You must have a legitimate reason to act this way, at least, to tell me that I could have made an unnecessary sacrifice.

"Listen, Roland, I would act childishly to take offense of your telling the truth."

"But, Joshua, I have told you the truth. I will never stop telling the truth."

"You have a great acumen. You must always cultivate it.

"The first revelation about Paula may shock you. That woman, for reason I will reveal to you later on, has given her heart up to someone else, from age fifteen."

"What! You have just told a joke!"

"No, I don't play with such important matter; I wouldn't allow myself to play with love affair."

"Who did she love at the age fifteen?"

"One day, she has presented you to a certain Marilee Thomas?"

"Yes, Paula presented her to me as a longtime friend.

"They work both for a real estate company. Marilee has acquired great wealth now.

Bitter disappointment

"Apparently, she helped Paula find a lucrative position in the same company.

"But, does Marilee know Paula's lover? Has she introduced her friend to that lover taken in consideration?

"If that is case, this affair has a long history. Those women are the same age.

"My following question is then legitimate: why did Paula make believe that she loved me passionately?"

Roland breathed deeply before answering, "She made believe that she was madly in love with you, for two reasons…"

"Roland, speak up.

"We have past the time for hesitancy. I have learned to accept things.

"You have put me in a contingent situation inviting me to live once more. You have enough power to rearrange the elements of reality.

"I bow to your greatness. I take you for my guide. Then, tell me the whole truth."

"First, Joshua, Paula wanted to put her lesbianism to test."

Joshua remained with wide-open mouth. He had a sweaty head, neck and spine.

Roland believed he should give Joshua a glass of orange juice; the more so as he hadn't eaten since his suicide attempt.

Actually, Roland had realized that it was time for breakfast. He asked Joshua to wait.

A stranger's wonderful chronicles, Book II

He made omelet, slice of bread and butter and other dishes. Then, he invited his protégé to follow him into the dining room.

"I will go on with my explanation while eating," he advanced. "I do believe that good food strengthens us physically and morally."

Then, as promised, he started to speak again, "Marilee and Paula had started their intimate relationships since adolescence. One day, Marilee, a little too abusive, had rubbed Paula the wrong way. Then, a nice handsome young man arrived. Paula thought having a chance to change her sexual orientation. However, she saw Marilee again at work and thought that her life would remain empty without her partner's love."

"And, Roland, what is the second reason?" asked Joshua.

"I will come to it.

"Marilee knows you better that you think.

"She has learned that your architectural project presented as thesis concerns a skyscraper capable of withstanding earthquakes and hurricanes of great magnitude."

"Roland," pointed Joshua, "You are simply incredible. But go on."

"Marilee doesn't lack ambition and boldness.

"She had advised Paula to bear your caresses a little longer; therefore, she would find out where you have kept your portfolio; for, apparently, they have looked for it in vain.

"She intends to use your skyscraper project to build a nice and fancy condominium for wealthy families living in a windswept area.

Bitter disappointment

"Then, yesterday, in the afternoon, Paula had finally put her hand on the precious document, which you have kept under your bed."

"Roland, you have the foresight of God.

"Definitively, I agree with you when you claim to know the alpha and the omega of reality."

"Wait! I want to deserve the title. I will reveal more on this situation.

"Listen to the following.

"Marilee, having the portfolio, has invited the most skillful architects of her enterprise to study the construction plan and rush to implement it.

"Unfortunately, these experts have given a disturbing piece of news to her: the plan is incomplete.

"Indeed, it is.

"As you have anticipated an act of industrial espionage of this kind, you have divided the construction plan in three parts."

"Roland, stop! You have taken the game too far. More and more, you have emerged as a vulgar spy. Kill me, if you want, but I won't listen to you anymore."

"I have emerged as a vulgar spy! You insult the man who has just saved your life?"

Joshua seemed confused. He wondered the reason why this stranger had saved his life. He had no obligation to do so. He could have ignored him and taken care of his personal business.

A stranger's wonderful chronicles, Book II

Like everybody, he would watch the news about his death, during the evening edition.

Additionally, as he knew everything, he could just put his hand on his project and turn richer, along the way, while letting Joshua kill himself. Actually, he would manage better without his presence.

At least, Joshua should owe Roland an eternal debt of gratitude.

"Roland," he pointed aloud, "forgive me to have insulted you. You render great services to humanity and me.

"Don't let me discourage you.

"I have just sunk into confusion about your generosity and your divinatory skills.

"Then, keep enlightening me."

"Joshua, I was about to tell that your decision to divide your portfolio betrays a manifestation of great discernment. It will allow you to implement your project before Marilee.

"You should know that she hasn't given up. She has sent burglars to your apartment. To have an idea, let's go and assess the damages with your own eyes."

This being said, Roland, sitting at his car wheel, took Joshua to his own apartment he had shared with Paula, for a short period.

Police officers stood in front of the entrance door. They asked the two friends to identify themselves. Then, they let them enter the apartment, since Joshua still had the key.

Bitter disappointment

When they opened the door, Roland and Joshua cried out in terror.

The apartment looked like a deserted area hit by a powerful tornado."

Joshua asked Roland to help him move the sofa. Then, he lifted the carpet and retrieved two large envelopes.

"Roland, with God's mercy, the addenda to the project remain intact.

"I must apologize to you.

"I have learned my lesson; and, from now on, I won't have any doubt about your words.

"But, let's go. We would lack wisdom to stay here."

"Joshua, my dear friend, you have guessed right," acknowledged Roland. "Let's get out of here. Evildoers might return to the scene."

Actually, as they rushed downstairs, they saw in the distance sinister-looking characters who were getting on the elevator, and who, once they spotted them, changed their mind and set out to catch them.

Fortunately, Roland had parked his car in front of the building, in which our friends rushed and got lost in the city street mazes.

Six months have elapsed. Joshua worked for *Fabricote*, one of Roland Badu's companies offering prefabrication houses. Joshua had also received a great deal of money for incorporating his project into Fabricote technique.

One day, he visited Roland in his office for a chat.

"Roland," he started, "how can I thank you for all you have done for me. My life has completely improved. You have shown me that I had conducted myself in a silly manner, when I had made an attempt to put an end to my life for that adventuress' beautiful eyes only."

"Indeed, you had conducted yourself foolishly," acknowledged Roland, "the more so as a young lady loves you passionately. She has never stopped loving you, since her adolescence."

"What are you talking about, Roland?

"Now, you try to make fun of me.

"Who would love a coward like me, who has almost committed suicide, instead of facing reality?"

"As I have said, that woman has fallen in love with you, even before your attempted suicide. She still loves you, even when she thinks that you have ceased to exist."

"Who is that woman?"

"Sylvania!"

"Sylvania! Our neighbor! My sister Cecilia's schoolmate! But I took her for my sister."

"She is not your sister.

"Additionally, she has changed into a young beautiful person. She emerges as a more genuine woman that your monstrous Paula. She is glowing with charm.

"You haven't observed her with a man's eyes, but with a brother's. Then, you should know that she has round breasts, dove's eyes, sensuous lips, robust and well-shaped legs.

Bitter disappointment

"After your wedding, you will have a charming woman in your bed, whom you will possess with passion."

"Roland, stop! You are crazy and a womanizer."

"Wait until I tell my wife. She will laugh her head off. Then, she will undoubtedly call the police to take me to a madhouse."

"Ah! You are married!

"Of course, I am.

"This office is in my general headquarters, while I follow your progress."

"But, how many general headquarters do you have?"

"I have one in almost all the corners in the world."

"And you have a spouse in each corner of earth. Have I guessed right?"

"Jo, you should curb your curiosity."

"Yet, at the beginning, I thought that you have sunk into perversion! You rather chase women."

"You've said it.

"By the way, I feel so happy to see you. You should make up with your family, for two reasons."

"What are they?"

"A wealthy real estate company has completely renovated your family's neighborhood, which has built up houses for the rich and famous.

"Now, only Sylvania parents' and yours look quite dilapidated."

"Oh, Roland, that's sad."

A stranger's wonderful chronicles, Book II

"Not for long.

"Use my cellular and call your mother. You must act cautiously, for everybody thinks you have gone forever. However, you speak first to your mother. Then, we go to see her."

Joshua followed his benefactor's advice to the letter.

Cecilia, one of his siblings, picked up the receiver and stated, "Who is he?"

"My name has no importance. I would like to speak to Mrs. Melon."

"Wait a minute."

She picked up again the receiver and informed, "My mother thinks that you can tell me what you have in mind. She has no intention of speaking to a stranger."

"Tell her that I am one of her secret admirers."

"You are one of her secret admirers!

"You are mad. My mother doesn't lead a disorderly existence like you.

"Well, here is my mother. She is very angry. She will tell you off."

There was a deadly silence in the meantime. Then, his mother stated, "Why do you want to harass me? How can I have a secret admirer at my age?

"Listen, mister, I love my husband. You must sink into madness and escape from a madhouse."

"Mrs. Melon, only uttered Joshua."

Then, the woman felt a cold sweat flowing on her spine.

Bitter disappointment

She would like to say something meaningful, but she couldn't make any sound. Finally, she had a motherly intuition and screamed: "Jo!"

Next, she felt dizzy and dropped to the floor.

Her husband grabbed the receiver and started, "Listen, my dear sir, why do you want to harass my wife...?"

"Papa, it is I, Joshua."

"Jo! You are not dead!"

"No, papa, I am not.'

"But, my son, why do you want to give a heart attack to your mother."

"I didn't want to come unannounced; which could have turned worse.

"She would take me at the most for a ghost.

"Well, papa, I will see you in half an hour. I will tell everybody what happened."

At the windows, the Melons anxiously looked out for Joshua.

Sylvania and her family joined them, once they had told them about the good news.

A huge dark red Hammer passed by in the street, turned left at the next crossing and, finally, stopped in front of the Melons' home.

The watchers couldn't believe their eyes when they saw a very expensive vehicle, which only wealthy people could own.

At last, Joshua get off that truly sophisticated truck, wearing a blue navy suit, a tie with blue and white dots.

A stranger's wonderful chronicles, Book II

The driver, a man in his thirties, followed him.

The watchers' eyes opened even wider, as the two friends got closer and closer.

Hortensia Melon, Joshua's mother, couldn't help it; she opened the door and rushed to her son. They fell flat on each other. Then, the father, Roger Melon, the sisters and brothers: Cecilia, Claude, Mildred and Jerome joined them outside.

The neighbors also took part in the family reunion.

As Sylvania hugged Joshua tight, the latter turned around and winked at Roland.

Everybody entered the house.

The parents and others pulled Joshua aside, occasionally, to ask him a lot of questions.

"I thought you were dead," said the mother in tone of emotion. "I saw you jumping from the skyscraper top. As I closed my eyes, I didn't know what happened.

"Later on, nobody seemed to have any idea about your whereabouts; for, others had also closed their eyes. We thought that the government took care of your body, as you didn't have any id card on you, according to the media.

"But, Jo, if you were alive, you should have let us know."

The son gagged the mother. Then, he advanced, "Mom, Dad, my friends, I was ashamed. I took myself for a coward.

Bitter disappointment

"Instead of facing my dilemma, I had chosen to commit suicide.

"A woman had pushed me to despair; yet, she didn't have an iota of love for me. She only intended to steal my architectural project.

"Fortunately, my friend Roland, unknown to me at that time, had an intuition of my foolish action and had saved me.

"My friends, I don't know whether this man belongs to this world or not, but he had extraordinary powers. Anyway, he has saved my life and allowed me to hope again."

Roland, remaining alone, got a kick out of the family reunion excitement.

Some point in time, he made motion with the hand and, then, he paged, "Sylvania!"

The young lady started.

She put her hand on her bosom to have a confirmation of the masculine paging.

"Yes, I have called you, Sylvania. I would like to speak to you."

The young lady went to Roland.

"But how do you know my name?"

"Sylvania, for some obscure reason, I know the real in its entirety."

"Impossible, Mr...."

"Call me Roland," he advanced.

Then, after a short pause, he inquired, "Do you want some proof?"

A stranger's wonderful chronicles, Book II

"Yes, Roland, I do."

"You have just finished nursing studies, but you haven't found any position yet."

"You may have learned this from Jo."

"No, he doesn't know it yet."

"What else do you know about me?"

"You have a secret in your heart.

"You had it since you were thirteen."

The young woman had a penetrating look at Roland.

She had an intuition about what he had referred to, but how would he know something like that.

To the best of her recollection, she had never revealed it to anyone.

"Are you a magician?" she inquired.

"Yes, I am one in my free time."

"What do you have in mind, Roland?

"You may want to trick me in order to make me open up to you; thus, unknowingly, I will reveal things about me and justify what you call a secret."

"Sylvania, I don't want to give you a puzzle to solve. Let me tell you what I have alluded to.

"From age thirteen, as soon as you had reached adolescence, you felt, first, a certain spiritual confusion.

"However, later on, you would identify the object of your confusion."

"Then, name it. I would like to know its nature. You only want to guess.

"Certainly, once you run out of guesses, you will give you tongue to a cat."

"I will never behave like that.

"No, I wouldn't give my tongue to a cat. I need this part of my body to speak."

Roland and Sylvania burst out laughing, which drew the others' attention.

"What is going on?" asked Cecilia.

"Nothing is going on" answered Sylvania. "Roland emerges as a good conversationalist."

Then, turning to the man, she asked him to tell her everything in his mind.

"Tell me if I am wrong but you have always had a weakness for Joshua."

"What!" exclaimed the young lady.

Once more, the others returned.

Roland beckoned to Joshua to come to him and said, "Jo, tell Sylvania what you think about her.

"Remember, you have told me so many beautiful things about her."

Joshua opened wide his eyes. Then, for the first time, he discovered the symbol of voluptuousness in Sylvania, as he remembered Roland's lewd description of her.

A stranger's wonderful chronicles, Book II

Finally, he pronounced, "Sylvania, I've told Roland that there is one woman, a neighbor, my sister's schoolmate, who would make me happy if she accepted to marry me."

The young woman stood there mouth-opened, as if she witnessed a situation taking a tragic turn.

Joshua stretched out his arms. She fell in them without a murmur.

They remained embraced for a long time, letting their heart beat in unison.

Then, Cecilia understood her childhood friend's "strange" reaction whenever she had seen Joshua. Even if she had started a conversation, Joshua's presence would have always reduced her to silence.

Joshua and Sylvania parted from each other. The former beckoned to the others to come near. "My friends," he stated, "again, let me introduce Roland, my rescuer, to you. This man has great gifts from Nature or God, and has the ability to know everything. He has made me revelations about Sylvania as if she has told him in person everything about herself.

"However, my beautiful Sylvania, I won't tell her anything more until our honeymoon."

"Honeymoon!" screamed Hortensia.

"Honeymoon!" shouted the others.

"Yes," answered Joshua, "we will get married and will go on a honeymoon trip. We shouldn't let pass certain occasions. This woman will fulfill all my dreams in life."

Bitter disappointment

A deep silence reigned over the place. Apparently, events unfolded at a rapid pace.

Finally, Joshua broke the glass to announce, "By the way, my friends, Roland comes with me for one specific reason.

"You should know, once and for all, this man leaves a trail of kind deeds behind him.

"He believes that men and women, all over the world, should live like brothers and sisters.

"Roland, speak up. I know you are not shy."

Roland kept silent for a moment to weigh down his words; for, on may easily hurt people's self-esteem.

Then, he started, "Hortensia, Roger, Maude, Pascal…"

"But who has given you our names?" asked the persons paged by Roland

"My friends," rushed saying Sylvania, "Don't waste your time on this subject. This man knows everything.

"He has just told me secrets about my adolescence that nobody could fathom.

"However, I have an impression that he behaves like that without any malice."

"Thank you, Sylvania," said Roland.

Then, he came right to the point, "Hortensia, Roger, Maude, Pascal…, remember, a real estate company has offered you a great deal of money for selling them your houses; because your properties downgrade the neighborhood and need to be revamped.

"The property owners, go-getters, newly wealthy, have never stopped complaining."

"They may be right," cut Pascal, Sylvania's father. "Our homes look dilapidated.

"Nevertheless, we don't have a penny to rebuild them.

"Yet, we live here. Emotionally, we have some attachment to our homes."

"Wait, my friends," said Roland.

Next, he went and came back with two huge plastic boxes with covers.

He gave Roger and Pascal one box each.

"My friends," he went on, "in these boxes you will put your documents and precious belongings.

"Then, Roger, you will go with your family to this address. This is one of my model houses.

"You, Pascal, you will spend a wonderful time with your family in this house the address of which is on this card.

"I have taken all the steps to make your temporary stay heavenly.

"Don't forget to give me the keys to your houses.

"In two weeks, I will go and get you.

"Then, you will live in renovated houses in which the neighborhood will take pride of."

Bitter disappointment

Three hours after, the Melons and the Dubroses left for their temporary homes.

Joshua promised Sylvania to go and take her to a restaurant.

Roland, to keep his word, started the Joshua and Sylvania parents' house renovation the day after.

Things didn't go easy.

First, the wealthy neighbors had some apprehension about these works and called the developers and the local authorities. Roland had to present several times his developer's license and his permit to implement the renovation.

However, gradually, two avant-garde houses proudly stood up in the neighborhood and made the wealthy neighbors jealous.

In the meantime, Joshua and Sylvania met at the restaurant. They exchanged their first burning kisses. Before the end of the meal, they loved each other madly and decided to get married shortly, at everybody's surprise.

"And, my darling," stated Joshua, "I need you in the big house I live in.

"We will soon fill it with the concretion of our love, I mean our children…"

The young woman gagged the man, kissed him on his half-opened mouth and declared, "I accept this way of life, my love. I have never stopped thinking about something like that.

A stranger's wonderful chronicles, Book II

"Actually, you have awareness about my love you, which has started since adolescence (as you have learned thanks to your clairvoyant friend).

"Thus, Jo, we have just started a marvelous existence."

Everything went according to plan.

Roland had renovated the houses, which attracted the *Architectural Magazine* that presented them as models betraying "the sign of human creativity"

Joshua and Sylvania got married.

Roland, naturally, was the best man, while Cecilia, the best woman.

Sylvania worked as a nurse at Fabricote Company, to stay close to her husband, the man of her heart.

One day, the phone rang, while Sylvania visited her husband in his office.

She took the receiver and frowned.

"Darling, who is the caller?" asked the husband.

"My love, there is a woman who would like to speak with you. She said that her name is Paula."

"Let me listen to her little speech," said the husband sarcastically.

The ancient mistress declared,

Joshua, my love, good afternoon

Bitter disappointment

Listen, I have learned about your marriage.

Congratulations!

Well, I call you on behalf of our company. My associates think that if I personally present our offer to you, you will react positively.

We want to offer you one million dollars for your skyscraper plan.

Of course, you must give us everything; for your blueprint is divided into three parts. Our experts think that...

Joshua slowly put down the receiver.

The wife inquired, "Jo, what's going on?"

"Nothing, darling," replied the husband.

Shortly after, he added, "Nana, my love, you should know that I receive these phone calls from people who have nothing to do with their life.

"I work hard to please my beautiful wife and my children, as well as my partners and the customers.

"I take no interest in anything else."

They exchanged burning kisses; while the husband rubbed the wife's stomach.

She had just come from Doctor Morrison. Her malaise came from her pregnancy.

A stranger's wonderful chronicles, Book II

◻   ◻

◻

The reporter Brian Clifford rubbed his hand out of contentment, as he listened to Joshua's account.

"Brian," added the storyteller, "I often wonder if I lose my mind and think about a phantom.

"However, I have no alternative but to dismiss such possibility. I can just look at my parents' sumptuous life and at mine, to bow to the fact.

"You should know, my dear Brian that, to honor my benefactor's presence and satisfy his unexpressed wishes, I have never missed to spread abnegation and charity in the sphere of my activities.

"Joshua," cut in Brian, "like you, I have benefitted from the marvelous stranger's good deeds.

"First of all, the episodes of my chronicles have made me famous.

"Second of all, without him, I would keep ignoring, like you, the presence of my spouse, a special woman.

"I don't have to tell that, like you, I have done my best to keep my benefactor's good spirit alive."

The reporter took leave of Joshua.

In three days, he would visit the woman caught in *the turmoil of love.*

(20)

The

Turmoil

Of

Love

By Antoine Archange Raphael

*M*aureen told the reporter, Brian Clifford, that she looked so beautiful that day; for, she was on her way to get registered at the *Superior Normal School* to start studying literature and philosophy.

Some point in time, she became nervous: the bus, more than ever, turned late. She had just remembered that public transportation had announced a cut in services, following rushed hours that ended up at nine thirty in the morning.

She saw a big car coming, slowing down and stopping. A young man got off it, walked up and bow to her.

Next, he looked up, smiled and stated in a melodious tone, "Miss., good morning."

Maureen betrayed an instant of hesitancy before answering, "Good morning, Sir."

He breathed deeply before adding, "My name is Raymond Felix."

Maureen kept silent.

She wondered if she wouldn't lack caution to have a casual conversation with a stranger.

"Miss.," went on Raymond Felix, "I am sorry, but, while driving, I couldn't prevent myself from admiring you.

"Not only you looked chic, but also you happen to be extremely charming.

The turmoil of love

"Then, a wonderful song, while looking at you, has crossed my mind. It goes more or less as follows, "You are so beautiful, I shouldn't dare love you.""

Maureen couldn't resist to that handsome young man charm and said despite herself, "My name is Maureen Daudet."

"This lovely name does its owner justice.

"By the way, you are waiting for the bus."

"Yes, I am. However, after rushed hours, these buses turn slow like turtles."

She looked at her wristwatch before adding, "I am almost late to register at the *Superior Normal School*."

"Ah! You will become someone with a powerful thinking brain."

"I hope so."

"Miss., I would be overabundantly happy if you let me take you to the *Superior Normal School*."

"Can I trust you?"

"Why wouldn't you? Who would hurt a Venus like you?"

"Well, apparently, I don't have any choice. If I don't register today, I will have to go there next week.

"It's a chance I wouldn't like to lose.

"Then, dear sir, I put myself at your mercy, if I won't inconvenience you."

"No, Maureen, you won't."

A stranger's wonderful chronicles, Book II

No sooner had Maureen get on the car a jeep from the army came with the sirens on.

"Oh!" said the young lady, "I have forgotten about my father's spies!"

"Don't worry," ensured Raymond, "my car runs faster than the army jeep. Soon, we will get lost in the city street maze"

Maureen turned quickly and saw no police jeep. She closed her eyes and wondered if she had sunk into the dreamland or madness.

Raymond's car stopped.

The young lady opened her eyes and pushed a cry of surprise: the car had just parked in the huge courtyard of *Superior Normal School*.

"How did you manage to...?" inquired the young lady.

She didn't complete her question. She believed that she had a dream about the whole situation.

However, her perplexity increased when Raymond informed her, "Maureen, you haven't had a dream. Additionally, I want you to have awareness of my ability to implement tricks apparently odd.

"Without any explainable reason, once I get close to someone, his past, present and future open to me as if someone has written them on a piece of wood in fiery letters."

"I don't believe you, Raymond."

"Do you want me to give you some proof?"

"Yes, Raymond, I would like that."

"I will give you a proof, under one condition."

"What is it?"

"You have to believe that I will never hurt you. I have always behaved like an entity intended to spread the good."

"To show you my good faith, I believe you, Raymond."

"What I will tell you concerns not a distant future

"You will register for philosophy classes."

"Well, Raymond, you may have guessed my choice and, by a stroke of luck, you hit the mark.

"Indeed, I have a fascination for philosophy to such a par that I want to make it my specialty.

"What else?"

"Doctor Charlemagne Monfilston will have the responsibility for introducing you to such human activity.

"The first day, he will ask the students to return in three days a paper about their understanding of philosophy.

"Next, he would ask you, for the weekend, to conduct inquiry about the friendly philosopher, Henry Bergson, and to hand over a six sheet composition on this philosopher's concept of God."

He kept silent for a while before going on deeper with his revelations about Maureen, "A certain Victor Bonnet has never stopped chasing you for the last three years or so.

"Your father likes him and bears his presence at home. Your mother still has a mixed feeling about him. However, you can't stand him.

A stranger's wonderful chronicles, Book II

"For you, his arrogance and his contempt for women make it impossible for being the elect of your heart. Nevertheless, your father doesn't know his drawbacks.

"Fortunately, to your great relief, he started to decrease his visits. He had just found a woman who accepts his evil character."

"Who are you?" inquired the young lady. "Are you a ghost, a spirit, a Satan's emissary, God's messenger or an object of scientific experiment capable of storing millions and millions of data? However, you emerge more and more as an exceptional man."

"Maureen, I would feel glad to respond to your burning questions. However, I don't believe I fulfill a Satan's emissary function, otherwise, I would have embarked on hurting others and I, certainly, would have wrung your neck.

"Fortunately, you have inspired me the best feelings in the world. You look like a spring of fresh water…"

"Raymond, if I stay here to listen to you, I will not implement the task for which I come here."

"Please, forgive me, Maureen. Go and register. I will wait for you.

No sooner had Maureen completed her registration, she re-joined Raymond.

"Listen, Raymond," she said, "I will take the bus to go back home. Undoubtedly, my father and his employees are waiting for me in front of the family house."

"Listen, Maureen," pointed out Raymond, "I will drive you back home."

"Impossible."

"Look at the license plate."

Maureen did as he had recommended her. She had a shock: the license plate indicated "taxi".

"Thus, Maureen, to go to the *Superior Normal School*, you had taken a taxi.

"Then, you asked the driver to wait for you.

"By the way, I leave you with this note. You will open it at home, soon after my departure.

"Let's go."

The car stopped in front of Maureen parents' home.

Her father and other militaries were waiting.

"Maureen, where were you?" screamed the father. "What did you do…?

"Papa," answered the young lady mellifluously, "I have just finished my registration for philosophy and literature classes at the *Superior Normal School.*"

"But, the man…"

"What man are you referring to?"

"You did get on a man's car…"

"Dad, I took a taxi to go and register for the classes," replied softly the young lady. "Fortunately, to come back here, I did take the same taxi."

A stranger's wonderful chronicles, Book II

The father had a quick look at the car license plate and saw the sign indicating taxi.

"Didn't you hear a siren…?" inquired the father. "You should have gotten off the taxi."

"Yes, I did. However, I didn't pay attention to police sirens; for, to the best of my knowledge, I don't have any reason to fear for police activity. Additionally, I didn't want to miss the opportunity to register for the philosophical classes.

Otherwise, I would have to wait for another week to do over what I had accomplished today.

"By the way, many students have intended to take philosophy classes; then, the university has put a quota to the number of students registering for such course. Fortunately, I am the last student accepted into the program."

"Well, my beloved Maureen, all looks well," admitted the father. "This taxi…"

Everybody turned around to have a closer look at the commercial vehicle, but it had disappeared.

Fifteen days had elapsed. Maureen had already started her college studies of philosophy and literature, and had taken, as Raymond had predicted, the class under Doctor Charlemagne Monfilston's guidance.

The night of the first incident, the young woman had read over Raymond's moving note,

The turmoil of love

Maureen,

Don't be afraid of me.

Despite my amazing gifts that have never ceased to astonish others and make me look like a bizarre man, not to say evil, I will not harm you.

I love you a lot and I will feel great joy to stay close to you (all the time).

However, it depends on your feelings toward me.

You will find enclosed to this present my phone number. If you think that you could find happiness to become my lover and later one my wife, call me, as soon as you will have taken your decision.

If you don't call me, I will think that you haven't felt anything for me. Then, Maureen, you would never see me in your way again.

Raymond.

Maureen couldn't make up her mind. The spirit of the note had never ceased to bring confusion in her heart. She had no doubt about his love for this stranger; but he remained, actually, a "perfect stranger" with exceptional gifts.

A stranger's wonderful chronicles, Book II

In the meantime, her indecision had deeply troubled her to such par that she hadn't found the ideas or the introduction regarding the first paper she had to hand over soon.

Doctor Charlemagne Monfilston had formulated the subject in these terms, "According to you, what is philosophy?'

Maureen smiled, remembering that Raymond had predicted, in minute details, this homework, more than a week ahead of time. "How did he manage to guess it?" she thought. "That's a big mystery I have to decipher.

"Well, in three days, I have to hand it over to my professor, yet, I haven't had the faintest idea about it."

Her mother rejoined her in her bedroom and asked, "You look sad. What's going on, Maureen?"

"Mom, I get confused," she answered.

The mother sat on the bed edge; for, apparently, her daughter needed her advice.

"Maureen, I am your mother, you may confine in me. I can never willingly give you the wrong piece of advice."

The daughter, unhesitatingly, pulled Raymond's puzzling note and showed it to her mother.

The latter read it over. Then she turned pensive.

"Mom," started Maureen, "for the last fifteen days, I have found myself in a state of confusion.

"I feel attracted to Raymond; but he is still a stranger.

"Must I keep suppressing my feelings and preventing myself from giving him a call?

"In the meantime, I can't do my homework. Yet, three days from now, I must hand my paper over to Doctor Charlemagne Monfilston."

With her delicate palm, the mother gagged her daughter. Then, she said, "Maureen, you must clear your conscience. I will plead with your father for understanding you. You must call your Raymond; otherwise, you won't have your lucidity back. Leave the note with me."

After supper, Commandant Henry urged his other children to go and "amuse" themselves in their rooms. "I have something to discuss with Maureen," he added.

Remaining alone with his spouse and her daughter Maureen, the Commandant, first, got engaged in thinking: he had to weigh down his words; for, he had awareness of the situation importance. He had no right to deny his daughter happiness.

Then, some point in time, he got his feet wet, "Listen, Maureen, your mother has told me about you dilemma. Apparently, you don't love Victor Bonnet."

"No, Dad, I don't love him at all," rushed saying the young woman.

"Why don't you love him? He gives me the impression of being a nice young man.

"Don't you think?

A stranger's wonderful chronicles, Book II

"Additionally, I know personally his parents, while this Raymond Felix remains a black hole, a perfect stranger"

"Dad, Victor Bonnet will never make me happy.

"No, he won't. To tell you the truth, I don't have any feeling for him.

"For one thing, he gives me the impression of not granting women too much importance.

"During our conversations, he has often reminded me of the insignificance of my female opinion; for, we live in world ruled by men.

"While, dad, you have only to read Raymond's note to realize his natural tolerance, his open-mindedness. Because of his inner qualities, I believe that I may find delight in having nice conversation with him.

"I would like at least to give him a ring for putting out feelers and testing on my emotions once and for all.

"I can no longer live in such state of mind confusion...

"Additionally, I wouldn't behave wisely if I set out to meet that man in the street."

"You don't lack wisdom," conceded the father. "I trust you. You may call him if such action will restore your serenity. I don't want you to fail in your studies.

"Go ahead, my beloved; you may use the phone in the living room."

Maureen stood up, went around the table and kissed her parents on the cheeks.

"Mom, Dad, you will always take pride in me.

The turmoil of love

"I promise you to act wisely."

In the meantime, Raymond sat down in his office. He had never stopped thinking about the chic and beautiful young lady he had met at the bus station. "Everything looks silly; for, she has never called me. Yet, I know she loves me…."

The phone at the office rang. The man's heart pounded to the breaking point. He knew that Maureen had to be the caller.

He rush picking up the receiver and said in a clear voice, "Maureen!"

"How do you know who has called?"

"Well…"

"Ah! Don't answer my question. You know everything."

After a short paused she went on, "Listen, Raymond, I call you to tell you that you have confused me a lot."

"No, Maureen, I haven't confused anyone in my life."

"But, my friend, since I can't function, while thinking about you, it amounts to the same thing.

"Listen, as you have anticipated, I have a paper to hand over in three days.

"Would you believe if I told you that I haven't even started the introduction? Why haven't I? Your image, like an irresistible force, occupies my mind."

"Maureen, in this case, we are in the same bag.

A stranger's wonderful chronicles, Book II

"What do you mean?

"I have never stopped paying attention to my phone, in case you should call."

"No, we are not in the same bag; for, you have no obligation; while I have to hand over my paper in three days."

"You are right.

"Well, listen, Maureen, my dear friend; let's try outlining this paper together.

"Your professor, if I have guessed right, has framed the subject, I remember, as follows; "What do you think about philosophy."

"Raymond! You are a true witch doctor."

"Listen, we are both guilty of confusing each other, then, we must share the responsibility."

"What do you mean?"

"As accomplices in our mutual confusion, why don't we try to tackle the subject of your paper at once?"

"But, Raymond, I do have a paper to hand over to my philosophy professor.

"You and I know nothing about philosophy."

"Maureen, your approach to philosophy would take us nowhere."

"Wait, Raymond. Let me sit down to jot some notes. I have the impression you will put me on the right track, as far as my homework is concerned.

"Who could I have believed it?

"Is there a right way to approach philosophy?"

"What I mean, Maureen" went on Raymond, "philosophy doesn't constitute a body of knowledge following the example of the various branches of positive knowledge. One can't confuse it either with art. It doesn't have a methodology and doesn't lead to the truth following researches."

"Ah! Raymond, the forest starts getting me into its secrets. Would you tell me that philosophy has no method of approach?"

"It has only one."

"It has only one?"

"Yes, it's critical reflection. But, attention, reflection, which forms the common denominator for all the minds in situation, intensifies and remains constant in philosophy."

"Oh, my God! Raymond, you never stop amazing me. You keep emerging as a ghost, a spirit, a genius, and a bearer of enormous powers."

"Maureen, these powers, I gladly put them at your disposal."

"Raymond, let's resume our subject. I feel that I will understand it completely. When I understand something, I may work on it easily.

"I will ask you one more question. Your answer will serve as the key to the subject. From that point on, I won't need you anymore."

"Oh, Maureen, you will dump me?"

"No, Raymond, I won't dump you. I won't need your assistance for this paper.

A stranger's wonderful chronicles, Book II

"The question is as follows, Raymond: why do we have to philosophize?"

"Maureen, do you want to become my wife?" rather asked the man.

"Raymond, you haven't answer my question on which depends our future relationships."

"Ah! We are getting somewhere."

"Now, let's be serious. Raymond, tell me the reason for philosophizing?"

"Certainly, Maureen, I will tell you. However, my intention to pop up 'the question' aims at giving you a shock, to remind you that I also suffer from your absence.

"Here is the answer to your burning question.

"Humanity professes innumerable beliefs according to which it may set itself on the right track: track leading to success, to good conduct, to immutable values, to positive knowledge promising better improved existing condition, to religion promising a more humble and charitable humanity, to art presupposing disinterest. Yet, we haven't accomplished true human progress.

"Then, in the middle of this confusion, philosophy raises questions about the nature of our activities, about their values, about existential conditions."

"Raymond, you are marvelous.

"Now, I must leave you to organize these ideas."

"You must leave so soon?"

"Raymond, I will call you in three days."

"Will you?"

"I swear."

"I believe you."

"Bye."

"Bye."

The whole family was waiting in the living room.

The mother asked, "Is everything ok?"

"Yes, mom," answered Maureen. "However, we will talk tomorrow. During my conversation with Raymond, we have conceived of the response to my paper. I will work on the ideas to organize them and, eventually, to hand over a coherent presentation to my philosophy professor.

"We will talk tomorrow."

Maureen rushed in her bedroom and used her laptop to "put her ideas together".

Three days after, she returned from the university. She showed her paper to her parents and siblings. She had obtained an excellent score for it, not without mentioning Doctor Charlemagne Monfilston's glowing comment,

Miss.,

My congratulations!

A stranger's wonderful chronicles, Book II

Based on this preliminary performance, I may advance that you are on your way to become a learned woman.

Your ideas are well organized and original.

Then, she called Raymond to give him the good news.

"This first success, Raymond, I owe it to you; for, you have found a way to guide me toward the subject completion."

"Maureen," cut in the man, "I will go to the world end to please you."

"In that case, Raymond, you will consent to a small sacrifice on my behalf?"

"You name it, and I will please you. Don't forget that you may become my princess."

"Thank you.

"But, listen to me, my good friend, in five days, I must hand over a paper on the concept of God professed by a French philosopher named Henry Bergson. I have one of his books with me. However, I don't think that I will have time to do researches on the subject.

"Then, I need you to consent to this little sacrifice. You will receive your reward, one of these days."

"Maureen, why do I have the impression that this little sacrifice describes a tall mountain to get over?"

"I've seen you in action; the mountains can't stop you.

"Well, I don't want to forget, here is your little sacrifice.

"Come to see me to help me with my paper."

"What!" exclaimed the man. "Maureen, do you mean to harm me? Your father will send me before a firing squad with no question asked."

"And you will deserve to receive the ultimate punishment."

"Why will I deserve such harsh punishment?"

"Remember, you ask me for marrying you, during our last conversation."

"Maureen, it was a slip of the tongue."

"No, you have meant it. Nature has properly placed your tongue in your mouth, and you have control over it. Then, it articulates what you have in mind. So, if you don't want me to report your whereabouts to my father, you must come.

"Actually, what kind of girl you take me for, if you want to meet with me in the street, in a corridor, in your car.

"You must come to our home, therefore, my parents' inquisitive eyes will see what you and I are doing, and we will have no other alternative but to behave wisely. They shouldn't let a boy and a girl by themselves.

"Do you grasp what I intend to say?"

"Maureen, you are half-hearted."

"It's the only way to protect myself from a man like you, who makes marriage proposal without any warning.

"Listen, my dear Raymond, I will tell my parents right away about your imminent visit. I will call you back to give you the time."

A stranger's wonderful chronicles, Book II

Few minutes after, Maureen called Raymond back to tell him to come the day after, around six o'clock in the evening.

Indeed, at the specific time agreed upon, the doorbell rang out. The youngest child, Elena, ran up and opened the door. Raymond kissed her on her hand.

Elena remained gaping.

She wondered if this man took her for a little princess.

She had a greater shock when that man insinuated, "Yes, Elena, you are a little princess."

She screamed and ran up to her father to whisper to his ear, "Dad, what Maureen has said is true. The man kissed me on the hand.

"In my mind, I said that the man took me for a little princess. Then, the surprise came. He heard my thought; for, he told me, "But, Elena, you are a little princess."

"Nana," said the father tenderly to calm down his little girl, "without noticing it, you may have undoubtedly whispered your thought. And the man, having acute hearing, has heard you."

"No, dad, I didn't whisper my thought."

"Well, Nana, calm yourself. I will tell you what I think of all this."

The visitor walked in the dining room.

The yellowish light from the ceiling showed him in his entire "splendor".

The turmoil of love

He dressed himself with distinction: a dark brown jacket, a pair of beige pants, brown shoes and a tie with chocolate and cream lines.

That evening, all the family members, including Maureen, were sitting around the huge family table. Apparently, they had just finished to have supper.

Maureen made an effort not to jump at Raymond's neck and take him for a big chocolate cake.

As far as the mother was concerned, she smiled broadly at the man.

The father looked at the visitor up and down.

The latter kissed in turn Maureen, the mother, Carmen, her youngest child on the hand. Then he shook hand with Commandant Henry, Justin (the second child), and Paul the fourth child.

The Commandant stood up. Then, he put his hand on Raymond's back and said, "I will leave you soon with Maureen so both you can work on her paper; however, I would like to have a word with you.

"Certainly, Commandant," agreed the visitor

The other family members, including Maureen and her mother, thought that the Commandant, because of his unyielding principles, would make a mess. They even thought that he would frighten away Raymond who might feel offended by the paternal scolding.

In the meantime, the Commandant and the visitor walked side by side in the penumbra.

The others saw them gesticulating.

A stranger's wonderful chronicles, Book II

However, Raymond, because of his deep intuitions about reality, had anticipated the reason for which the Commandant would like to talk to him alone.

"Listen," said the latter, "for one reason or another, Maureen seems to find happiness by you. Similarly, my wife and the other children give you a warm welcome. With respect to me, I haven't decided yet.

"One of the reasons for my indecision comes from what you have told Maureen. You have claimed that you know the alpha and the omega of reality; that you can reveal the profound truth of each person getting near you.

"Between us, you know that you are joking."

Raymond raised his hand, as a sign of respect. Then, he pronounced, "Commandant, I know that you have studied physique, astronomy and organic chemistry.

"Therefore, you mind bathe in objectivity. I can't teach you anything in terms of epistemology.

"However, despite science progress, the existential conditions have worsened, the unknown exists and new animal species appear and reverse learned people's belief. We call these unusual facts new, odd, bizarre and so on. They look bizarre because of our lack of familiarity with them.

"Commandant, listen to me, the powers Maureen has told you about, I cannot explain them logically; except that I do have them."

"Come on, Raymond, you mean to joke."

The turmoil of love

"No, Commandant, I don't intend to joke. How could I face other if I acted as a joker?

"Commandant, I will give you some proof, but under one condition."

"Such as?"

"You must give me your word of honor to accept the happy ending coming out of my proof."

"Raymond, did you mention happy ending? What do you mean by that?"

"Well, I embody an entity intended to spread the good around me. Therefore, the consequences of my deeds always turn happy but bizarre."

The Commandant remained pensive for a while, to weigh up his following decision.

Then, without any murmur, he acquiesced, "Agree. I give you my word of honor, the more so, as you have promised to act in a way leading to a positive result."

Raymond tuned pensive. Then, he advanced, "Well, my dear Commandant, if I don't tell you the truth you will stop me at any time.

"As a Commandant concerned about the military administration under your authority, you have often used your own income to ensure its sound functioning.

"You just send a note to the headquarters that will always reimburse you. Yet, for a reason unknown to you, the reimbursement you have expected hasn't arrived yet.

A stranger's wonderful chronicles, Book II

"You only have five dollars in your pocket."

The Commandant's eyes opened wide.

"Listen, Raymond, you don't belong to this world. You must be the figment of my imagination. Therefore, your meeting with Maureen, your visit this evening, this conversation we have, all this comes from my imagination.

"Nobody, beside me, can assess the exact amount of money I carry in my pocket."

"Commandant," cut in Raymond, "you don't have a dream; you haven't sunk into madness; your imagination works well. I belong to this world.

"But, use patience and let me tell you something about your dilemma."

"You will tell me something about my dilemma?"

"Yes, I will.

"In fifteen minutes, your wife will ask you for your monetary contribution to this month mortgage payment. Additionally, your children, except Maureen, will remind you that school tuition and lunch contribution are due for this month.

"Apparently, you have no solution in mind.

"Despite your feigned poise, these imminent obligations have never left your mind.

"Then, commandant, the happy ending of my demonstration arrives."

This being said, Raymond pulled an envelope from his jacket pocket and handed over to the Commandant.

"Commandant, it's between us. You will go back to you family and act natural. You won't a word of our little agreement to anyone (above all to Maureen).

"When your wife and children ask you for money, you will pull the envelope and gracefully "comply".

"I swear, as a gentleman, to keep our meeting secret.

"By the way, I have no unrevealed motive for acting this way, except that I believe this is my duty as a fellowman to help another fellowman or woman; for, we are all brothers and sisters in humanity.

"It's time to rejoin Maureen with whom I will discuss her next paper on Henry Bergon's concept of God.

"It's a strange coincidence; that philosopher's first name is the same as yours."

Once returned to the living room, the Commandant invited his wife and their other children to follow him to the living room. "For," he added, "Maureen and Raymond will need the table to write."

As soon as they had reached the living room and they had sat down, the wife advanced, "By the way, Henry, my love, tomorrow, you will leave home early in the morning for military training. You must give me your portion of the mortgage bill."

The husband had a short pause. Then, he smiled before saying, "Of course, my darling."

A stranger's wonderful chronicles, Book II

He pulled the envelope from his pocket, pulled the amount of money that represented his portion of the mortgage payment and gave it to his wife."

Next, it was Carmen's turn to act as *spokesperson* for her siblings and herself, "Dad, it's time for our lunch money and tuition. Since you will leave early, you must give us the money now."

"Is it an order, Carm?"

"Yes, dad, it's children's order."

"What would happen if I don't execute it?"

"We will take you to court."

"What would the judge decide?"

"He would condemn you to receive one thousand kisses on your cheeks by all your children before a live audience."

"That would represent a harsh decision. My cheeks would bathe in an ocean of saliva.

"Phew! Let me give you the money right away to avoid such embarrassing moment."

He was about to put the envelope back to his pocket, but his wife stopped him and pulled out one extra twenty dollar bill and said, "This will allow me to have a good lunch on the job tomorrow. And this is a little gift from you, as I notice that you have plenty of money in this envelope that looks more a more like a cornucopia."

"Lynn, my darling," pointed the Commandant, "how observant are you!

The turmoil of love

"This envelope is a true horn of plenty."

Everybody burst out laughing, which made Maureen and Raymond jump, as they had embarked on the philosophic composition.

Maureen inquired, "By the way, Raymond, what do you know about Henry Bergson?"

After a minute of reflection, the strange visitor answered, "First, Maureen, my little darling, as I have entered the living room, you have taken me for a big chocolate cake. You have made every effort not to eat me alive in others' presence."

"What! Raymond, you become almost incredible. The way I see it, I can't have the least reflection on you! Do I look crystalline in your eyes?"

"Yet, Maureen, I have to make a confession."

"Did you say a confession?"

"Yes, my darling, you haven't been exempt from a great danger from me."

"I have incurred great danger from you?

"Raymond, my dear friend, why do you say something like that, which really frightens me? I do have the impression that you are not a killer."

"No, I am not. However, on entering the dining room, you have appeared to me as a huge glass of vanilla ice-cream."

Both burst out laughing.

The mother came at once and asked, "All is well, my children?"

A stranger's wonderful chronicles, Book II

"Yes, mom," rushed answering a jubilant Maureen, "except that Raymond has emerged as one of the funniest and most bizarre person I have ever seen."

A dead silence reigned over the dining room. Then, the young lady had a surprise by noticing that Raymond had heard her first question.

He said, "Maureen, in a way, I take myself for a product of Bergson."

"You have certainly sunk into madness."

"No, I haven't.

"According Bergson, we may fathom the secrets of reality via an effort of sympathy called intuition. At this stage, we reach the unique and the inexpressible."

Maureen remained with the eyes wide opened. She had immediately understood Bergson's philosophy and had seen the road leading to this remarkable philosopher's concept of God!

"Then, Maureen," went on Raymond, "according to Bergson, if we increase this intuitive process, if we enlarge on it, if we expand it, we will reach the very inner core, the essence of reality and grasp the conductor leading to God.

"By so doing, we will reach the kingdom of freedom and creativity."

Maureen, despite herself, kissed the man on the lips.

"Raymond, my little darling," she screamed, "you are marvelous."

"Ah! I won't stop talking about Bergson to receive kisses from you."

"Raymond, listen, you must stop talking. You deserve no reward."

"Why don't I?"

"Because, Raymond, you make no effort to think and to grasp the meaning of any subject. The way I see it, you embody, my dear friend, thinking in action.

"That's it! You embody thinking in action."

"Then, tell me, my friend, why should I reward you for your nature?"

The young lady took a short moment, before adding in a falsely devious manner, "Raymond, if you protest, you will have no more surprise kisses."

"My lips are sealed," rushed saying the visitor.

It was nine, in the evening, when he took leave of the whole family.

Maureen saw him to the exit door.

Before leaving, the man had kissed the young woman tenderly on the mouth.

Maureen, far from taking offense, had a broad smile on her face and returned the kiss.

Days and months had elapsed without any mishap. Occasionally, Raymond met with Maureen at home to discuss college papers, a good excuse for the man and the woman to exchange burning kisses, whenever it was possible for them to act "pas-sionately

One day, Lynette, Maureen's mother, went to *Celia Bank* to get some cash.

A stranger's wonderful chronicles, Book II

As she walked through the hall to go back to her place of work, after having secured a receipt from the cash machine, she found herself face to face with Raymond.

"Raymond!" she exclaimed. "It's a big surprise! What are you doing here?"

"One of my offices happens to be here."

"Did you say one of your offices?"

"Yes, I did.

"One must keep himself busy to make end meet."

After a short pause, he went on, "Oh, Mrs. Lynette Daudet, let me present you to the bank big shots.

"This is Marceline Gomez, the bank chairperson. She oversees all the bank operations.

"This lovely young lady, Anita Boisson, works in the capacity of the executive director

"This well-dressed young man, Anthony Just, fulfills the assistant director's functions.

"My friends (he turned around toward the employees), this is Mrs. Lynette Daudet. You should always give her a warm welcome."

Instinctively the three employees handed over their business cards to Mrs. Daudet.

Next, Raymond beckoned to Lynette to follow him to his office.

She couldn't believe her eyes.

The turmoil of love

The office bathed in an unprecedented luxury. Nevertheless, the woman bowed to Maureen friend's modesty. "This man may be wealthy," she thought, "yet he is not arrogant."

"Mrs. Daudet?" started the man.

The woman got started. Then, she got herself together and pronounced, "Call me Lynn. We know each other enough to stop being formal."

"I agree with you, Lynn.

"I have always wanted to give you a gift."

"Why?"

"Lynn, you have served as my advocate by Commandant Henry."

"Well, how have you heard about it?"

"Oh!" only exclaimed the woman.

Then, after a short moment, she rushed adding, "No, Raymond, don't say a word.

"They have mentioned your deep intuition to me."

She took another pause before explaining, "Raymond, I have pleaded Maureen's cause and yours, because I wanted to make my daughter happy.

"Apparently, she seems to feel great by you."

"Lynn, I share her feelings," answered Raymond.

He took one moment of hesitancy before pointing out, "By the way, give me your account number.

"I will deposit the gift I have in mind.

A stranger's wonderful chronicles, Book II

"It is not necessary to give me your secret code and other personal data regarding this account.

"I will just do a transfer of my gift."

Lynette handed over her banking card to Raymond. From his computer, the latter made a transfer of cash. Then, he returned the card to Lynette.

"Well, Lynn, I won't keep you any longer. I know that you have to resume your office."

By five thirty, the Commandant went and picked up his wife. On the way, she informed, "Henry, whom did I meet at the *Celia Bank*?"

"Lynn, darling, I have no idea."

"Raymond!"

"Raymond?

"But, what is he doing there?"

"I asked him the same question."

"What was his answer?"

"He told me that he is keeping one of his offices at the *Celia Bank*."

"Did he say one of his offices?"

"Yes, he did."

After a pause, she added, "Well, the most surprising part of the meeting came when he presented me to the bank chairperson, to the executive director and the latter's assistant.

"Here are their business cards.

"In addition, Raymond recommended them to give me a warm welcome if I ever need their services."

"This Raymond is an important person. But he is so young!"

"Henry, that is not all."

"What else do you want to tell me?"

"He told me that he had always intended to give me a gift. I asked him the reason for that.

"He told me that I had served as a good lawyer for him by Commandant Henry."

"Ah! You did react like a warm and charming advocate. The night following that pleading, you did behave like a high school girl."

The spouses burst out laughing.

The Commandant turned serious.

"Is something wrong, Henry?" inquired Lynette

The husband didn't answer at once.

He slowed down the vehicle, drove alongside the sidewalk and turned off the engine. In an almost tearful way, he informed, "Lynn, I have also benefitted from his generosity.

"Do you remember when he came to visit Maureen the first time? While conversing, I told him to start making Maureen believe that he had special gifts allowing him to read people's mind and to know the alpha and omega of reality. He made me swear to accept the "happy ending" of his disclosures about me.

A stranger's wonderful chronicles, Book II

"He told me that I was like a cat on a hot tin roof; for, my wife would ask me for my portion of money for the mortgage.

"By the same token, my children would ask me for lunch and tuition money.

"Finally, he told me that I only had five dollars in my pocket.

"He gave the reason for my penury: I had spent, as usual, my income to facilitate the good functioning of the administration under my authority, hoping that they would reimburse shortly after. Unfortunately, the general administration has taken its time to do so.

"Finally, as promised, I accepted the "happy ending" of his display of powers, as far as I was concerned. He gave me an enveloped full of money.

The women opened wide her eyes. "Ah!" she exclaimed, "You mean the famous envelope that I picturesquely called the *horn of plenty!*"

"Listen, my darling," pointed the Commandant, "that man has made me more human, more understanding, and more aware of my Promethean role on earth.

"Lynn, my darling, we are so lucky to meet with such great character…"

The husband turned on the key again and kept on driving to the family home.

As they reentered their bedroom, the wife said, "Henry, I really don't know the amount of the present."

The turmoil of love

"Lynn, I can't help you, in this respect. Why don't you use the laptop we keep in the bedroom and get access to your bank account?

"In the meantime, I will take a shower."

"It's an excellent idea," acquiesced the woman.

She screamed.

The Commandant only had time to cover himself with a beach towel to run up to his wife and find out what was going on.

The woman has temporarily lost her speech faculty. She only had the strength to point to the *gift amount*.

The husband had also a shock when he saw the *lavish present*.

One year had elapsed. Maureen and Raymond met on a steady basis.

The young lady's family had finally recognized that the lovers live in harmony. Even the Commandant bowed to her daughter lover's civilities.

One night, Raymond came with a parcel cover wrapped with flower design paper and tied by a green silk ribbon.

In the living room, in presence of everybody, the lover kneeled down and handed the parcel over to Maureen.

Then, he stated, "Maureen, do you want to be my wife?

"Today, it's your birth date and the anniversary of our first meeting, a year ago."

Maureen looked around and saw nothing but smile on everybody's face. Then, she declared, "Yes, Raymond, I want to be your wife"

The young lady meticulously opened the box.

A stranger's wonderful chronicles, Book II

First, she pulled an expensive-looking diamond ring; then, a broach, finally a golden fine-knit chain. She showed the jewels to her family to see.

She got ready to put the box on the table, but she saw a note.

She read it,

Maureen, my beloved, you must use caution and put the box away at once. It contains other gifts that you can't show to others now.

Maureen turned toward Raymond and made a gesture expressing her understanding.

In her bedroom, Maureen, eaten by curiosity, reopened the box and pulled another note,

Maureen,

Now, we belong together.

We will get married and we will know an existence of happiness. In the meantime, I allow myself a certain liberty. I have enclosed in the present a bankcard and a checkbook. As your fiancé, I don't want you to have any urgent need.

Thus, concentrate yourself on your studies and our love.

I don't mean anything else.

I adore you.

Raymond.

The year after, Maureen and Raymond got married; since the parents and relatives didn't think that their intimacy would jeopardize her studies.

Together, they worked well on her school compositions counting among the best ones in this school.

Two years after, Maureen received her philosophy professor's license.

She would pursue superior studies, while teaching, the more so, as her husband had never stopped being one of her most knowledgeable advisors.

◘   ◘

◘

"Mr. Clifford, I have just told the story of my life, concluded Dr. Maureen Daudet Felix.

"Without my encounter with the mysterious stranger, I would not become what I am now.

"And I am sincere."

"I believe you, Doctor." Assured Brian Clifford, "I will take great delight in adding your story to *"the wonderful chronicles of a stranger"*, a weekly magazine known to the world.

The reporter got happily on his car.

A stranger's wonderful chronicles, Book II

He drove straight to his office to have time to edit his most recent account and entrust it to the secretary, his lovely wife.

He thought about his next episode. He would entitle it *"avoided tragedy"*.

(21)

Avoided

Tragedy

By Antoine Archange Raphael

*M*ax Paul returned from a business meeting. He looked happy; for, once more, Joseph Carbone, a guru in the petroleum business, had recourse to Max Paul's architectural skill to build his prefabricated villa.

For one reason unknown to the engineer, he engaged his big car in the *Great Alexandria Boulevard.*

He had the impression of driving on a highway: all the traffic signals had turned green.

When he reached the intersection between *Great Alexandria Boulevard* and *Angel Street,* he saw a crowd of people gathering in front of *Duccio Pharmacy.* Police officers, ready to take extreme measures, rested on the lookout before the drugstore entrance door.

Through the glass door, his gaze met a woman's, who could be around twenty-five and a girl's, standing close to her.

Then, he had one of his *intuitions.* He had to act fast to prevent the unnecessary occurrence of a great human tragedy.

He parked his car along the sidewalk and got off it, despite vehement protesting gestures made by a police officer. Then, he walked slowly toward the troubled location.

A lieutenant tried to make him spin on his heels to search him, but the authority instead spun around.

"What's going on," stated the police officer. "I intend to make you spin."

"Nothing is going on, Lieutenant Boston. Since I am innocent of any wrongdoing, then, I can't spin.

"Officer, try once more."

The police officer tried and underwent the same experience.

The driver said in a pleasant fashion, "My dear Lieutenant Boston, what do you expect to find on me? As a civilian, I don't have any right to bear arms. Additionally, I share others' opinion according to which we may only find lasting solutions to human problems around a conference table.

"Thus, you will find nothing suspicious on me."

"Shut up!" yelled the high-ranking police officer. "You must sink into madness and escape from a health center. However, we don't have the time for joking. You must leave now."

"No, lieutenant Boston, I can't leave now. I have to carry out a mission."

"Wait just a minute, Mister! You have called me by my name twice. Who told you my name?"

"Oh! I just know you, as I know the alpha and the omega of reality."

"I did guess right! You have sunk into madness."

"No, I haven't sunk into madness.

"Let me make a disclosure about you. You have pushed me to behave like, because of your incredulity.

"I know that, one day, you have received an envelope from a certain Mr. Marino Luciano."

A stranger's wonderful chronicles, Book II

"Be quiet!" exclaimed the police officer.

Then, after a short pause, he inquired "What do you want?"

"Liliane's uncle, that young woman inside the drugstore along with her three children and her lover, has called me to ask me to go and pay the prescription intended for one of that woman's children. That child's name, as far as I can remember, is Yvonne. She suffers from arrhythmia.

"Thus, let me solve this dilemma once and for all."

"Does the young woman know you?"

"No, she doesn't. However, her uncle and I have attended *Architectural University.*"

"Yes, I know that university. Are you an architect?"

"Of course, I am. And I specialize in prefabrication."

"Then, let's see what we can do. Definitely, you may emerge as this problem solver."

He followed the police officer.

Once they had reached the drugstore entrance door, the authority ordered the other officers to let them through.

Max and the young woman looked at each other. For some unexplained reason, she smiled.

He beckoned to her to open the door.

She complied.

"Don't worry, Liliane," said Max in a sweet tone. "Your uncle, Ernest Champion, has called me to come to your assistance."

Then, he went to the pharmacist and inquired, "How much she owes you."

"She owes me two hundred dollars."

"Then, hurry up. Here is the money."

While the pharmacist completed the transaction, the lieutenant entered the drugstore and inquired about the situation.

"Officer, all is well," answered Max. "In five minutes, we will leave the drugstore.

"And everything will fall in its proper place.

"By the way, I would like to have a chat with you Lieutenant "Boston. Here is my business card. I would like you to close that deal with Mr. Marino. He happens to be a heartless negotiator."

"Would you help me really?"

"Yes, I would."

"Why would you?

"You will have another Damocles' sword on my head."

The officer kept silent for a short while before recognizing, "All the extortionists behave in the same heartless way."

"I have never practiced extortion," stated Max.

"Then, why do want to help me?"

"Officer Boston, I want to help you because we are brothers in humanity."

"You have certainly resumed your madness.

A stranger's wonderful chronicles, Book II

"Did you say brothers in humanity?

"My dear fellow, what happens to the truth according to which man acts as wolf to man?"

"Lieutenant, this truth doesn't mean anything to me. It only expresses a pessimistic viewpoint. Actually, we are not wolves, why would we act like them. We belong to the category of men, women and children, imbued with reason, imagination, love and the sense of justice. Why would we opt for a wolfing life instead of helping each other? "

"You sound incredible, my friend, but you are right."

The police officer scratched his chin, the time to think. Then, he asked, "Max, when may I call you?"

"Listen, you don't have to call me. I stay away from politics. When I want to help, I act fast.

"Tomorrow, around ten in the morning, I will come to your home. You will be off tomorrow, won't you? Tell your wife to make, as usual, her best cappuccino."

The lieutenant couldn't believe his eyes and his ears. He contented himself to shake this *marvelous stranger*'s hand, left the pharmacy, ordered the other police officers to go back to the police station.

The prescription, once filled, Max invited the woman, her lover and their children to follow him...

"I will take you home," he said.

"Do you know our address?" inquired the lover, by the way Abner Vincent.

"Certainly, I know. You live at thirty-five Bellevue Street."

"You are quite correct."

The lover turned towards the woman and advanced, "But, darling, you have never said anything about that uncle of yours; what's his name?"

"His name is Ernest Champion," cut in Max.

"Yes, my darling, you have never said a word about your uncle named Ernest Champion."

"Well, Abner, I didn't know that my uncle took any interest in me," finally replied the woman. "I have met him once, in my life, when I was twelve. He lives in opulence.

"Thus, like you, I have a big surprise at his intervention to pull us from a bad situation."

A deadly silence reigned over the car. Suddenly, the lover stated furiously, "Ah! I see now. This man here called Max Paul is your former lover.

"You give the impression that you don't know him. Believe me, Liliane I didn't expect such deception from you."

"What!" screamed the woman. "You have the nerve to insult me in my children's presence. "You have gone too far."

She burst out crying.

"Darling, forgive me," rushed saying the lover.

A stranger's wonderful chronicles, Book II

After a short pause, he went on, "Darling, you must understand my state of mind. I have no money. As a father, I can't provide for my family. We must pay the rent; but, I don't know how I will manage to honor this obligation. Soon, we will turn homeless."

Max made a gesture of the hand; then, he pronounced, "My name is Max Paul. For some unknown reason, today, I had some urge to drive at random and found myself near the drugstore. I have a gift for understanding the whole reality of people in distress.

"Liliane, I have mentioned your uncle name to pacify lieutenant Boston; however, I have never met your uncle…"

"But how do you manage to know my name and my family ties?" asked the woman anxiously. "Who are you?"

Abner opened his arms before cutting in, "The situation gets confused by the minute.

"Where do you come from, Mr.? You must answer my question; for, I must know your intentions. I have the duty to protect my family if need be."

"Abner, you know how to fight. You have obtained your black belt from *Judo Institute*…"

"What? Mister…"

"Max Paul. My name is Max Paul. Let's go back to your martial combat skills. One of your instructors, Mr. Azikawa, told you, one day, that you must not use violence for the sake of violence."

"What?"

"Why would you aggress me, while I have just pulled your family from a bad situation?"

"But, Sir…"

"My name is Max Paul. I know the alpha and omega of reality."

"Ah!" exclaimed Lillian, "Abner, my children, we are experiencing a case of collective hallucination. This Mr. Max Paul doesn't exist. We haven't received the medication for our beloved Yvonne. Soon she will die…"

"Liliane, my friend, you have made a mistake to think like that," argued Max. "You can just open the bag to see the bottle with the medication inside."

The woman acted as he had suggested and stated, "Yes, the bottle in there. Therefore, Yvonne won't die.

"I believe, mister, that you have exceptional gifts."

Finally, they reach the vicinity of the building where Liliane, Abner and their children lived. Max got off the car and rushed opening the door to let the woman and the children get out. Then, he said, "Would you invite me in your home? I would like to speak to you. Don't have any fear of me."

"Mr. Max, I have no fear of you," said Yvonne.

The parents opened wide their eyes.

"Yvonne, why haven't you any fear of him?" asked the father.

A stranger's wonderful chronicles, Book II

"Dad," answered the girl, "clearly, this man has enough power to hurt us. However, he didn't. Then, mom, dad, he must act as a messenger of God."

Max bent forward and kissed the girl on the cheek.

"Thus, Yvonne, you see the reason why I won't let you die. You need only to have an operation to correct one of your heart valves.

"Your operation will cost ten thousand dollars. I will take care of the expenses.

"Your parents, siblings and you should know that you will be, one day, a senator, representing your district people."

"I will be a senator!"

"Yes, you will."

"But, sir, I had a dream…No…How do you manage to know something like that."

"Yvonne, I know everything.

"However, I can't tell you the source of my power. I don't know it my-self."

Max left, soon after having supper with the family, not without given an envelope containing money to the parents. Then, he handed over two other envelopes containing each a letter of introduction to Berkeley Institute where Lillian would teach math, and one to Bernier House where Abner would work as a certified mechanic.

Avoided tragedy

A fourth envelope had the address of *Good Wish Medical Center* where they would operate on Yvonne.

Liliane, spontaneously, hugged Max.

"Would you ever forgive me for having lent you malicious intentions?

"In this respect, Yvonne turns out to have more perspicuity than we, in terms of grasping your unmatched generosity."

Abner, with tears in his eyes, cut in, "Max, I have badly treated you. I don't know the reason for my behaving in such uncouth manner."

Max breathed deeply. Then, he cast a kind look at the lovers. Finally, he concluded, "My brother, my sister, evil has always kept its presence in human history, as evidenced by the bloody wars, homicides, ethnic cleansing, acts of betrayal, politicians' heartlessness… Men and women suffer so much from all these nonsensical actions that the good, whenever it seldom appears, turns suspect.

"You understand the reason why a nation, occasionally, elects a sadistic to power, who has promised to make him suffer all the ills in the world, while a candidate full with compassion has been available.

"The nation believes that the latter, because of his courteous manner, must have hidden bad feelings.

"Anyway, my brother and sister, you will never be the same persons, following our encounter. Don't forget to spread the good in your way."

He got to his car in time; for the female employee, assigned to enforcing traffic rules, nearly gave him a summons for illegal parking.

A stranger's wonderful chronicles, Book II

He patted her on the back and said, "Julia, you haven't got lucky with me!"

"Sir, how do you know my name?" astonished the public employee.

"Julia, it is long story.

"I don't really have the time to tell you about it.

"However, here is my business card. Call me this evening. I will help you with paying your rent for this month. So far, you have no idea how you will get any extra money to honor your obligations; for, you have so many credit cards to pay."

"Sir, wait a minute."

"Listen, my name now is Max Paul. I will help you out.

"By the way, it wasn't my luck preventing you from having the time to write me a summons; you were just thinking about these obligations you have to meet."

"Are you sure, someone can help me out?"

"I will."

"Thank you so much Max. You must act as a messenger of God."

"Bye, Julia. Listen, to free your mind from any fear for me, Come to see me with your husband and children. I will give you cause for satisfaction.

"Your husband happens to be an unemployed electrician. He may work for my company if he wants to.

"Bye."

Max parked his car in front of a family home, in a neighborhood populated by middle-class people. He sat down in an apparently pensive manner; he was thinking about his good deeds that he had provided Julia and her family with.

Then, unhesitatingly, he got off the car, went and pressed the buzzer without any ceremony.

The door opened at once and revealed a very beautiful woman in her late thirties.

"It's Louise?" he inquired.

"Yes, it's I, Mr...."

"I am Max Paul."

"I am glad to meet you, Mr. Max Paul. My husband has told me about you."

"Louise, don't be formal with me. You should take me for your brother."

Soon afterward, the visitor gave Mrs. Jordan a bunch of flowers.

"Max," acknowledged the woman, "these flowers are beautiful and fragrant. Apparently, you have just picked them out. Would you have a flower bed?"

"No, Louise, I don't have one. I have produced them magically while knocking at your door."

The woman remained open-mouthed.

A stranger's wonderful chronicles, Book II

Then, after pulling herself together, she admitted, "Whatever the means you have used to produce these fresh and dazzling flowers, I must recognize that you behave like a true gentleman.

"Come and sit in the living room. Let me page my husband."

Indeed, the woman screamed, "Darling, it's Max. He has just arrived."

Few minutes after, Lieutenant Boston Jordan rejoined his wife and the visitor in the living room.

After given a vigorous handshake to the latter and a tender kiss on his wife's lips, he said to her, "Darling, is breakfast ready?

"We won't go on a mission on empty stomach.

"Additionally, Max wouldn't help me without his cappuccino of which you have the secret."

The woman nodded. Then, the men followed her.

She presented her two children to the visitor, who had sat peacefully and waited for the adults to show up.

"Max, this is my daughter, Melanie," she said. "She is seven. This is my son Daniel. He is five."

"My children, how are you?" inquired Max.

"Very well," answered the children together.

"Indeed, my children, you are the picture of health.

"Are you happy to stay home for this holyday with Mom and Dad?"

"Yes, sir," replied Melanie. "We love our parents very much."

"I am glad to hear that."

Avoided tragedy

Shortly after, people around the table took delight in the foods prepared by Louise Jordan.

She was a cordon bleu who had studied culinary arts in Europe. She had thought of opening a restaurant, but she had received an anonymous letter telling her that a "powerful organization" would burn down "such restaurant" if she opened it. The letter concluded,

You should know Mrs. Louise Jordan that in this neighborhood, nothing takes place without my consent. If you yield to my demands, we will meet one day. In the meantime, don't make the mistake to open a restaurant. You will lose all your resources, as well as the life of your husband and your two children.

You have just received a warning. Salute!

Strangely enough, for some unexplained reason, all banks in Louise Jordon's neighborhood had denied her financial assistance.

The moment for cappuccino arrived.

"Louise," said Marx jovially, "they haven't exaggerated your skill. It's the best cappuccino I have ever savored.

"Don't worry. Your brother Max would feel honored to help you open your restaurant."

The woman opened wide her eyes. That Max knew everything about her.

A stranger's wonderful chronicles, Book II

"Well, Lieutenant Boston Jordan, let's go to our meeting," suggested the visitor."

The wife held Max by the wrist and said, "Max, I trust you. Protect my husband. He is my only source of joy and hope."

"Louise, your husband will come back home free of all worries, and you will have your restaurant."

"Thank you in advance"

Lieutenant Boston Jordan and Max entered a tavern. It plunged into almost darkness, since its owner hadn't reopened it yet for business.

Two sturdily built men searched the visitors for concealed weapons or microchips.

After their "illegal search", they shook their head to inform their boss that the visitors hid nothing that would compromise him.

"Who is he?" asked the extortionist, Marino Lucien, while pointing his chin at Max. "Didn't I advise not to visit me with anyone else? This man may act as a spy for the police or the national security, which intend to interfere in my business..."

"He is a good friend," answered Boston Jordan. "I want a witness' presence when I have to pay you off a debt I don't owe you.

"Frankly speaking, I thought, as a childhood friend, you have intended to give me a gift..."

With a brisk motion of the hand, Marino Lucien stopped the lieutenant. Then, he stated, "I don't run a goodwill organization. I don't care about your lousy income which allows you barely to survive. I gave you money to serve me…"

"How could have I served you?"

"I wanted to know what the police and other security people say about my organization…"

"No, I couldn't betray the police department. I was a police officer (and still am), not a criminal.

"In addition, if you remain straightforward, you won't need to worry about the police.

"As your childhood friend, I think that I must give you such piece of advice."

"I don't need advice from a loser. You live from hand to mouth.

"Anyway, since you refuse to serve me, then you must reimburse me."

"How much does my bother owe you?" cut in Max Paul.

"I don't remember speaking to you."

"If you don't want to speak to me, you won't have any reimbursement; for, the money will come from me."

"Oh! I see.

"Well, listen, your brother has received an envelope containing more two thousand dollars."

"More than two thousand dollars!" protested the lieutenant.

Max Paul touched lightly Boston's shoulder, inviting him to remain calm.

A stranger's wonderful chronicles, Book II

Then, he asked the extortionist, "How much does he owe you?"

"Let me see...Well, according to my calculation based on the length of loan, he owes me five thousand dollars."

The lieutenant tried to grasp Marino by the throat to strangle him, but he stopped short: more than six handguns aimed at him.

"Don't worry my brother," insinuated Max. "We will pay the money."

"I only want cash. I would not accept a check which would put me in a compromising position."

"Of course, crooks like you only use cash. They can never go to regular financial institutions to take care of their shady activities."

"Listen, Max, watch your mouth."

"Why do you feel offended by my remark? It expresses the truth.

"You embody a vermin..."

"Well, enough speech. Give me the money."

Max opened his briefcase, counted five wads of bills and handed them over to the extortionist.

"Well, I hope you will leave my friends alone and that you will not interfere in their family business.

"Otherwise, I will come back to get you.

"You don't want me to come back!"

Max kept silent for a while. Then, he added, "We know that you have sent his wife an anonymous letter to prevent her from opening her restaurant in the neighborhood..."

Avoided tragedy

"Listen!" yelled Marion Lucien. "I don't care about what you learn, but nobody tells me what to do. I still have the picture showing the moment at which the lieutenant has received the envelope from me.

"Additionally, nobody can open a restaurant in the neighborhood without my consent.

"Did you hear me?

"Besides, that Louise Jordon won't receive any banking assistance; for, I control these financing institutions."

Max went closer to the criminal.

Instinctively, the latter and his henchmen pulled their handguns. The lieutenant feared for incurring a grave danger because of his accidental friend's action. However, he had a big surprise when Marino Lucien and his assassins screamed with pain and dropped their mysteriously overheated weapons.

Then, slowly, Max pronounced, "Listen to me, dirty little vermin.

"Look in your safe; you won't find any picture of Lieutenant Boston."

"But who are you?"

"I become the projection of you criminal conscience," replied Max.

Marino remained perplexed.

"Well, Marino, here is the picture," went on Max, while showing the snapshot. "Let me get rid of it once and for all.

"As far as the negative is concerned, I will take care of it as soon as possible.

A stranger's wonderful chronicles, Book II

"From now on, you can't touch even one hair of the Jordans' head; for, if you do, I will come back to you and show you the full range of my power.

"However, to give you an idea of what you will face, let me show you the file I draw up on you."

Next, he pulled a minicomputer from his jacket interior pocket, turned it on and, like a recording magnetic film, he showed the odious criminal acts perpetrated by Marino Lucien and his henchmen.

"Let me tell you that less than twenty-five percent of your criminal activities will be enough to send you to jail for life or to receive a death sentence.

"You have committed many acts of genocide. You shouldn't have the right to live in society.

"If you are not careful, I will come back and kill you personally."

Then, Max rejoined the lieutenant and suggested, "Let's go. This place makes me nauseous."

Before reentering his house, the police officer observed, "Max, I felt like killing these scoundrels once and for all. I swear that enveloped has contained only two thousand dollars. That day, like now, I didn't have more than ten dollars in my pocket. However, days after, that criminal tried again to give me a gift; but I flatly refused. I realized his bad intentions.

"As a representative of the law, I didn't want to compromise myself."

Max, with a motion of the hand, cut in. Then, he said, "I can't tell the content of that envelope, which has vanished.

"However, I believe you since you claim that envelope couldn't have more than two thousand dollars.

"But, today, my brother, you haven't said the truth about the amount of money you have just received from…"

"What!

"Max, you are too kind to insult me. I have just told you I have ten dollars in my pocket."

"Are you sure, Boston?"

"Max, I swear that I have no more than ten dollars in my pocket. I live from hand to mouth. My income only allows me to pay my obligations."

"Boston, my dear brother, believe me. You have more than two thousand dollars in your pocket. I have always completed my mission…"

"Since you insist, here it is…"

Boston Jordan couldn't believe his eyes; he had a thick wad of bank notes in his hand.

"Max, when did you put so much money into my pocket…? You are incredible."

"Let's go, Boston. I must rush saying good-bye to your wife and your children."

In the living room, Max, remaining standing, stated, "My dear friends, I must take leave of you. My little friend, at the hospital, needs me.

A stranger's wonderful chronicles, Book II

"I have an intuition of that."

"But, Max," said the woman, "I know that you hold powers that baffle our mind and transcend possibility of action. Are you from Lucifer in person or an envoy of God?

"Why do you want to help others and us?"

"Louise, I can't answer your first set of questions," replied the benefactor. "I don't know the origin of my magical divinatory powers.

"However, regarding the second set of questions, I may tell you that I am sincere when I take men, women and children as my brothers and sisters."

After a short pause, he rushed saying, "My friends, I must leave you. Louise, tomorrow, you will go to *Promotion Bank*. You will get the funds you need for opening your restaurant."

"Max!" yelled the woman. "Is it true?"

"Yes, it is.

"Besides, I have recently built a new condominium on Saint Antoine Boulevard. I intend to use the first floor units for commercial activities. Here is the key of one of the units. It's the location of your new restaurant. You may go now to see it with your family."

Max kept silent for few seconds, before concluding, "Well, I believe I have covered everything.

"My dear sister Louise, in this envelope, I put some money, which will allow you to meet certain expenses.

"Don't forget my little friends, Melanie and Daniel.

"Then, bye, my friends."

Instinctively, the police officer, his wife and their children gave each a kiss on Max's cheeks.

Apparently, the hospital became the center of a big confusion. The specialist who should operate on Yvonne, showed eagerness to act accordingly; however, he had to wait for the administration authorization to proceed, because of absence of any information about Yvonne parents' health benefits.

The nurse in chief yelled, "Listen, who will pay for such expensive surgical procedure?"

The parents felt embarrassed; for, the staff and the visitors had overheard the nurse's question.

The mother went to that employee and said, "Miss., you must lower your voice. It is a very delicate matter."

"Listen, Miss., you don't have any qualification to tell me how I should behave," screamed the employee.

The specialist asked the mother to have a chat with him in private.

Then, he inquired about the financial aspect of the deal.

"Dear Doctor," replied Liliane, "a Good Samaritan, named Max Paul, has promised to help us."

The doctor went to the nurse to ask her if a certain Max Paul had paid the amount of ten thousand dollars.

A stranger's wonderful chronicles, Book II

"Ah!" spoke out the nurse. "These people depend on a Good Samaritan! He may be a bit of a joker, a liar or a penniless pedant. I know these kinds…"

Yvonne overheard that nurse's derogatory remarks and replied (despite a strong parents' opposition), "Madam, my friend Max Paul is not a bit of a joker, a liar, a penniless pedant. You have made a big mistake. You will see. He will keep his words."

Only then, the nurse had awareness of her lack of tact.

"Well, Yvonne, be patient," urged the doctor. "I am willing to wait for the solution of this situation; for, you will not go back to your home without undergoing the corrective surgery. I will save your life, my little friend. I give you my word, even if I don't get paid."

"Thank you, Doctor," said Yvonne's father. "Professionals like you become as seldom as the most precious pearl in the world."

Suddenly, Yvonne shouted for joy when she saw her benefactor, Max Paul, arriving.

He took the girl in his arms and covered her with kisses. Then, he went to the nurses' station and said, "Madam, you have missed your profession."

"What! You have no right to speak to me like that."

"Listen, Elisabeth…"

"How do you manage to know my name?"

"I know more about you than you think.

Avoided tragedy

"You love gossips. However, you have made a mistake about me. Nobody takes me for a bit of a joker, a liar and a penniless pedant."

After a moment of silence, Max Paul went on, "I thought you would have changed with time. However, if you want I can give you a rundown about your childhood and your adolescence. You have never been a person with a heart. Do you remember how much you had hurt your younger sister, Violeta?

"You have also given such hard time to your cousin Beatrice and your classmate Monett.

"For reason of decency and charity, I won't go beyond these recalls. However, you must use caution."

The nurse remained open-mouthed.

Then, Max Paul spoke to the clerk, "Miss., did you call the department of finance regarding a payment made by a certain Max Paul intended for covering my friend Yvonne's surgery costs?"

The clerk breathed deeply before answering, "Not yet."

"What keeps you from acting this way? You should have done so a while ago."

"Sir, you are right. I will do it now."

"That's not your fault; for, this nurse, very prompt to criticize others, has said nothing to you."

Few minutes after, the secretary passed the phone receiver to the doctor.

He had a broad smile on his face.

A stranger's wonderful chronicles, Book II

"Let's go, my friends," he then said to Yvonne's parents. "We have lost too much time unnecessarily."

Next, they took Yvonne to the operating room, while the parents and Max remained anxious in the waiting room.

Two hours after, the specialist rejoined them to tell them about the good news.

"As far as you are concerned, Mr. Max Paul," went on the doctor, "we don't know how to thank you.

"I seize this opportunity to present you the general manager's apology, the chief of service's and mine for the uncouth manner in which the nurse in chief has treated you. The big shots think that she should go."

Max touched slightly the doctor's shoulder and said, "Doctor, I have divinatory skills and I know the alpha and omega of reality."

"Is that so?"

"I will give you a little proof of that.

"You have always dreamed of having a wife who would fulfill all your wishes; for, you are still a single."

"Oh! You are a very interesting man."

"Such woman you have yearned for exists.

"I mean an old childhood friend you haven't seen for more than fifteen years."

"My friend, wait just a minute!"

"Yes, she is the one.

"Marilyn Thomas.

"Like you, she works in the capacity of a cardiologist. She has never forgetting you. Your image has remained engraved in her charming head.

"I have here my cellular. Her number is in my phone memory. Go ahead. Don't be shy."

The specialist opened wide his eyes. Then, he said, "Well, if you don't see any inconvenience, I will be in your house in one hour...Yes, now, I have the address...Mary, it's a long story, a mystery...

"Yes, I have just become a believer, thanks to Max's divinatory skills...Yes, he stands by me...Bye."

The specialist returned the cellular to Max; then, he hugged him.

"My dear Max," he said, "you must be an envoy of Providence."

Max made a large motion of the hand and pronounced, "My friends, I must leave, but, not before I give a kiss to my little friend Yvonne."

The specialist beckoned to the parents and Max to follow him.

Yvonne had just coming from the general anesthesia influence. She smiled at the sight of friendly faces.

Max walked up to the bed, bent forward and kissed her tenderly on the cheek.

"Yvonne," he said, "I must take leave of you."

"Will have ever seen you again?"

"Yes, when you become Senator."

The girl nodded.

A stranger's wonderful chronicles, Book II

"However, Yvonne, you must use wisdom," added the man. "Don't reveal your future to anyone."

The girl nodded again.

Max turned around, kissed the parents, the other children and the specialist.

He whispered to the latter's ear to suggest to him, "If you value my advice, my good friend, do your best to prevent the firing of the nurse.

"If they fire her, she will commit suicide.

"We don't want something like that to happen to any human being.

"Actually, she has received a psychological shock that will make her a better person in the near future.

"I am sure of that."

The specialist kissed Max on the cheek, who set out to leave the premises without delay.

"My dear Max, I thank you for everything. I will never forget your boundless generosity.

On the way, he said to the secretary, "Mona, you must always practice the good.

"Then, you will always feel happy if you follow my advice throughout your existence."

"I will follow your advice to the letter," replied Mona in tones of emotion.

"Bye, my friends," said Max loud and clear.

Next, he disappeared.

◘   ◘

◘

This time, Brian Clifford felt that he hit the jackpot, since, by a stroke of luck he had four testimonies about the marvelous stranger.

He received the testimony of Yvonne who became Senator, representing her district, an outcome predicted by Max Paul years ahead. She gave the reporter all the details of the events taking place from the time of her parents' confrontation with the pharmacist to the time of the marvelous stranger's intervention.

Brian got another account from Louise Jordan who received him at her restaurant always attended by all kinds of people. Louise's husband and their two children added to their wife and mother's report.

The journalist also had an account of the events from the cardiologist who had married to his childhood friend, another cardiologist.

Finally, he received the testimony of Julia (the traffic agent), her husband and their children.

"He must be a messenger of God," concluded the woman.

Brian Clifford smiled at the thought that he would get another account on his *mysterious friend's* beneficial activity. He would visit "la petite Lucinda"

(22)

Little

Lucinda

By Antoine Archange Raphael

*A*rmand Hubert drove at moderate speed. He returned from a business meeting and headed to his home. When he reached the toll bridge, he had the choice between the highway and the local route. He opted for the former, for no apparent reason.

Billboards showed up everywhere, announcing a variety of possible business activities.

Armand Hubert stopped the car to read something about the sale of a huge real estate property in a large billboard advertisement.

The driver saw the possibility for building houses (at least a condominium) intended for a community of middle-income people; the more so as that piece of land found itself close to two urban centers having an abundance of factories, administrative activities, health centers, colleges and many other similar businesses.

Homeless people composed of men, women and children had erected temporary shelters with plywood and boxes.

That day, Armand Hubert, suddenly, found himself in the middle of a manifestation of violence: military aimed their automatic weapons at the homeless trembling all over.

Apparently, the property caretaker had called the law enforcement people to get rid of these destitute the sight of whom might discourage prospective buyers.

Armand Hubert pulled his cellular phone from his jacket pocket and dialed the phone number written on the billboard in dark red.

A stranger's wonderful chronicles, Book II

"May I speak to this property caretaker," he said. "I am in the car stationed by the sidewalk…"

A well-dressed man, standing by the military, answered the call. He turned around and saw Armand Hubert leant against the car body.

He beckoned to the military to stay on the lookout and joined prospective buyer.

They shook hands. Then, the caretaker said in a drawl voice, "I am Nicholas Diva, the administrator of this beautiful piece of land.

"Would you be interested in it?

"By the way, don't pay any attention about what you see. These scoundrels take advantage of a guardian's absence to occupy this splendid property.

"If they pay no attention, they will pay dearly for their unlawful occupancy."

The visitor cut in, "My name is Armand Hubert. Yes, I am interested in this piece of land. However, let me set my first condition: you have to ask the military to leave and stop frightening these destitute."

"But…"

"There is no but, Mr. Diva…I have no intention and no time to joke.

"The intervention of organized force may always endanger others' lives, including yours.

"The world should never solve its problems forcibly, but rather around a conference table.

"These people you call scoundrels happen to be human beings like you and get dreams to fulfill, like you and me.

"You should never forget it.

"Well, go and tell the military to leave the premises, otherwise, I will go and look for another piece of land. There are many in this area."

The peremptory tone in which the prospective buyer spoke made Nicholas Diva act without any murmur.

He went to the superior officer who ordered his men to leave, to the great relief of Armand Hubert and the destitute; for, by accident, an officer could fire a shot at the crowd and cause someone's death or an unnecessary bloody commotion.

"Well, Mr. Diva," said the buyer, "let me go to these destitute. Now, they no longer trust you."

Max acted as he had suggested.

"Listen, my friends," he started, "I will buy this piece of land to build a condominium.

"Do you have another place to live in?"

"No, sir," answered many of these destitute together.

"Dear sir, by our foolishness, we put ourselves on the fringe of society," stated one of them. "Now, we can't find any job, any decent place to live at."

"What's your name?"

"My name is Phelps Renault.

A stranger's wonderful chronicles, Book II

"This is my wife Bertha, my daughter Lucinda, my son Robert and another girl whose name is Clarisse."

"Mr. Renault, are there any other families living on these premises?"

"Yes, sir, there are."

"My name is Armand Hubert."

"All of us almost live with our families."

"Well, my friends, we will find a satisfactory solution together."

"Thank you, Mr. Hubert," stated Phelps Renault. "God will bless you."

Armand Hubert spoke to the caretaker in these terms, "Nicholas Diva, let's go to your office to finalize the deal."

"Certainly, Mr. Hubert, we should."

"Call me Armand."

"I will."

As he walked up to his car to follow the caretaker's, Phelps Renault's five year old girl, by the way, the little Lucinda, followed him closely, despite the parents and neighbors' scream in protest.

"Lucinda," yelled the mother, "leave Mr. Hubert alone. Did you hear me, Lucinda?

"You don't wear clean clothes."

"Lucy," implored the father, "why do you have to behave like that?

"You embarrass us. What happens? You have always behaved wisely."

"Mr. Armand Hubert," the father spoke to the Good Samaritan, "Lucinda has never behaved like that.

"Actually, she is shy and always stays close by us."

"Ladies and gentlemen, don't worry," stated Mr. Armand Hubert. "Probably, Lucinda takes me for a good and trusting friend.

"We don't reject friendship. It represents a rear pearl in the world."

At these words, Armand Hubert turned around and said, "Come to me, my little Lucinda."

To the destitute and the caretaker's surprise, Armand Hubert opened his arms and lifted the child.

The general surprise changed into consternation, then into admiration, when the child threw her arms around the man's neck and kissed him on the cheek.

The man whispered few words to the child's ear. Then he released her, not without saying, "Go, my little Lucinda. Don't have any fear. You will certainly enjoy a better lot in life. I give you my word.

"Now, my little friend, go back to your parents. I will see you later."

Then, he waved at the destitute and pronounced, "My dear friends, I will see you in one hour.

"I promise you a better lot. I will do my best to keep my promise to you."

The destitute, instinctively, applauded the harmony between the man and the child.

One hour later, Armand Hubert rejoined the destitute. But he didn't return empty-handed.

A stranger's wonderful chronicles, Book II

He came with two trucks filled with foods, toilet product, clothes and camping stoves.

Next, Lucinda, her brother Robert and her sister Clarisse wore new clothes and shoes.

Other children of different destitute families had also received new clothes and shoes.

Armand Hubert beckoned to the men to ask them to help him put up a huge tent. Then, he invited everybody to an emergency meeting.

Despite Armand's obvious generosity, the destitute thought that he would ask them to leave the place. However, at their big surprise, he had a smile on his face.

He beckoned to Lucinda to join him and asked her to sit by him.

He started, "My friends, you owe Lucinda a debt of gratitude. She has touched me deeply. Believe me, she will succeed in life."

The man stopped to stroke the child's face.

Then, he went on, "I have a plan of action beneficial to all of us, if you really want to change."

"Sir…"

"Call me Armand. Take me for your brother. Don't have any fear of me. I will not hold you empty promises"

"Oh, thank you," said a woman who stood by the man who was about to speak.

Then, she burst out crying.

Other women patted her on the back to calm her down.

"What's you name?" asked Armand to the man who wanted to speak.

"My name is Berea.

"Armand, we will follow you everywhere; for, seemingly, you mean to open a world of hope to us.

"We have intended to live anywhere, under any condition until we die.

Nobody wants to have anything to do with us. However, if you think that we can still recapture our human dignity, then, we will follow you in your pilgrimage that will also be ours."

"First," suggested Armand, "you must show an irreproachable attitude.

"Stay away from alcoholic beverages and illegal drugs. The prospective buyers of my condominium units would not welcome their coexistence with scoundrels.

"Second, besides the condominium, I will build one-floored complex not far from the great construction. I will kill two birds with the same stone: these among you with a profession will put their skill at the owners' disposition.

"Are they car mechanics among you?"

At least three destitute raised their hands acquiescently.

"Well, I will provide you with a garage and all the modern equipment. We will become associates. An office clerk will issue invoices and will entrust the takings to a security company specialized in transferring funds to bank accounts.

A stranger's wonderful chronicles, Book II

"Of course, you will have an income."

After having written the mechanics' names, Armand Hubert proceeded by order of importance, that is to say masons, cabinetmakers, tailors…

"You will participate in your home construction, then in the condominium.

"Specialized and experienced workers will join you to guide you throughout your activities.

"What do you think?"

A woman raised her hand and made the following observation, "Armand, my name is Louisa Mentor.

"Do you intend to hurt us? For, people don't give up their wealth to assist others. Are you an envoy of Satan or God?"

"What gets into you Louisa?" yelled another woman named Zealand Lavoie. "What difference does it make? A Good Samaritan comes along and you want to discourage him."

"Listen, shut up!" yelled a man.

Then, he presented himself, "My name is Beaumont Mentor, Louisa Mentor's husband.

"I do lover her very much, however she often talks too much.

"Armand don't take offense at her questions. We need someone like you…"

Armand Hubert made a large gesture of the hands. Then, he stated without beating about the bush, "My friends, Louisa is right. You shouldn't incriminate her. Many often wear sheep clothes, while they are actually wolves.

"Additionally, you must welcome women's opinions. Like us, they have something to say in the unfolding of reality.

"However, Louisa," Armand turning toward the woman, "let me tell you that your friends and you are lucky to meet a Good Samaritan who doesn't know if he is an envoy of Satan or God.

"All I know, well, this morning, instead of taking the local route, I took the highway. I do have sometimes these kinds of intuitions leading me to people in distress.

"Where do they come from?

"I can't tell you.

"However, my good friends, I strongly believe that I rather act as an envoy of God; for, I always feel anxious and happy to help others.

"Listen, my friends, I can't spend my life just eating, drinking, acquiring money.

"I would then live like a pig happy in its muddy bath (there was a collective burst of laughter). I want to spread the good around me; for, I take you all for my brothers and sisters. I take great delight in bringing you joy…"

The destitute, Louisa and Zealand included, burst out crying.

Then, Armand Hubert stood up and joined the crowd to appease everybody.

A stranger's wonderful chronicles, Book II

He shook hands with some, hugged many, and whispered encouraging words to others' ears.

He had never stopped holding Lucinda by the hand.

As he had anticipated, a month after, he had changed the neglected property into an urban center, with all the services required by a modern community, such as department stores, health centers, garages, beauty parlors, supermarkets...

The men and women with professions had participated in the construction of the complex intended for the former destitute and the condominium.

One day, Nicholas Diva, the former land caretaker, revisited the area and couldn't believe his eyes.

He said to Armand Hubert, "My friend, what happens to the destitute?"

"They become important members of our little nascent community."

"What!"

"There were many professionals among them and they helped me build their own complex building (the one-floored building you see over there).

"Then, they also helped building the condominium.

"Additionally, they start their own business, in partnership with me, and offer their services to the community.

"I would say that the area functions like an autarchy, meetings all its needs and pouring joy in the heart of the neighborhood members."

After a moment of silence, he insinuated, "Nick, how do you manage?"

"Armand, I am doing ok, considering," answer the real estate agent.

"You can trust me.

"I know that you have apparently insurmountable problems. But we can solve them."

"Ah! Armand, you are a good fortune teller."

"Let me tell you a secret."

"Did you say a secret?"

"Well, Nick, my dear brother, I do have a profound intuition of reality.

"Let me explain myself.

"When someone stands close to me, I know all the aspects of his life as if that person has written them in a book."

"Armand you have expressed something impossible. I don't believe you.

"You must be simply joking."

"No, I am not.

"For example, you are not an evil man."

"Armand, you want to make fun of me. You have seen me in action, last time, when I have exposed the destitute to police brutality.

"However, you have saved them and give them reason for enjoying life again."

"You have acted against your will."

"What do you mean?"

A stranger's wonderful chronicles, Book II

"Nick, your heart bled when you exposed the destitute to unnecessary violence. Yet, you didn't have any choice. The owner of your real estate agency, a man of steel heart, threatened to fire you if you didn't call the police.

"He had given you the same order three times, and you had turned a deaf ear.

"Nevertheless, you didn't have any choice. You need your job to take care of your family composed of four people: Camellia, your wife; Teresa, your eldest child; Gabriel, your son and you.

"You have a small income, yet, you prefer your wife to stay home, as she is not robust, and that you would rather welcome her presence in the house to raise the children.

"You live in a building located in the heart of crime-infested neighborhood.

"Your only guarantee consists in shutting up at home, after seven in the evening; for, drug dealers kill each other and kill innocent people in the process…"

Nicholas Diva pinched his own arm to make sure he wasn't sleeping.

Then, not saying one word, he took leave of that strange Armand and resumed his office.

He told his colleagues about the happy transformation of that area.

"My dear friends," he went on, "you must see it with your own eyes to believe what I am talking about.

"I am talking about an area that used to look like a desolate savannah."

His colleagues closed their ears with their fingers to express their "indifference".

Nicholas resumed sadly his office.

Martina Metallo, a female colleague, joined him.

This woman, extremely beautiful, educated and reserved, had been always dressed up.

She was twenty-one and had never had a lover in her life. She always said that she would, one day, meet with the man of her dream. "Otherwise, I will live alone with my parents," she concluded. "There is no law of nature or society, which will make me marry a man I don't love. Such decision, in this respect, will have the complexion of a suicide.

"Nick," she observed suddenly, "the owner of that condominium fascinates you."

"Indeed, Tina, the man is sympathetic, as they said," replied Nicholas.

Then, after a short pause, he added, "However, his most fascinating side comes from the fact that he knows the alpha and the omega of reality."

"My God!" exclaimed Martina. "Nick, you have always been naïve.

"That man tried to fool you. I understand now the negative reaction of my colleagues to your account."

After a short moment of silence, she added, "Well, since I think about it, they could also be jealous of you."

Nicholas opened his eyes wide.

A stranger's wonderful chronicles, Book II

"Nick, must I call the ambulance?" inquired Martina turning anxious.

After he had calmed down, he said, "No, Tina. Don't call the ambulance. You wouldn't believe me, Tina, if I told you…"

"What is happening to you?"

"Well, Armand told me that a young woman in my office, called Martina would express her doubt about my sayings."

"I don't believe you. You have just made up a story."

"He also said that woman, if she is not careful will remain unattached all her life."

"He said that!"

"He said more."

"What else did he say?"

"No, I can't tell you."

"Nick, you must tell me. You have started it, you have to finish it."

Nicholas kept silent. He wondered if he was raving.

"Nick, listen, tell me what he said about me."

"You want to know?" said Nicholas.

"Yes, I do."

"I will tell you, under one condition."

"What is this condition?"

"You must apologize for calling me a naïve."

"Yes, I will apologize if the man's prediction materializes."

"Yes, he said more about you."

"He said more about me? You are raving. The man has never met me."

"Do you want to know?"

"Oh! I am sorry.

"Speak up."

"He said that, until now you haven't found the man of your dream...You have even argued that there is no natural or social law that requires that you should marry a man you don't love. Your decision, in this respect, would have the complexion of a suicide.

"Tina, I have told the truth. The man has said that."

"You are joking."

"No, I am not."

"Nick, my good friend, that man, can he have access to a stranger's mind?

"What else did he say?"

"Tina, I fear for letting you know. If his prediction doesn't materialize, then, you will take me for a naïve or a funny fellow. But, believe me, I wouldn't take a joke that far."

"Nick, please, tell me."

"Well, he clearly stated that today, you will meet with the prince charming."

"I will?"

Martina went away in her office. She didn't want to hear more from her colleague's "ranting".

A stranger's wonderful chronicles, Book II

As she thought about it, Nicholas Diva had always had a vivid imagination. "He, then, misses his profession," she whispered. "He could have turned a prolific writer…"

Yet, she had received a shock. "If that man has the power to describe me without knowing me," she thought, "there is the possibility for him to tell the truth…

"Come to think of it, my opinion about my personal decision has never left my mind…

"We will see…"

Someone knocked at the office front door.

Nicholas Diva's colleagues stood instinctively to welcome a prospective wealthy-looking client.

He dressed himself with elegance: he wore a brown suit, a dark shirt and tie.

A broad smile radiated through his face.

For some reason, he walked straight to Nicholas, gave him a vigorous handshake and said in a suave manner, "My name is Antoine Megara.

"They have placed an advertisement in this newspaper concerning a real estate property.

"I think, if my memory serves me right, (he pointed a finger at the real estate section of that paper), that the agent's name is Martina Colona."

Nicholas Diva, for some unexplained motive, experienced a moment of weakness and sat down on the chair nearby to avoid collapsing.

He just had some kind of intuition about that Armand's predictions.

"My dear sir, is everything ok?" inquired anxiously the well-dressed visitor.

"Yes, everything is ok," replied Nicholas. "I had a passing moment of dizziness."

Then, he screamed, "Tina, come over, a client comes to see you."

The woman entered the waiting room, while she lowered her head to glance through a magazine.

The visitor couldn't prevent himself from *devouring* her with his eyes. He had never seen such beautiful pair of legs. Then, he cast an interesting eye over the employee's entire body and couldn't prevent himself from nodding.

On her turn, Martina looked up to welcome the visitor and had a shock.

"Miss., have I caused any disturbance by coming here?" inquired the client whose appearance seemed to trouble others. "You look very per-plexed. Have you confused me with someone else?"

She didn't answer at once. She turned around and looked at Nicholas Diva who nodded.

"No, sir, nothing is wrong," she said loud. "I will attend you and do my best to give cause for satisfaction.

"I may come back…"

"Oh! Everything works fine," rushed saying the young woman. "Come to my office."

A stranger's wonderful chronicles, Book II

He followed her unhesitatingly.

"Have a seat, sir," she stated, while pointing to a chair set behind her desk.

Both noticed their spontaneous decision not to act formally, as if they had formed longtime friendship with each other.

"Miss. Colona, I would like to visit this property advertised in this newspaper."

"Certainly, you may.

"However, before we do, let me show it on video."

"That's an excellent idea."

After the film projection, Antoine Megara acknowledged the beauty of that property.

"To tell you the truth," he went on, "I have always dreamed of living in that neighborhood. However, for one reason or another, I have never found the house of my taste.

"Additionally, Miss, I don't know why I want to live in that house.

"My condominium apartment has plenty of space for a hardcore single like me.

"Are you married, Miss.?"

Martina betrayed a moment of hesitancy before answering, "Not yet, Mr. Megara. I am waiting for the prince charming."

"Miss Colona, what a strange coincidence! I also yearned for a princess."

"Indeed, Mr. Megara, I must acknowledge the strange nature of this coincidence," added Martina.

Next, she stood up.

"Let's go and visit the property," she suggested. "Will we use your car or mine?"

"I would like to drive such distinguished woman like you."

"Thank you."

On the way, Antoine Megara slid a folded note to Martina. She opened it and read,

Martina,

I am sincere. At first sight, you have caused such a strong impression on me. I should have said a strong commotion. It's the first time I have such feeling. I want to confuse it with love

And you, what do you feel for me? Do you find me at least acceptable?

Martina jotted down a line at the note bottom and returned the folded paper to Antoine Megara. He opened it and had great joy in reading the answer,

Antoine,

A stranger's wonderful chronicles, Book II
Yes, I have a feeling similar to yours.

How can we explain something like that?

It could be one of the mysteries of life.

Next, the client and the real estate agent kept silent while making a tour of the house on sale.

The prospective buyer had never ceased to have awareness of the agent's competence, her enthusiasm, her eloquence and her diction…"

Soon after, they had returned to the office, Antoine signed all the papers and application forms relating to real estate transaction.

Since it was a Saturday, Martina's colleagues, except Nicholas, had left.

Finally, Antoine broke the ice, "Martina, tomorrow, business is closed. You will have time to have some rest. Do you want to accompany me to a restaurant?

"One of them, I know, serves nothing but succulent foods that will please your palate. I promise to let you go as soon as we will have finished eating."

"Wait just a minute, Antoine!

"I must let my parents know the reason I won't join them, tonight, at the family table."

After having a good supper at the restaurant, Antoine, as promised, "let Martina go free".

Nevertheless, before he did, he asked her for "a warm goodbye kiss".

The woman joyfully acquiesced.

"My beautiful lady, what do you plan on doing tomorrow?" inquired the man.

"I have nothing to do tomorrow. Why do want to know, Antoine?"

"Listen, I don't mean any harm. However, may I go to see you at your parent's home?"

"Why can't you?"

They parted from each other.

In the meantime, Nicholas, remaining alone in the office, was about to close all the doors and windows, and to turn off the electric appliances, when his cellular phone rang.

He rushed putting the receiver to his ear and had a shock to hear Armand's voice, "Nick, all is well?"

"Yes, as you have anticipated it."

"Martina will make a good choice. This Mr. Antoine Megara is a good guy."

He took a long pause before asking, "By the way, Nick, what do you intend to do, tonight?

"Why don't you visit me in my office?

"Come on, Nick, my brother, go and get your wife and your children.

"I would like to meet them."

"Armand…"

"I know.

A stranger's wonderful chronicles, Book II

"You won't resume your apartment in time and will expose your family to great danger, which seems really unnecessary.

"Listen, my friend, go and get your family.

"You will spend a marvelous time somewhere else, not beset with dangers.

"Your wife, above all, will have great pleasure in a change of atmosphere."

"Armand, you know that I don't have this kind of money allowing me..."

"Nick, let me handle the expenses, since I take upon myself to invite your family."

"Agree, Armand. I will go and get my family. We will reach your office in forty-five minutes."

"I am waiting for you."

Nicholas, discreetly, knocked at the administrative door.

He asked himself if he wouldn't create unnecessary trouble to his family, in case Armand wouldn't keep his word.

"Please, my friends, come in" Armand warmly beckoned the visitors.

Then, he went on, "Nick, don't tell me!

"It's your beautiful wife Camellia, your daughter Teresa and your son Gabriel.

"Nick, my good friend and brother, your wife loves you very much.

"Engineers, physicians, even a Senator have expressed their willingness to marry her, but your image has predominated over theirs...

"She couldn't picture life without you."

Without any warning, Camellia grabbed Armand by the hand, to the husband and the children's surprise.

Next, she yelled, "Armand, who are you? Do you belong to this world?

"Are you a stranger from distant places, some kind of spirit, coming from nowhere?

"How do you manage to know so much?"

"Camellia, my sister, you have a strong grip" acknowledge Armand. "However, even if you torture me, I won't be able to tell you the nature of my strange person.

"It's another way to tell you, I don't know it myself."

Everybody burst out laughing.

"Please, forgive me," rushed saying the woman. "I didn't intend to hurt you."

"No, you didn't hurt me. However, if you grab Nick by the neck, you will certainly strangle him."

Everybody had another burst of laughter.

"Well, my friend," Armand went on. "I have promised you a good night sleep.

"However, before I do, I would like to show you one unit of this condominium."

A stranger's wonderful chronicles, Book II

Shortly after, he added, "It's another mystery to decipher."

"Another mystery to decipher!" screamed Teresa

"Tell us about this mystery," added Nicholas.

"Well, my friends, in one week, I have sold all the condominium units; which anyone can understand. I have sold them at an affordable price.

"Additionally, the condominium is located not far from urban activities. Yet, I kept one of the units. Why do I behave like that? I have no idea.

"Let's go and see it, and you will tell me what you think about it.

"For some unexplained reason I value your opinions, my dear brothers and sisters."

While in the lobby, Nicholas' cellular rang several times. He put the receiver to his ear and almost had a heart attack.

The call came from Martina.

"Tina, you won't believe me. My family and I, for the first time have left my dangerous apartment at this hour to visit Armand."

"Nick, did you say Armand?" said the caller astonishingly

"Yes, Tina, I did."

"May I speak to him?"

"Certainly, you may."

Nicholas passed the cellular phone to the *marvelous stranger* who pronounced, "Hello! Tina!"

"Did Nick tell you…?"

"No, he didn't.

"I know that you would call me, as I know the alpha and the omega of reality.

"I have no power to arrange things, but I may anticipate them. Nita, it's your last chance.

"Don't hesitate when he proposes to you tomorrow, at your parents' home."

"You know that he will visit me tomorrow and will propose to me?"

"Yes, I do."

"Will you come to our wedding?"

"You will have a sign of my presence."

"May I send you a kiss?"

"Why not, since Antoine won't see you misbehaving?"

She laughed heartily. Then, she said, "Bye, my lord."

"Ah! I am your lord?"

"Yes, you are. And I will never forget you."

Shortly after, she added, "My lord, would you forgive me for having doubt about your sayings?"

"Of course, I would. Additionally, you are not the first one who has doubt about my predictions. Sometimes, I have doubt about my own skills."

"Bye."

Armand opened the entrance door of the unit door located on the ground floor.

A stranger's wonderful chronicles, Book II

Nicholas and his family couldn't believe their eyes.

Camellia remained wide-mouthed in seeing the sophisticated kitchen.

Her daughter would like to spend the rest her life in one bedroom; while the boy would like to occupy another bedroom and take it for the delight of his childhood.

With respect to the parents, they had such a big surprise on opening the master bedroom door.

"What do you think, my dear brothers and sisters?" inquired Armand.

The whole family had lost the speech faculty.

Finally, he made a large gesture of the hands and invited the family to pay attention.

Then, he pulled a set of keys out of his jacket pocket and handed it over to Nicholas.

Next, he declared, "When I have seen you, I have understood the mystery behind my reluctance to sell this unit. I strongly believe that a family will have great joy to occupy it. And this family is you, my dear brothers and sisters.

"Camellia, Nick, my children, you will spend the night in this unity and you will spend many other nights in it.

"Tomorrow, go and get your belongings from your apartment and leave your old pieces of furniture.

"Return the keys to the super, not without telling him that you have just found better accommodations.

"He will feel so happy to rent that apartment to a criminal, with your old furniture."

As Armand was about to leave, Camellia said, "Armand, may I hug you?

"I feel some kind of urge to do so."

"Certainly, you may."

She passed to action.

"I would like to hug you too," added Nicholas.

"Who prevents you, my brother?" asked Armand. "Well, come over, everybody.

"Let me hug you.

"Well, enjoy yourselves"

This being said, the man took leave of Nicholas Diva, as well as his family, went out of the unit and disappeared in the city and the world.

◘　　◘

◘

The reporter, Brian Clifford felt great pleasure to speak to these people who, less than two years, had lived on the fringes of society.

They became professional and, from that point on, turned useful to society.

The children of these destitute attended a neighborhood school. Occasionally, Armand Hubert visited them, above all to have news about his little friend Lucinda.

A stranger's wonderful chronicles, Book II

She emerged as a genius, according to her teachers. She acquired knowledge fast.

As the *marvelous stranger* had predicted it, she would have a bright future.

Brian had the opportunity to speak to that girl who had primarily touched Armand's heart and urged the latter to start the process.

Additionally, Martina and her husband, as well as Nicholas, Camellia and their children, and other people concerned had confirmed all the events occurred in the course of this episode and had nothing but a great debt of gratitude for the man who had shown his civility and humanness through his transcendent behavior.

The reporter felt very happy and anticipated another joyous occasion to proceed with his *marvelous chronicles of the stranger*, with his next visit to the "hopeless".

(23)

The

Hopeless

By Antoine Archange Raphael

Ferdinand Gaston, alone in his helicopter, flew over an area bathed in a dense forest, running alongside a river apparently peaceful but twinkling. Ferdinand Gaston, undoubtedly, thought about the deceptive appearance of the river course revealing only its depth to aircraft pilots.

With respect to the desolate area, giving the impression of the end of the world, it had the reputation for endangering car travelers' lives. Police had reported cases of assault, armed robbery…

These rumors had never stopped to intrigue Ferdinand Gaston. "As for me, I would show caution against venturing in this area," he had always said whenever, for any reason, he had to fly over this region.

Indeed, that day, returning from a visit to one of his clients living far away from him, as he didn't have any choice, he flew over that untamed area.

He had noticed a helicopter on the ground and had the time to identify the flying vehicle: it belonged to the great TV chain WGGEC.

Three men, coming from the forest, walked up to the grounded helicopter. They looked frightening with their long machetes and axes.

They wore rags, which made them look like gorillas.

First, Ferdinand Gaston had downplayed the scene, thinking that the televised team would soon have a live interview with those criminals who used to stalking unfortunate travelers lost in this area by accident.

Then, Ferdinand Gaston wondered if the pilot hadn't landed because of mechanical failure.

The hopeless

In this eventuality, the reporter, the camera operator and the pilot incurred great danger.

For conscience's sake, Ferdinand Gaston made a sharp turn and decided to land his helicopter to have a clear idea and, if need be, give a helping hand to the TV crew.

The men, coming from the forest, kept walking up to helicopters. Suddenly, they started running while screaming like wild beasts.

One of them stated, "Get ready to die, unless you accept to empty your pockets and your wallets. This is a hold-up."

The TV people trembled like leaves. They thought that, unwillingly, they found themselves in a deadly situation, the more so as they had no guarantee that those barbarians wouldn't kill them, even after giving up the monetary contents of their pockets and their wallets to them.

These scary people got on the helicopter and locked the doors; but they knew that those criminals would also climb up the aircraft to harm them.

Suddenly, they heard Ferdinand Gaston's stentorian voice giving the criminals a warning, "Stop! Otherwise, I will act accordingly."

"You must be kidding, my friend," said one of the criminals.

"If you want to die, try to attack us.

"We only want money. But we may also kill you as if you were meaningless flies."

Slowly, Ferdinand Gaston pulled a boomerang set in motion by remote control.

A stranger's wonderful chronicles, Book II

The device, attached to a long nylon cord, shot forward at about the height of a person. It whistled to the criminals ears, who instinctively clung together. Then, it started to turn around them and tied them up like giant sausages. Next, they fell to the ground and stay there still, under the helicopter occupants' stunned eyes.

Then, Ferdinand Gaston beckoned to them to open their aircraft doors.

He recognized the female reporter, Bethany, a very ambitious woman who believed that she embodied the most beautiful and important female reporter in the world.

She wouldn't stop at anything to shine.

Actually, she had succeeded, so far, thanks to her immediate supervisor, Melvin Pollard, another ambitious person and that woman's secret lover.

They usually fabricated the facts together to make them work in their favor.

That day, Ferdinand Gaston, had an intuition about the TV helicopter problem.

He said, "My friends, all will go well."

"I don't think so," cut in the pilot, whose name was Jetsam Sullivan.

Then, after a short pause, he added, "You want only to impress us."

"Why do you think so, Jetsam?"

This one had his eyes wide opened. Next, he inquired, "Dear sir, how do you know my name? I have seen you for the first time. Would you be as dangerous as these scoundrels you have just overcome?"

The hopeless

Ferdinand didn't get offended. On the contrary, while smiling, he pronounced, "Oh! Forgive me, my friends, my name is Ferdinand Gaston."

"Nice meeting you," rushed saying Bethany.

"I am also delighted to meet you, Ms. Bethany Manropes."

"Ah! What's going wrong here, dear sir?" inquired the woman anxiously.

"But, Ms. Manropes, all is well."

"But who are you? You have called our pilot by his name. You have just mentioned my name and surname. I strongly believe that that you know our cameraman's name."

"Actually, Bethany, your cameraman's name happens to be Seneque Romain."

"But, sir," cut in the pilot, Jetsam Sullivan, "it amounts to what they call 'jumping out of the frying pan into the fire'. You have saved us from the criminals tied up by you; but, now, your mysterious person gives us such a fright.

"What do you intend to do, dear sir?"

"My friends, you are no longer in a state of danger, replied Ferdinand. "I only intend to help you overcome your deadly situation.

"You should have no worry about my calling you by names.

"Your images have spread all over the world. Don't forget that you are in the media business."

"You are right, Ferdinand," cut in Seneque Romain.

A stranger's wonderful chronicles, Book II

"My friends (he turned around to speak to his coworkers) we are too nervous. Don't forget that Ferdinand has undoubtedly saved our lives."

"Seneque, you are full of wisdom," argued Ferdinand.

After a short pause, he went on, "Listen, my friends, you are lucky to meet someone with such profound intuition about reality, to such a par that I wouldn't hesitate to inform you that I know the alpha and the omega of reality."

"Impossible," stated the woman.

"I profess the same opinion," added the pilot.

The camera operator, Seneque Romain, raised his hand to signal his intention to speak.

"Seneque, shut up!" exclaimed Bethany

The camera operator shook his head to express disbelief and then smiled.

Next, he argued, "Bethany, Jetsam, you have surprised me. I thought that you have practiced some wisdom. Don't you think that your reaction lacks objectivity?"

"We don't want to hear your cheap opinion," observed Bethany. "Don't forget that you are a simple cameraman."

"Yes, my friends, I am a simple cameraman. However, without my services, you wouldn't have pieces of news acceptable to the public.

"Thus, whether you want it or not, I fulfill an important function in the media.

The hopeless

"Additionally, I don't need your opinion to have an idea of the importance of my function.

"I represent more than a simple cameraman. I have a college degree from the State University, specializing in technologic photography.

"Yet, I insist on your lack of objectivity. For, the man proclaims to know the alpha and the omega of reality; then, you must ask him to prove his claim."

There was a deep silence only disturbed by the whisper of the wind through the flora and the sea waves from afar.

"Seneque, this time, you have betrayed some wisdom," ac-knowledged Jetsam. "Apparently, our telephonic communications have been temporarily cut off. Soon we will plunge into darkness.

"Why can't we recourse to the doubtful omniscience of this lunatic?"

Suddenly, the camera operator had an intuition: he had never missed the delightful Brian Clifford's episodes "The marvelous chronicles of the stranger".

He wondered if he and his colleagues didn't have an unexpected stroke of luck to receive assistance from that *mysterious man.*

However, he was careful not let his colleagues know about his intuition, who would take him for a fruitcake.

"Hi! Mr. Gaston!" yelled Jetsam Sullivan. "Apparently, we must trust your "profound intuition".

"We don't have any choice.

A stranger's wonderful chronicles, Book II

"Will you help us reset the helicopter in motion, or whatever you may call it? We have tried to get in touch with the mother studio, but in vain."

"Perhaps, the communications satellites have stopped working for a while;" answered Ferdinand. "The surrounding mountains may have blocked the signals.

"However, you no longer have any need to call the mother studio. I believe that this helicopter problem comes from the transmission shaft. A screw turned loose from the central shaft and the whole mechanism fails.

"You are lucky to get away with no injury.

"Let me see."

Ferdinand Gaston climbed up the flying vehicle and confirmed his opinion.

"Listen, my friends, wait for me. I will go and get a screw from my toolbox and a wrench. You will fly in less than twenty minutes."

Indeed, the TV company helicopter flew away. However, the camera operator asked his benefactor, before leaving, what would become of the thugs.

"Seneque, I will drop them at the center of rehabilitation," had replied Ferdinand. "Two years from now, you won't recognize them."

The camera operator had a big surprise at noticing that Bethany and Jetsam, on reporting the incident, didn't mention Ferdinand Gaston's assistance. Then and only then, he understood that the televised station kept misinforming the public with the sole purpose of keeping their place among the greatest news information companies."

In a vast room filled with colleagues (including the TV station owner), Bethany said that the pilot and the camera operation had overcome the three criminals.

"We have here their pictures" she went on. "We have tied them up. Now, the justice department remands them for trial. Who knows, they are certainly watching the news."

The camera operator tried to cut in, but the pilot and the reporter prevented him from speaking.

The woman whispered something to her immediate supervisor's ear, who went straight to the owner.

The latter beckoned to the camera operator to follow him to his office; then, he spoke to him in these terms, "Seneque, according to Bethany, our star, the pilot and their supervisor, you have betrayed the company on several occasions by trying to contradict the station statements.

"You should know that millions count us among the best televised station in the country. By your action, you intend to hamper the development of our business."

"What did I do wrong?" protested the camera operator. "To the best of my recollection, I haven't expressed any bad feeling about my place of work. Sir, those who have reported my dissenting opinions…"

A stranger's wonderful chronicles, Book II

"Listen," cut in the owner, "you must stop whatever you are doing and leave the premises."

"What?"

"We have a replacement.

"My dear sir, return the Camera at once. Otherwise, I will call security."

Actually, the owner pressed on a buzzer.

Seneque didn't have any choice; three sturdily built men stood at the entrance.

At home, Seneque kissed his wife and their three children. Then, he collapsed on the sofa.

"Darling, is something wrong" inquired the wife. "You give me the impression of sinking into depression."

The man kept silent.

The wife sat down by him, put her hand around his neck and repeated her question.

"Moe," finally answered the husband, "they have just dismissed me from duty."

"My God! What did you do wrong?"

"Nothing I know of."

Few minutes after, Mogette concluded, "Well, darling, we have to accept our fate. You are an expert in photography; you will survive.

"We have to survive."

"That's true, Moe. However, I didn't have the time to work enough to have some savings.

"If I could buy a professional camera like the one I used at the TV station, I would turn an independent photographer, would travel all over the world seeking for exclusive shots and would sell them to companies involved in interesting researches.

"However, Moe, a commercial camera costs more than five thousand dollars.

"What should I do?

"In the meantime, you are expecting our fourth child. Then, the others children have so many needs. Phew!"

Seneque burst out crying. His wife patted him on the back to calm him down.

Someone knocked at the entrance door.

"Sen," said the wife, "let me see who the visitor is."

"Listen, Moe, I don't want to speak to anyone. Tell the visitor that I don't feel well.

The wife opened the door and saw a well-dressed man. She said, "Mr., how may I help you?"

"Moe, as your husband calls you, I am Ferdinand Gaston…," replied the man.

"Listen, my dear Mr. Gaston, how do you manage to know my nickname?"

A stranger's wonderful chronicles, Book II

"Well, I know everything. As soon as I see your beautiful face, your whole history popped up in my mind. How may I explain something like that? I don't know.

"However, for nothing in the world, I will part from my natural gifts.

"Additionally, I am your husband's good friend (his only good friend, for the moment). His name is Seneque Romain. I know that he has found himself in bad humor.

"Tell him my name, and he will see me. As I have told you, I know the alpha and omega of reality.

"Maybe he didn't tell you everything; however, they have fired him because he has tried to tell the truth to his colleagues."

"Darling!" yelled the woman. "Come to speak to this man. His name is Ferdinand Gaston.

"He told me he is your good friend."

"Moe, I am coming!" shouted the husband. "Don't let him go. I am coming!"

Shortly after, Seneque came in.

His wife couldn't believe her eyes; for, her husband seemed to have regained his optimism.

The excited men hugged each other, as if they had stricken a longtime friendship.

"Moe," said the husband, "let me introduce Ferdinand to you. He has a lot of skills."

"Darling, I have an idea," pointed the wife.

"Ah!"

The husband got near the wife and whispered something to her ear.

The woman opened her eyes wide.

Ferdinand had understood everything. The woman had just learned from Seneque that the visitor embodied the "marvelous stranger".

"Listen, Sen (as your wife and your relative call you), let's go to the commercial area. Your family will accompany us. I would not advise anyone to leave his house without his family, except to go to work.

"Don't forget, my friends, the family members have a common destiny, in some extent. Diversity comes later in life, with the adult status of the children who may conceive of their own destiny."

Once in the commercial area, Ferdinand gave money to the woman and urged her to go shopping at the big supermarket in that neighborhood.

In the meantime, he would take Seneque to the house specialized in selling professional cameras.

On the way, he told Seneque about the latter's studies of photography at the university. He would certainly sell his snapshots to magazine and scientific organizations interested in professional illustrations for their presentations.

"I know a magazine you may go to as your first client," added Ferdinand. "I have its address here.

A stranger's wonderful chronicles, Book II

"Tomorrow, you will call that place and will mention my name."

On their way back, he would announce an alarming piece of news to Seneque and his family, "My friends, I have a sad piece of news to tell you."

"Oh! Ferdinand, did you say a sad piece of news?" asked the woman anxiously. "What can it be?

"What is it?" inquired the husband in his turn.

"Well, you won't recognize your apartment."

"Ferdinand, why do you have to behave like that?" said the woman.

"I have done nothing wrong. I will never hurt you. Besides, I am with you now; how can I participate in your apartment ransack.

"However, someone has stolen, at the TV station, the tape recorder showing the scene by the forest.

"The first person they have suspected is your husband. They have sent criminals to ransack the apartment in search of that bloody tape recorder.

"Thus, my friends, in some extent, I have saved your life when I urged you to accompany me at the commercial center. These criminals wouldn't hesitate to kill all the apartment occupants."

"This time, Ferdinand, I don't believe you," cut in the husband. "You want to simply scare us. You speak as if you have witnessed an event, while driving."

"Don't forget, Sen, I have a profound intuition about reality."

"I want to see this occurrence with my own eyes."

240

"Let's go."

While they reached the vicinity of their apartment, they could see, through the vehicle glass, fire trucks and police cars which brightened up the whole neighborhood of their flashing spotlights.

When they got off the car, police officers approached the Romains.

One of them suggested, "My friends, you must look for another accommodation. Your apartment is not habitable."

Indeed, not only they had knocked over and damaged pieces of furniture, but also they had set the place on fire. Thanks to the fire department, the rest of the building was safe.

"Do you have a place to go to?" asked another officer.

"Yes, they do," replied Ferdinand. "I will take care of the family."

Shortly after, Ferdinand took the Romains to a beautiful family house.

"Listen, my friends," he said as he was leaving, "all is well that ends well.

"Sen, you have the magazine address and telephone number. Tomorrow, by ten in the morning, give them a ring.

"Don't worry about your new home. It belongs to a series of prefabricated houses I have built, which you can see all around you.

"For some unexplained reason, I haven't sold this unity. Now it belongs to you."

"But, Ferdinand, our benefactor, who are you?" asked Mrs. Romain. "Do you intend to hurt us, after you have showered goodness on us?"

A stranger's wonderful chronicles, Book II

"Madam, I will never hurt your family for any reason in the world. As I said to all my protégés, your husband, your children and you represent my fellow creatures, my brothers and sisters in humanity and nature. I feel happy to have the power and the possibility to help you. At least, tonight, once more, I have brought a smile on your faces.

"Speaking of hope, I must go now; otherwise, they will kill the pilot, Jetsam Sullivan"

"My God!" exclaimed Seneque. "What's going on? You give me a scare."

"Sen, he has stolen the recorded tape, hoping to blackmail Bethany and her lover. If the criminals find that man before I do, they will kill him.

"This tape may badly damage the TV station reputation."

This being said, Ferdinand hugged all the Romain family mem-bers. Then, he left, not without saying, "My dear friends, I will see you, one of these days."

The pilot, Jetsam Sullivan, while he tried to insert the key through the entrance door lock of his fiancée's house, felt an iron grip around his wrist.

He turned quickly to identify his aggressor; then, he acknowledged Ferdinand Gaston's presence.

He was about to hurl insults, but, Ferdinand, with a gesture of his index finger, advised him to keep silent.

The hopeless

He pulled him in a dark corner; put his hand in the pilot's interior jacket pocket and retrieved the recording tape.

"Your life is in danger," whispered Ferdinand. "Let's go back to the studio at once.

"You will give the impression that you have never left.

"Listen to me, my dear brother, If the TV security people reach you here, in the house, these heartless goons will kill your fiancée, your son and you."

Jetsam Sullivan had his eyes wide open with panic. He sensed Ferdinand's extraordinary powers. He followed him without a murmur.

As soon as he had reached the TV station waiting room, he became the target of ten gunmen.

"What's going on?" he inquired for conscience's sake.

"Give back the tape," yelled Bethany

"You have disappointed us," added Melvin Pollard.

"You will die," observed the owner.

"But I don't have the tape," answered the pilot.

"Search him," ordered the owner.

One of the assassins made him spin around and searched his pockets. Then, he lowered his shoulders before saying, "No, there is no trace of the tape recorder on the pilot."

"Then, dear ladies and gentlemen, who has stolen the tape?" screamed the owner.

A stranger's wonderful chronicles, Book II

"I have!" yelled someone at the reception room entrance door.

Shortly after, he added, "Here it is."

A criminal snatched the tape from Ferdinand's hand.

"Yes! It is he!" pointed out Bethany. "What will you do to him? He is capable of harming us."

"Sir…," she went loud.

"My name is Ferdinand Gaston," the visitor indentified himself.

"You know that you have to die," observed the patron. "We won't let you ruin us."

"Just a minute!" exclaimed Ferdinand

"What do you want?"

"I have made a copy of the tape, which shows everything, including the shots you have erased. If you remain quiet, nothing will occur. However…"

He didn't have the time to complete his thought; for, the gunmen had shown willingness to riddle him with bullets.

He dashed out.

The criminals set off in pursuit of him, but he disappeared (like in thin air).

Few minutes after, Bethany went to her immediate supervisor and lover, and closed the door.

Contrary to the man's expectation, she didn't show any exuberance; she rather turned pensive.

"Baby, what's going on," inquired the man.

She didn't answer at once.

She glued to him to whisper something to his ear; for, what she would tell him could have disastrous repercussions on their future in the bosom of the TV station, in case that the owner should know about it.

The latter might even order their physical elimination.

"Darling," she said, "we have committed the biggest mistake in our lives."

"What are you talking about, my baby?" inquired the man. "We have always used caution. Nobody knows anything about our affair."

"No, I don't want to talk about us."

"Then, what is going on?

"Why do you have such mysterious attitude?"

"We have him close by and we let go such a great opportunity."

"What are you talking about? Bet, you are serious!"

"Darling, we have missed the exceptional luck to meet with the marvelous stranger!"

The lover at once realized the veracity of the female assertion and gagged her with his palm to enjoin "absolute silence". If the owner of the TV station learned about this event, he would at once dismiss the lovers and order their elimination.

The man contented himself to whisper, "Brian Clifford will always enjoy the exclusiveness of the events connected to this entity."

A stranger's wonderful chronicles, Book II

He added, after a pause, "So, baby, the man who had the recording tape…, this Ferdinand we wanted to riddle with bullets...!'"

The female reporter nodded.

The door burst wide open, and the owner showed up.

He stated, "I like to see you living in harmony. I have always drawn my employees' attention on your perfect harmony in the bosom of our corporation."

Once the owner had left, Bethany concluded, "Fortunately, that Ferdinand has a reputation as a good man. He will never disclose the truth of the incident, as he knows that many employees will suffer from his indiscretion."

"Baby, you understand the reason why I love you so much! You are very perspicacious."

"Thank you, my love."

Shortly after, she added, "I also trust your judgment."

Few minutes after, she left with a new camera operator in search of scoops.

◘   ◘

◘

The journalist, Brian Clifford, visited several eyewitnesses to corroborate this episode about the "marvelous stranger'" deeds: the Romain family, the hopeless who used to terrorize car travelers as well as the TV station.

The hopeless

They had all the impression of having dreamed of their experiences during their encounter with Ferdinand.

However, this man certainly existed in the matrix of tridimensional reality.

The hopeless, by the way Merlin Prowess, Osmond Concedes and Reginald Tortellini, had respectively received intensive training in electricity, automobile mechanic and plumbing.

Seneque Roman became a renowned photographer.

They saw him with his camera, in every corner of the planet, in search of unprecedented shots, which magazines and other similar businesses bought like warm pies.

As far as the pilot was concerned, he still worked for the TV station.

Nevertheless, he had the good fortune to fly a brand new helicopter.

Actually, to urge him to silence, the TV station had doubled his salary and benefits.

He had just married his fiancée after years of engagement, since they had no excuse for remaining single.

Apparently, lack of money had prolonged these illegitimate but delicious moments.

His wife was waiting for a set of twins.

A stranger's wonderful chronicles, Book II

The journalist, Brian Clifford, thought already about the delight he would take in visiting the *marvelous stranger's* recent beneficiaries: *the poor family at the courthouse.*

(24)

The poor Family

At the

Courthouse

By Antoine Archange Raphael

*T*he journalist, Brian Clifford, parked his car alongside the sidewalk, in front of a pretty two-story family home. Sturdily, he walked up to that house and knocked three times at the entrance door. The smile on the face, a ten-year-old girl welcomed him.

She said without any hesitancy, "You must be the journalist, Brian Clifford"

"In person, my little friend," answered the visitor.

"Wait in the living room. My parents will join you soon. They know that you are coming."

Indeed, few minutes after, Acacia and August Présilien, Leila's parents, came into the living room and shook the reporter's hand.

"I am August Présilien," said the man. "This is my wife Acacia."

"Please to meet you," said Brian.

"Thank you for coming to see us," went on August. "Acacia, Leila and I have thought that we had a kind of collective dream that would soon go away.

"However, we know that we intend to fool ourselves; for, how can you explain that we live now comfortably, without the existence of that marvelous stranger who have pulled us from our nightmarish dire poverty?"

Indeed, the man, his wife and their daughter had joined the crowd of homeless. They had lived from building to building, after the closing of business hours, in which they had intruded without security agents' knowledge.

The poor family at the courthouse

That day, they had intended to spend the whole night at the *Justice Palace*.

Nobody had noticed their presence until then, because an animated debate between a certain Justine Solage's lawyer and the attorney of the industrialist, Roberto Maher, a multimillionaire, had retained everybody's attention.

The former had adamantly accused the latter of raping her in his office.

According to the plaintiff's lawyer, Justice Solage received a phone call from the industrialist, asking her to come to assist him with the office operation; for his secretary, Angela Bijoux, had called sick.

No sooner Justine Solage had entered the industrialist's office, the latter, without any warning, had raped her.

She had tried to defend herself, but she had succumbed to Mr. Roberto Maher exceptional strength.

Next, she yelled.

Employees, security officers and many more came and noticed her disheveled hair, torn up blouse and skirt, as well as bruises on parts of her body.

The police arrived, arrested the industrialist without any ceremony.

Few hours later, the court would have released him on his own recognizance.

Lucien Leptis argued for his client's innocence.

A stranger's wonderful chronicles, Book II

That lawyer's speech for the defense greatly fascinated August Présilien and his wife, who, despite their lousy appearance and their miserable existence, had enough education to appreciate that lawyer's eloquence.

He had said among others,

Your honor,

Ladies and gentlemen of the jury,

Ladies and gentlemen of the audience,

If you have known my client's moral orientation, by the way Roberto Maher, you will find him innocent.

He treats his employees with great deference and compassion.

He gives them a decent salary, and, contrary to many corporations spread all over the country and the world, he takes interest in his employees' health care.

Not only he has opened a clinic on the premises, which the workers and their spouses and children may attend but also, he gives them health insurance accepted by any health provider in the world.

Finally, he gets involved in his employees' lifestyle, by helping them when they want to buy decent homes to live in with their families.

The poor family at the courthouse

I think that such compassionate man wouldn't go as far as to rape a woman.

Your honor,

Ladies and gentlemen of the jury,

Until then, my inquiries have revealed that all his average and high-ranking employees feel happy working for him.

Ladies and gentlemen,

You should know that the woman appearing before the court asking for justice, accusing my client of rape, isn't at her first try. She had already accused other men of raping her.

They have all one common denominator: a great wealth.

"Objection!" yelled the plaintiff's lawyer, not without waving his hands desperately

"On what ground?" inquired the judge.

Your honor,

Ladies and gentlemen of the jury,

The rapist's lawyer tries to wake up a sleeping cat. However, the police officers who base their action on the DNA test run on

A stranger's wonderful chronicles, Book II

the plaintiff will prove soon that my client, present at the tribunal, is a victim of rape.

Besides, a crime shouldn't go unpunished, because a multimillionaire has committed it.

Of course, the rapist's lawyer talks about him in glowing terms to receive an important fee; yet, all those millionaires are heartless.

How can you explain that they have acquired so much money while the rest of the world can barely survive?

Ladies and gentlemen, you know the answer.

With a large motion of the hand, attorney Lucien Leptis asked to speak,

Your honor,

Ladies and gentlemen of the jury,

Ladies and gentlemen of the audience,

I don't come to this courthouse with the purpose of assessing that woman's misdeeds, by the way, Justine Solage.

By the way, ladies and gentlemen, not only I have awareness of the numerous skeletons in this female pervert's closet, but also in her legal representative's.

The poor family at the courthouse

Attorney Roquet Montrouge thundered.

Objection!

Attorney Lucien Leptis rushed saying,

I squash the last statement. However, to put an end to this travesty of justice, allow me, your honor, ladies and gentlemen of the jury and the audience, to tell you how the events have unfolded to reach this false accusation.

The judge said almost happily,

We are listening, honorable counselor.

The lawyer proceeded,

Thank you, your honor.
We have here an act of extortion concocted for a long time.
Justine Solage and her accomplices have infiltrated the corporation.

A stranger's wonderful chronicles, Book II

As you can see, she is extremely beautiful.

Yesterday, the executive secretary of the industrialist Robert Maher, by the way, Ms. Angela Bijoux, called her boss to tell him that she couldn't make it, since she had to take her mother to the doctor.

Someone intercepted the phone conversation and thought he could turn this simple unfortunate incident to his advantage.

By eleven o'clock in the morning, Mr. Roberta Maher, my client, saw Justice Solage coming to his office. Then, without warning, she yelled and drew everybody's attention.

Justice Solage's lover had made a huge blunder when he gave her instructions to follow to make 'this operation' successful. He said among others, 'This industrialist keeps in his office an important some of money. If he wants to avoid a scandal, he will accept to give you one million dollars in cash.

'We won't accept a check'.

Since my client refused, Justine Solage made a scene drawing other employees' attention as well as security agents'.

Before this act of extortion, Justine Solage and her lover had sex. The sperms they took a sample of, from the alleged victim's vagina, belongs to that lover.

The poor family at the courthouse

Well, your honor,

Ladies and gentlemen of the jury and the audience,

That lover has the nerve to sit peaceful in the audience like someone with a clear conscience.

My dear friends, I am referring to Ricky Tambo, sitting in the first row.

The designated extortionist saw no way out, stood up and was about to dash out, but the judge ordered the security agents to have a hold of him.

Next, they handcuffed the lovers and took them to the State Prison.

The judge apologized to the industrialist who was joined at once by his wife, his three children and loyal friends

The industrialist excused himself to go and speak to his "brilliant lawyer".

"Thank you, attorney Leptis," he pronounced in tones of emotions. "You have done a wonderful job. I don't know how to thank you.

"Accept this check. If the amount doesn't satisfy you, tell me; for, your performance has no price."

Attorney Lucien Leptis had a glance at the check and almost collapsed.

After pulling himself together, he stated, "Mr. Roberto Maher, your generosity has no bounds. The amount should largely cover my services."

"Well, honorable counselor, how did you manage to uncover this well-planned extortion?"

A stranger's wonderful chronicles, Book II

"Let me tell you a little secret, Mr. Maher.

"I have a profound intuition of reality. I know the alpha and the omega of existence."

"What do you mean?"

"I can't explain it to you."

"Well, we do have a little secret to keep," concluded the industrialist. "Once more, thank you so much.

"If a friend needs a good lawyer to pull him from a mess, I won't hesitate to send him to you."

Attorney Leptis headed towards the exit, not without waiving at the judge, at his client, his family, their friends and the lawyer for the plaintiff.

People and reporters had invaded the courtroom.

The lawyer almost reached the exit door when he heard a din. Police officers yelled at a group of three people namely a nine-year-old girl, a woman and a man in their thirties. Wearing filthy clothes, they sat down on a bench.

The police officers were about to snub them and to violently push them away, but, with a gesture of the hand, the lawyer, at everybody's surprise, stopped the authorities and stated, "Listen! Don't mistreat them."

"Sir, don't interfere with the police activity," yelled one the policemen.

"Sir, I don't intend to interfere with police activity. However, these people have an appointment with me."

The poor family at the courthouse

Turning around and recognizing attorney Leptis, the aggressive police officer screamed, "Well, attorney Leptis, you have alluded to an impossible situation.

"These filthy people can't be waiting for you! Can they…?"

"Yes, Officer Merlin Thompson, they are waiting for me.

"You know my name, attorney Leptis," said the officer astonishingly. "To the best of my recollection, I have never met you."

"Officer Thompson, don't get alarmed. I know everything…"

"You know everything?"

"Yes, I do.

"However, don't worry. These poor people mean no harm to anyone."

After a short pause, he went on, "Well, Officer Thompson, we have in front of us a family. The father's name is August Présilien; the mother, Acacia.

"As far as the girl is concerned, well, her name is Leila."

The beggars couldn't believe their ears.

They thought they had plunged into a dream from which they would wake up soon.

With a motion of the hand, the lawyer invited them to come closer to him.

"Let's go, my friends. Your dirty clothes make others nauseous; which you may understand."

They walked to a great shop carrying almost everything.

A stranger's wonderful chronicles, Book II

The security agent firmly stood to the lawyer and his slovenly friends' way and started "Where do you think…"

He didn't finish his sentence, for, the lawyer, in a sweet tone inquired, "Carlyle Jefferson, don't you remember me? I am Lucien Leptis…"

The so-called Carlyle Jefferson opened wide his eyes. He remembered a great service the *marvelous stranger* had rendered him.

Like his slovenly friends, he had no place to live in; but a man embodied the person of attorney Lucien Leptis had pulled him from the pit of despair and had recommended him to someone else, who had found him his current position as a security guard.

He bored to the lawyer and made a gesture meaning, "the coast is clear".

One look at the dirty family made the well-dressed customers howled with disgust.

The owner, Ms. Constance Reynaud put her hand to her nose and meant to ask the security agent to "get rid of" these people, but the lawyer stretched his arm to shake her hand.

She ignored him and rather advanced, "I don't know you; but whoever you may be, do you intend to ruin me? How can you brink these dirty people to my shop?"

The lawyer beckoned to the owner to get closer to him. Then, he whispered to her ear, "Ms. Constance Reynaud, you have to listen to what I have to say

"No, listen to me…"

The poor family at the courthouse

"You know my name!" said the storeowner, while opening wide her eyes.

"Yes, I know your name," answered the lawyer. "To tell you the truth, I know the alpha and the omega of reality, above all your reality as the Reynaud's unique child.

"I don't intend to ruin you, but to boost your business.

"Well, Ms. It's a long story.

"For the time being, listen to my suggestion. Go and get to the microphone and announce that it's a publicity stunt aiming at showing that even if someone reaches *Good Welcome Shop* in rags, he will leave the store in style from head to toes."

The owner complied reluctantly. Soon after, the clients started smiling again.

"Now, Constance," suggested the lawyer, "You will allow them to have a shower.

"Then, your employees and you will strive to get these poor peopled well dressed.

"As soon as you will have completed the change, you will announce the result once more. Don't forget to remind the clients that they have participated in the advertisement making and that they have appeared on candid camera.

"Don't worry; I will cover all the expenses."

Everything occurred as attorney Lucien Leptis had suggested.

A stranger's wonderful chronicles, Book II

Acacia, after being dressed, became a beautiful, cute, young lady, with her radiant face, her robust arms and legs, and her dove's eyes.

Leila, in her dress and her shoes with metal buckles, looked like an angel freshly fallen from heaven.

As far as August was concerned, one would easily confuse him with a distinguished professional such as a lawyer, a professor, an engineer…

The commercial bore fruits and spread like wild fire. The clients felt so important to have participated in it; the more so as television channels, thanks to attorney Leptis' skill and financing, started to show it throughout the country. Consequently, the number of clients, in the blink of eye, had increased to the owner's great joy.

Attorney Leptis took his friends to the restaurant section and ordered food they loved.

The owner joined them, a smile on the face.

Some point in time, she stated, "Attorney Leptis…"

"Please, Constance, call me Lucien," he cut in. "Would you believe it if I told you that I feel so great by you."

"I am so glad to hear you saying it. I also feel great happiness to know you.

"After all, you have emerged as the most generous and inventive man I have ever met."

Shortly after, she asked perplexedly, "Where do you come from, my knight? You generosity and your perspicuity seem unreal.

The poor family at the courthouse

"Listen, no one I know of would act with such lucidity and panache.

"Again, where do you come from? Does God or Satan send you on a mission?

"Listen, you must enlighten me; otherwise, I will believe that I have plunged, temporarily, into madness and that you represent nothing but an anxious woman's projection of her own state of mind.

"For example, you come with people apparently poor and you make a commercial I benefit from.

"These beggars, are they actors?"

"No, Constance, my dear, they are not. They used to live in the streets and in abandoned house (often in plain air). I have just met them.

"However, despite their dire poverty, they have never stopped forming a family, the basic social unit; they have never stopped belonging to mankind.

"Then, why wouldn't I help them?

"It costs me almost nothing to assist them. Actually, my dear Constance, when I help them, I feel tremendous joy. They allow me to go beyond my animal contingencies consisting of drinking, eating, sleeping, and indulging in pleasures...

"I rather become a man, an unfolding project."

Constance couldn't believe her ears.

"Well," she said, "how can you explain your choosing my shop among thousand."

A stranger's wonderful chronicles, Book II

"Constance, my love" replied Lucien, "I can't answer your question. Except that my inspiration always guides me towards people in distress."

"In this case, Lucien, this commercial, ensuring my success, you didn't plan it?"

"No, I didn't. However, my dear sister, its workability has dawned on me."

The new friends, like the owner, would like to have a reassuring answer from this presumed lawyer.

This one felt their concern and said, "My friends, once more, I am in the dark like you."

"Incredible," said Leila.

"Yes, my child," insisted Lucien Leptis, "It's incredible, but true.

"This morning, I felt the need to drive by the courthouse.

"As I saw a large audience, I said to myself that I would lose nothing to enter the sanctuary of justice and to see what was going on.

"Then, I had a profound intuition, realizing the innocence of the accused, by the way, that millionaire with an angelic heart, like you, Constance, and I decided to represent him.

"On my leaving the court, I saw you, my friends (he turned around to face formerly poor people). In spite of your distress and your lousy appearance, you did make me aware, as I had said it to Constance, of the notion of family, its homogeneous unity the multiplicity of which form the community and the nation.

The poor family at the courthouse

"Then, my dear friends, I had no choice but to save you, using my skills and my resources.

"I sincerely take you for my brother and sisters. Whatever I do for you comes from my duty as a true brother or father. You owe me nothing.

"Well, mysteriously, your shop, Constance (he turned around to face the store owner), happens to be close to the court. At the entrance, I saw the security agent, Carlyle Jefferson, whom I had pulled from a predicament.

"He had recognized me; then I knew that I was on the right track.

"Now, all is well that ends well.

"Here you are, Constance, with renewed optimism; for, you did have some moments of worry about the future of your business. You have even thought of closing it down, if business keeps slowing down.

"Fortunately, ever since this commercial, your shop has blossomed."

The owner raised her hand indicating her willingness to speak, "But, Lucien, your divinatory power goes beyond all bounds. How did you know that I had some moments of worry? It's the first time I have seen you"

"Constance, as I have just said it repeatedly, I embody a living mystery. No sooner had I met with someone, I knew everything about him.

"I have a profound intuition of things.

"For example, my friend and brother August is a professional mason."

"I am a professional mason!" echoed Mr. Présilien.

A stranger's wonderful chronicles, Book II

"Leila is a buddy genius.

"She will shine at school and become later a respected professional."

"Which school is that?" asked the girl.

"The one you will attend tomorrow."

"Sir, I believe you."

"No, Leila, I am not a sir for you. I am Uncle Lucien."

"Thank you, Uncle Lucien," said the girl showing all her white teeth.

"As for you, Acacia," started Lucien.

"Lucien, I know," argued the woman. "I am dreaming now. When I wake up, I will look dirty, wear rags and smell like a horse."

"No, Acacia, you must believe me when I tell you that you don't have a dream and no longer smell bad.

"However, it will come as a shock to you to learn that you only need a comfortable house to rest more often.

"Now, my dear Acacia, don't ask me the reason why you need so much rest."

"Lucien, you have suggested the question," stated the woman against her will. "Now, Lucien why do I need so much rest?".

"Acacia, my sister, you need more rest because you are pregnant."

"Oh!" exclaimed everybody together.

Then, overcome by emotion, they cried, including Constance.

Instinctively, they stood up and kissed Lucien on the cheek, to express their feeling of gratitude.

The poor family at the courthouse

"Thanks for everything," said August. "You give my wife more than I can have ever offered her. But I do love her."

"She knows that, August.

"Leila also knows that you love them a lot."

Lucien stood up in one bound. His new friends and Constance did the same.

"Constance," he said, "we have no alternative but to take leave of you.

"My friends yearn after a house to rest themselves; which you may understand. They have spent more than six months sleeping on the ground itself."

"Will I ever see you again?" whispered Constance.

"Yes, I will see you again."

"Thank you so much, Lucien. You have given me your word; it is enough.

"You should know in advance that your presence will fill me with joy. You fascinate me."

"I will come back to see you."

Lucien walked to the owner and whispered something to her ear, which made her smile.

She drew the man against her and kissed him tenderly on the lips.

The employees and the clients witnessed this manifestation of tenderness and gave a thunder of applause.

A stranger's wonderful chronicles, Book II

Constance felt a little embarrassed and put her hand on her chest.

As far as the employees were concerned, they ran up to the man to shake his hands, to hug him, gave him a kiss or to whisper nice words to his ears.

In the street, the Présiliens followed their benefactor to his car parked in a private parking.

"Sir...," started August.

"Please, August, call me Lucien. I am sincere. You are my brother."

"Well, Lucien, I feel very confused. So, don't laugh at me if I ask the following question: Are we dead?

"Don't be afraid of telling me the truth.

"As we have suffered a lot on earth, God takes pity on us and welcomes us in paradise.

"For, my dear friend and brother, don't make me believe that my wife, my daughter and I wear fine clothes, have eaten in a clean restaurant, sit in a car, and will occupy soon a house.

"Lucien, tell me that we are not dead or we don't have a collective dream."

"August," answered Lucien, "I won't gain anything to appease you, to agree with the product of your imagination and to let you know that you have a collective dream. My dear brother, you are alive, as well as your spouse and your daughter.

"Let's go. In the great book of destiny, they didn't write down that your family and you will always live in dire poverty."

The poor family at the courthouse

They drove at the heart of the city. For the first time, the Présiliens, for years, saw streets so clean, as well as buildings, family homes. These former destitute had lived, as they say, on the fringes of society and strove to avoid men and women's company.

After a forty-five minute drive, they stopped in front of a beautiful family home, in a nice neighborhood.

Lucien gave August a set of keys and pointed to the beautiful house.

"Here is the house you will live in from now on," added Lucien. "From here, you can see the supermarket. I mean the building you can see over there.

"My friends, you will find there foods and whatever you need.

"The car in the garage belongs to you."

"But, Lucien," cut in Acacia, "How will we manage to keep this house?"

"This house is yours.

"I am an engineer by trade. I have a company specializing in prefabricated homes.

"As owner of the company, I have the right to give away a house to those who really need it.

"You are homeless, then, logically and humanely speaking, you deserve this house.

"Don't you think so, my friends?"

Lucien cellular phone rang.

269

A stranger's wonderful chronicles, Book II

He had a long conversation with Constance Reynaud.

Then, he put the phone back to his jacket inside pocket and followed his friends to the house.

"Listen, my friend, things seem to get better."

"How things can be much better, Lucian?" inquired Acacia. "What are you talking about, Lucien?"

"Well, the *Welcome Shop* commercial has drawn a lot of attention.

"Constance has just called me to let me know that many commercial and publicity agencies will ask you to represent the image of the ideal family in their commercial announcements."

"Really!" cut in the girl.

"Yes, they will.

"Tomorrow, the company *Milk for All* will send their publicity agents to you, in the neighborhood of five in the afternoon, for shooting a commercial.

"Leila will have the time to return home from school. You will receive a big check that you will deposit. You have a checking account at the *Local Bank*. It is located not too far from the supermarket.

"Here are the checkbooks.

"Tomorrow, by eight in the morning, you will take Leila to the *Sisters School*.

"From the living room window, you can see the school establishment.

"The superior sister Margaret Dugan is waiting for Leila."

The poor family at the courthouse

Lucien took a short pause to catch his breath. Then, he stated, "Well, I believe I have covered everything.

"You have enough money in your pockets to meet the immediate expenses."

The spouses put at once their hands in their respective pockets and pulled wads of notebooks. They looked at each other and hunched their shoulders.

"Then, goodbye, my friends," said Lucien.

Leila put her hands around his neck and showered kisses on his neck and cheeks.

"Do you have to leave?" she asked.

"Yes, Leila. I have to help other children like you in distress."

"I understand."

On her turn, the mother hugged Lucien, while weeping bitterly.

Finally, August hugged Lucien tight. "I hope to see you again, Lucien," he advanced. "I am too overcome by emotion to express my gratitude."

"You will hear from me, August. It's not a promise; it is an expression of certainty."

This being said, he left the house.

◘   ◘

◘

The reporter, by order of elimination, visited the new beneficiaries of the *marvelous stranger*.

A stranger's wonderful chronicles, Book II

He started with the industrialist, Roberto Maher who told him among other things, "Brian, until today, I can't clearly accept the idea that the marvelous stranger has really visited me and has pulled me from the grip of that dangerous extortionist and his accomplice, Justine Solage.

"You should know that few days after the trial, I have conducted inquiries on the Internet. I have found no trace of a lawyer by the name of Lucien Leptis.

"I have also used the competence of an investigative agency, which hasn't been more successful.

"Then, my wife, my parents, my children, my in-laws, my friends, my associates and I have concluded that I did have a nightmare or something of this nature.

"However, if I had a nightmare, some mental confusion, how can you explain the signification of this letter?"

He handed over an unfolded sheet of paper to the reporter who read the following:

Robert,

Salute.

Don't concern yourself too much about identifying me.

Nevertheless, I take this opportunity to tell you that your wife, your children, your friends, your secretary and you don't have any dream about me. Like all of you, I exist.

The poor family at the courthouse

Yet, if I am a renowned international lawyer, under the name of Lucien Leptis, defending countless innocent people exposed to human injustice, you will be Napoleon Bonaparte or Toussaint Louverture (the great Haitian leader).

Anyway, on the day the extortionist and his accomplice were about to tarnish your reputation, I believed it was my duty to defend you; for, you were ready to let people walk all over you. What you must know, my dear brother, whenever my heart and my mind mixed with each other to argue a case, they work wonders.

Your check, I have deposited into my saving account to increase my funds that I put at the anonymous and distressing humanity disposal.

I send my best thoughts to your wife, Juliana, to your daughters, Rena and Paula, to your sons, Christian and Marvin, and to your secretary, Marilia whom you love like your own daughter. Keep on acting right.

Your improvised attorney, Lucien Leptis.

After reading the note, the reporter contented himself with saying, "Mr. Maher, a different turn of events would surprise me.

A stranger's wonderful chronicles, Book II

"However, this manifestation of the marvelous stranger falls in line with his exploits.

"Well, I must leave.

"The foods you have given me have done justice to your fin gourmet reputation.

"From here, my friends, I will go to visit the Présiliens who, like you, have benefitted from the marvelous stranger's magnanimity.

One hour after, he reached the Présiliens' home, who, like the industrialist, expressed their impression of plunging into a collective dream of which they would wake soon.

August went on, "Yet, irrefutable facts come to confirm our encounter with the marvelous stranger.

"First, from the discouraging homeless status we pass to property owners'

"Then, all that extraordinary man's predictions have materialized to the letter; I mean my wife's pregnancy and Leila great intelligence.

"My wife and I have now a new born child; my oldest daughter shines in school.

"Finally, as you know, Brian, we become the ideal family used in commercials."

After some thinking, the reporter stated, "My friends, as for everybody who has met with the marvelous stranger, he is mysterious but real.

"Since he spreads the good, we have the right to wish him longevity.

The poor family at the courthouse

"Thank you for the carrot cake and the glass of grapefruit juice with milk.

"These foods seem to come from out of this world.

"Well, my dear friends, I will close my inquiry with my visit to *Welcome Shop*."

When he reached the shop, a jubilant Constance Reynaud welcomed him.

For the first time, the staff and the customers had seen her so joyful.

She never stopped humming her favorite songs, all day long, while taking care of business.

That woman observed, "Brian, I don't want to hide my feeling. Since my encounter with the marvelous stranger, namely Lucien Leptis, I can't stop believing that I am bathing in the fountain of youth.

"First, I have completely regained my optimism. He let me know, right after the commercial, that I will never stop acquiring wealth until I die.

"My former husband has abandoned me to have a nice time with an opulent woman.

"He has left me with four children. Now these are so proud of their mom.

"Somewhat, I strongly believe that I have taken my revenge against that rascal.

"How?

A stranger's wonderful chronicles, Book II

"A friend of mine has informed me that, last time, that man has expressed his regrets to have abandoned me.

"Frankly speaking, Brian, I don't know why he has to complain now.

"As far as I am concerned, he has already reached either paradise or hell, you get my meaning.

"However, Brian, I would rather lose a fortune to spend delicious moments with the marvelous stranger, the embodiment of generosity and civilization."

After letting out a heave of sigh, she went on, "Oh! He is handsome, elegant, charming.

"His voice soothes me."

She closed her eyes and took another pause as if she took delight in drinking the most delicious fruit juice in the well.

Next, she touched Brian's forearm and said, "I apologize for my strange behavior.

"Well, Brian, my dear brother, you may understand my euphoric state of mind: my dream, as if by magic, comes true and feels me with joy.

"That exceptional man, to my great surprise, visited me yesterday, and we spent such exquisite time, something out of this world."

Constance shook her head repeatedly before continuing, "Once more, Brian, this man astonished me when he said and I quote, 'Constance, don't get scared of me. I mean no harm. I want you to be wealthy and happy all your life.

The poor family at the courthouse

"I mean it.

"Listen, my beautiful little Constance, I know you will consent to great sacrifices for enjoying my company.

"However, you don't have to lose a fortune for my beautiful eyes on.

"No, you don't have to go this far. You will see me from time to time.'"

Brian stood up, kissed Constance on the cheek and walked away, not without saying, "Constance, you are my sister in our love for the marvelous stranger."

In three days, the reporter will visit the *woman in the isolated parking lot.*

(25)

The
Young woman
In the
Isolated
Parking lot

Antoine Archange Raphael

*A*nne Scylla reached the end of her tether. She didn't know what else to do. She often thought of hurting herself or going away, at random, until she got exhausted and died. Nevertheless, she would always stop in time to reconsider her ultimate decisions.

Her friends and neighbors, without forgetting her coworkers, took her usually for an inviting woman who seized the least opportunity to help others.

Yet, for unknown reason, her supervisor, Ms. Andrea Cocteau, had never stopped scolding her and making her function as cashier at the *Pell Market Enterprise* almost impossible.

Indeed, Ms. Cocteau showed displeasure at whatever the employee did. She would remind her of her *great friendship* with the customers.

"Anne," added the supervisor, "you don't come to work to turn to a star. I have been watching you closely. You are the only one who stops the customers for a chat. The job hardly responds to the description of a place appropriate for chasing a husband."

She also reminded the employee of her *overdressing*.

"For," she added, "we have here a place of work, not a church. You simply have intention to make yourself look more important. As for me, you act simply as a little schemer, looking for something unknown to me.

"Perhaps, you intend to conquer the heart of one of these wealthy clients who attend our business for one reason or another. But you won't succeed…"

A stranger's wonderful chronicles, Book II

One day, Anne Scylla felt so frustrated that she could barely prevent herself from going for her supervisor's throat and strangling her.

That day, she strong believed that *clingy* had gone beyond all bounds, when she tried to "teach" the employee how to behave personally.

As usual, Anne Scylla paid an extra attention to Gabrielle Bison, a ninety-year-old woman who meant to leave independently in her home until she would die. Her children and grandchildren had tried in vain to send her to a nursing home.

Anne Scylla admired that old woman's courage, who, after she had finished shopping, would always go to Anne to pay. She took advantage of her closeness to the employee to have a chat, while the latter helped her reloading the cart.

The employee, to some extent, identified herself to that old woman. The more so as she had learned that Gabrielle Bison was once glowing with beauty and charm.

Additionally, she had attended the best schools of her time and had a vast culture.

"However, old age, like a sneaky river, had surprised her. Anne Scylla thought that old woman deserved everybody's respect (more than one could imagine).

That day, Gabriel Bison could barely walk in spite of her cane. She had to stop, once in a while, to catch her breath. Yet, as usual, she didn't lack determination and meant to go back home.

The young woman in the isolated parking lot

Anne Scylla, after she had finished helping her reloading her cart, went and got a nice maintenance man, Joseph Badu, and asked him to see Gabrielle Bison to her car which was as old as she.

Yet, something strange to recall, despite her debility, Gabrielle Bison, once seating behind her car steering wheel, regained her youth vigor.

Andrea Cocteau, that heartless woman, went closer to the cashier and heckled her, "Anne, as for me, you are a disgrace to our enterprise."

"What did I do wrong, Ms. Cocteau?" inquired the employee. "You have clearly lost your mind."

"How dare you speak to me like that?

"I am your supervisor. I can report you to the administration and get you fired.

"Go ahead, Ms. Cocteau. You will render me a great service, by making me stay away from you. I don't have the courage to quit, but I will feel great joy not to remain victim of your harassment."

Then, after a pause, she asked, "By the way, Ms. Cocteau, what do you complain about?"

"Well, as usual, you waste the company time to put the customers at a false scent.

"You behave as if you have more compassion than anyone in the world..."

For the first time, colleagues and customers had seen Anne reaching this level of anger.

A stranger's wonderful chronicles, Book II

She screamed, "Andrea, if you don't get off my face at once, I will harm you.

"I feel tired of you mood swings. As far as I am concerned, you behave completely as an unreasonable person. I won't spend my entire life being your scapegoat. Get out of my face. You make me nauseous."

The supervisor walked backward and disappeared.

The executive director of *Pell Market Enterprise* was walking by and heard Anne's voice.

He walked to her and inquired, "Anne, is everything ok? It's the first time I have seen you mad."

"Mr. Gilbert Melon, I do have respect for you and I regret to expose you to the negative aspect of my personality. I will strive not to behave like that in the future.

"However, as you can see, I have to serve a long line of customers.

"I must give them cause for complete satisfaction.

"I may simply add, Mr. Melon, that I feel great now. Yes, I do, I have just happily discovered that I have a person status, not a dog's."

The director patted the cashier on the shoulder and stated, "Anne, who would mistake such a beautiful and kind young woman like you with a dog?

"You must tell me if someone bothers you. You can always reach me at my office."

"Thank you, Mr. Melon," said Anne Scylla.

The young woman in the isolated parking lot

Shortly after, she proceeded, "According to many, you deserve your position of trust."

Coworkers temporarily left their cash registers either to give a kiss to their "coworker", a good word of encouragement, or to express their joy at seeing her reacting to Andrea Cocteau.

This latter toned down her animosity towards the angry employee, not without thinking about vengeful actions to take against her in the future.

She let anyone know that she had influential friends in the bosom of the corporation. She wouldn't stop until she got rid of that "shrew"

"In my annual report, which reaches the committee direction of the conglomerate," she told her close friends and relatives, "I will mention that Anne Scylla is the only trouble-maker who prevents the commercial unit to keep its *number one* status."

She would not also fail to let the big shots know that the unit director strangely showed too much leniency towards Anne Scylla.

As she was leaving, Andrea Cocteau concluded, "Who knows? These two perverts can change the directorial office into an orgy room. Apparently, this director and that schemer had an affair. I will put an end to it. I will kill two birds with the same stone: I will get rid of this shrew and will accede to the unit direction."

Indeed, secretly, Andrea Cocteau had never ceased to covet that commercial unit direction. "I have more seniority than anyone else (included the actual director).

A stranger's wonderful chronicles, Book II

"They told me that he owes his promotion to influential friends working at the general headquarters.

"However, I will find a way to get rid of him."

Until then, she had looked for Gilbert Melon's drawbacks and had found nothing.

This director conducted himself as a very meticulous man, who, every morning, devoted himself to a tour of inspection of the entire unity.

One morning, he had a big surprise when government inspectors came to him and gave him a formal warning about missing documents required by the *Health Department*, which summarized the dangerous nature of certain chemical products sold to the public.

"Mr. Melon," stated one of the inspectors, "as this unit has violated the health code the first time, we won't report this breach of law to the *Health Department*.

"However, my dear friend, you must comply as soon as possible.

"We will come back next week to see if you have taken all necessary steps to put an end to this violation."

"Thank you, Inspector Baines," said Mr. Melon. "I will take care of everything now.

"However, I must tell you that this morning I saw the missing documents glued to the shelves."

"You saw them with your own eyes?"

The young woman in the isolated parking lot

"Yes, I did."

"In that case, we may have a case of sabotage in our hands. Use extreme caution."

Mr. Gilbert Melon turned very disturbed about this breach to public safety. "Something is wrong," he thought.

He invited the employee in charge of these documents, by the way Mr. Gideon Polis, to come to his office.

The employee protested, "Mr. Melon, I don't know what has really happened. However, yesterday, until two in the afternoon, the appropriate documents were at the customers and staff members' disposal. I took care of this myself, the more so as the *Health Department* inspectors had announced their imminent visit to our unit.

"Someone, with evil intention, may have removed these documents."

The director trusted Gideon Polis. Then, he started to think over this unfortunate incident.

During lunchtime, Marinella, a good friend and coworker of Anne, whispered to her ear the rumor according to which Andrea Cocteau could have secretly ordered the removal of the damaging documents.

"Marinella, my sister, why would she behave like that?" ask Anne Scylla anxiously. "What can she gain from something like that?"

"Anne, my good friend, you are so thoroughly naïve," answered Marinella. "Andrea lets everybody know that she should have obtained the unit director's position."

A stranger's wonderful chronicles, Book II

"Oh! I understand now. Melon's friendship seems to infuriate that old bat.

"Listen, I must tell that man to be careful."

"Yes, you must."

"Anne, keep your mouth shut. I think that woman may go the extremes.

"Therefore, don't trust anyone. Cleverly, you must warn Mr. Melon.

"However, Anne, you can always count on me."

Three days after, Anne Scylla stopped at the director's office for a chat.

Geremia Casey, an office clerk assigned to the director's office, was a very talkative woman.

Usually, she drew everybody's attention on the least incidents occurred at the place of work. Andrea Cocteau, a good psychologist, often invited Geremia Casey to her table, during lunchtime, for a chat.

That day, as usual, Geremia and the supervisor Andrea Cocteau shared the same table at the cafeteria and conversed in a low pitch of voice.

As Anne Scylla arrived, Geremia touched slightly Andrea's hand and whispered, "Here is your enemy."

"Ah! That one!"

"Listen, Andrea, I call her your enemy to spice our conversation. However, I know Anne. She is harmless.

"Why don't look for her friendship?"

"Geremia, I don't know," replied Andrea. "For some reason or another, I don't trust her."

The young woman in the isolated parking lot

"Why don't you?"

"I don't know."

"By the way, Andrea, your 'enemy' gets along well with the director."

"How do you know something like that?"

"Once in a while, Anne pays Mr. Melon a visit. And I have overheard more than once Mr. Melon sings the praises of Anne.

"Actually, three days ago, Anne visited the director. They don't have an affair. No, I don't think so. They spoke loud enough to let me hear the nature of their conversation."

"What did they talk about?"

"They talked about the incident concerning the missing chemical products documents…"

The loudspeaker announced a general meeting at two-thirty.

During that meeting, the director put accent on the incident mentioned by Geremia.

He concluded as follows:

The Central Office of Investigation will send three of its agents to conduct a thorough inquiry.

Once identified, the Justice Department will arrest the guilty person, and our corporation will dismiss him from the enterprise.

A stranger's wonderful chronicles, Book II

Which is understandable: he puts in danger not only the employees and the customers' lives, but also the future of the enterprise.

I ask all employees to collaborate with the agents from the Central Investigation Bureau.

If anyone gets some pieces of information that may facilitate the investigation, he or she shouldn't hesitate to contact us at the main office.

Andrea felt like a cat on a hot tin roof. She asked herself if her accomplices, Angelo Kabob and Bobby Lester, hadn't left any clue about the theft of the documents they could trace back to her.

Andrea pulled her cellular phone and dialed a number. She only said, "Tonight, about six PM. She must go; otherwise, they would know what really had happened. We will be in a jam...I will manage to let her leave the last..."

As usual, the cashiers, before going back home, had to submit their reports to the supervisor; for the amount of money in the cash machine had to match the printout.

For one reason or another, Andrea found a way to make Anne the last cashier to submit her report, despite the employee's endeavor to get near her supervisor.

The young woman in the isolated parking lot

Finally, Anne entered the parking lot.

She had a moment of panic when she noticed the absence of people and cars, except hers.

She got on it quickly and tried to turn on the engine. Nothing happened. She had the impression that the starter had turned dead.

Anne burst out crying. For, without a car, she couldn't go back home and return to work the day after.

Without a job, she couldn't pay her rent and other obligations required by modern living.

Her parents lived more than one thousand miles from her.

Then, two men, with long knives, headed toward her.

She thought that her last hour had come; for, in the same parking lot, about six months before, in almost under the same circumstances, they had found a female teacher dead, after they had stolen her bag.

Additionally, not too long before, they had raped a female employee and left her for dead.

She still remained hospitalized.

As the criminals approached, Anne's legs gave away.

One of the criminals stated, "Anne Scylla, you are a nuisance to everybody. Today, you must go on your eternal trip."

Then, the woman fell to the ground.

In some kind of twilight sleep, she saw a car arriving full speed, which stopped between the criminals and her.

A stranger's wonderful chronicles, Book II

Then, she believed that a man got off the vehicle and had a fierce fight with her aggressors.

The struggle lasted some time, during which, the man graciously made daring judo and karate moves. He jumped in the air, rolled on the floor and hit the criminals hard with his feet and his fists.

When Anne regained conscience, she saw the criminals tied up, her rescuer on the phone and several police cars arriving with siren on.

The police officers handcuffed the criminals.

As to the rescuer, he walked up to Anne and shook her hand to pacify her. Then, he said, "Anne Scylla, my name is Jerome Bell"

The woman made a gesture of the hand before saying, "Mr. Bell, how do you know my name?"

Suddenly, she started to panic again; for, as far as she was concerned, this man had rescued her from the criminals to put his own diabolic plan to execution. "My God!" she thought. "I find myself alone with this stranger.

"I should have drawn the police's attention! What have I done? Here am I in the parking lot, at the mercy of a man, a well-dressed man but a street fighter!"

"Anne," stated Jerome, "don't have any fear of me and don't confuse me with a serial killer.

"Although I am a street fighter, I do not intend to hurt you. I use my martial skill to help others…

The young woman in the isolated parking lot

"Well, my behavior may confuse you, and you wouldn't be the first one to get confused by my conduct.

"For one reason or another, I have a profound intuition of reality and some kind of sixth sense to detect people in distress and pull them from their predicaments.

"I have the impression of reaching something close to the totality of knowledge."

"No, Mr. Bell, I don't believe you. Only God knows the alpha and the omega of reality. Don't insult my intelligence."

"I know," cut in Jerome. "You have attended college studies at the State University. You have a Master Degree in Market Economy.

"You live alone. Your parents live at more than one thousand miles from you. You have no other choice but to work as a cashier for *Pell Market Enterprise*.

"Your supervisor, Andrea Cocteau, has given you a hard time. Geremia Casey, a talkative woman, has told her about your recent visit to the director.

"Andrea, now, thinks that you know the person responsible for the document theft at the chemical department. Then, she asks her accomplices to mess up with your car, while she has made sure that you would be alone in the parking lot.

"The criminals could have killed you.

"You are in a constant state of worry.

A stranger's wonderful chronicles, Book II

"You wonder what would happen to you.

"You are beautiful and young, but you wouldn't give yourself up to the first man met with in your way; for, many of your female friends and relatives have known a hellish life with their husbands and lovers…"

Anne Scylla remained wide-mouthed. She wondered if she wasn't under the influence of a dream or if she hadn't lost conscience.

Undoubtedly, Jerome Bell (if that was his name) was a ghost, a projection of her own soul, an envoy of God, the Creator of the world, or Lucifer in person.

If he came from Lucifer, he would have already hurt her or killed her.

The man opened his arms. After, a minute of hesitation, Anne Scylla fell in them and rested her head on the male chest and closed her eyes.

She happened to realized that his chest could be the softest in the world.

"Jerome, I give up," she said. "If you want to kill me, I won't put up a fight.

"As a matter of fact, how can I fight someone who has just overcome two heavily armed assassins?"

"Anne," reassured the man, "once more, I have no intention of hurting you."

Few minutes after, Jerome gently pushed the woman away, not without saying, "Well, Anne, my friend, I will soon set your car in motion.

"Then, you will follow me if you want to; for, I still have the impression that you don't trust me.

The young woman in the isolated parking lot

"You believe that I am using friendly manners to deaden your watchfulness and then hurt you."

The man got on his car, and Anne, on hers.

Next, she followed the man, while she still wondered if she used wisdom.

She should have taken advantage of her freedom of action to get lost in the street labyrinths, as she thought that the man ignored her address.

"But, why would I behave like that?" she wondered. "If he wanted to hurt me, he would have done so longtime ago. Additionally, this man's great generosity and divinatory powers have aroused my curiosity.

"Actually, this man, with such acumen, may have already known my address.

"Let me follow him. If something bad happens to me, the Creator of reality will have written my misfortune in the great book of destiny, since time immemorial."

Some point in time, the man turned to the right on Bailers Boulevard, a busy area, and parked his vehicle in front of a car dealer.

Anne parked her vehicle behind Jerome's. He beckoned to her to get nearer. Finally, he presented her to a man.

"Ms., my name is Robert Gentiles," said the latter. "We will keep your old car."

"You will keep my old car!" Anne echoed him.

"Yes, we will keep it. You won't need it.

A stranger's wonderful chronicles, Book II

"You do have a new car now. Here it is."

Anne couldn't believe her eyes. Like a robot, she signed the forms. The salesman, Robert Gentiles, gave her the new car keys.

Before leaving, she walked up to Jerome and said, "How can I explain such great generosity, Jerome? I don't do prostitution. If I don't sell my body, I won't, certainly, sell my soul.

"Listen, you have already saved my life. Now, you anticipate my need for a new car. Then, again, why do you display such incredible generosity?"

"Anne," finally said the man, "you are my sister, my beautiful sister."

"I am your beautiful sister!"

"Of course, Anne, you are. Otherwise, I wouldn't feel obliged to help you.

"Then, tomorrow, my beautiful sister will go to work in a brand-new car. You will also find money in your bag to buy new clothes.

"You will have a good surprise on the job. From now on, you will keep blossoming like a rose in the morning, exposed to the sun."

"You won't come back to get paid?"

"No, I won't."

"You won't create any reason for hurting me?"

"No, I won't."

"Then, let me give you a kiss on the cheek."

"Why shouldn't you?"

The young woman in the isolated parking lot

"I will never see you again?"

"Yes, you will see me in spirit."

"Jerome, why won't I see you in flesh and blood?"

"It's possible."

"Bye, Jerome."

"Bye, my little Anne."

The woman started up the car engine and headed toward the commercial area to buy news clothes, as suggested by her Good Samaritan.

Yet, she kept asking if she didn't experience mental confusion.

The day after, her coworkers congratulated her on her "impeccable bearing".

For the first time they reacted like one man to tell Andrea Cocteau, that "mean supervisor", to let "their friend" alone.

At lunch time, Anne showed her brand new car to her coworkers.

They asked her if she had hit the jackpot.

"Yes, to some extent," she answered.

"What do you mean?" inquired Gaston Bator.

"Well, if someone saved my life; next, he took me to a car dealer and gave me a brand new car, then, as far as I am concerned, I have hit the jackpot."

Returning from lunch, they saw a big crowd in the great hall. They also noticed a reporter's presence; by the way it was Brian Clifford flanked by his cameraman.

A stranger's wonderful chronicles, Book II

The director and other big shots of the enterprise wouldn't miss such gathering for any reason in the world.

The employees didn't know what to think about the reason for such gathering.

Suddenly, the director pointed a finger at Anne Scylla; then, he beckoned to her to get closer.

Without beating about the bush, Brian Clifford asked, "Anne, I just come from jail. The criminals, Angelo Kabob and Bobby Jeter, have told me something about a spirit coming from nowhere, which has overcome them, tied them up and saved your life.

"Provided they have told the truth, I would admit that the fortune has smiled on you.

"Anne, do you think that the criminals have succumbed to mental aberration or that they have told the truth?"

Anne kept silent for a while before admitting, "I don't know the nature of the man who has saved my life. He may embody an angel or a fiend of Satan; I can't tell.

"I know that he has displayed unprecedented strength, which has defied imagination. For a while, I have rested at the mercy of that powerful entity. If that man wanted to hurt me, I wouldn't have any means of defense against him.

"However, today, I feel so glad that exceptional man arrived in time to pull me from the claws of death.

The young woman in the isolated parking lot

"I owe him a debt of eternal gratitude; for, all the wealth in the world, all the inventions, all the splendor of our planet couldn't keep me alive.

"Someone has paid those criminals to kill me.

"As the money they have received has more importance than my life, without the intervention of this outstanding entity, I would have belonged to history today, which would have faded away with time, without the marvelous stranger's intervention.

"Brian, that great man must have an exceptional nature. And I strongly believe, based on the seriousness of the situation I found myself in, that I must have God's blessing to have seen that *wonderful stranger* in action."

A deep silence reigned over the place.

The customers momentarily forgot the personal reasons for visiting the enterprise.

The employees also had their eyes glued to Anne, waiting for the conclusion of her account.

Finally, the authorities and the rest of the crowd couldn't believe their ears.

"My friends," went on Anne, "that man has unstoppable powers I saw with my own eyes, despite my frozen fear and my blurring perception of reality.

"However, he has himself made an allusion to his unlimited gifts. He has told me that he has a profound intuition of reality and can reach the inexpressible.

A stranger's wonderful chronicles, Book II

"In other words, he knows the alpha and omega of reality, in any context.

"I didn't want to believe him, reminding him of the fact that only God has omniscience.

"Then, to convince me, he made revelations about my life in minute details. He told me that he knew me because he felt in harmony with me, as if he had changed into me.

"However, the highest point of his personality comes from his unprecedented generosity: he has given me a brand new vehicle. Then, without my knowledge, he put money in my bag. I had only fifteen dollars in it, before his generous action.

"He has clearly predicted that I would have a nice surprise today.

"How may I confuse this entity with the figment of my imagination or a disintegration of my mental synthesis?

"I keep on living and enjoying the company of good people like you, don't I?

"The criminals, still alive, have mentioned the man's intervention, haven't they?

"I park my brand new car in the parking lot?

"The wonderful man gave me the criminals' identities and their leader's, didn't he?

"I must bow to the evidence."

Brian Clifford got near Anne and shook her hand. Next, he stated,

The young woman in the isolated parking lot

"Thank you, Anne. More than you think, you have just reminded me of the marvelous stranger's qualities. I have no doubt about his existence.

"I won't fail to include this episode into the next edition of "The marvelous stranger's chronicles".

The clients and the employees had no choice but to resume their activities.

One of the authorities handed over two sealed envelopes to Gilbert Melon, respectively addressed to Andrea Cocteau and Anne Scylla.

The latter cried with joy when she learned that, from that point on, the administration promoted her to the supervisor of the unit in which she had worked for five years or so.

Her friends ran up to her to congratulate her.

"At least," added Sonia Koch, a beautiful cashier, "we won't have Andrea's eyes glued to us looking for trifling reasons to blame us."

"What will happen to her?" inquired Philip Brown, another Anne's coworker.

"I don't know," replied the lady.

Andrea kept silent about the content of the letter received from the central administration, hoping to make others forget it.

That woman could have felt joy at her promotion as the *assistant director* of a unit located at *Montpellie*r, in the northern section of the country;

A stranger's wonderful chronicles, Book II

however, an addendum made her nervous and caused her to exclaim, "Ouch! What are they talking about?"

"What's going on?" screamed the employees together. "Have you seen Lucifer in person?"

"Listen, stay cool, everybody! Don't forget that, until further notice, I am still in charge," she answered angrily. "Don't forget it. And mind your business."

The note underlined:

Andrea Cocteau,

 Since you belong to the first generation of employees, we don't want to dismiss you.

Rest assured this is the only reason for which you still keep your job with the company.

However, a friend of the company who wants to remain anonymous has told us that you have taking part in the theft of the documents required by the Department of Health. For the same reason, losing your composure, you have ordered the killing of Anne Scylla.

Thus, you have committed all the sins in the world by behaving like that.

Normally, you should be in jail by now instead of working here.

The young woman in the isolated parking lot

Morally speaking, you don't fit to work around good people.

According to the anonymous friend, you deserve a second chance, since you will have your mistakes and your misdeeds to serve you as guiding light.

However, the slightest lapse of behavior will cause your dismissal.

Signed: The Administration.

Three days after, as Anne Scylla sat peacefully in her office, the director came.

"Anne," he said, "you do have all the reasons in the world to rejoice.

"However, I can't prevent myself from noticing some sadness on your face.

"What's going on with me? Am I a bad director? Does my presence inconvenience you?"

"Actually, Mr. Melon…"

"Anne, call me Gilbert. No more formalism between us."

"Yes, Gilbert, I should have rejoiced.

"Contrary to what you think, you emerge as an excellent and compassionate director. Your presence doesn't inconvenience me at all.

"However, for some unexplained reason, I can't prevent myself from thinking about my *Good Samaritan*, the one that pulled me from the abyss of death and poverty. Without him, I would become a piece of history today. As I have said, I owe him an eternal debt of gratitude.

"Frankly, I would like to see him again."

She stopped talking. Gilbert's face turned somber.

"Now, Gilbert, it's my turn to ask you for the reason for your sudden bad humor."

"Anne, while listening to you, I have lost hope of seeing better days in my life…"

"You have lost hope…What are you talking about?"

"Anne, it's better to keep silent."

"But, yes, we should talk about the cause of your unexpected sadness."

"Do you know, Anne, that I am a single?"

Anne frowned. She had always believed that her director happily lived in the bosom of his family.

"Anne, I have told the truth. I am single.

"Deliberately, I get surrounded by people to avoid loneliness, namely my parents, my brothers and sisters."

"What are you waiting for, Gilbert. You should marry a glamorous woman. You have plenty of charm and education. Additionally, you have a good position with this company. Then, what prevents you from getting married?"

"Yes, Anne, all that you have said represents a positive asset; except that my heart hasn't spoken yet."

The young woman in the isolated parking lot

"I see.

"Then, let's go back to what we have said. Why did you say that you lost hope…"?

"Anne, let me go away. I am in such a pain."

"Gilbert, I am a good listener.

"Tell me what is going wrong. Perhaps, I would find some good piece of advice to give you."

"Listen, Anne, for a while, I thought that I would conquer your heart."

"What!"

"Yes, Anne, I've loved you for a long time.

"But, apparently, you don't love me. You rather love that Jerome…"

"I didn't say that.

"Besides, I don't even know if that Jerome exists. If he does he won't look like an entity known to us. I do believe in that man's purely spiritual nature. How can I love a spirit?

"However, I can't prevent myself from wishing to see him again to express my gratitude.

"That's all."

After a moment of silence, she went on, "Gilbert, do you want me to tell you something?"

"Yes, Anne, if you want to soothe my pains."

"No, Gilbert, you have made a mistake. I want to do more than console you."

A stranger's wonderful chronicles, Book II

"Do you want really to console me? Yet, Anne I don't need consolation and pity!"

"Gilbert, I do also love you.

"But I didn't want to tell you about it in fear for others to accuse me of chasing a husband.

"Additionally, I don't know how your parents and relatives' would react."

"My parents have nothing to do with my intimate life.

"On the contrary, they worry about my single status. I have already told them about you…"

"Listen…"

She didn't complete her sentence; for, Jerome stood at the doorway.

Anne remained wide-mouthed, pointing only to the door.

The director followed her finger direction and he also saw Jerome.

"It is you, Jerome?" he inquired hesitatingly.

"Yes, I am Jerome, Gilbert Melon, Anne's future husband."

At these words, the woman lost conscience (and undoubtedly, the man also sank into mental confusion).

When she pulled herself together, she found herself unrestraint in Gilbert Melon's arms.

They saw a note on Anne's office top.

She rushed unfolding it. She then smiled. Next, she showed the note to Gilbert,

The young woman in the isolated parking lot

Anne and Gilbert,

Salute!

This is your good friend, Jerome. I didn't mean to frighten you. The way I see it, you belong together. You must not thwart your destiny.

My best wishes.

Jerome.

They turned around; Jerome had left.

"Darling," said Anne, "did I have a dream?"

"No," answered Gilbert, "you didn't have a dream. The man stood at the doorway. I saw him.

"However, some point in time, he found a way to get us closer to each other.

"By the way, how do you explain his note?"

Someone exclaimed, "Oh! Excuse me."

Gilbert beckoned to Geremia Casey and said, "Well, Geremia, this is the future Mrs. Gilbert Melon.

"Let everybody know.

"By the way, the administration has promoted you to the rank of supervisor at the unit located at Montpellier. You will join your good friend Andrea Cocteau."

A stranger's wonderful chronicles, Book II

"Congratulation, my friends," said Geremia anyway.

This being said, she went and spread the news.

Three weeks after, Anne and Gilbert got married, in the presence of a big crowd composed of their respective parents, friends and relatives, colleagues and many others.

As they paged the names of gift donors, one of them was Jerome.

Anne and Gilbert froze.

They wondered about the content of this envelope.

Then, the new bride took it and opened it with the eagerness and excitement of a girl unfolding a Christmas gift.

She couldn't believe her eyes. She showed the content to her new husband. He almost dropped to the ground. It indicated the newlyweds' house...

There was a note saying,

Anne and Gilbert,

My congratulations!

I know that two marvelous people like you will change the communal life into heavenly adventure. Then, this little gift is from me, which will allow you to experience the perfect love in your new home.

As an architect, I have built it to fit all your desires and dreams.

The young woman in the isolated parking lot

Your friend forever,

Jerome Pell

Anne and Gilbert would live like two pigeons, in harmony with their mysterious friend's wish.

◘   ◘

◘

Brian, as usual, took great pleasure in recording this new marvelous stranger's episode.

He anticipated the satisfaction he would have, following his next visit to the man who thought that he was the author of an « impossible homicide ».

(26)

The Impossible Homicide

By Antoine Archange Raphael

*L*aurent Saint-Jean left his home in a state of anger. His wife had tried in vain to calm him down; but he couldn't take it anymore. This time, he would go to extremes, by killing that reporter who had just written a misleading article about him; which would certainly minimize his chance of having the important position at *Syndrill & Co House*.

He sped up his car on the highway, without paying attention to the traffic rules and the speed limit prescribed by the law.

Highway policemen saw that vehicle zoomed past and were about to chase it, but they lost sight of it; for it had left the highway to enter the great boulevard in which stood up the condominium unit the reporter Louison Calliste had bought and occupied, for quite a while.

Laurent Saint-Jean parked his car in a *no parking zone* and entered the building, holding a gun.

It was exactly ten in the morning.

He saw Mathew Aden, sitting behind the superintendent's office and went straight to him.

"Listen, sir," he yelled, "don't give me a hard time. I don't have a fight with you. All that I need is to show me Louison Calliste's unit."

"Certainly, sir," rushed saying Mathew Aden.

"It's number twenty-two, on the second floor."

"Thank you."

A stranger's wonderful chronicles, Book II

No sooner had Laurent Saint-Jean entered the elevator that Mathew Aden dialed the nearest police station phone number.

"Officer, the man is holding a gun," he explained. "You must act fast."

In less than fifteen minutes, police officers occupied the hallway.

Mathew Aden, with his index finger, showed the way to the stairs.

The police officers cautiously opened the access door and headed to the second floor.

They walked furtively, hugged the walls, to protect themselves against any possible aggression.

Suddenly, they heard three gunshots. They rushed into the reporter's apartment and saw him lying dead on his bed, while the aggressor stood up holding a revolver.

He shot Louison Calliste three times in his stomach.

The police chief yelled, "Drop the gun!"

Laurent Saint-Jean complied at once. Many police officers grabbed him and dropped him to the floor. One of them handcuffed him.

He asked, "What's your name?"

"My name is Laurent Saint-Jean.

The police chief pronounced,

Mr. Laurent Saint-Jean, you are in a state of arrest for the murder of Louison Calliste.

All that you say, society will use for or against you.

The impossible homicide

We will keep you in jail until a judge hears your case.

Do you understand me?

"Yes, Officer," answered the presumed assassin in a strangely serene fashion, in the manner of someone who has just fulfilled his duty.

A stormy crowd occupied the court, the stairs leading to the flight of steps and the street.

This crowd turned overexcited when they saw the accused getting off the police van, with hands handcuffed and legs chained up.

Some yelled, "Assassin! Assassin!"

"How can you kill such important personality?" screamed someone.

"You will have what you deserve," shouted another.

"You have killed a great man!" argued another. "You will undergo the ire of justice."

Finally, they introduced the accused into the courtroom where they would decide on his case. According to the media, if they found him guilty, he will go to jail for life. Some lawyers went as far as to mention death penalty by lethal injection.

In the meantime, someone knocked at the main door of the Saint-Jean family's home. Laurent's discouraged wife sluggishly went to the door and, slowly, opened it. Her two children, Irene, a ten-year-old girl, and Roger, an eight-year-old boy followed her closely.

A stranger's wonderful chronicles, Book II

A well-dressed man gave a handshake to the woman and pronounced, "You are Irene, Laurent's wife.

"This charming young lady must be Bettina. This handsome young man is Roger."

"But, sir, how do you manage to know so much about us. It's the first time we have seen you in our life. If you are a joker, you have chosen the wrong time to try entertaining us. Do you know…"

"My friends, I have a profound intuition of things, and I possess the alpha and omega of reality."

"It's refreshing! It's simply refreshing!" exclaimed Bettina.

The mother pointed a nervous finger to her daughter and yell-ed, "Shut up, Bettina! What's wrong with you?"

"Mom," said the boy.

"What's going on? It's the first time these children behave this way.

"Sir, have you done something to them?"

"Madam," rushed saying the visitor, "sometimes, children feel close to reality. Their warm welcome means to tell you that you don't find your-selves in a state of danger."

"Sir, listen.

"You knock at my door and welcome my children and me as if we were good friends. You frighten us."

"I understand your fear.

"Let's me introduce myself.

312

The impossible homicide

"My name is Luckner Marion. I am a lawyer who would like to represent your husband at the court. He had foolishly put himself in a dangerous situation."

"Counselor Marion, you should have put yourself in my husband's shoe to understand his situation. The man he has killed has pushed him against the wall."

After a pause, she added, "Counselor Marion, we can't afford to have a lawyer. My husband and the family must rely on the judges and the jurors' clemency, after having heard Laurent's motive for murder."

"I know."

"What do you know?"

"You have only twenty dollars in the house. The children and you have only a cup of coffee for food. You don't know what else to do.

"It's too late for you to look for a job, because you can't leave the children alone in the house.

"Because of the article written by Louison Calliste, who has falsely accused your husband of grave mistakes, the latter has lost the hope of being hired by *Syndrill & Co House* and by any other respectable business."

Irene couldn't believe her ears and held her forehead to prevent it from exploding.

"Ah! I see," said the woman. "I have a dream. You are the figment of my derailed imagination."

"Madam, you don't have a dream.

A stranger's wonderful chronicles, Book II

"Your children and you may touch each other to ascertain your physical presence.

"Telle me, how could you feel your body resistance in a dreamy context?

"When I speak, your children perceived, like you, the vibration of my voice. How can you explain that distinct persons have the same perception if they are dreaming?"

Bettina, for no clear reason, hugged the visitor.

"Bet, what's wrong with you?" inquired the mother. "You have never behaved like that."

"Mom, remember what I have told you last time?"

"Yes, I do remember. You have said something about a savior…"

The mother remained wide-eyed.

Then, pulling herself together, she stated, "Sir, you know our unfortunate situation.

"We can't afford to hire a lawyer.

"Additionally, there is nothing…"

"Irene don't finish your sad thought in presence of these angels. Your husband couldn't commit this homicide."

"You have said that as a joke?"

"No, I haven't.

"However, we must act fast. I anticipate that your husband will make his case worst because of his anger. I can sense that he would have the desire to strangle the lawyer put at his disposal by the court, who tries to advice him to plead guilty and to rely on the court and the jury clemency.

"Let's go to the courthouse."

Irene and her children got on the visitor's car and headed to the courthouse.

They reached the sanctuary of justice in the middle of a chaos.

Laurent Saint-Jean had seized his lawyer by the neck and tried to strangle him, while the security agents kept doing their utmost to free the lawyer from that stronghold.

Irene couldn't believe her eyes: the scenario anticipated by the visitor unfolded like a melodramatic action.

The visitor suggested, "Irene, go and speak to the judge. Tell him that you are Laurent's wife and to say it loud and clear through the microphone."

The woman followed the man's advice. The judge screamed on the top of his lung, "Mr. Laurent Saint-Jean, your wife Irene is here…"

The prisoner calmed down at once.

The lawyer, freed from the stronghold, had a sigh of relief and kept his distance from his alleged client.

"Mr. Laurent Saint-Jean, added the judge, who will represent you?"

"I don't know, your honor. However, this lawyer has insulted my intelligence by asking me to admit that I was a serial killer…"

"What!"

A stranger's wonderful chronicles, Book II

"Yes, your honor. Then, I saw red. Your honor, adversity keeps hitting me hard. I regret to create such commotion in the courtroom."

"But…"

The wife beckoned to the judge. Then, she said, "Your honor, may I have a word with my husband for about five minutes."

"You must act fast, Mrs. Irene Saint-Jean.

"We have lost too much time."

"Thank you, your honor."

Irene introduced the visitor to her husband.

"Darling, this lawyer wants to help."

"But, who is he? Actually, darling, you know we can't afford a lawyer"

Luckner Marion asked the woman to go and sit down in the audience. "Leave me with Laurent," he added.

Remaining alone with the prisoner, he stated in a natural fashion, "Laurent, I know the alpha and the omega of reality."

"What!" exclaimed the prisoner. "It's jumping out of the frying pan into the fire.

"You are a fruitcake."

"Laurent, I don't accept your expert opinion.

"I may reveal your life starting from your most tender youth to the present.

"For example, at the age of fourteen, you made love to Josephine Milord."

The impossible homicide

"Shut up. Who are you?"

"I am the man with a profound intuition of reality.

"Someone saw you having sex with Josephine."

"Who is he?"

"It's your mother. But she didn't say a word to your father."

"Shut up.

"Don't say one more word. You want to represent me, then, let it be. Nevertheless, you are wasting your time.

"I have emptied my handgun to that rascal's stomach. The policemen and policewomen have seen me with the gun in my hand, standing close to the body."

"Laurent, listen to me carefully. You speak too much. Don't keep repeating something impossible. You must trust me. I will pull from this mess.

"How would you do that?"

"First, as I have said, you should know that you couldn't murder the reporter."

"My dear Mr. Attorney, let me apologize in advance about what I will say: you have certainly sunk into madness."

"No, Laurent, I haven't. Once more, you must trust me. I will prove your innocence."

Laurent opened wide his eyes. Then, he grabbed Luckner Marion.

Everybody thought he would try to assault him.

A stranger's wonderful chronicles, Book II

The police, eventually, would intervene, once more, and the judge would have no choice but to order the transfer of the prisoner to a psychiatric facility.

However, what followed let everybody stunned. The prisoner kissed his lawyer on the cheek.

Then, returning toward the judicial authorities, he addressed himself to the legal panel as follows, "Honorable judges, I want the distinguished Attorney Luckner Marion to represent me.

"I absolutely trust him."

"Alleluia!" exclaimed the chief justice, namely Honorable Romain Lagrange.

Then, without beating about the bush, he pronounced, "Mr. Laurent Saint-Jean, you are accused of killing the reporter Louison Calliste. How do you plead?"

"I am innocent!" screamed the prisoner to everybody's dismay."

"Mr. Laurent Saint-Jean, if your lawyer has advised you to plead innocent, he has the intention to mislead you. He may be a joker."

Counselor Luckner Marion raised his hand and stated, "According to the judicial system of our country, a man accused of a crime must have the innocent's status until proof to the contrary."

"You are right, acknowledged the judge."

Then, after a short while, he inquired, "What's your name?"

"My name is Attorney Luckner Marion," answered the lawyer.

The impossible homicide

The judge jotted down the lawyer's name on his notebook. Then, he beckoned to the district attorney and stated, "Mr. District Attorney, by the way, Mr. Hector Devon, you may present the count of indictment and proceeded with the witnesses' examination.

The district attorney started,

Your honorable justices,

Ladies and gentlemen of the Jury,

Ladies and gentlemen of the audience,

During my professional career, it's the first time I have experienced such evident case of homicide.

The man sitting in the dock went to the building where the late honorable reporter, Louison Calliste, lived and emptied his pistol to his stomach.

There are many eyewitnesses to this horrible crime, namely the condominium superintendant, Mr. Mathew Aden, and more than twenty police officers.

Without beating about the bush, I believe the accused deserves harsh punishment.

Let me call the first witness for the prosecution, Mr. Mathew Aden to the witness box.

A stranger's wonderful chronicles, Book II

Mr. Mathew Aden sat peacefully at the witness box. Then, the district attorney started, "What's your name?"

"My name is Mathew Aden."

"What's your profession?"

"I am a well-known condominium superintendent called "City Residence"."

"Tell us, Mr. Mathew Aden, what happened last Sunday, at ten in the morning?"

"I saw the accused arriving with a gun in his hand. He told me not to worry; for, he didn't have any quarrel with me. Finally, he asked for late Louison Calliste's apartment number. If I refused to tell him, he would be very mad."

"Then..."

"I called the police that arrived in about fifteen minutes. I heard shots. I had an intuition that the worst had happened. I wouldn't have any surprise at learning there were two dead persons. But later on, I would learn that the accused had emptied his revolver to the victim's body."

The judge invited attorney Luckner Marion to cross-examine the witness.

"Thank you, your honor," stated the defense lawyer.

The district attorney, under the influence of emotion, pronounced, "Your honor, isn't it a waste of our time? With such avalanche of evidence, this lawyer will make us waste our time unnecessarily..."

The impossible homicide

"Mr. District Attorney, we need order in the court," warned sharply the chief justice, Romain Lagrange. "You haven't had the right to speak"

The lawyer for the defense ignored the district attorney's comment and started the cross-examination.

"Mr. Mathew Aden, you said that my client entered the building at ten in morning."

"Yes, I did."

"Are you sure?"

"Objection!" screamed the district attorney.

"On what grounds, Mr. District Attorney," asked the judge.

"What difference will make the timing, under these circumstances?"

"Mr. Marion?" said the judge.

"The timing will make a big difference, under these circumstances," answered the lawyer for the defense. "However, we need patience, which the district attorney seems not to have."

"Mr. District Attorney," said the judge, "your objection, not having any basis, is denied.

"Counselor Marion, go ahead."

"Thank you, your honor.

"Mr. Mathew Aden, you said that my client reached the building at ten in the morning, holding a gun in his hand."

"Yes, honorable counselor."

"How do you know exactly the time?"

A stranger's wonderful chronicles, Book II

"Well, as a superintendent, when I sit down in my office, I take pleasure in looking at the passing of time on the clock of the wall. I have contracted this habit as a means of distraction from the slow motion of moments."

"It's fascinating."

"Honorable attorney, would you say that I have misbehaved to watch the passing of time and that I have sunk into mental disturbance."

"I wouldn't say that at all, sir. I wouldn't reach such conclusion. On the contrary, I mean to congratulate you. Because of your habit, you will contribute to showing my client's innocence, without the shadow of the doubt."

"Is it true, honorable attorney? Will I contribute to save the life of an innocent man? In this case, I am fortunate."

"Yes, Mr. Aden, you are.

"What did happen, between nine-thirty and ten in morning?"

"Almost nothing of importance occurred, honorable attorney," answered the witness. "It was a Sunday. Usually, the unit owners get up late on Sundays."

"Mr. Aden, take your time to think about all that you had seen that Sunday morning."

"Honorable attorney Luckner Marion, as I have said, I didn't see anything worthy of my attention. However, as far as I can remember, I saw a thin man leaving the elevator and heading toward the exit."

"Well, you saw a thin man leaving the premises.

The impossible homicide

"Can you describe him, Mr. Aden?"

"Certainly, I can, honorable counselor. He carried a pair of blue-jean pants, tennis shoes, a kepi, dark glasses, and a set of keys in his hand…"

Attorney Luckner Marion kept silence for a minute or so. Then, he asked the judge if he could approach his bench.

"This is very unusual!" yelled the district attorney.

Shortly, he added, "According to us, this devil's advocate makes us waste our time.

"The evidence is overwhelming, showing that the accused is guilty, beyond the shadow of doubt."

The judge drummed on his desktop before declaring, "Mr. District Attorney, I preside over the unfolding of justice. To my recollection, you haven't had the authorization to speak. If you continue this way, I will ask the attorney general to send me another representative."

"Your honor, I am sorry," conceded the district attorney. "The victim's parents and relatives, as well as the lawyer for society have temporarily lost patience.

"Of course, my outburst has no justification.

"However, your honor, at the end of the trial, I will conduct a thorough inquiry about the legitimacy of Mr. Luckner Marion as a lawyer."

"You have the right to act as you please, Mr. District Attorney. In the meantime, do approach the bench to listen to attorney Marion's suggestion."

A stranger's wonderful chronicles, Book II

No sooner had the two party's lawyers had stood by the judge's bench, Attorney Marion whispered,

"Before going on with my witness' cross-examination, I ask you honorable judge, to put the security agents in a state of alertness."

"Why, Attorney Marion, should I put the security agents in a state alertness?"

"Come on," cut in the district attorney, "this man believes that this legal process is nothing but a game."

Turning towards the lawyer for the defense, he added, "Dear counselor Marion, you must wake up from your dreams.

"Yes, you are dreaming!"

"Mr. District Attorney, you put my patience to the test," yelled the judge. "One more word and I will hold for contempt to the court. And I mean it.

"Go ahead, attorney Marion," added the judicial authority.

"Your honor, some point in time, a well-dressed young woman in the audience will try to leave the courthouse. You must prevent her from leaving."

"Why?"

"She is the assassin!"

The judge and his assistants opened wide their eyes.

As for the district attorney, he made a simple gesture of the hand and had no other alternative but to wait and see, convincing himself that, some point in time, the court must stop Attorney Marion for "mental aberration" and his attempt to make a mockery of justice.

The defense lawyer went on with his cross-examination.

"Mr. Aden, how do you know for sure that the man you saw leaving the elevator wasn't instead a woman? Don't have any doubt about the person's gender?"

"Honorable attorney, to tell you the truth, I thought to have seen a man. However, since you have just raised the question, I am no longer certain of that person's gender, who had left the premises by nine-thirty. Indeed, I can make a mistake; the more so as men and women, in these days, almost dress the same way. How can we lessen this margin of error?"

"We can do it easily, Mr. Aden. Let's project the camera film showing people's whereabouts, on that Sunday morning, between nine-thirty and ten in the morning."

A court expert complied.

When the film reached the image responding to the description given by the superintendent, Attorney Marion exclaimed, "Stop!"

Then, he proceeded, "Mr. Aden, don't you think this is a woman? You must look hard."

"Yes, Honorable Counselor, this is a woman, if I go by the thoracic cage and the rest of the morphology. The breasts and the behind certainly remind me of a female's."

A stranger's wonderful chronicles, Book II

There was a burst of laughter.

Soon after, a beautiful woman, wearing a flowered dress and high-hilled shoes, stood up and tried to leave hurriedly, but, the informed police officers accosted her.

"What's going on?" she screamed. "I have the right not to assist to the court session. Do we live in a country practicing dictatorship?"

"Miss.," stated the judge, "they have pointed to you as being Louison Calliste's killer."

"I am the reporter's killer! I don't understand.

"Didn't they say that the so-called Laurent Saint-Jean has killed that man?

"The District Attorney and all the witnesses profess such opinion."

"By the way, what's your name?" inquired the judge.

"Rose Lewis"

"Do you know late Louison Calliste?"

"No, I don't know that man.

"Additionally, I was home, that whole Sunday morning, at the time of the murder."

"No, that morning, you did go to the condominium in which late Louison Calliste lived."

"No, I didn't."

The judge beckoned to the technician assigned to the Justice Department and ordered, "Show the film once more."

The technician complied. The thin person's image reappeared.

"Miss, isn't it you on the film?"

The woman burst out crying. Few minutes after, she recognized, "Yes, it's I."

"Then, Miss Lewis, I have no choice but to place you under arrest until further notice."

Two police officers, with no further ado, left with the woman to Central Booking.

"Your honor," argued the district attorney, "Ms. Lewis' presence at the condominium doesn't invalidate the fact that Mr. Laurent Saint-Jean has emptied his revolver to the victim's stomach and killed him."

"Mr. District Attorney," stated the judge, "before answering your question, let me get further explanation from Attorney Luckner Marion."

Having said that, he turned around and proceeded, "Attorney Luckner Marion, I don't know how you have anticipated Ms. Rose Lewis' reaction; however, I must recognize that you do have a gift for detecting unprecedented events.

"I hope you will present irrefutable proofs of Mr. Laurent Saint-Jean's innocence."

"Your honor, I will take great delight in proving my client's innocence."

After a short moment of silence, he went on, "Your honor, are you in possession of the ballistic report?

"I hope you are."

A stranger's wonderful chronicles, Book II

"Yes, honorable Attorney," replied the judge. "By a struck of luck, Doctor Polémon Danton, the forensic expert put himself at our disposal."

"Good.

"Doctor Polémon Danton, you have probably removed two sets of bullets from the reporter's body. There are three in the stomach and two in the head. These bullets didn't come from the same gun?"

"No, they didn't.

"The ones that I have removed from late Louison Calliste's stomach have come from a forty-five caliber revolver. These I have pulled out of the victim's head have come from an exceptional caliber firearm.

"Evidently, the killer has used an assault rifle with a silencer; otherwise, the whole condominium would have heard the shots."

"Did someone shoot these two series of bullets at the same time, I mean in the neighborhood of nine-thirty?"

"No, he didn't. The bullets in the victim's head were shot in the neighborhood of nine-thirty."

"Based on your expertise, Doctor, could the victim survive his wounds, following the shots from the assault rifle?"

"No, he couldn't. He died instantly."

"Thank you, Doctor Polémon Danton," concluded the defense lawyer.

Then, turning toward the audience, he concluded, "Your honor, members of the judicial panel, ladies and gentlemen of the jury, my client has emptied his gun to a cadaver stomach.

The impossible homicide

"Consequently, he couldn't commit a homicide.

"The real killer, Ms. Rose Lewis has certainly slid the assault rifle under the bed…"

A dead silence reigned over the courtroom.

Nobody could anticipate the decision of the judicial panel that held an emergency meeting.

One hour after, the panel returned.

The chief justice stated,

Ladies and gentlemen of the jury,

Mr. District Attorney,

Members of the audience,

The defense lawyer has put forth argumentation that proves the impossibility for his client to commit the homicide. For one reason or another, we have agreed with him.

However, ladies and gentlemen, before a final decision, we would like to have recourse to the lawyer expertise to allow us to access to the absolute truth.

Attorney Luckner Marion, how can you enlighten us further?

The lawyer complied with the judge's request and smiling replied.

A stranger's wonderful chronicles, Book II
I will be delighted to do so, your honor.

Then, he presented his findings to the astonishment of the judicial panel, the district attorney, the jurors, his client and the other members of the audience.

Ladies and gentlemen,

The reporter, late Louison Calliste, had reputation for being an excellent investigator having the ability to unravel skeletons from others' closets and expose them to the public.

In reality (and the public ignores it), that man had hurt so many innocent people.

To start with, he created a criminal organization specialized in blackmails.

He had accomplices all over the world, who had acquired the skills to discover others' secrets, whether these go back twenty years or not.

Once the pieces of information obtained, the organization got in touch with the victims and threatened to expose them to the public, unless they paid large monthly fees the reporter kept a lion share of them.

Worse still, this reporter had recourse to cruel sadism: if the victims became penniless, he divulged their so-called secrets (which he had often made up from appearances, insinuations, and bawdy innuendoes, on his televised program entitled "The moment of truth".

To this day, that organization has done harm too many and has prevented them from moving ahead on the social ladder.

Many of its victims, such as the late congressional representative George Dumont, the school superintendent of secondary school, Raboto Saint-Ange and many more, have lost their cool and committed suicide.

As far as my client is concerned, the late reporter Louison Calliste, a year before, called him up to tell him about his knowledge of his extramarital relationship with a woman.

Despite the inaccuracy of the revelation, my client accepted to pay five hundred dollars a month to a bank account designated by the criminal organization.

My client didn't want to create a scandal in the bosom of his family and another one.

Finally, my client became unemployed, despite his great education: he holds a Master Degree in the fields of political science and public administration. Such lousy situation has reduced his family to the shadow of itself. Next month, the bank will probably repossess the family house.

The family's hope comes from a job offer made to my client by Syndrill & co House.

However, since he turned penniless, he no longer had the money to give that criminal organization; thus, the reporter, late Louison Calliste, without any kind compassion, started last Sunday an assassination character campaign against Mr. Saint-Jean.

He stated during his last broadcasting the following, 'Syndrill & Co House would make a big mistake by offering Laurent Saint-Jean such important function, in the capacity of administrative division chief.

'This man doesn't have enough morality to fulfill such function. During my next Sunday broadcasting, I will be more specific.'

It was a warning to my client against his decision not to continue to pay.'

My client saw red; which anyone may understand: he has a charming wife and two lovely children.

The impossible homicide

Then, out of despair, he took his licensed handgun and tried to remove that monster from the surface of earth, even if he had to spend the rest of his life in jail.

I seize the opportunity to ask the justice department to show leniency toward Rose Lewis who has also fallen victim of black-mail from the criminal organization.

For the first time, in her life, she has found the man of her dream.

However, Louison Calliste threatened to expose her on TV because of an alleged indecent background, which the diabolic reporter had totally fabricated.

Like my client, Rose Lewis had lost her cool and had shot the blackmailer twice in his head.

I regret to have designated the true author of the homicide in order to exculpate my client.

If Ms. Rose Lewis is listening to my statement, I want her to believe that she will enjoy better days in the bosom of society.

A deep silence reigned over the courtroom. Nobody could grasp attorney Luckner Marion's perspicuity scope.

The chief justice pronounced,

A stranger's wonderful chronicles, Book II

Ladies and gentlemen,

I must recognize Attorney Luckner Marion's explanation valid-
ity. Having said that, I declare that, you, Laurent Saint-Jean,
are innocent of any crime. You are free to return to your family.
However, you must keep living straight.

"Thank you, your honor," said the accused feelingly.

"But, just a minute!" went on the judge. "Attorney Luckner Marion, did your client and Rose Lewis let you know about the blackmail."

"No, your honor, they didn't."

"How do you manage to know all these facts in their minute details?"

"Your honor, do you want really to know?"

"Yes, all of us in this courtroom want to know."

"Well, you may not want to believe, but I have a profound intuition of things.

"I know the alpha and the omega of reality.

"Nevertheless, ladies and gentlemen, I can't tell you anything else.

"I am glad to have a bent toward goodness."

The judge opened wide his eyes and pointed to Marion. He had just understood everything; for he always took delight in Brian Clifford's *"Marvelous Stranger's Chronicles."*

"Impossible!" shouted the District Attorney. "I knew it. That man is a joker. But I would find the truth."

The impossible homicide

Attorney Luckner Marion stood up, walked to the judge and handed an envelope over to him, with the note written on it: "to be opened in private".

Then, he got closer to the District Attorney and whispered to his ear, "Now, you are an irreproachable District Attorney.

"However, ten years ago, you did accept money from *Big Papa Marc-Laurel…*"

The district attorney looked at him straight in the eyes.

"Fortunately," he went, "this is our secret which nobody will know; for, you behave now in a straightforward fashion."

He shook hand with him. Then, he beckoned to Laurent Saint-Jean and his family to follow him.

He took them to a supermarket and asked them (including their children) to buy whatever they wanted to.

Next, he took them home and remained standing.

Finally, he kissed everybody good bye, not without saying, "Laurent, the owners of Syndrill & Co House will call you, one minute from now. They have seen everything on TV. Their offer hasn't changed."

Indeed, the phone rang. It was Bob Mansoura of the Syndrill & Co House. The others in the house overheard Laurent saying, "Mr. Mansoura, I am free tomorrow. I will be there by ten in the morning. I will be there."

Laurent jumped up and down with joy.

"Listen, my friend," cut in a happy Luckner Marion, "I must leave.

A stranger's wonderful chronicles, Book II

"All is well that ends well. Laurent, you have enough money in your pocket to manage before receiving your first check from your new function.

"As for you, Irene, you have enough money in your bag to handle the current family obligations."

Instinctively, Laurent went for his pant pocket and Irene for her bag.

They shook their head in disbelief; for, they didn't know when that man could give them monetary gifts without their knowledge.

Once more Luckner Marion hugged all members of the family and left the house.

The Saint-Jean rushed going outside to wave him goodbye, but they didn't see any sign of the *marvelous stranger*.

In the meantime, the judge opened the envelope in his office and couldn't believe his eyes.

He saw an important bundle of dollar bills, as well as a note saying,

Your Honor,

I don't mean any disrespect.

You are poor because of your honesty. For days, your family and you have badly eaten.

For the same reason, you have been paying your mortgage late.

Call you wife to tell her to wait for you at the house door.

The impossible homicide

You will take her and your children to the supermarket to buy substantial foods. Then, you will pay your mortgage on time.

By the way, your Honor, you haven't mistaken: I am the marvelous stranger.

◘   ◘

◘

The reporter Brian Clifford visited Saint-Jean family, as well as Judge Romain Lagrange and his family. They all expressed their astonishment with the *marvelous stranger*. As many beneficiaries of this man did, they had doubt about his existence, which doubt they had to dispel at once, since the gifts received from that stranger were real.

Rose Lewis, freed from jail fifteen days earlier, gave the reporter a big surprise, by welcoming him warmly and offering him something to eat.

Some point in time, she broke the silence, "Brian, you understand my dilemma, as you keep chasing the marvelous stranger for more than a year. That man has confused my mind.

"I tried to stay objective; however, how can I explain his having detailed information on me?

"Well, I have resumed my work. The owner of the business and his wife don't think that society should ostracize me after I have freed everybody from a vermin, posing as a great reporter. Then, life continues.

A stranger's wonderful chronicles, Book II

"Once in a while, I think that I have dreamed of the *marvelous stranger*. However, how to explain this letter I have received from him, as well as the content of the envelope.

Rose Lewis handed over the letter to Brian who eagerly read it at once,

My beautiful petite rose,

As all roses, you have had cactus responsible for putting an end to blackmailer's life. However, you have never ceased to practice the good.

Would you forgive me for having identified you as late Louison Calliste's killer? I could have caused you greater harm; except I didn't know how I could assist my client without the revelation.

My beautiful petite rose, from now on, I won't turn a hurdle in your way.

To prove it, I have enclosed a small amount of money as your marriage gift.

Signed, Luckner Marion.

Nota bene: don't waste your time looking for a certain Luckner Marion who has embarked on this legal affair. He has existed for the occasion.

The impossible homicide

The man behind the occasional lawyer is everywhere and assumes a multitude of names.

You will have a marvelous communal life.

Brian Clifford, after having read the letter several times, returned it to Rose.

"Well, who is the prince charming?" he inquired.

"I have no idea, Brian," replied Rose. "I have one lover in my life. This devilish Louison Calliste's blackmail may have cooled him off.

"What infuriates me (the woman closed her fists), the blackmailer has simply made up a story of my intimacy with my boss, Mr. Rambour, while his wife takes me for a member of their family…"

Rose stopped talking. The phone rang. She took the receiver. As the caller took his time to speak, the woman was about to hang up.

"It's Ricoh," announced the ex-lover.

The woman beckoned to Brian to tell him that someone close to her was calling.

"Ah! You call me to insult me. Otherwise, what do you want?"

After a short moment of silence, Rose argued, "You just heard a rumor, and you dashed out…

"My dear friend, do you call that love…?

"I want to know."

"Please, darling, wait for me. I am coming over."

A stranger's wonderful chronicles, Book II

Rose hung up and said to Brian, "My ex-boyfriend has called me from a phone booth nearby. He told me that he would be here in five minutes.

"Stay. You will undoubtedly be the first one to know his intentions."

Prudently, Ricoh entered the house and had a surprise to see Brian Clifford and his camera operator. He had a moment of hesitation, not knowing what to think.

Then, without any specific reason (maybe under the influence of a great emotion), he rushed getting near Rose Lewis, kneeled before her and pronounced, "Darling, would you ever forgive me?"

The woman took some time before answering, "Yes, my love, I forgive you."

"Do you want to marry me next week?"

"Yes, Ricoh, I want to…"

"Amen!" exclaimed Brian.

Next, he took leave of the lovers, not without reminding them, "Once more, the *marvelous stranger* has given proof of his existence."

Alone with his lover, Ricoh would like to know what was going on.

"I don't want any secret between us," he added.

"Ricoh," stated the woman. "you should know today that I don't keep any secret from you.

"The Marvelous Stranger has sent me this."

Then, she handed over the envelope to him. He opened it and had a big surprise at seeing the check amount.

The impossible homicide

"Yes, my love," pointed out Rose, "he has been my guardian angel, during my trial time…"

(27)

The family Without Electrical Power

By Antoine Archange Raphael

*F*or days, Marceau Polarde had an intuition that his family would experience bad days. Actually, the family situation had never changed positively. Marceau, the only employed family member, worked for a big department store and earned a derisory income.

His wife, Edith, having a frail constitution, couldn't take the pressure of waking early in the morning to go to work. Her doctor advised her to stay home for a while to have absolute rest until further notice.

Marceau's income could barely help the family to meet its monthly obligations, which kept on increasing with the galloping inflation.

Additionally, the Polardes had three children, namely Aida, a young lady of seventeen, Paulette, another one of fifteen, and Patrice, a young man of ten.

Soon, Aida would finish high school and would start college studies, a coming step that gave the parents cause for worry, because of the exorbitant college tuitions.

Paulette attended the secondary school in the neighborhood and reached eleventh grade.

As for Patrice, he would complete soon his primary studies.

For quite a while, the electric bills had tremendously increased. Marceau had sent e-mails and notes enclosed with the return facture envelopes. However, the company NEE (National Electrical Energy) had never addressed Marceau's reason for concern. The man had also phoned the company, but the employees sounded as confused as he.

A stranger's wonderful chronicles, Book II

As a last resort, he wrote to the department of energy, but the government answer gave him no hope.

That answer was as follows,

Dear Mr. Polarde,

We have granted your request a great deal of consideration. Within three months, we will let you know about our finale decision.

Usually, we leave the primary decision to NEE. It often finds a better solution than us.

In the meantime, Mr. Polarde, receive the expression of our sympathy

Signed, Beatrice Paulson.

Division Chief.

After having read over the government letter, Marceau Polarde realized that, in a modern society, the wealthy corporations impose their rules.

He mumbled, "I can't believe that the government leaves its subjects at the mercy of people actuated only by profits. It's like asking a cat to watch over a piece cheese.

One day, he received from NEE a disconnect warning within the following ten days, unless they received one thousand and five hundred dollars owed by the family.

The family without electrical power

In their statement, the corporation people didn't allow the family to pay on account.

They offered one option: either the family paid the total amount or it had to face interruption of service.

Marceau, Edith and their children wondered if they were living in a world made for human beings in situation. How can society reach such degree of insensitiveness?

They didn't need to go too far to have the answer to their question; the media had spoken daily about the high rate of unemployment, homelessness, starved…, while the wealthy enjoyed themselves, made fun of the poor, made a show of their fortunes.

One day, Edith, out of despair, asked, "Did God send us to this world to experience a hellish life forever?"

"Oh! Mom," cut in Aida feelingly, "God has nothing to do with the lousy situation of the planet.

"On the contrary, He gave it to us as a gift. It depends on us to manage this gift.

"We must simply recognize that our leaders stop having a heart and living like human beings who should manage this planet as good fathers and mothers.

"That's all."

After a pause, Aida went on, "Mom, there is a poem written by an author who has, maybe, shared your concern.

A stranger's wonderful chronicles, Book II

"This poem, for some unexplained reason, has a strong effect on me. Would you like to hear it?"

"Of course, Dada, I would."

"I would like also to hear it, Dada," cut in the father. "It would certainly distract our minds from worry."

"Then, here it is,

God,

As the Creator of galaxies
And their beings,
You should know that
They have associated Your Name
With the entire world
Misdeeds
And injustice.

Tell me:
That
You are not,
Like

The family without electrical power

Our masters and dictators,

A seeker of praise

And absolute obedience;

Tell me,

That,

Unlike our powerful

And policy makers,

You don't believe in the formula:

Might makes right;

Tell me,

That

The association of your name

To all the world misdeeds,

And injustice

Results from frauds;

Tell me

That,

In the mist of time,

A stranger's wonderful chronicles, Book II

Because of your boundless love,

You've embarked

On free creativity;

Tell me,

That,

If You wanted to,

You would have kept

All the gold

And all the wealth,

Of the galaxies

And our planet's,

Sources, origins and results

Of unlimited and unwise Power,

As well as of misdeeds,

Scorns and animosity;

Tell me,

That,

You wouldn't hold

These words full of hatred,

The family without electrical power

Antagonistic sects

Heap on each other;

That You wouldn't practice

Prejudice against anyone;

And that You wouldn't be scornful

Of the underdog.

God,

Tell me Yourself

What You really are.

Edit couldn't believe her ears.

She had just discovered her oldest child thoughtfulness, who had chosen such meaningful piece of literature.

She pulled her against her bosom and kissed her on the hair. Finally, she recognized, "Aida, my beloved daughter, how deep are you in thought!

"Let me tell you, today that I am pride having a learned young woman for a child."

"Oh, mom!" the daughter exclaimed. "I am not a learned young lady."

"You will have a bright future."

"My dear Edith, I do have the same impression," added the father.

A stranger's wonderful chronicles, Book II

After a pause, he advanced, "My friends, this author allows me to grasp an aspect of reality I didn't quite understand. Nobody knows God's intentions."

Indeed, this little conversation and the reciting of the poem had temporarily distracted the Polardes from their worry. They had to face again reality and wondered what they would do to pay the company such a large sum of money.

Actually, how to explain such invoice, while they lived in a small house and only used electricity to cook food, to give light in the house at night and watch television?

The Polardes got excited.

For several days, they started to call everywhere to find out what course of action they could adopt, under such circumstances; for, in this twenty-first century, how could the live without electricity that makes all the appliances work?

For some unexplained reason, these great corporations have lost personal contact with the public. Actually, they have programmed major part of the services, to such a part, they have left the operations to computerized machines.

When you find a human employee, he is incompetent and sends you to another incompetent employee…

Finally, the day of service interruption arrived. In few seconds, the electric appliances at the Polardes' home plunged into deep silence.

The family without electrical power

The Polardes could still enjoy the sunlight. However, they wondered how they would proceed at night.

Fortunately, Edit had still kept her propane stoves and would do her best to feed her family.

The Polardes overheard an animated conversation going on not far from their home.

They looked through the window and saw a well-dressed man in discussion with the NEE employees.

"Listen, my friends," said the well-dressed man, "how can you reduce people to live in darkness?"

"My dear sir," replied one of the NEE employees, "we are soldiers. We have order to terminate the Polardes' service because of nonpayment."

"That's strange."

"What is so strange, sir?" cut in another employee.

Shortly after, he added, "Interruptions of services keep going daily. Why should you worry so much about them?"

"Well, electricity, like water forming the rivers, blood in our veins, oxygen we breathe, comes from our common *Mother Nature*.

"If she turned off the electric supplies, as you have just done, what would you say? What would be the NEE's reaction?"

"We don't have time to philosophize, sir. The Polardes must pay if they want our services back."

A stranger's wonderful chronicles, Book II

"Sir, you are mistaken," argued the well-dressed man. "The Polardes will have their electrical supply free."

"Impossible."

"In my dictionary, I don't include this predicate."

"Perhaps, you have alluded to clandestine connection."

"No, I have referred to another source of energy."

"You just talk nonsense. These people don't have the means to pay their electric bill, how would they access to more expensive sources of energy. You are rambling."

"What will be, will be."

The NEE's employees left in their truck, not without laughing their head off and pointing at the well-dressed man. They thought that he was mentally disturbed.

The *civilized man* knocked at the Polardes' residence door.

Slowly, Edit opened the door to greet the visitor. A board smile opened his face.

He said, "It's Edith Polarde?"

"Yes, I am," replied the woman.

"Are you Marceau Polarde's wife?

"You are the fourth child of Gamelan family. You attended the Catholic Sisters School, located at Mount Mouton, a clean neighborhood. Then, you pursued literature studies at the State University. But you suffer from poor health condition and can't find employment."

The family without electrical power

The woman made gestures of the hands. Then, she stated, "Since we find ourselves on familiar ground, I don't have any choice. Where do you come from, my dear sir? I don't know you at all; but, you know my life in minute details.

"Did you conduct any inquiry about me before visiting me?"

Having overhead this conversation, Marceau and the children joined the man and Edith at the entrance door.

"What's going on, Edit?" cut in the husband.

"All is well?" asked the children together.

"Sir, Listen…," started the husband.

The visitor made a gesture of the hand to stop him. Then, he rushed saying, "I know that the family is in a gloomy mood. I have just met the NEE's employees who have told me that they have suspended your electric service.

"I have told them that they have misbehaved; for, electricity, like water we drink, blood running in our veins, is a gift from our common *Mother Nature*.

"What would happen to mankind (including NEE) if our common mother cuts off our electric supply?"

"Mr.," cut in Edit, "you sound strange, but you represent a breeze of fresh air.

"Your optimism is contagious."

"Thank you, Edit.

A stranger's wonderful chronicles, Book II

"My friends (he spoke to the whole family), don't worry too much about your predicament. Together, we will find a better accommodation."

"But, who are you, sir," Marceau raised his voice. "How can you know so much about us?"

Edith touched slightly the husband's face to calm him down. Then, she stated, "Darling, we must never lose our civilization. As much as we stay together with our wonderful children, we will keep our civilization.

"This gentleman hasn't done us any harm. Despite our poverty, he stops by for a little chat. This is the expression of civilization, isn't it?"

"Darling, you are right," finally recognized the husband after having kissed his wife on the lips.

The children, in their turn, hugged their mother.

Marceau beckoned the visitor in and invited him to occupy one of the armchairs in the living room. Finally, he stated, "Sir, my wife is right. I have no justification to make you responsible for my predicament. On the contrary, you intend to distract our mind from worry."

"Marceau Polarde…" started the visitor.

"You know my name?" inquired Marceau

"My name is Marc-Laurel Nicholas.

"I have a deep intuition of events and I know the alpha and the omega of reality."

"Mr. Nicholas, aren't you a little too presumptuous?"

"First, I would like you to stop being formal with me," said the visitor.

The family without electrical power

Then, shortly after, he stated, "I will give you proof of my divinatory skills, once I finished with your wife."

"Oh!" advanced, Edith. "Marceau, children, your joining me have prevented me to hear a complete revelation about me.

"I don't know how he has managed, but the man knows me better than I do."

"Is it true, Edith?" inquired the husband.

"It is true.

"Now let him go on with his revelation about me."

"Well, Edit," continued Mr. Nicholas, "your children don't know it, but you have studied, as I have said, modern literature at the State University."

"Is it true?" asked the children together.

"Yes, my children," answered the mother. "You are the living proofs..."

"How can we be living proofs of your education?" inquired Aida.

"Why do you speak so formally?

"Because, from the cradle to the time you have to go to school, I have only used formal English."

"I understand now," cut in Paulette.

"But, everybody, keep quiet," suggested Edith. "Let me hear the oracle."

"Well," went on Mr. Nicholas, "without others' knowledge, you have written two books.

The first one is entitled, *From the girl to the woman.*

A stranger's wonderful chronicles, Book II

"The other one, at which you are still working, you call it, *The woman in the world.*"

Edith grabbed the visitor by the wrist. Then, she screamed, "You are a spy! Nobody, even my husband, can know something like that...

"Additionally, how would I complete the first novel? They have just cut off my electric connection."

"Edith, you must forgive me. For one reason or another, my steps have led me to your house.

"But, be a little patient. I will tell you about another source of electricity, once I finished with my revelation about Marceau.

"You will make revelation about me?" astonished the husband.

"Why won't I? You don't stand above revelation, as far as I am concerned.

"You are the second child of the Polardes. You attended University and majored in modern technology. For one reason or another, you have never found a position in your field of activity.

"You have conceived of a car tire..."

"Marc-Laurel, I take my hat to you," cut in Marceau. "How can anyone explain these qualities of yours?"

"My friends, let me tell you a little secret. I don't know the origin of my talents. However, I can grasp reality in its totality.

"For example, I already know that Aida will become a physician."

"What!" exclaimed the young lady.

The family without electrical power

"Paulette will be a lawyer."

"Incredible!" said the latter. "I have always yearned for such profession."

"As far as you are concerned, Patrice," went Mr. Nicholas, "you will study, like your father, modern technology."

The Polardes remained dumbfounded. Finally, Marc-Laurel stated, "My friends, I have wasted too much time to prove you my skills; while the true reason that pushes me to your house, I haven't touched on it.

"I am an engineer by trade. I specialize myself in prefabricated houses.

"Along the way, I sell almost everything.

"I have just launched a company specializing in solar power. I have chosen your home as a pilot in your neighborhood. With your authorization, I will install solar panels on your house roof. You will certainly draw your neighbors' attention. One never can tell, they will become my customers.

"What do you think?"

"Marc-Laurel," intervened Marceau, "If you are telling the truth, I will take you for God in person."

"My dear Marceau, look at the window. The technicians wait for my signal."

"My dear friend," said Edith, "since you have conquered the heart of the house master, let the light shine once more in the house."

"Amen!" said the children together.

A stranger's wonderful chronicles, Book II

"Marc-Laurel," added Edith, "once we have electricity again, you must keep your word."

"Which one is that?" inquired the benefactor.

"You promise to help me publish my first book."

"I will do it. By the same token, I will advise you, Marceau, on the way to let concerned people take an interest in your car tire project."

"Oh! You haven't forgotten," cut in Marceau.

"Never," replied Marc-Laurel.

The technicians received authorization to install the solar panels on the home roof and completed their connection with the main electric cables.

By six P.M., the Polardes' home shone brightly.

As promised, Marc-Laurel helped Edith to follow the different steps leading to the publication of her first book on the internet.

First, he converted the manuscript to *PDF*, then, chose an image and colors for the cover and, finally, downloaded the whole book to an editor specialized in *books on demand.*

Edith, her husband and their children couldn't believe their eyes.

This woman had just fulfilled her dream to become an international author.

As for Marceau, Marc-Laurel helped him downloading his project to the *Society of Inventions.*

Soon after, the inventor had received a statement from that business, letting him know they will be in contact with him within forty hours.

The family without electrical power
"Your project looks great," concluding that society's employee.

The neighbors, sympathetic with the Polardes, marveled at the goodness of solar energy enjoyed by that family, and had recourse to Marc-Laurel Nicholas competence. Shortly after, other neighbors followed in the Polardes footsteps.

Marc-Laurel Nicholas' customers had never ceased to receive brochures from NEE letting them know that it would strive to make things better for them if they rejoined it. But those clients, fully satisfied with solar power, could no longer live without this new source of energy; thus, the NEE's brochures went straight to the garbage cans.

◘　　◘

◘

The reporter Brian Clifford contacted the Polardes as soon as possible, with a view to making his "Marvelous stranger's chronicles" going.

Before gathering the pieces of information, Brian sat at the family table and enjoyed foods prepared by the Mrs. Polarde.

"Edith," confessed the reporter, "I must tell you that you are a true cordon blue. You know how to season these dishes to flatter the most delicate palace.

"With good foods like these, you will always keep your family happy."

"Amen!" exclaimed Marceau.

"It's our mother," said the children together.

A stranger's wonderful chronicles, Book II

As usual, the Polardes let Brian know that Marc-Laurel Nicholas' intervention had a variety of meanings.

To start with, he looked like a mentally unbalanced person. However, they had no other alternative but to bow to the evidence that he wasn't rambling; for, he had made revelations about Edith and Marceau, which looked like tape recording events.

Next, the Polarde had to bow to the fact; for, the NEE had actually cut off the family electrical supply.

Therefore, since they didn't have a penny, they had to recognize that solar panels installed by Marc-Laurel worked perfectly (even better than the conventionally lighting received from NEE).

In the same line of thought, the monetary gift from Marc-Laurel didn't fall in the realm of fantasy; for, the Polarde had used it to go shopping, honored some obligations and many other things.

Brian Clifford couldn't prevent himself from having a shock when Edith told him, "Brian, my dear friend, the mystery doesn't stop there."

"What is it?" inquired the excited reporter.

"As I have mentioned it, the man has helped me publish my first book…"

"Just a minute!" cut in Brian. "You want to refer to 'From the girl to the woman'?

"But, it is you, Edith!

"Oh! Edith, don't lose any minute. Tell me exactly what did happen."

The family without electrical power

"Brian, the man has helped me publish my first book through an agency specializing in *books on demand*.

"Three months have elapsed. I have received a check amounted to five thousand dollars: my book has won the grand prize of a literary contest. And, since then, they have been buying my book at the rate of ten per day.

"The man has allowed me to have, like anyone else, an income and the possibility to meet my family's needs.

"It's crucial.

"Before meeting with Marc-Laurel Nicholas, or the one who had borrowed this name, I lived with no hope. Because of my frail constitution, Marceau thought it was wise to stay home. To fill up my hours of loneliness, I started to write, without knowing that I represented a gold mine.

"Fortunately, that man's perspicuity makes me enter the tunnel of creativity and glory.

"Brian, my friend, there is more, but let Marceau tell you in person."

Marceau took a while to gather and order his thoughts. Then, he said, "Brian, my dear friend, to this day, I don't know if I can affirm under oath that I have met a real man or a spirit.

"You know what I mean…

"All I can say, we do have now a source of electricity other than the one we used to receive from NEE.

"Additionally, the man in question has helped me present my inventive idea which, soon, will bring me some cash.

A stranger's wonderful chronicles, Book II

"Yesterday, Brian, I received this letter from the *Society of Invention, Co.*"

Having said that, Marceau handed over the *saving letter* to the reporter

Dear Marceau Polarde,

I am writing to let you know that I have good news to tell you.

Your inventive idea, according to reliable sources, has reached its final stage.

If all is well, the International Tire House will send you a contract as soon as possible and other participation rules, within few days to come.

From that point, the sky will be the limits.

I present my congratulations to you Mr. Polardes.

Bob Cutler, the Chairman.

Marceau, from that point on, regained his optimism in life, with his wife being a well-known writer and above all, with the news according to which *The International Tire House*, the most important tire manufacture in the world, he would make money on every tire sold.

The reporter Brian Clifford had no choice but to take leave of such remarkable family.

The family without electrical power

He would go straight to the magazine office to edit this family's account on its meeting with the marvelous stranger and to entrust the executive secretary, by the way his lovely wife, with the transcript.

He smiled, thinking about his next visit to an old acquaintance: Sabina in "Sabina's daughter in a state of danger"

(28)

Sabina's Daughter In a state Of danger

By Antoine Archange Raphael

*A*s they say, time flies. George Musa remembers his encounter with Sabina, as if it was yesterday. He sees in his mind that beautiful woman who, first, seemed to sink into madness, by taking him for a prince charming of whom she had dreamed, while she was only twelve.

By the way, Sabina intended to stay far from her cruel husband who had confused her with home ornament.

George Musa remembers to have presented all sorts of arguments to persuade her to get off his car and rejoin her husband and her children; but Sabina had insisted on taking George Musa for that prince charming dreamed of in her adolescence.

Later on, she would attend the State University and obtain her doctorate degree in sociology, with a view to founding an organization aiming at helping women in distress throughout the world.

Since, then, George and Sabina have lived in harmony, the more so, once she thinks about his *prince charming*, he feels like an irresistible desire to spend delicious time with her.

Yes, time flies. Sabina's organization has blossomed and has acquired international reputation.

With respect to her children with George, they have grown up, to such a par, they are attending university.

Since George, assuming a multitude of names and personalities designated so picturesquely by the reporter Brian Clifford by the expression,

A stranger's wonderful chronicles, Book II

"marvelous stranger", travels all over the world, leaving a trail of good-ness behind him, Sabina has raised his children, namely Rose-Yolande and Rainier, in a sweet but firm manner.

Their mother doesn't prevent them from having friends; but she has never stopped telling them, "Rose, Rainier, don't ever stop using judg-ment. If you have doubt about a friend's wisdom, you must manage to avoid his or her company.

"I believe that your father, an exceptional man, would condone my viewpoint."

On the other hand, Sabina has never missed the opportunity to remind them of her intention to remain not only their mother for life (since destiny wants it this way), but also their friend and advisor.

She also advises them to trust their father, "a man extremely generous and intellectually brilliant".

One day, Sabina thought to have detected some sadness on her daugh-ter's face.

As the latter sat on the loveseat in the living room, with her hand to her chin, the mother joined her, having an intuition that she would confine in her.

She pulled her daughter against her bosom before saying, "Rose, I have never seen you so pensive before. What's going on, my dear?"

Sabina's daughter in a state of danger

The daughter betrayed an instant of hesitation before answering nonchalantly, "Mom, everything is ok."

"Do you have an affair of the heart?"

"Oh, mom!"

"Listen, Rose. As I have said it, I am your mother for life. For the same reason, if you want, I will act as your friend and advisor for life.

"I don't forbid Rainier and you to have lovers. However, I can already draw your attention on the fact that if someone really loves you, he won't have any fear for meeting your parents. You must never accept a secret affair. Above all, do you best to have intimate relationships after marriage. Many men take interest in you as a symbol of beauty and sexuality. Nevertheless, you have gone beyond this simple image.

"Don't behave like those loose women who go to bed with everybody."

"Mom, as usual, you don't lack wisdom," cut in the daughter. "I will never fail to follow your advice."

Shortly after, she went on, "Listen, mom, I don't really know how to explain my dilemma.

"A schoolfellow called Joseph Montluc comes to me, once in a while, to tell me that he loves me.

"I must confess that he pleases me."

"Rose, my beautiful darling, it's a nice beginning.

"Nevertheless, why do you have some reservation about him, my dear?"

"Mom, I can't explain this strange impression I have about him."

A stranger's wonderful chronicles, Book II

"You have strange impression about him! Rose, what do you mean?"

"Mom, I am serious. Whenever he gets near me, for reason unknown to me, his body gives out unpleasant, frightening vibes."

The mother smiled at her daughter's possible ingenuity.

"Rose, my darling," she acknowledged, "as you have awareness of it, I have studied sociology and psychology and obtained a doctoral degree; but this is the first time I have heard a phenomenon of this sort.

"How can you describe these vibes?"

"Mom, whenever he gets near me, intense heat comes out of his body

"Mom, I don't want to take a joke too far; I mean that an intense heat emanates from that man's body, to such a par that I will get burned if I try to touch it."

The mother thought hard and believed that maybe her daughter had taken a certain foresight after her father. She had no doubt that Joseph Montluc could have uncontrollable drawbacks. "What may they be?" she concluded.

"Mom, you turn pensive."

"My darling, why do you think that man's body gives out so much heat?" inquired the mother.

Then, after a pause, she suggested, "Why don't you speak to your father?"

"No, mom," replied the young woman. "I have no intention to bother him, as soon as I had a hitch."

Sabina's daughter in a state of danger

"Rose, my darling, come on. What you have just told me is not a hitch.

"By the way, our meetings may bring us joy, as they may bring us a world of bitterness."

"I understand. However, mom, my father, because of his great divinatory skills could prevent me from finding happiness.

"Please, mom, hear me out!

"We are not perfect. Maybe, the intense heat I have felt by Joseph Montluc comes from my vivid imagination. "

"Rose, I don't know what to tell you

"You don't want to tell your father about it; but, believe me, he has already known it."

"That's impossible, mom,"

"You should know that this predicate doesn't exist in your father's dictionary.

"Besides, he and I live in perfect harmony, as I am close to you. He must know what happens to my children. I don't have to tell him anything. He has a profound intuition of my family reality."

"Mom, I don't believe you."

"Well, whenever you see him, ask him what he knows about you. You will see."

"Mom, I will prove you wrong."

"Rose, you will see."

"He won't know anything, unless, you tell him about me in person."

A stranger's wonderful chronicles, Book II

"No, I will never divulge my daughter's secrets without her consent (even to your father)."

"Then, mom, forgive me."

Rainier returned from university. He saw his mother and sister sitting on the sofa and joined them.

The mother stroked his hair and asked, "Handsome, everything is fine?"

"Yes," responded the son, "everything is fine, except that I am dying of starvation."

"We were waiting for you to have supper. The table is ready. Let's go."

As usual, they ate peacefully, not without mentioning the breaking news.

Then, they watched their televised programs. Finally, Rainier went to bed.

As for Rose-Yolande, she followed her mother to her bedroom to continue the conversation.

"Rose, listen," whispered the mother, "I need a good night sleep after having worked hard the whole week. Today is Friday. We will have time…"

The mother turned silent. She had the intuition that her daughter needed her advice.

"Come, my darling," she said while pointing to a chair. Then, she pulled a stool and sat down close to her.

Sabina's daughter in a state of danger

"Rose," she only had the time to utter.

The daughter made a gesture of the hand. Then, she advanced, "Mom, you won't believe me, but I don't know how to explain what I saw today."

"What you saw today? Rose, do you intend to give me a heart attack?"

"No, mom, I don't.

"Mom, listen.

"I have told you about the unpleasant vibes I felt by Joseph Montluc?"

"Yes, you have. I strongly believe that they signal something not too rosy."

"I have bad more bad experiences to tell you about my encounter with that man."

"Rose, don't tell me that you have gone beyond the boundaries of…"

The daughter gagged her mother with her palm and rushed saying, "No, mom, I didn't go beyond the boundaries of wisdom or whatever you have in mind.

"Today, on our way home, since it was Friday, my friends and I hugged each other.

"However, as I got closer to Joseph Montluc, I had to stop short; for some unexplained reason, his face horribly changed into something awful…"

"Rose, what you are talking about?" cut in the mother. "You may want to sleep."

"Mom, I don't want to sleep.

A stranger's wonderful chronicles, Book II

"What I have said betrayed the expression of the truth, beyond the shadow of a doubt."

"But what did go wrong with this Joseph Montluc? My God'! You must use caution about that man."

"Let me tell you what I saw, and you will understand the gravity of the situation."

"What did you see?"

"When I got closer to Joseph Montluc, his face changed into Lucifer's, with a set of horns. Fire came out of his eyes."

"Rose! You have just made up such story, haven't you? You mustn't rely on the figments of your imagination."

"Mom, why would I come to your bedroom, at this hour to tell you a joke? I have told you the truth."

"Rose, excuse my reaction. This vision, you have told me, has gotten me so scared."

"How do you feel now, my darling?"

"Well, mom, since I reach home now and get near you, I have no longer any fear."

The daughter stood up, kissed her mother good night on the cheek and went to her own bedroom.

The mother remained pensive.

She knew her daughter well. She always called her "a learned young woman".

Sabina's daughter in a state of danger

Rose majors, like her mother, in sociology.

She will soon have her master degree and intends to pursue studies until doctorate degree.

She doesn't lack objectivity. Therefore, that day, she wouldn't make up such horrifying story just for fun.

That night, Sabina, alone in her bedroom, put on her nightgown. As she got near her bed, her cellular phone rang. She grabbed the receiver from the nightstand and put the receiver to her ear.

She remained dumfounded: George Musa was on the other end of the line.

"Darling, did I wake you up?" he said.

"No George, you didn't wake me up."

"Rest assured, darling, at any time of the day and the night, you your voice always makes me warm."

Then, after a pause, she inquired, "But, my sweet little George, where are you calling from?"

"Darling, don't get scared. If I tell you, you won't believe me. "Look through the windowpane."

Sabina "complied" as quickly as possible and had the wonderful surprise at seeing a smiling George standing on the sidewalk.

"George, come over," she said. "Don't make any noise. I don't want the excited adults to disturb the peaceful children..."

Soon after, George and Sabina rushed in her bedroom.

A stranger's wonderful chronicles, Book II

The day after, by eight in the morning, Sabina and her children sat at the family table for breakfast.

The children noticed the presence of a fourth set of plate, knife, fork and spoon and asked for "clarification".

The mother didn't answer verbally. With her thumb, she pointed to her bedroom.

Soon after, George showed up, smiling, with arms stretched all the way.

The children rushed towards him to welcome him and cover him with kisses.

"Ah!" observed the father, "you should know, my angels, that family reunions have always created a warm atmosphere and good feelings."

"Dad," observed Rainier, "the word reunion doesn't quite do justice to what I feel now. As far as I am concerned, you look like the messiah coming from heaven."

"Rainier, my dear son, I know that you have a vivid imagination," cut in the father. "You would take an elephant for a mouse."

"Dad, can you blame us?" inquired an overexcited Rose-Yolande. "With a father like you, with unmatched acumen, our imagination must grow wings to match up to your inventive mind."

As the father and his children headed to the table, he said to their mother, "Nana, my darling, what have I you told these children?"

"George, my darling, leave me alone," answered Sabina. "You know very well that their power of imagination comes straight from you."

Sabina's daughter in a state of danger

Shortly after breakfast, George went and sat down on the sofa.

Rose-Yolande sat on the father's laps and rested her head on his chest.

As for Rainier, he pulled a chair, sat behind the sofa and threw his arm around his father's neck.

Sabrina remained seated at the table, surveying the family scene amusingly.

"By the way, George, my darling" she said, "you have surprised me. To the best of my recollection, it's the first time you come to visit me unannounced."

George didn't answer at once.

He took some time to gather his thought. Then, he stated, "My darling, to tell you the truth, I didn't have any intention to visit you tonight."

"Oh!" exclaimed the woman. "How do you explain your presence here?"

"Well, I had an intuition telling me that my beloved daughter is in danger…"

Rose-Yolanda stood up at once and screamed, "Mom!"

"Rose, I have already told you that I will never divulge my children's secret to anyone, even to George.

"How many times do I have to say it?

"You are now adults. You should know how to behave. Thus, I must respect your decisions."

A stranger's wonderful chronicles, Book II

George pulled his daughter all away against him and replaced her head on his chest.

"What's going on?" inquired Rainier.

"Rainier, your sister has incurred serious dangers," answered the father.

Then, speaking to his daughter, he stated, "First, Rose, you have misunderstood me if you believed that I would prevent you from reaching happiness.

"I would never wish you evil.

"Then, once your mother has given you her word, you should not have any doubt about her sincerity.

"My children, you must always pay attention to certain vibes emanating from people; they signal their goodness or their wickedness.

"For example, you, Rose, should ask yourself questions when you felt this intense heat coming from Joseph Montluc's body."

"Dad, you want to tell me that you have the power to detect something like that?"

"Rose, because of our closeness, I will never fail to grasp your reality.

"I have a profound intuition of reality in general; I know the alpha and the omega of our world."

"The alpha and the omega of our world!" echoed Rainier.

"Yes, Rainier, I do. Emmanuela represents no danger."

"Dad!" exclaimed the son.

"Emmanuela!" screamed the mother.

Sabina's daughter in a state of danger

"Oh, mom, it's a recent relationship…" explained the son.

"Good, Rainier. I don't prevent you from looking for your happiness. However, in due time, you must let us know about your activities.

"You shouldn't become a woman's chaser and jeopardize your future career."

The daughter touched lightly her father's chin and said in tone of emotion, "Dad, I feel so sorry to have rejected your assistance. Will you ever forgive me?"

"Rose, you are my daughter. I must forgive you. I have no other choice."

"Thank you, dad.

"But, dad, this is the puzzle I have to decipher: how should I evaluate the unpleasant sensations I felt by Joseph Montluc, while I didn't hate him?"

The father kept silent for a short while. Then, he stated, "Rose, that young man's charm doesn't come naturally; he has learned it after days of rehearsal."

"Dad, I don't understand."

"Rose, my beloved daughter, have you ever heard of modern slavery?"

"Yes, I have."

"Joseph Montluc and many other handsome young men have received training in charming—if I may say so. They seduce beautiful young women, attract them in their homes, drug them and, finally, give them to an association that sells them to rich hedonists, living all over the world, who have nothing else to do beside yearning for young and charming women.

"When these women start coming to age, or time has taken the bloom from their faces, the criminals stop taking any interest in their bodies and, unhesitatingly, give them a drug overdose and kill them.

"You understand now the meaning of intense heat vibes emanated from this *Romeo's* body and the scary image of Lucifer appearing on his face.

"My dear daughter, this handsome and charming Joseph Montluc belongs to a criminal ruthless organization.

"His father is one of the owners."

Rose-Yolande and her brother opened wide their eyes.

The siblings thought they had dealt with adolescents like themselves, but their friends had rather reached a point of no return in terms of rottenness.

"I have more to tell you," went on the father.

"What else, dad?" inquired Rose. "You must tell us everything."

"Yes, dad, you must tell us everything," added Rainier. "I didn't know that others had put my beloved sister in serious dangers."

Sabina stood up and came to sit down on the sofa close to George's left side. Then, in a melodious tone, she entreated, "My love, I don't have to remind you that you have chosen to help others. You don't need any encouragement from anyone to act accordingly.

Sabina's daughter in a state of danger

"You should also remember that people need you."

The man kissed tenderly Sabina on the lips and acknowledged, "Nana, you are right."

"Listen, my sweet little darling, because of our closeness, I start to know you."

"In this case, I must use caution and should be on my best behavior all the time."

"Well, let me tell you the reason why you hesitate before continuing your revelations.

"Rose's attitude…"

"My attitude!" screamed the daughter.

Then, shortly after, she wondered, "Mom, what have I done unknowingly?"

"Well, your father has received a big blow when you have thought that his divinatory powers may interfere with your happiness.

"Since then, he keeps asking himself if he shouldn't let life go without his anticipation of others' problems and let people alone."

Rose, tears in her eyes, threw her arms around her father's neck "Listen, Dad," she said, "don't make others suffer because of my foolishness."

She took a long pause to calm down.

Then, she went on, "Here I stand close to a human wealth and goodness and I take it for granted… Dad, please, tell me all the ramifications of such organization misdeeds."

A stranger's wonderful chronicles, Book II

"Your mother is right," stated the father.

He took a short pause and went on, "Well, here it is.

"You have a close friend, a schoolgirl. If I don't make any mistake, I believe that her name is Huguette…"

"Yes, Huguette Badu…She is my best friend. What's happened to her?

"Nothing has happened yet to her.

"However, is she in danger? Yes, Rose, she is, even more than you are."

"My God! Dad, what will happen to her?"

"Joseph Montluc has presented her to his buddy, Clarence Comings.

"You must act fast to prevent your friend from going out with Clarence.

"Like Gisele Marcus, Viviane Salit and many more, she will disappear…"

The mother, the girl and the boy had their eyes wide open with fear.

As far as Rose was concerned, she had just had the answer to the puzzle concerning her schoolmates' disappearance, whom they had never seen again.

"What can I do, dad?" she inquired in tones of emotion.

"Rose, my beloved daughter, call your friend to tell her that you will go to her home to pick her up. We must warn her at once.

"Don't forget to tell her that your father has the gifts for astonishing people and that he will visit her parents."

"Dad, will you drive me to her home?" inquired Rose. "Remember, I have owned yet a car."

Sabina's daughter in a state of danger

The father didn't answer at once.

The mother rushed saying, "Rose, Rainier, your father brings you an important gift each, which I didn't approve of, to start with."

"Why didn't you approve of our father's gifts to us, mom?" stated Rainier

"Yes, mom, why didn't you?" cut in Rose-Yolande. "You must have a good reason; for, Rainier and I have the privilege to have one of the best mothers in the world."

"Thank you, Rose," stated Sabina.

Shortly after, she indicated, "I didn't approve of gifts for security reason.

"However, according George, you have enough wisdom to handle the gifts he intends to give you."

Rose kissed her father on the cheek, while Rainier rubbed the paternal shoulder.

"Dad, what is it?" inquired the boy.

The man stood up and asked his children to follow him. Once by the window, he pointed to two brand new cars, namely a yellow one and a grey one.

"Rose, the yellow one belongs to you."

The daughter buried her head in her father's stomach to hold back her cry of joy.

"Rainier, the grey is yours."

A stranger's wonderful chronicles, Book II

"Dad, I don't believe my eyes.

"You have thought of everything. You have gone beyond the boundaries of generosity."

"Yes, my children, I have thought of everything. I believe you deserve a car now.

"However, you must prove to your mother that you have enough spiritual maturity to use wisely a car. Don't give ride to friends who could make you act foolishly."

"Dad, don't worry, you will be proud of us," state Rose-Yolande.

"Dad, you and Mom will have an idea of our degree of wisdom," added Rainier.

Next, the father pulled two sets of keys from his jacket pocket and handed them over to his children who shortly after disappeared.

Rose-Yolande went to pick up her friend, while Rainier went to visit Emmanuela.

George and Sabina would have two hours of intimacy. They would take full advantage of their "free time" (of course, as I had said Sabina, as excited adults).

Indeed, they "acted wisely" for, after one hour or two, the children returned home.

Rose-Yolande presented Huguette Badu to her parents and her brother.

When she was close enough to her father, she whispered, "Getty, this is my father."

Sabina's daughter in a state of danger

Instinctively, the young visitor hugged George tight as if she took him for a saving tree.

"Ms. Badu, what have I done well or bad to deserve such warm welcome?"

"Huguette, my good friend," cut in Sabina, "this man is too modest. However, he leaves behind him a long trail of good deeds."

This being said, Sabina took her son Rainier by the arm and said, "Rainier, take me to the supermarket.

"George, I will be back in one hour."

George sat down on the sofa, between Huguette and Rose-Yolande.

The latter stretched her arm and touched slightly her friend. Then, she said, "Getty, my father has stopped his international activities to come in person to warn me about a great danger I have been expose to. When he has described it, I have almost passed out.

"Then, in the heat of her predictions, he has told me that my friend named Huguette might incur greater danger…"

The friend opened wide her eyes.

"Mr. George, what can it be?" she finally asked. "Oh, my God, protect my family and me!

"Listen, my friends, because of my parents' lousy financial situation, we won't survive a disaster or a piece of bad news. I am sure of that."

With a large gesture of the hand, George invited the visitor to calm down.

A stranger's wonderful chronicles, Book II

Then, he reassured, "Huguette, call me George. Rose's friend is like my own child. I will do my best to protect you against all comers."

"Oh, George, Thank you!"

Following a short pause, she added, "I would be so happy to have a father like you. To start with, I would live in a fancy house like this one."

"Thank you, Huguette."

Then, after a pause, he went on, "Rose may have inherited foresight from me, otherwise, she wouldn't have unpleasant vibes by Joseph Montluc. The second time, last Friday, at the time of parting from each other, Rose tried to get closer to him, but she had to stop as that young man head changed into this of Lucifer, with a pair of horns and fiery eyes."

Huguette, instinctively, placed her palm on the man's back. "Is it an appalling story you have just imagined, George, to urge me to wisdom?"

"Getty, my father has told the truth,

"Don't forget that I have warned you about his deep intuition of reality?"

"But Rose, you have to understand my reaction. What George has said seems incredible. How can someone create such vision...?"

Then, shortly after, she added, "George, forgive me to have interrupted you.

"I am not rude, but scared and excited at the same time."

George Musa went on, "This Joseph Montluc and his family get involved in the activities of an international organized crime specializing in a kind of modern slavery: they sell young beautiful sexy women to wealthy old sadistic hedonists.

"Montluc has received training in seducing young women who have disappeared without leaving any sign of life.

"Among the victims of that organization, we count your schoolmates who has vanished in thin air, in spite of thorough investigation conducted by several security agencies…"

Huguette Badu remained dumfounded.

Yes, George told the truth! Three or four of her schoolmates had simply disappeared.

Then, she really found herself in a state of danger!

The man didn't carry a joke too far!

On the contrary, because of her friendship with his daughter Rose-Yolande, he intended to save her. In this case, she would do her best not interrupt him anymore.

Indeed, she wanted to know everything to spare her parents a life of sadness; for, she represented their ultimate family hope.

"George, please, excuse my interruption," she state beseechingly. "Keep talking. I want to know everything about this sad affair."

"Joseph Montluc has introduced his friend Clarence Cummings to you?" went on George.

"Yes, he has."

"He is one of the seducers."

A stranger's wonderful chronicles, Book II

"You must be kidding!"

"No, I am not."

"Sorry, George, my reaction comes from fear. However, you should keep talking."

"Huguette, he has invited you to accompany him to a restaurant, this weekend. You have told him that you would give him a ring to let him know about your decision.

"I would advise you to stay away from that man. If you go to this restaurant, they will put you on drug and you will disappear without leaving any sign of your existence on this planet.

"Believe, Huguette, you are a beautiful woman they will sell like hot cakes."

"George, what should I do?" inquired Huguette.

"Don't worry. These criminals, by exposing my daughter to danger, will pay for their boldness. The organization won't be around in less than two days. Then, all the associates in crime will go to jail."

The man took a pause, the time to look for the best way to shift the conversation to another unpleasant subject. Then, he went on, "Now, tell me about your family and you.

"If I am not mistaken, you wish you could be my daughter to live opulently."

"George, I was kidding. My parents wouldn't appreciate my complaining about their poverty."

Sabina's daughter in a state of danger

George and his daughter looked at each other conspiratorially. Finally, she made a nod to her father, which Huguette had seen.

"Listen, Huguette," said George, "may I visit your parents?"

"Oh, no, George, you may not!" rushed saying Huguette. "I won't advise you to visit us. We live in a raggedy house, an inheritance from my maternal grandfather.

"My friend, because of our financially stress, we can't even renovate it."

"Call your parents and tell them about my intention to visit them."

Huguette made a gesture of the hand to have her schoolmate's consent. The latter nodded.

Huguette used her friend cellular. She went to a corner of the living room for privacy.

"Mom," she said among other things, "these people live in a palace looking like a dream house.

"What should I tell them…well, let me put him on the phone."

She handed over the cellular to George, not without telling him, "My parents said that their house…"

"Yes," stated George, "let me tell you Niella…I know everything, the alpha and omega of reality…You don't believe me…Well, let me make a revelation…You have always dreamed of having a stand by the prestigious company called *The Great International House*. Your brother Conrad Benjamin, a security agent for that enterprise has mentioned your idea to the company chairperson. The latter hasn't seen any inconvenience to such idea. However, you don't have the funds for something like that...

"Oh! You are waiting for me...Well, I am leaving now before your husband and you change your mind..."

George, Sabina, their children accompanied Huguette to the Badus' house.

Huguette's parents, to the best of their ability, gave a warm welcome to the visitors.

Some point in time, without beating about the bush, everybody went to *The Great International House* and obtained from the chairman the official authorization to have a stand in which Niella would sell almost everything: sandwiches, coffee, milk, chocolate, fruit juices, cakes, socks, cellular phones, batteries...

In a short time, *Commercial Prefabrication*, a company specialized in building kiosks and stands put together a lovely stand with a huge electric stove, a large freezer, a commercial coffee maker, cabinets and other objects.

Huguette's parents couldn't believe their eyes.

The mother didn't waste any time; she opened business the day after.

As far as Huguette's father was concern, being a professional mason, he would join the team of George Musa's workers.

With the Badus' consent, George completely revamped the family's home.

Sabina's daughter in a state of danger

In the meantime, George parked his car facing the imposing building announcing *The International Home of Exchange*. He walked straight to the director's office and presented himself to the secretary as follows, "My name is George Musa. I would like to see the person in charge of this business, namely a certain Roland Montluc."

"Do you have an appointment?"

"No, I don't."

"Then, Mr. George Musa, you can't see him without an appointment.

"I tell, give me your name and your phone number. He will call you."

"Ms., tell him that you have in front of you Rose-Yolande Musa's father. He will certain have some eagerness to see me immediately."

The secretary through the intercom transmitted the information to someone.

Soon after, four built men came out and beckoned to the visitor to follow them "without a murmur".

They took him to a spacious office.

A tall and healthy-looking man yelled, "Sir, I am Roland Montluc.

"You have mentioned a certain Rose-Yolande Musa. To the best of my recollection, I have nothing to do with someone by this name."

"Ask your son if he knows her."

"My dear sir, did you say, my son? Listen, what are you talking about?"

"Of course, you understand me. Actually, you do have awareness of the reason for my coming here.

A stranger's wonderful chronicles, Book II

"However, to joggle your memory, let me remind you of your son's name: Joseph Montluc."

"Listen, George Musa or whatever your name may be, apparently, you know too much to stay alive."

"No, I won't die."

Then, shortly after, the visitor pronounced, "Listen to me, your organization will stop functioning today. For, you have the effrontery, the audacity to expose my daughter's life."

Roland Montluc and his employees burst out laughing, while pointing their index fingers at George Musa.

Then, the chief criminal turned sour and yelled, "Do you really know whom you are dealing with?"

"Certainly," replied George Musa, "I know whom I am dealing with. You have a criminal organization with international ramifications.

"This organization is responsible for the disappearance of hundreds of women.

"You have killed many and have forced others to give sexual satisfaction to wealthy depraved persons.

"Listen. You have launched an army of young handsome men to seduce young beautiful women, put them on drug and sell them as slaves, haven't you?"

The strong-looking men pulled their pistols and, at their patron's signal, they got closer to George, with a view to killing him on the spot. However, to their great surprise, their pistols let out intense heat, to such a par, the criminals had no other alternative but to drop them to the ground.

Then, George stated, "Commandant, have you heard everything?

"Then, it's time."

In a flash, hundreds and hundreds of police cars arrived, with their sirens on.

Then, security officers took over the building and thoroughly searched, hoping for finding victims and documents which would allow the national security to track down the criminals and their international ramifications, and to alert the international security agencies.

Commandant Nelson, the chief investigator, got near George Musa and gave him a handshake.

"Thank you, my dear friend," he said. "You have allowed us to put our hands on one of the most sadistic international organizations.

"By the way, my dear friend, haven't you had any fear for your life?"

"No, Commandant, I haven't. My action was as easy as drinking a glass of water.

"If you have allowed me, I would have taken these criminals straight to hell."

"What?

"Do you have some understanding with Lucifer and his fiends?"

"Not only have I some understanding with Lucifer and his fiends, but also with all the forces in the world."

A stranger's wonderful chronicles, Book II

"In that case, my dear George Musa, I must conduct some inquiry about you."

"You won't find anything on me."

"Well, good bye, sir…"

Commandant Nelson turned around. There was no sign of George Musa.

"It's as if the man has never existed," thought the police chief.

Shortly, after catching his breath, he concluded, "Well, I am glad that he stands on the side of decency and justice."

In the meantime, Huguette Badu called the Musa up.

"This is the Musas' residence.

"It's Sabina on the phone."

"This is Huguette."

"Ah! Huguette, everything is ok?"

"Things get better than my parents and I have thought.

"George, as far as we are concerned, doesn't come from this world. His generosity has no bounds."

"You are right.

"By the way, I know what you are talking about.

Huguette, you should know that man has pulled me from an abyss of despair."

"But, Mrs. Musa…"

"Please, Huguette, call me Sabina."

Sabina's daughter in a state of danger

"Sabina, I am in heaven. However, besides the goodness showered on my family, I would give a fortune to know how he has managed to put an enveloped full with money in my bag and with a note saying,

Huguette,

You are now my daughter. I want you to reach happiness. Like your sister Rose-Yolande, you will find happiness one of these days.

Take delight in my little gift.

George.

"Huguette, I don't know that man's secret," insinuated Sabina. "I can't explain the powers of that mysterious generous soul. I believe that you must follow his advice and make the best out of 'his little gift'."

"Good bye, Sabina. Tell Rose that I will see her at the university on Monday."

"Bye, Huguette."

That Sunday, Rainier, by two in the afternoon, returned home, accompanied by a beautiful young woman. A board smile opened up his face.

"Dad, Mom, Rose, here is my friend Emmanuela."

"Ah!" uttered the mother. "You are the ravishing Emmanuela Rainier has talked so much about?

—Oh! exclaimed the visitor.

A stranger's wonderful chronicles, Book II

"Anyway, I am glad to meet you, Mrs. Musa. I have often thought that Rainier's mother must be a beautiful woman to give birth to such handsome man."

"Well, you are charming," went on the mother. "It's a great female quality."

Then, Rainier pointed to his father and said, "Emmanuela, this is my father."

George rubbed his fingers against each other; then, magically, he made a bunch of flowers and handed it over to the visitor.

The latter opened wide her eyes.

"Emmanuela," rushed saying Rainier, "I forget to tell you that my father has extraordinary powers."

"Welcome to our home," stated George.

After a pause, he added, "What my son Rainier meant, I have a profound intuition of reality.

"For example, yesterday, as usual, you expected to see Rainier on Monday.

"Yet, sitting down in your parents' living room, you had a strong intuition that you would see him sooner.

"Then, ten minutes after, here was Rainier, with his smiling face.

"My dear Emmanuela, don't have any fear, I belong to this world."

The visitor put her hand to her mouth to prevent her from screaming; for, George had expressed her own thought in minute details.

Sabina's daughter in a state of danger

Finally, Rainier showed her sister Rose-Yolande and said, "An old acquaintance."

The two young ladies hugged each other.

"Emmanuela, you are welcome in our home," pronounced Rose-Yolande.

"Thank you, Rose."

Emmanuela ate dinner at the Musas.

She happened to carry herself as a young reserved woman but full of sense of humor.

At five in the afternoon, she took leave of the Musas to return to her parents.

Rainier drove her back home, not without promising his parents to rejoin them with forty-five minutes.

◘ ◘

◘

Brian Clifford remembered the first episode during which he had met with Sabina. He had great joy to see again this exceptional woman.

He acknowledged the effrontery of this criminal organization that had gone as far as to endanger the "powerful" George Musa daughter's life.

The reporter reached to conclude that organization had received what it deserved.

The reporter also visited the Badus, while the husband and the daughter were helping Niella.

A stranger's wonderful chronicles, Book II

According to them, at first, they had the impression of living in a world of dream, which couldn't be possible, considering these concrete proofs of the marvelous stranger's visit and action.

"How to explain this stand," added Niella Badu, "the raggedy house renovation, my husband's employment to a prefabricated company, the money we handle…"

"Niella," stated Brian Clifford, "The marvelous stranger has thrown many families like yours into confusion.

"However, he exists.

"Believe me, my dear friends; I know what I am talking about. I have also benefitted from his generosity.

"It's a long history requiring hours to tell you.

"I seized this opportunity to promise you that I will add this episode to the "Marvelous chronicles of a stranger"

Finally, Brian Clifford visited Commandant Nelson who also believed that marvelous man came from nowhere, but not from this world.

"Brian, my friend, I have never seen someone like him, in my entire existence.

"By the way, Brian, my dear friend, he has told me himself and I quote, 'I am in communication with all the forces of the universe.'

"Frankly, Brian, I don't see how I could deny my encounter with him."

Brian Clifford took leave of the commandant.

Sabina's daughter in a state of danger

He smiled to the idea that he would have a delicious time with the most recent beneficiary of the marvelous stranger: *the neighborhood moron.*

(29)

The Neighborhood Moron

By Antoine Archange Raphael

Marie-Therese Mercier had never understood the mistreatment received from her affluent family, which was known to people everywhere and which put that young woman in very embarrassing situations.

 Since childhood, her parents had never missed any opportunity to remind her of her clumsiness and her lack of intelligence.

They strongly believed that Marie-Therese's trying case had to result from a curse put on the family for a deadly sin committed unknowingly by the parents or by their ancestors in the past.

"You know, these things occur sometimes," admitted the father, one day.

Nevertheless, for Marie-Therese Mercier, her parents' backward attitude had no rationale behind it.

Indeed, her father, Jerry Mercier, had obtained a civil engineering title.

Certainly, he had acquired objectivism through his studies, since scientific philosophy belonged to the engineering study curriculum.

With respect to her mother, Luciana Mercier had attended Normal Superior School and secured a PhD in history.

She had, evidently, received training in research techniques from the university and had been exposed to the history of philosophy, starting with the ancient Greek thinkers to reach the contemporary philosophers among whom have appeared the positivists.

Then, Marie-Therese, supposedly idiot, couldn't understand her educated parents' negative attitude towards her.

A stranger's wonderful chronicles, Book II

Actually, they had never taken any time to have a serious conversation with her and to assess, along the way, the depth of her intelligence.

At the family meetings, they managed to keep her away, and rushed to go and apologize to anyone who struck conversation with their daughter.

"Listen, my friend, Marie-Therese is a little awkward," they often added. "You must not pay her too much attention, considering her level of…"

They would stop in time to avoid hurting too much their daughter's susceptibility (if any).

On the other hand, Marie-Therese's siblings represented the family's pride and joy.

Indeed, Colbert, Nadia, Catherine, Randolph and Paula attended university after finishing high school.

Yet, these elements of the new generation didn't have enough patience to complete their college studies.

As the time went by, Colbert became a renowned singer selling his cassette like hot breads.

One day, Nadia had dropped out to marry the son of a real estate tycoon.

Catherine pursued an acting career.

She had already played several extra roles. She might become a great movie star overnight.

Randolph worked as an agent for an important real estate company specializing in condominium construction.

The neighborhood moron

As far as Paula was concerned, she became an executive secretary for a company named Style Magazine, after she had married the chairman of the board.

The parents, Jerry and Lucinda, didn't believe in the wisdom of sending Marie-Therese to college.

"Darling," acknowledged the mother, "it's a mystery that oaf could obtain her high school diploma. Certainly, the level of studies has lowered."

"Lucy," explained the husband, "you must not forget that those schools have to reach a certain quota of graduate students to keep receiving governmental subsides."

Again, Marie-Therese couldn't seize the rationale behind this type of reasoning; for, her brothers and sisters, before her, had attended the same high school.

How could her diploma have less worth in her parental balance of appreciation?

The whole neighborhood tried to avoid that *oaf's company*, who seemed to talk about "silly things" and who had probably sunk into folly.

To make matters worse, a leading psychiatrist, Doctor Martin Gene, Jerry Mercier's old schoolmate in high school, and a good friend of the family, had "discovered", from the parents' say-so, that Marie-Therese suffered from *mild imbecility* and *schizophrenia*.

On weekends, the siblings, along with their spouses and children, went to visit their parents.

A stranger's wonderful chronicles, Book II

They made a lot of noise.

Marie-Therese would then experience the worse moments of her life; for, everybody completely ignored her or referred to her in insulting terms.

During weekdays, Marie-Therese stayed home with the housekeeper who took care of almost everything: house-cleaning, preparation of foods and other chores.

Additionally, Ms. Francesca Sernela had received "instructions" to watch over Marie-Therese, *the oaf of the family and the neighborhood.*

Marie-Therese could stay home all day or, from time to time, she may go to the public square nearby, under the watchful housekeeper's eyes that may perceive everything from the windowpanes.

Marie-Therese would take advantage of her solitude to read good books.

One day, the housekeeper became alarmed when she saw a well-dressed man taking seat by Marie-Therese.

Without beating about the bush, she called in turn Mr. and Mrs. Mercier to report the incident.

"Don't lose sight of them!" exclaimed Jerry Mercier. "I am coming."

Lucinda Mercier also left what she was doing to go back home and straitened things out.

"That clumsy girl will drive us to despair, one day," she whispered.

The neighborhood moron

In the meantime, the man, who joined Marie-Therese, spoke to her in these terms, "Good morning, Marie-Therese Mercier. My name is Jonas Hippolyte. "

"Mr. Jonas Hippolyte, you have called me by my real name," stated the young woman. "By any chance, do you know me?"

"Marie-Therese, I appreciate the fact that you don't speak to me in a formal manner. Then, I would say that we are on friendly grounds.

"Well, to answer your question, I would ask you not to have any fear of me."

The man took a pause before telling Marie-Therese the following, "Listen, I have a profound intuition of reality. Additionally, my closeness to a person allows me to know the truth about his or her life.

"Then, I may say that I know the alpha and the omega of reality."

"Mr. Hippolyte…"

"Marie, call me Jonas."

"Jonas, is what you have said possible?"

"As far as I am concerned, I will say yes, it is possible.

"Let me give you a proof of that.

"You are the youngest child of Mercier family.

"The Merciers have six children.

"For some odd reason, your parents take you for an idiot.

"A friend of the family, Doctor Martin Gene, has confirmed such diagnosis."

A stranger's wonderful chronicles, Book II

"Apparently, Jonas, you know everything. But let me give you a little test before trusting you completely."

"What do you think of me?"

"Do you want me to be sincere?"

"Certainly, I do."

"You are a genius."

"I am a genius! Hum!"

They kept silent for a while.

Marie-Therese, in her mind, tried to figure out the meaning of the stranger's statement, which might express or not her true reality as a person.

Then, in spite of herself, she admitted, "Jonas, I trust you. Why do I? I don't know.

"Even if you intend to harm me, your approach sounds more humane than my family and neighbors'. For them, I embody some kind of plague-stricken person."

"Do you know why?"

"Their oddness remains a mystery to me."

"Marie, believe me, human beings in general take interest in appearances, in whatever pleases. In this respect, we behave exactly like lower animals.

"This endless itch to pleasure affects everything around them, even the subjects of conversation.

The neighborhood moron

"Your parents, your siblings, your neighborhood people talk about mundane things you take no interest in. When you open your mouth to speak, you invite others to transcendence. Then, they don't understand you and find you annoying. Instead of recognizing their lack of spiritual insight, they rather minimize the depths of your thoughts, and try to make you look small-minded."

The young woman touched the man's hand to indicate her intention to speak.

"'Jonas, my dear friend," she recognized, "you've said it all. In the same line of thinking, I may add that human reality has two aspects: an external one and an inner one.

"The way I see it, the others see my external side, but ignore my inner one.

"Jonas, believe me, our conversation allows me to admit that I have never suffered from idiocy."

"You haven't."

"Thank you so much Jonas for opening my eyes."

"Marie-Therese, I want you to believe in your acumen. Actually, let me give you an instance of your genius.

"In the classroom, during your twelfth year..."

"Wait a minute! How do you know?

"Oh! Don't answer me. You know the alpha and the omega of my reality.

A stranger's wonderful chronicles, Book II

"In this case, you may embody a ghost, expressing the figments of imagination."

"Marie-Therese, don't ever speak like that again. Others would really believe that you have sunk into madness."

"I agree with you, Jonas.

"Then, go on."

"Yes, in the classroom, during a discussion, you had sustained a thesis that had fascinated your professor and your schoolfellows.

"The discussion was about the principle of identity and its consequences.

You have argued then,

Our first impression may lead us to believe that principle falls down through a lack of accuracy; for, reality is in a state of change, flux and reflux.

The beings are born, turn old and disappear in a continuous flow.

However, all things being equal, the principle of identity makes great sense. It seems more convenient and realistic than we think.

Human intelligence would find it impossible to understand the real if it couldn't, abstractly, keep in our mind and our memory characteristics of individuals such as men, women, children, animals and things.

We would end up in an endless reassessment…

"Jonas, definitely, you are not from this world," admitted the young woman

The man touched his chin before inquiring, "Marie, what do you intend to do?

"Quite frankly, you would represent an enormous loss to mankind if you spent your life vegetating and responding to the poor image given of you by others."

"Jonas, I don't really know. I rest at the mercy of parents, siblings and others, who don't quite understand me."

"Do you want to put yourself at my mercy?"

"Yes, I do, with all my heart."

"Then, Marie, let's go and get your transcripts from high school.

"They are in your bag. Then, we will go to register you at the university."

"You said university!"

"Yes, Marie, I did.

"I will take care of everything. If your parents don't want to, will you trust me and follow me?

"Jonas, my dear friend, I will follow you without a shadow of hesitation.

A stranger's wonderful chronicles, Book II

"I mean it."

In the meantime, the parents, the siblings and their families had an emergency meeting.

They called the police and doctor Martin Gene who reached the place as soon as possible.

In a flash, the neighborhood looked like a war zone.

The housekeeper had to repeat her observation for *one thousand times,*

A well-dressed man sat down by Ms. Marie-Therese. They had a long conversation. Some point in time, Marie-Therese entered her bedroom, while the man was waiting on the pavement. Then, they left in the man's car...

By seven o'clock, Marie-Therese resumed the family home and had a shock to see all these people, including police officers and her bizarre psychiatrist accompanied by three other employees namely a woman and two men wearing white uniforms.

The father yelled out, "Where did you come from, idiot, imbecile?"

The mother cut in, made gestures with her hands and invited everybody to calm.

"Darling, my children, my friends," she added, "we must do our best to use tact. We are dealing with a mentally disturbed child."

The neighborhood moron

The siblings and their spouses agreed with the mother, to avoid a scandal.

Marie-Therese looked at her parents and the others in turn. Then, she stated, "Don't call idiot, and, contrary to your belief, I haven't sunk into mentally disturbance.

"My birth certificate has clearly spelled out my name: Marie-Therese Mercier."

Colbert, the family eldest child cut in, "They saw you with a man at the public square."

"Yes, I had a stimulating conversation with the man.

"His name is Jonas Hippolyte."

"Good heaven! Tell us what happened," asked the mother in an irritating voice.

"Mother, nothing you have in your mind has happened. Contrary to your belief,

"That man is not depraved. We only had a chat."

"Then," cut in the father.

"The man took me to the university to register me as a student," replied Marie-Therese.

"The man has registered you at the university as student?" inquired Nadia

"Yes, Nadia, he has," replied Marie-Therese. "Do you find this bizarre?"

A stranger's wonderful chronicles, Book II

"Certainly," intervened Randolph. "You have no aptitudes for pursuing high studies."

"Randolph, my dear brother, you have expressed your personal opinion, which rests on nothing and which certainly means nothing for Jonas and me."

"Then, Marie, we understand," cut in Paula. "It is your prerogative to go to college. Give us the name of the university you will attend?"

"If I tell you, Paula, everybody will know it and will come to disturb me in my studies to prove my idiocy."

"But why do you take suddenly this decision?" inquired Catherine.

"My friend and I have decided, because of my acumen, that I should attend university."

The parents and the siblings didn't know what to do, since Marie-Therese didn't act illogically.

Additionally, she had reached adulthood and could make a decision; unless that Jonas, a diabolical mind, had the time to brainwash that *poor woman*.

The father inquired, "This Jonas, who is he?"

"According to me," replied Marie-Therese, "he is a great man, a marvelous human being.

"Actually, I told him that his divinatory powers and his acumen, having surpassed the limits of human nature, seem to draw a picture of a mind, a ghost, a God's envoy.

"He asked me to stop repeating my deduction and he reminded me that I had just used a language others might turn against me to justify their belief in my mental dullness."

The father turned around towards the psychiatrist and suggested, "Martin, you must give her the injection to calm her down. Then, she will spend some time at the center for observation."

"What!" screamed Marie-Therese. "What's going wrong with you, people?

"How can you take such backward decision?

"I should return the compliment and take you for mentally disturbed persons..."

She didn't have time to complete her sentence; the male employees grabbed her and forced her to sit down on a chair, while the doctor was ready to inject her.

He felt the woman's arm in search of the vein into which he would inject his sedative, when a well-dressed man with a confident bearing suddenly entered the living room.

Then, with an iron grip he seized the doctor's hand and pressed it hard to immobility.

"Who is this man?" protested the psychiatrist.

"Doctor Martin Gene, I am Jonas Hippolyte," the intruder presented himself.

Everybody cried of surprise.

A stranger's wonderful chronicles, Book II

Police officers pulled their guns together and turned them against the intruder.

The police chief yelled, "Sir, I ask you to let go of the doctor's hand. Otherwise, we will have no other alternative but to take extreme measures."

The so-called Jonas Hippolyte slowly turned around towards the police officers and stated, "Officers, look around you, there are many witnesses who will swear that I haven't touched you at all.

"However, if you pull the trigger, you will hurt yourself."

Everybody (including the police officers) looked towards the hands supposedly armed; the nozzles of the guns had turned against the officers' stomach.

"Now Doctor Martin Gene," went on Jonas Hippolyte, "why do you think of pumping this nonsense into the veins of a person sound of mind and body?

"Tell me, Doctor!"

"Marie-Therese suffers from a mild case of imbecility and schizophrenia," replied the physician unequivocally.

"What!" astonished Marie-Therese. "Doctor, the word schizophrenia derives from the Greek compound skhzein (split) and phrên (thought), which presupposed a separation of the patient and the external world.

"Do I give you, Doctor, the impression of losing awareness of reality?"

"Marie," acknowledged Jonas Hippolyte, "you have said it all."

The neighborhood moron

"You see that I am right about your intelligence."

"Yes, Jonas, you are right, and I do take you for my savior."

"As for you, Doctor," argued Jonas Hippolyte, "I have friends in the psychiatrists and psychologists association. I can go to them and report this fake diagnosis you have ascribed to my friend from her parents' say-so."

He had never ceased to look the doctor straight in the eyes. Finally, he relaxed his grip and reached out to hold Marie-Therese by the hand.

"Let's go, Marie."

"My friends, Marie follows me," he added loud, shortly after. "You will have an idea of her becoming within six years. I promise you, she will become an educated young lady.

"As for you Jerry and Lucinda, at Marie's return, you will regret not having loved her because she is the youngest child and that her birth has come to trouble your bourgeois lifestyle.

"As for you, Colbert, Nadia, Catherine, Randolph and Paula, as Marie has resisted following you in your superficial life, you have reinforced the parental animosity towards her.

"Yet, despite everything, you should know that she has never stopped loving you.

"Bye, my friends."

Shortly after, the *marvelous stranger* and Marie-Therese left the house arm in arm.

A stranger's wonderful chronicles, Book II

When the others got themselves together, they rushed out and ordered the police officers to stop the couple; however, Jonas and Marie-Therese had disappeared.

A feeling of shame and regret assailed the Merciers.

They ended up wondering if that Jonas Hippolyte wasn't a serial killer they had mentioned often on the media, who had eluded all the police inquiries.

Undoubtedly, they would never see Marie-Therese again. They would learn soon, from the news media that they would have found her body floating on the surface of an ocean or in an isolated place.

"Lucy," lamented the father, "we pay the price of our prejudice. As the Lord has noticed that we have rejected our daughter, he rushes removing her from our care."

"You may be right, Jerry," whined the spouse. "I have failed my maternal duties.

"I should have included her in the same motherly love I showered on all my children."

Doctor Martin Gene and the police had no other alternative but to alert the *International Office of Investigation.*

Soon after, many agents started their inquiries from the neighboring universities.

Doctor Benjamin Macro, the chairperson of *National University* promptly welcomed one of the agents named Marc-Charles Burin.

The neighborhood moron

As the university authority smiled, the agent asked, "Doctor, you are smiling.

"Would you, by any chance, know what's going on?"

"No, I don't, agent Burin," answered Doctor Benjamin Macro, the university chairman. "I am the last persons to get involved in local gossip.

"However, agent Burin, if I were Marie-Therese Mercier, I wouldn't fail to run away from my parents' home.

"According to some rumor, that woman's parents have abandoned her since childhood."

"I get you, Doctor," stated the agent.

Then, after a short while, the agent took leave of the university authority.

What he didn't know, this chairman belonged to the group of persons, who had benefitted from the *marvelous stranger's* generosity, who would move heaven and earth to allow that immensely generous man to continue his beneficial endeavor along the way.

Nobody would have a surprise at learning that Marie-Therese used a coded name to pursue her studies.

Years have elapsed with no sign of Marie-Therese. The security agencies thought it was wise to put an end to the inquiries.

The parents and the siblings kept going on with their existence, not without feeling a twinge of sadness.

A stranger's wonderful chronicles, Book II

A weekend, while, as usual, the parents, the siblings and their families gathered in the living room to chat, Paula cried with pain.

The others, including her husband, rushed towards her to calm her down.

"Oh!" she exclaimed, "I can't get over the mistreatment I gave my sister as if she was a dog.

"If the serial killer murdered her, did she suffer a lot? Oh! God! How wrong can we be! The more so as the killer has reminded us of the fact that she has never stopped loving us. Do we deserve her love?

The mother patted Paula on the back. "Lala," she stated, "I feel your pains.

"Listen, Jerry and I have never found happiness.

"We miss this woman who seemed to have more intelligence than we thought. Now we have a great love for her, as it may arrive too late.

"Because of our guilty conscience and our love, we have never touched her bedroom."

"Is it true?" inquired Nadia.

After a pause, she added, "I would like to see this room again."

"Let's go to see it again, together," urged the father. "We have nothing to lose."

Once in the bedroom, Catherine thought that something unusual had occurred in it.

What could it be?

She couldn't answer her own question.

Then, suddenly, she noticed the absence of Marie-Therese Teddy Bear. She remained dumbfounded, while pointing to the bed.

"What's going on?" asked Randolph. "Cat, you have lost your speech power.

"Should I call the ambulance?"

Pauling Moab, Catherine's husband hugged her tight. "Cat, I understand," he said. "The emotion is too strong for you. Let's go, my friends, leave the bedroom."

Catherine didn't move, while she kept on pointing to the bed. Finally, the others seized the meaning of her emotion: the teddy bear, a doll Marie-Therese loved so much, had disappeared. When did they take it away?

Who was responsible for something like that?

Nobody had the answer.

The mother got near the bed and saw a written note at the spot previously occupied by that doll.

The note said,

My friends,

As you know, I don't go anywhere without my teddy bear. It belongs to me. It's perhaps my only possession. Then, with the expert assistance of my friend Jonas, I did go back home to retrieve it.

A stranger's wonderful chronicles, Book II

I had the time to open my parents' bedroom, who were sleeping

soundly. Yet, I read sadness on their faces. They certainly have

a guilty conscience.

I am alive. Jonas didn't kill me, contrary to what others believe.

A man of such high degree of civilization wouldn't allow him-

self to kill his fellow creatures

Signed: Marie-Therese.

The parents, the agents of *International security Agency* and others couldn't decide whether to resume the inquiries or to let things go their way. Myriad questions popped up in their mind; no one could answer them.

Did this taking away of the Teddy Bear occur at the beginning of Marie-Therese's disappearance?

If yes, this event was years old.

Did the missing daughter come in person to steal the doll or did that devilish Jonas Hippolyte come in person to create confusion in the mind?

Six years had elapsed.

On a bright Sunday, about midday, all the televised programs underwent a temporary interruption to allow the diffusion of a *special bulletin.*

The neighborhood moron

The Merciers, as usual, sitting in front of the huge TV screen in the living room, waited impatiently for the diffusion of this *special bulletin* by the media.

Millions of viewers, like them, asked themselves if the world would soon undergo a catastrophic commotion of great magnitude.

The TV announcer state, in a tone full of emotion, the following,

Ladies and gentlemen,

Don't worry, your favorite programs will return within few minutes.

Now, we find ourselves at the National State University at which they will hold soon commencement ceremonies held for the outgoing classes.

We have here the chairman of the university, Doctor Benjamin Macro who will make an opening toast.

Doctor Macro, you have the microphone.

The chairman slowly took the microphone from the announcer, cleared his throat and stated,

Ladies and gentlemen,
My dear students,

A stranger's wonderful chronicles, Book II

I won't be long; for, today, the emotion and the suspense of this commencement more than ever have overcome me.

Once you have heard the story I will soon tell you, you will understand the reason for losing my usual eloquence.

A mysterious stranger approached me, six year ago.

He told me that his name was Jonas Hippolyte.

He advised me against accepting his name for granted.

I understood at once his message; for, fifteen years ago, a stranger had pulled me from the abyss of despair and had taken me straight to the university, after he had paid for my tuitions and accommodation.

Now, I am Doctor Benjamin Macro.

There was a thunder of applause at the auditorium.

However, millions of people in their homes and their cars started to cry instead.

The speaker went on,

I can't tell you, ladies and gentlemen, if, this time, I have dealt with the same stranger, but he is as young as I am (laughter and applause).

sity and to become later on professionals, my dear fellow students, we have categorically expressed our intention to join the guiding lights of humanity.

The speaker, had a sustained standing round of applause from the audience.

Mr. University Chairman,

My dear professors,

My dear follow students,

I can't find the best way to conclude my little speech except that I will recite a poem composed by Jonas Hippolyte, while he was waiting for me in the university reception room.

The poem is entitled 'At the museum'.

When did my benefactor visit that museum (explosion of laughter)? This is highly debatable. For, in spite of his apparent youth, he believes he is the father of mankind (thunder of applause). Has he imagined such visit (another burst of laughter)?

However, ladies and gentlemen, his poem has impressed me a lot. Here it is,

A stranger's wonderful chronicles, Book II

At the museum

With no motive I may think of,

And out of curiosity,

I stop for a short while at the museum.

I find delight in seeing

Works of art,

Scientific specimens

And past cultural artifacts:

Rocks from the Moon,

Dinosaurs,

Indian outfits,

Pictures and attires,

 Reminding me of earlier

 Men,

Women

And children.

Of course, my mind travels back in time,

Allowing me to shake hands

The neighborhood moron

With all my ancestors,

From the Pithecanthropus,

The Neanderthal,

The Zinjanthropus,

The Atlanthropus,

To the ones belonging to

A more distant past

And got lost in the mists of time.

Somehow I sense their actions

In order to survive and

Scatter all over the planet.

I salute those giants

Who had conquered nature

In its worst shape.

I take pride in being descendant of them

And, later on,

In acquiring the status of a person.

Only, then, I understand that

The idea of belonging to humanity

A stranger's wonderful chronicles, Book II

Bears a great deal of responsibility:

Men and women should shy away

From participating

In savagery and chaos.

They should make Mother Nature

So proud of them.

Shortly after the audience sustained applause, the speaker concluded,

Then, Ladies and gentlemen,

My schoolfellows, bye!

I wish you success in your endeavors. And, above all, I wish

longevity to our University.

Thank you,

ladies and gentlemen.

And God bless all of us!

Doctor Marie-Therese had a standing ovation from the audience and a cry of approval from the media listeners.

Instinctively, the Merciers, in the living room, stood up to express their respect and admiration for their daughter and sister.

The neighborhood moron

Everybody had to recognize that, against all odds, she had just covered herself with glory and honor.

The father, Jerry Mercier, tears in his eyes, suggested, "Let's go and pick up our beloved Marie. Let's hope she still finds us worthy of her."

"Dad," assured Paula, "I know Marie enough to anticipate her positive reaction towards us.

"Additionally, if I am not mistaken, her mysterious benefactor has told us that she still loves us."

"Let's go, my friends," concluded, the mother, namely Lucinda Mercier with a sob in her voice.

Then, shortly after, she added, "We shouldn't have any minute of hesitancy."

At the gate, the security guard approached the car driven by Jerry Mercier, followed by about a dozen others. On behalf of the parents, the security guard opened the portal and welcomed the family and relatives in these terms, *"Jonas Hippolyte has authorized us to let in the Merciers and their friends"*.

Marie-Therese had a big surprise to see this "population" coming into her room.

The reconciliation caused great emotions: tears, onomatopoeias, kisses, hugs.

"Where is Jonas?" inquired the father.

A stranger's wonderful chronicles, Book II

Marie-Therese burst out crying.

After she got herself together, she stated, "Why did he abandon me? He gave me his word to attend my graduation. I know. He has never existed; he is only a fancy of my imagination…"

"Marie, what a beautiful bunch of flowers!" exclaimed Nadia.

"A bunch of flowers!" inquired Marie-Therese. "Someone has invaded my privacy.

"Let me see…"

That bunch of flowers came from Jonas Hippolyte. There was a note attached to one of the branches saying,

My congratulations, Doctor Marie!

I hope you will love these flowers that have come from my imagination and my magician fingers

The key attached to the bunch of flowers will introduce you to one of my condominium units.

It is located on Mont Alban Avenue.

You will find the unit number on the cardboard box.

Next Tuesday, you will go to Psychological Research Institute where you will start putting your competence at the service of humanity.

Now, have a nice time with your family.

The neighborhood moron

You will have a princess' reception in your childhood neigh-borhood.

Jonas.

Marie-Therese said good-bye to her schoolfellows and professors, and then got on her father's car.

On the way, the father received a call from his friend, Paul Tosca, living in the neighborhood for years. The conversion was short. The father had his eyes wide-open.

"Darling, what's wrong?" asked the wife.

"Nothing, Lucy," answered Jerry Mercier. "In fact, reality turns brighter."

A mile from the family house, the father stopped the car and asked everybody, except the drivers to proceed on foot. Then, there was jubilation. A population full of emotions occupied the street to express their sympathy to the "learned woman of the neighborhood". They embraced Marie-Therese, kissed her, and hugged her, not without expressing words of regret and welcome back.

Finally, there was a great reception in the family living room, on the porch and in the street. People ate, drank and spoke about their *learned daughter*.

By eleven in the evening, as Marie-Therese was ready to go in her bedroom, Catherine inquired, "This Jonas Hippolyte, is he your lover?"

"Oh!" exclaimed the others outrageously. "Catherine, what's wrong with you?"

"No, Cat," replied Marie-Therese. "For the time being, he is my second father."

Next, the young woman entered her bedroom.

The day after, the whole family accompanied her to her new home.

The Merciers and the in-laws couldn't believe their eyes. The unit looked like a dream house.

Yet, Marie looked anything but happy. She felt a little empty with Jonas' absence.

"At least, he could have visited me," she whispered, "to make me believe that I don't have a dream. How can I understand that man?

"I do ask a childish question. Nobody understands this man. Perhaps, I will never see him again."

Someone knocked at the door. Marie-Therese turned around and remained dumbfounded. Jonas appeared so handsome, splendid and magnificent. He carried a dark grey suit, black shoes and a multicolor tie.

Marie-Therese rushed towards him and covered him with kisses on the neck, the cheeks, the hair, the lips…

"Jonas, my beloved, did you hear my prayer?" asked the woman.

"Yes, Marie, I did."

Then, the father, the mother, the siblings and their spouses, their children embraced the man.

The neighborhood moron

"Thank you, my friends," he said. "Men, women, children should behave like one big family, and should help each other. Providence and Nature have shown the way to wisdom, by giving us free all that we need to survive: blood, a heart, a brain, a vital impetus. However, we know that mankind has turned its back on this existential simplicity…"

He got near Marie, held her by the hand and stated, "You will always stand on the top of the mountain."

"But, Jonas, will I see you again?"

"Yes, my beautiful Marie, I will always make you feel my presence."

"My knight, that's a lot, knowing that you have a gigantic schedule."

"Listen, my friends, I must leave you. If I don't go now, I will have trouble with the national security agents."

Soon after, he kissed Marie-Therese on the hand and disappeared.

Less than five minute after, a dozen police cars invaded the neighborhood. The chief police officer and three others knock-ed at the door and asked if anyone had seen the so-called Jonas Hippolyte.

"No, officers," rushed saying the father.

"It's strange," insisted the chief. "An anonymous phone call has let us know that a man has just visited you, who seems to respond to Jonas Hippolyte's description.

"Actually, we have passed a grayish car. The driver seemed to be in a hurry…"

"Oh! Officer," assured the father, "it was the real estate agent."

A stranger's wonderful chronicles, Book II

"Well, my friends, we are sorry to disturb you," finally acknowledged the chief.

Doctor Marie-Therese, for more than a week, has started to put her skills at the service of psychological researches.

◻   ◻

◻

Brian Clifford had a brief conversation with the chairman of *National State University*, namely Doctor Benjamin Macro who, by the way, kept urging the journalist to maintain the publication of "A stranger's wonderful chronicles, such exciting magazine."

After a pause, he added, "For, my dear Brian, despite my professional status, I have no other alternative but to bear to the evidence of apparently unusual facts.

"However, Brian, what fascinates me the most, this man has the power to destroy with impunity; yet, he has chosen the road to goodness."

"Chairman, you have told the truth," acknowledge Brian. "As far as keeping the program 'A stranger's wonderful chronicles' alive, it's settled. It ensures my daily bread.

"Additionally, as I have said on various occasions, I have also benefitted from that great man."

As far as the National Security Chief was concerned, he confessed, "Brian, I am so glad that the man spread goodness around him.

The neighborhood moron

"You may understand that we had no alternative but to conduct an inquiry about him.

"However, his way of behaving, although disturbing at the beginning, always aims at others' well-being.

"Thus, the man rather fascinates us, while creating a puzzle to decipher."

Doctor Marie-Therese stated in her turn, "I can't identify him, but my professional success would make no sense without ascribing it to that man who has presented himself to me as Jonas Hippolyte.

"The man, however, didn't touch one hair of my head. He embodies civilization in action.

"I rest persuaded that one day, he will visit me, with the best intention in the world."

As usual, Brian took leave of everybody, with a smile on the face.

He was very anxious to take this new account to the executive secretary; for, it would have to appear on the next magazine issue.

He thought about his next episode entitled "The seed of love".

(30)

The

Seed

Of love

By Antoine Archange Raphael

*T*he agronomist, Gertrude Melon, opened her eyes wide, while her jeep swung between the precipice and the road. The woman feared for making any move. She wondered if she wasn't on the brink of dying any minute; for, this precipice measured one thousand feet in depth.

Gertrude's heart, in case that the jeep should fall into the abyss, would have stopped by fear and the pull of gravity, even before she reached the bottom.

Gertrude Melon felt a sharp pain at the left ankle. She asked herself if she didn't get hurt while she put suddenly on the breaks to avoid the jeep from plunging into the abyss.

A big beige SUV stopped. A tall man got off it. He beckoned to the lady to remain still, while he walked slowly towards the endangered vehicle.

He understood the whole situation and believed that the driver swung between life and death.

He grabbed the jeep crossbar with one hand and, with the other hand, unbuckled the driver security belt. Then, he advised the woman to gradually slide towards him.

Next, she lost consciousness in the stranger's arms. She thought to have heard loud noise, but she couldn't give the exact account of the following events.

When she regained conscience, she found herself in a hospital room, with one leg hanging by a string attached to a pulley.

A stranger's wonderful chronicles, Book II

"Here you are!" said a nurse.

"Ms., what's happened?" inquired the agronomist.

"My name is Angela Crouton" answered the nurse. "According to identification documents found in your pockets, you are Gertrude Melon, living at 56 Palisades Street, Monte Pin. Fortunately, we have seen your phone number among your papers and we have called your parents.

"They have just arrived and sit in the waiting room. Let me go and pick them up."

"Ms. Crouton…

"Call me Angela."

"Angela, what's happened really?"

"Well, according to your rescuer, you did make a false maneuver and almost plunged into the abyss.

"Ms. Melon, you are lucky. Many cars have fallen into this particular abyss with their passengers who have died in the process."

"Is my rescuer around?"

"No, he is not, for the time being."

The nurse left the room to go and get the accident victim's parents.

Few minutes after, Mr. and Mrs. Melon, as well as their other children, entered the hospital room.

Under the influence of emotion, they contented themselves to cover Gertrude with kisses, while crying bitterly, touching the patient on the arms and the stomach, and saying incomprehensible, meaningless words to her.

"Trudy," finally said the mother, "would you believe it? We have almost lost you."

"Darling, how would we manage without you," added the father.

Then, after breathing deeply, he added, "You represent a great source of joy for us.

"I haven't mentioned thousands and thousands of peasants who count on you for your expertise.

"Phone calls came from all over to inquire about your health condition."

The patient smiled before saying, "By the grace of God, an exceptionally strong man has saved my life."

"Have you ever seen him before," asked Sophia, one of the sisters.

"No, Fifi, I haven't seen him before," answered the patient. "I don't know what I will do to see him again to express my gratitude to him.

"I must let you know that, without his assistance, I would belong to history, today."

By eight in the evening, the family took leave of the patient. The parents and the siblings felt so happy to learn that Gertrude would leave the hospital, the day after. She had to have some rest at home for at least one week.

A stranger's wonderful chronicles, Book II

Gertrude overheard a conversation in the nurses' station. Apparently, the nurse Angela Crouton had just received a bunch of flowers from a man; for, she stated, "These flowers are gorgeous!"

"Angela, my lovely nurse, these flowers came from my flower bed."

"Well, this is very irregular, but how can I turn down such a gracious man like you."

Few minutes after, Gertrude saw Angela arriving with her rescuer.

"Gertrude," she said, "Mr. Prosper Mericourt wouldn't like to go back home without saying good night to you."

With a gesture of her fingers, Gertrude urged the man to get closer.

He gave a handshake to the patient.

"Mr. Prosper Mericourt…"

"Please, Gertrude," said the man, "call me Prosper. And don't be formal with me."

"But, sir, I have just had the opportunity to meet you, under exceptional circumstances," argued the woman.

"Apparently, yes, we have just met.

"However, believe me Gertrude, my lovely friend, a superior entity has planned this meeting, in its minute details, since the beginning of time and has carefully written in the book of destiny that we should meet at the crossroads…

"Don't you think so?"

"Prosper, my friend, you express yourself in a very stranger manner."

The seed of love

"Gertrude, I strongly believe that the events have occurred according to plan.

"I could have taken another road, but for one reason or another, this morning, I have taken Prodigy Boulevard and saved your life in the process."

"You are right, Prosper. Destiny wants to keep me alive on this planet. Otherwise, I would have belonged to history, by now.

"I don't know why I made this wrong maneuver that has almost claimed my life."

The man smiled.

"Why are you smiling, Prosper?" asked the woman. "'have I said something nonsensical?"

"No, Gertrude, my beautiful young lady, you haven't said something nonsensical," stated the man. "But, don't be alarmed if I tell you that you certainly know the reason for making the wrong maneuver, which almost caused your death.

"Prosper, do you call me a liar?"

"No, I don't. I mean no disrespect. However, you know the reason…"

"It is impossible for you to know something like that."

"The predicate impossible has no meaning for me.

"Gertrude, let me tell you a secret."

"Prosper, this conversation has gone too far. You may be a sadistic fellow…"

A stranger's wonderful chronicles, Book II

"I would have let you die if I was sadistic…"

The woman breathed deeply.

Then, she advanced in a regretful manner, "Prosper, my friend, forgive me to use a poor choice of words and to call you sadistic.

"Of course, you behave without malice and you don't wish me any harm.

"Actually, I rather owe you an eternal debt of gratitude…"

The so-called Prosper Mericourt didn't take offense. He kept on telling Gertrude the secret, "Gertrude, I have a profound intuition of reality and I know the alpha and the omega of people's life I have been close to…

"So, don't be alarmed and take me for a lunatic."

"You are rambling, Prosper."

"You want some proof?"

"Certainly, I do."

"Well, Gertrude, you have made a false maneuver at the wheel when you heard on the radio that they had kidnapped Justin Montaigne."

Instinctively, Gertrude grabbed the man by the hand.

"Prosper, you don't belong to this world!" she exclaimed. "Really, you don't.

"To know my unexpressed thoughts you have to act as a projection of my person in time and space. Then, this projection looks like a man imbued with omniscience and boundless generosity…"

The seed of love

"Gertrude, my lovely friend, how can you reach such conclusion?"

"Prosper, you understand the magnitude of your power? You speak about the elements of my intimate thoughts. I should be the only person to have an awareness of them."

"Yet, Gertrude, I have such power. Where doesn't it come from? I can't tell you.

"However, what do you see behind me?"

"I see a big mirror, a cabinet and a painting."

"How can you believe in the existence of objects, while casting doubt about my existence?

"You may touch my hand. Actually, this hand you have grabbed, haven't you felt its firmness?"

A dead silence reigned over the room. Gertrude and Prosper could overhear the arrival of ambulances carrying, undoubtedly, victims of accidents or other sick people.

"Well, Prosper," Gertrude broke the glass, "since you have started it, you have to finish it. What kind of relationship do I have with Justin Montaigne?"

"Now, Gertrude, you become the woman after my own heart."

"I become the woman after your heart? Prosper, what do you mean?"

"Oh! Don't get offended. I have no intention of acting fresh with you. It's a figure of expression.

"I mean that you have trusted me now.

A stranger's wonderful chronicles, Book II

"One day, you were thirteen and attending junior high school. It was a Tuesday. During the time of recess, you rushed going to the store at the street corner to buy a bottle of soda. You bumped against Justin Montaigne girlfriend's stomach. Despite your reiterated excuses, that girl, coming from a wealthy family, heaped verbal abuses on you.

"She said the following 'Little whore! You must pay attention to where you are going and put you little miserable person in a corner.

"Did you hear me little whore? You should never touch me. You must be careful. I may crush you like a meaningless insect.'

"Justin Montaigne had a shock and blamed Carmen Petty (that's the name of that haughty girl) for her rudeness and lack of compassion.

"That Carmen Petty turned so mad that she also heaped verbal abuses on Justin and walked away without any ceremony.

"In the meantime, the young man apologized to you and took you to the store. That day, he bought you a sandwich. He also bought one for himself.

"For some reason or another, he felt happy by you, despite his quarrel with his girlfriend.

"He saw you to your school. You presented him to your principal.

"He promised him to talk about the school distressful appearance with his father.

"The day after, Justin Montaigne and his father, Melvin Montaigne, visited your school, at the time of recess.

The seed of love

"You were happy that he recognized you and drew his father's attention on you.

"You reached out and tried to shake Mr. Melvin Montaigne's hand, but your hand remained in the air; for, the man leant forward and kissed you on the forehead.

"You didn't know what to think.

"Few days after, a construction company renovated and enlarged your school."

Gertrude made a gesture of the hand to stop the flow of her own childhood memories told by a perfect stranger, with the exactness of a movie camera.

"But, Prosper Mericourt, who are you?

"Do you come from beyond?

"Has God sent you on the mission to console me?

"Do you live in my mind?

"Have I sunk into madness?

"Nobody on earth can have such power…"

The man, with gestures of the hands, invited Gertrude to calm down. Then, in a melodious tone of voice, he told her, "My friend, your questions are justified. However, I can't give you any answer. I am born this way, with divinatory powers and magic which I use, fortunately, to help my brothers and sisters."

The patient burst out crying.

A stranger's wonderful chronicles, Book II

Few minutes after, she calmed down and stated, "Prosper, my heart bleeds.

"Justin, his parents and their wealth associates have used their fortune for the good of my school and mine.

"After junior high school, I pursued secondary school, then college.

"Now, they have kidnapped Justin, and I can't help. They can even kill him."

"Yes, Gertrude, they will kill him, even if the family pays the ransom of one million dollars."

"They will kill him!"

"Yes, Gertrude, these criminals act under the command of an invisible hand behind the kidnapping."

"Can anyone help the Montaigne family?"

The man stood up.

"Prosper, don't leave me," implored the patient. "How can you save my life and abandon me later on, without telling me something?"

"If you keep me waiting here, I won't be able to save your friend Justin."

"You will save his life!" exclaimed Gertrude. "Oh, Prosper, I trust you.

"You can do everything."

"Then, bye, Gertrude."

Shortly after, the man left the hospital in a hurry.

The seed of love

Gertrude called the nurse and asked her to catch up with Prosper; for, she would like to tell him something else.

The nurse returned with a concerned face.

"Gertrude, the man seems to vanish in thin air."

"I believe you," said the patient. "He has just disappeared."

On Friday night, the *International Mines Company* usually closed down its operation until the next Monday. They also locked up the office, a modest three-room house. However, that weekend, if someone watched it, he would notice some unusual people's comings and goings.

At the front door, two security guards stood up; they had submachine guns in their hands.

Inside that office, one could see three well-dressed men and another one, with his hands and feet tied up to the armchair in which he sat.

Some point in time, one of the well-dressed men picked up the receiver and had a long conversation with someone.

Suddenly, he put the receiver to the prisoner's ears, who spoke fast. Then, the man, who had held the telephone, put it down and slapped the prisoner on the face. Finally, the three standing men left the office, gave instructions to the gunmen, resumed their car and got lost in the big city's street labyrinths.

Prosper Mericourt thought that the moment of action arrived. He walked on the sly and reached the back of the house with one window protected by iron bars.

A stranger's wonderful chronicles, Book II

He pulled a small bottle from his jacket pocket and poured a liquid on the lower end of the bars. The acid melted the attachments.

Then, he slowly bent the bars up while trying not to break the other ends.

He slid into the room, to Justin's big surprise. He beckoned to him to remain silent.

Next, he cast off Justine's chains, asked him to follow him outside, he returned the iron bars to their original position and, finally, he invited Justin to get on his car and drove away.

He handed over his cellular phone to his protégé and suggested, "Justin, call your father at once to prevent him from paying the ransom."

The rescued victim complied and few minutes after, he stated, "Dad…, it's Justin. I can't tell you anything with certainty… I am in a stranger's car, who manages to make me escape through that house backside window… No, don't pay the ransom… I am telling you the truth.

In the meantime, Prosper Mericourt presented himself to Justin as follows, "My name is Prosper Mericourt. I am an architect and have a company specializing in prefabricated homes. You wouldn't expose yourself to danger if you have come to me to build your dream home."

"Just a minute, Mr. Prosper Mericourt…"

"Please, call me Prosper."

448

"Listen, Prosper, it's the first time I have met you. How could I go to you for your expertise in prefabricated houses or things of this nature?

"Additionally, I have already solicited the service of an old school-fellow, Robespierre Salomon…"

Prosper smiled.

"Prosper, my friend, what it is?" inquired Justin turning anxious.

"Well, even if your parents had paid the ransom, you would die; for, behind the kidnapping stands up your ancient schoolfellow, Robespierre Salomon. He intended to enjoy part of the ransom and shoot you."

Instinctively, Justin grabbed Prosper Mericourt by the hand and squeezed it heard.

"Who are you?" he asked.

"Justin, you may call me Prosper Mericourt now. I have a profound intuition of events. By the same token, I know the alpha and the omega of reality."

"Prosper, stop it! I don't believe you. You have simply sunk into folly."

"My dear Justin, I don't have to justify myself.

"However, if you want to believe me, I will feel so much better."

"But I don't have any choice. If you intended to hurt me, you would have done so a while ago.

"At least, tell me what did happen. Why should I have to die?"

A stranger's wonderful chronicles, Book II

"You know that Robespierre has married Carmen Petty who had lost her temper with you, you had prevented her from heaping verbal abuses on a pretty, charming schoolgirl called Gertrude.

"Robespierre can't stand you; for, daily, the name of your family and yours turn the talk of the town, reminding of your charitable organization throughout the country and the world.

"Additionally, his wife has never stopped calling your name as someone she knows, who has succeeded in life.

"Then, that Robespierre, not only he would have kept part of the ransom, but, his men had order to kill you."

"But, how can you know so much, my dear Prosper?" cut in Justin.

"As I've told you, my good friend, I have a profound intuition of events.

"Additionally, reality often makes me believe that the cosmos bathes in logic; the elements of reality intertwine with each other to give an impression of continuity…

"Don't you agree with me?"

"One moment, Prosper!

"Now you want to confuse my mind with your profound philosophy.

"I have the impression that you intend to tell me something personal."

"Ah! Justin, if you stay by me, you would turn a profound mind.

"Listen, I wouldn't claim that I willingly save you from such deadly situation; for, I didn't know you from Adam and Eve.

450

The seed of love

"To some extent, a good deed you had done in the pass to someone has saved your life."

"Prosper, no more parables from you! What's going on? Who put you in my way?"

"Do you really want to know?"

"Yes, Prosper, I do.

"You must tell me everything; otherwise, I will always believe that I have a dream."

"Be ready for a pleasant surprise: your little friend Gertrude has saved your life."

"How did she do that?"

"First of all, I must tell you that she has grown up and has turned such a beautiful, dazzling young woman, with gorgeous legs, round bosom, dove's eyes…"

"Prosper!"

"Well, she was driving her jeep to go to work…"

"What she is doing?"

"She becomes an agronomist appointed by the government to assist peasants to cultivate their lands in a more efficient manner."

"Oh!"

"Do you want to know…?"

"Yes, Prosper, I do. "Excuse my rudeness. Because of your powerful mind, your acumen and your ability to read people's minds, you make me confused to the point of taking you to a figment of my imagination..."

"Well, on her way to work," went on Prosper, "she learned from the radio the news of your kidnapping and, losing her composure, she made a false maneuver which put her vehicle on the edge of an abyss of more than thousand feet

"For one reason or another, I drove at random in the area. I thank Providence that put me on the path of that beautiful creature. I saved her. All is well, besides her twisted ankle.

"Like you, she had surprise at my natural gift for reading people's minds and for revealing to her the reason for her distraction that almost killed her.

"It's the one who has put me on your track."

Ten minutes after, the kidnappers called the parents to learn if they had put the ransom at the indicated spot.

"No, I didn't," stated the father, namely Melvin Montaigne. "Well, if you kill my son, you will go straight to jail for life. I may not have the power to prevent you from acting as you please, however I will turn heaven and earth to send you to jail."

He put down the receiver.

Melvin Montaigne let out a sigh of relief when he saw his beloved son arriving with his rescuer, Prosper Mericourt.

The seed of love

The latter received a phone call on his cellular phone and excused himself to take the message. Next, he rejoined the Montaigne family and told them, "The security people have arrested the kidnappers. Commandant Gaston has just called me to tell me the news.

"Thus, those kidnappers and maybe killers won't be a nuisance to anyone anymore."

Prosper received another call. They heard him saying, "Yes, he is safe and sound...

"If you want...

"Well, I will come..."

Turning towards the Montaignes, he stated, "Well, my friends, I have accomplished my mission; I must take leave of you..."

Justin grabbed him by the hand and rushed saying, "Not too fast.

"You have just begun your mission."

"Justin, you find yourself now in the bosom of your family," acknowledged Prosper. "What else do you want from me?"

"First, I must show you the land you will build my house on."

"Oh, I forget!"

The father cut in, "Just a minute! I thought that your old schoolfellow, Robespierre, has the contract.

"What's going on, my son?"

"Dad, I have changed my mind," answered Justin. "Prosper has advised me to stay far from those people."

"Yes, but Prosper…," insisted the father. "He is your old school-mate…"

"Dad, you see this man called Prosper Mericourt? He knows every-thing.

"Impossible."

"Well, Dad, we won't have time to talk about it.

"For the time being, he has told me that Robespierre had participated in the kidnapping."

"Oh, my God!" exclaimed Gina, Justin's mother. "This world is fall-ing apart.

"Is it true?" inquired Medita, Justin's sister.

"How can I explain my kidnapping at the time of my business meet-ing with that man to go and see the land?

"Did he call?

"Then, he had an idea of what had occurred."

He lowered his voice to speak to Prosper, "The second phone call is from Gertrude?"

"You start using your intuition."

"I would like to see her."

"Why would you?"

"Prosper!"

"Let's go."

"My friends, Justine will be back…," announced Prosper.

"Justin will go out, under one condition," suggested the father.

"What's the condition?" asked the savior.

"Prosper, you will return with him. I don't trust anyone else."

"Melvin, I shall return."

On the way, Prosper insinuated, "Justin, Gertrude has remained unattached.

"Why does she remain unattached? I have no idea. However, since you have no interest in marriage, I will make a pass at her…"

"Prosper, you have done your best to discourage me, but you will not succeed. Gertrude belongs to me."

"No, Justin, my dear friend, she belongs to me. I have saved her life."

"Oh, Prosper, you may have all the women in the world. Leave Gertrude to me.

"Listen, my dear friend, I promise you to take good care of her."

"Can I trust you?"

"Yes, you can."

The car made a right turn in a back street and stopped in front of a small family house.

Prosper knocked at the door. It opened at once to show a beautiful and smiling Gertrude.

She recognized her rescuer from her car accident and hugged him without any ceremony.

A stranger's wonderful chronicles, Book II

"Thank you, my friend, to save my life" she said. "And my eternal feeling of gratitude for saving Justin's life. He is the man with the golden heart.

"How is he, Prosper?"

"Gertrude, the man may answer your question in person.

"Here is he."

Justin stepped into the house.

Then, without any ceremony, he opened his arms to welcome Gertrude who, instinctively, fell into them, to the great surprise of parents and siblings.

"Gertrude," said Justin in tones of emotion, "thank you for saving my life."

"I didn't. Prosper did."

"He has told me everything about all the ramifications coming from the men event: my kidnapping.

"You have cried and asked this man to save me."

Justin took a long pause, the time necessary for weighing up his ultimate decision to get engaged and married.

Then, he said in tones of emotion, "Listen, Gertrude, I don't know about you, but I am a single.

"If you don't see any inconvenience, I would like you to be my wife."

Gertrude turned around to face her parents and siblings to have their unexpressed approval.

Then, she stated, "Justin, if you don't see any inconvenience to marry a woman of small economic condition, then, I am yours."

"Gertrude, remember the circumstances under which we met the first time?

"Money didn't play any role in it."

"Yes, I do," replied the beautiful lady.

Finally, Justin and Gertrude exchanged their first kiss.

Prosper smiled.

As he had promised before, Prosper took Justin back to his parents' home.

"Prosper, my friend," said the father, "Now, I trust you completely."

Mr. Montaigne remained silent for a long while: he had all sorts of ideas crisscrossing his mind.

Finally, he went on, "By the way, Prosper my dear friend, since you become Justin's architect, I believe that you should advice him against building a house; for, he is single and doesn't show any willingness to have an affair or get married…"

"Melvin," argued Prosper, "there will be a Mrs. Justin Montaigne in the house."

"What!

"Justin!"

"Papa, allow me to tell you that I have found the woman of my dream.

"She has remained unattached, waiting for me for over ten years."

A stranger's wonderful chronicles, Book II

"You mean a woman waiting for you! But, who is this lucky woman?"

"Papa, more than ten years ago, a girl fascinated you so much that you gave her a kiss..."

"What!" exclaimed Melvin's wife. "You gave burning kisses to girls?"

"Darling, you have heard Justin. Such manifestation of sympathy happened over ten years ago."

"Dad, I have just referred to the little Gertrude, the one who had captivated you during your visit to the school you have renovated."

"I remember this little girl!"

"Now, since time has elapsed, she has turned a blossomed woman.

"She went to college and became an agronomist, working for the government."

"Justin, my dear son, don't say one more word. That woman will make you happy.

"Additionally, she will make us happy, as she is an agronomist."

"Wait just a minute, dad! You are not going to hire her..."

"Two weeks after your marriage, I will hire her..."

In the meantime, Justin's sister, Medita pulled Prosper apart in a corner of the room.

"Prosper," yelled Melvin.

"Yes, Mr. Montaigne, I am listen to you...," answered former.

"Apparently, you have conquered everybody's heart in this house..."

"Oh, dad," argued Medita, "stop being jealous."

"I strongly believe that Prosper has enough love to please all of us."

Everybody burst out laughing.

"Prosper," started the daughter.

"Medita, let me tell you that you find yourself on the right track," cut in the man.

"What! You know the question I will ask you?"

"Tata," yelled Justin, "this man knows everything, the alpha and the omega of reality..."

"My dear brother, I have just noticed it.

"Now, my beloved Prosper, what do you mean?"

"Tata, as I said it, you find yourself on the right track by loving Gregory Dillon."

The young lady remained dumbfounded for a while.

Prosper went on, "I understand your reluctance. They have accused that man of all the sins in the world.

"Some said that he has organized a criminal association terrorizing banks, jewelries—you name it.

"Others accused him of participating in orgy clubs.

"Finally, some firmly believed that he is rapist."

"Then, Prosper! Don't tell me that man has no criminal records?"

"Tata, the man hasn't committed any of these crimes they have accused him of."

A stranger's wonderful chronicles, Book II

"Then, my dear Prosper, what's going on? Why do they want to fool me?"

"Do you want the answer?"

"Prosper, do you want me to strangle you?"

As Medita spoke louder, the father jokingly insinuated, "Tata, don't strangle our friend and rescuer."

"Tata," added the mother, "don't give us the reputation as killers."

There was a burst of laughter.

"Tata," answered Prosper, "you don't have to take such extreme measure.

"The chairman of the company you work for, namely Paul Monet, loves you madly.

"However, he had an intuition of your love for Gregory.

"Then, to discourage you, he managed to spread malicious gossip about the object of your love.

"Listen, Tata, as far as I am concerned, it's time to accept to work for your father, my good friend.

"By the same token, you can ask your father to hire Gregory. Then, both you will stop being at the mercy of this evil admirer Paul Monet and you will certainly live like two pigeons, forever and ever."

Medita jumped to Prosper's neck and kissed him on the lips.

"Thank you, my sweet Prosper…"

Justin got near them and asked, "Prosper and Medita, what's going on?

460

The seed of love

"You have to behave yourselves."

"Justin, don't get involved in my business," answered the sister.

"Justin, my dear friend, you have heard the woman," added Prosper.

Suddenly, the media announced,

Breaking news:

We have just learned that the police have freed Justin Montaigne in time to prevent the payment of one million dollar ransom.

Police officers have also arrested the kidnapers. Apparently, they behave as hired killers and henchmen. Their leader, nobody (including the kidnapers) knows him. They confessed, a while ago, that they had only received instructions from him, but they didn't know him and couldn't identify him.

They always met with him in a dark place. He wore colored glasses and always remained behind his vehicle wheel. He only told them when the kidnapping should take place.

Police continues to investigate.

Melvin Montaigne put his hands on Prosper's shoulders and admitted, "You have told the truth.

"You don't lack generosity and acumen.

"However we can't find appeasement…"

A stranger's wonderful chronicles, Book II

"Melvin, don't complete your sentence," cut in Prosper. "I won't miss to give the leader a warning. Yet, I wouldn't like him to go to jail.

"I think about his wife and children who may get hurt in the process, while they are innocent..."

"Prosper, you embody goodness and compassion—to say the least"

"Thank you, Melvin, so do you…"

As it was getting late, Prosper thought of taking his leave of the Montaignes.

"Justin," he remarked, "you will have your house in three days.

"In three days? Good. I will make a deposit at the bank tomorrow. In three days the business will get settled.

"Take care of my 'friend'; otherwise, I will return you to the kidnapers."

"Which is impossible," cut in the father; "for, thanks to you, the kidnapers are in jail."

"Ah! I forget. Then, I will think of something else to punish him.

"Well, good bye, my dear friends. I know that you have a lot to talk about."

On the way, Prosper called Robespierre and stated, "I am aware of your misdeeds.

"From now on, dear fellow, you must leave my friend Justin alone. Otherwise, I will reveal your participation in the kidnapping.

"If you don't believe me, then, try to defy me.

The seed of love

"I have evidence connecting you to your participation in this dirty action. Again, I advise you to stay away from Justin. You don't deserve his friendship."

Robespierre's face paled. His wife noticed it and inquired about it. "My love, is there something you haven't told me? Remember, I am your wife. You will gain to let me know about all your problems.

"Darling," he answered, "nothing bad has happened to me. I have just lost a client.

"He has told me that the bank, for no good reasons, hasn't approved of his loan.

"Well, there will always be another client."

"That's the spirit, my love," concluded the wife.

◘　　◘

◘

Brian Clifford, once more, had some difficulty to sort out the data.

He visited, first, the Montaigne family that confirmed all the facts.

Actually, the marriage between Justin and Gertrude, as well the one between Medita and Gregory, would remain unexplainable without the marvelous stranger's intervention, whose name was this time Prosper Mericourt.

In addition, the prefabricated house inhabited by Justin and Gertrude reminded the elegant style of real estate concepts only known to the marvelous stranger.

A stranger's wonderful chronicles, Book II

All his customers seemed thoroughly satisfied.

Finally, Medita and Gregory have accepted to work for the Melvin Montaigne Corporation.

From that point on, they live like two pigeons, safe from malicious rumors.

The reporter headed to his office to edit this account from the Montaignes and Gertrude Melon, before entrusting the manuscript to the executive secretary (his wife).

On the way, he smiled at the prospect of meeting, in three days, with another beneficiary of the *marvelous stranger* in the episode entitled "The real godsend", in Book III.

End of Book II

www.ingramcontent.com/pod-product-compliance
Lightning Source LLC
Chambersburg PA
CBHW070750030726
47504CB00003B/505